Kingsley Amis's (1922–1995) works take a humorous yet highly critical look at British society, especially of the period following the end of the Second World War. Born in London, Amis explored his disillusionment with British society in novels such as *That Uncertain Feeling* (1955). His other works include *The Green Man* (1970); *Stanley and the Women* (1984); and *The Old Devils* (1986) which won the Booker Prize. Amis also wrote poetry, criticism and short stories.

Rachel Cusk was born in 1967. She has won the Whitbread First Novel Award and the Somerset Maugham Award, and is the author of two works of non-fiction and seven novels, including *In The Fold*, longlisted for the 2005 Man Booker Prize, and *Arlington Park*, shortlisted for the Orange Broadband Prize 2007. Her non-fiction book, *A Life's Work*, was published to huge acclaim in 2001, and her account of a summer spent in Italy with her family, *The Last Supper*, was published in 2009. Her most recent novel, *The Bradshaw Variations* was published in 2009. In 2003 she was chosen as one of *Granta's* Best Young Novelists. She lives in Brighton.

KINGSLEY AMIS

Complete Stories

With a Foreword by Rachel Cusk

PENGUIN BOOKS

PENGUIN CLASSICS

Published by the Penguin Group
Penguin Books Ltd, 80 Strand, London WC2R ORL, England
Penguin Group (USA) Inc., 375 Hudson Street, New York, New York 10014, USA
Penguin Group (Canada), 90 Eglinton Avenue East, Suite 700, Toronto, Ontario, Canada M4P 2Y3
 (a division of Pearson Penguin Canada Inc.)
Penguin Ireland, 25 St Stephen's Green, Dublin 2, Ireland (a division of Penguin Books Ltd)
Penguin Group (Australia), 707 Collins Street, Melbourne, Victoria 3008, Australia
(a division of Pearson Australia Group Pty Ltd)
Penguin Books India Pvt Ltd, 11 Community Centre, Panchsheel Park, New Delhi – 110 017, India
Penguin Group (NZ), 67 Apollo Drive, Rosedale, Auckland 0632, New Zealand
(a division of Pearson New Zealand Ltd)
Penguin Books (South Africa) (Pty) Ltd, Block D, Rosebank Office Park, 181 Jan Smuts Avenue,
Parktown North, Gauteng 2193, South Africa

Penguin Books Ltd, Registered Offices: 80 Strand, London WC2R ORL, England

www.penguin.com

First published in Great Britain by Penguin Classics 2011
Published in paperback 2013
1

Copyright © Kingsley Amis, 1955, 1956, 1962, 1958, 1962, 1972, 1960, 1958, 1964, 1972, 1986, 1960, 1972,
1978, 1979, 1982, 1972, 1980, 1993
Foreword © Rachel Cusk, 2011
All rights reserved

The moral right of the author and the author of the Foreword has been asserted

Set in 11.5/15 Sabon LT Std
Typeset by Palimpsest Book Production Limited, Falkirk, Stirlingshire
Printed in Great Britain by Clays Ltd, St Ives plc

978-0-141-19529-2

www.greenpenguin.co.uk

ALWAYS LEARNING   **PEARSON**

Contents

Foreword

What is today's reader offered by the work of Kingsley Amis? This may not seem an especially pertinent question to ask of a writer who only died in 1995, but in art the recent past can sometimes appear more outmoded and inaccessible than distant history. The living writer is close to the common well of experience; once the writer has died, and can no longer articulate our contemporary world for us, he is exposed to the more brutal judgement of time. What in his work is timeless? What, if anything, makes it worth preserving? Of course, definitive answers to these questions aren't always found: dead writers continue to go in and out of fashion, their work suddenly meaningful again in one era then failing to make sense in the next. It is often the most passionately contemporary writers – Kingsley Amis was one – whose reputations decline most steeply in their absence, for obvious reasons. Relevance becomes irrelevance; the same devotion to the here and now that brought them popularity and fame ensures their obscurity once here and now have become there and then. Yet the observation of ordinary life nearly always forms the cornerstone of great and lasting art. It is the quality of that observation that is put to the test over time, that will determine whether the work is trivial or lastingly true.

Kingsley Amis made his name in the 1950s with the publication of his first novel, *Lucky Jim*, a work that seemed to define a new era not just in its portrayal of the evolving world of higher education that is its setting but in literary values too, advancing as it did a more youthful and democratic conception of literary style and subject matter that reflected changing modes of social behaviour. In *Lucky Jim* Amis reprised the black comedy of Evelyn Waugh and re-clothed it in the provincial workaday garb of the ordinary middle classes, and if in doing so he belied something of his artistic seriousness, he was rewarded for it with instant acclaim. His story of a young provincial-university lecturer's sufferings at the hands of academic bores, pretentious snobs, prissy disapproving women and spoiled culturally elitist young men was a huge commercial and critical success. It laughed at everyone who needed laughing at in that cramped, class-bound decade; it gave a likeable validity to the new forms of life, to social and sexual freedoms it showed as modest, funny, authentic.

Amis was himself a university lecturer during this period – he taught at Swansea, where he lived for many years with his wife and three children – and so he knew whereof he wrote. Indeed, the integrity of *Lucky Jim*, and of Amis's work generally, derives from its autobiographical impulse. Though he wrote assiduously in different forms and genres – he considered himself a poet first and a novelist second – it is for its hold on unadorned life that his writing was and is esteemed. Yet if Amis kept close to the sources of his own experience, it may partly have been out of a kind of humility, almost a shyness in the face of questions of art. Self-deprecation, usually in the guise of comedy, is a hallmark of an Amis project; humour was his mode of attack and of address. And if humour is also a defence, against, among other things, the accusation that one is taking oneself too seriously, Amis may have relied on his identity as a comic writer to shield him from the larger consideration – both private and public – of his stature as an artist.

Nowhere is this clearer than in his handling of the short story form, whose particular possibilities for advancing the representation of modern experience he understood and acknowledged while firmly distancing himself from them: 'the things that only the short story can do,' he wrote, 'the impression, the untrimmed slice of life, the landscape with figures but without characters, make little appeal to me.' His own stories, he said, were mere 'chips from a novelist's work-bench'. He goes on, more revealingly, to observe that the contemporary short story tends to be published in 'those pale and sickly present-day equivalents of the Victorian fiction magazines, the periodicals subsidized by the Arts Council or one of its offspring. A writer, or any other kind of artist, who partly or largely need not depend on pleasing the public, who in effect has his fee guaranteed whatever the quality of his product, is tempted to self-indulgence and laziness.' Better to stick to the novel, 'which as yet is unlikely to contain any material subsidized by the Arts Council'.

Amis's fear of art being viewed as pretence and the artist as lazy or dependent is clear from these remarks; and who would accuse an artist of being lazy? The answer might be: a working man. With his talk of product and work-benches, Amis is trying to create the image of the writer as an ordinary worker, to dispel art's associations with foppishness and pretentiousness and self-aggrandizement. These associations were evidently painful to Amis – but why? It is as though, in the modernist possibilities of the short story, he perceived a threat both to his masculine and his writerly identity; yet for a generation of American male writers emerging contemporaneously with Amis, the short story was a sort of 'working man's' – indeed almost a macho – form. The story-writer Amis claimed most to admire was Rudyard Kipling: despite being hailed as an innovator with *Lucky Jim*, Amis's anxiety was after all perhaps that of being thought old-fashioned. As far as the short story was concerned, he may have affixed that label to himself before anyone else could do it for him.

Any reader for whom these stories constitute the first encounter with Amis's work will find them nonetheless to be a sample-case of his qualities as a writer. As his remarks about the short story suggest, he did not take either himself or the form in new directions; instead, he brought to it valuable fragments of his gift, 'chips from a novelist's work-bench'. Chief among these is his vigorous observational prose, so assertive and deft and concise:

The Mess occupied a Belgian provincial hotel and this was its lounge, a square room lined with burst leather-padded benches. Officers sat on them reading magazines. Only the fact that two or three or them were also drinking stopped the place looking like a barber's waiting-room. Outside it was raining a little.

('Court of Inquiry')

And of course the astringent of humour, cutting and re-cutting the description as though in the (unfounded) fear that it might be found over-rich, or worse, over-serious:

The part of Frank that could be seen above the back of the pew seemed to Alec to offer a good deal of information. The thick black hair was heavily greased; the neck bulged in a way that promised a roll of fat there in due course; the snowily white shirt-collar and the charcoal-grey suit material did somehow or other manage to suggest, not lack of taste exactly, but the attitude that money was more interesting.

('All the Blood Within Me')

These stories, spanning Amis's career, also of course span his interests and preoccupations, his choices and changes of subject matter, his formal experiments, his writerly moods and declensions, his tics and trademarks. There are army stories, literary genre stories (sci-fi, plus a Sherlock Holmes spoof from which Sherlock Holmes is absent), as well as stories about literature (in 'Mr Barrett's Secret', Elizabeth Barrett Browning's father discloses his reasons for his estrangement from his daughter after her marriage to the poet); and then there are stories that are more than chips from the work-bench, stories in which Amis's piquancy as an artist, his essence, can be experienced, such as 'Moral Fibre', 'All the Blood Within Me' and 'Dear Illusion'.

This essence, composed as it is of social frustration, fleshly appetite, critical disquiet and the sometimes painful bridling of personal emotional power, is most detectable in Amis's portrayals of relationships, where his hilarious, faintly misanthropic

grasp of human character ('The first person he saw on entering
the dining-car was Bob Anthony, wearing a suit that looked like
woven vegetable soup and reading a newspaper with awful
concentration') creates scenes whose bristling surface activity
conceals undercurrents of profound desolation, of alienation and
loneliness, of despair at the meagreness of the world's offerings.
Amis's characters, generally speaking, aren't glamorous or liber-
ated or even particularly empowered; mostly they are entrapped
at the local level of British life in the second half of the twentieth
century, subject to the grating irritations of the ordinary. Few
writers of Amis's calibre observe their world from such a level
today; and it is for his accounts of human pettiness and small-
mindedness, of small-scale tyranny, of big emotions felt in exigent
places, of the tensions of local shop and street and flat, that we
should continue to read him.

In 'Moral Fibre', a domineering social worker encounters one
of her charges in the narrator's kitchen:

'Ah, good morning, Betty,' Mair said bluffly. 'How are you getting
on? Do you like working for Mrs Lewis?'

'Aw, all right.'

Mair's lion-like face took on the aspect of the king of beasts
trying to outstare its tamer. 'I think you know my name, don't
you Betty? It's polite to use it, you know.'

At this I went out into the kitchen again, but not quickly enough
to avoid hearing Betty saying, 'Sorry, Mrs Webster', and, as I shut
the door behind me, Mair saying, 'That's more like it, isn't it,
Betty?'

In 'All the Blood Within Me', a man attends the funeral of a
woman he has loved and for decades conducted an affair with,
an affair accepted within her marriage, to the extent that the two
men are friends and may even live together now that she's gone.
With admirable delicacy Amis evokes the muted pain of this
arrangement, and the confining suburban world in which it has
occurred:

A handful of earth was thrown on to the coffin. Alec realized that he had been very afraid of the hollow noise this might make, but it was all right, the soil was dry and chalky, without noticeable clods, and when the spades got to work it could, from the sound, have been anything at all being buried. There were the beginnings of movement away from the graveside; Alec sighed and raised his head, and the whole scene shone brightly in his eyes: the people with their varied complexions and hair, the grass, the privet hedges, the vases of red and blue flowers on the graves, the great pair of cypresses by the entrance, all slightly over-coloured like a picture postcard.

What today's reader, and indeed today's writer, can learn from Amis is the value of the particular; a value that is higher now than ever, as the choices and possibilities for living become ever more homogeneous. It grows harder to represent by means of the particular – the perceptible detail – what makes people and places distinct from one another, what will signify their individuality. It may be old-fashioned to fear the decline of individuality; the writerly means of halting this decline may well be old-fashioned too. In the best of these stories Amis does so, constructing a solid surface of well-observed concrete fact, upon which the play of character through dialogue and voice can occur. One feels at such moments the presence of the novelist's workbench, in all its utilitarian beauty.

Rachel Cusk, 2011

Acknowledgements

These stories were first published as follows:

'My Enemy's Enemy' in *Encounter*, 1955
'Court of Inquiry' in the *Spectator*, 1956
'I Spy Strangers' in the collection *My Enemy's Enemy*, Victor
    Gollancz Ltd, 1962
'Moral Fibre' in *Esquire*, 1958
'All the Blood Within Me' in the *Spectator*, 1962
'Dear Illusion' as Covent Garden Stories no. 1, Covent Garden
    Press Ltd, 1972
'Something Strange' in the *Spectator*, 1960
'The 2003 Claret' in *The Complete Imbiber*, vol. 2, Putman &
    Co., 1958
'The Friends of Plonk' in *Town*, 1964
'Too Much Trouble' in *Penguin Modern Stories II*, 1972
'Investing in Futures' in *The Complete Imbiber*, Cyril Ray, 1986
'Hemingway in Space' in *Punch*, 1960
'Who or What Was It?' in *Playboy*, 1972
'The Darkwater Hall Mystery' in *Playboy*, 1978
'The House on the Headland' in *The Times*, 1979
'Affairs of Death' in *Shakespeare's Stories*, Hamish Hamilton,
    1982
'Mason's Life' in *The Sunday Times*, 1972
'To See the Sun' in *Collected Short Stories*, Hutchinson, 1980

All the stories listed above were published together for the first
time in *Collected Short Stories*, Hutchinson, 1980.

'Mr Barrett's Secret', 'Boris and the Colonel', 'A Twitch on the Thread', 'Toil and Trouble', 'Captain Nolan's Chance' and '1941/A' were first published in *Mr Barrett's Secret and Other Stories*, Hutchinson, 1993

COMPLETE
STORIES

My Enemy's Enemy

I

'Yes, I know all about that, Tom,' the Adjutant said through a mouthful of stew. 'But technical qualifications aren't everything. There's other sides to a Signals officer's job, you know, especially while we're still pretty well static. The communications are running themselves and we don't want to start getting complacent. My personal view is and has been from the word go that your friend Dally's a standing bloody reproach to this unit, never mind how much he knows about the six-channel and the other boxes of tricks. That's a lineman-mechanic's job, anyway, not an officer's. And I can tell you for a fact I mean to do something about it, do you see?' He laid down his knife, though not his fork, and took three or four swallows of wine.

'Well, your boy Cleaver doesn't impress me all that much, Bill,' Thurston, who hated the Adjutant, said to him. 'The only time we've tried him on duty he flapped.'

'Just inexperience, Tom,' the Adjutant said. 'He'd soon snap out of that if we gave him command of the section. Sergeant Beech would carry him until he found his feet.'

'Mm, I'd like to see that, I must say. The line duty-officer getting his sergeant out of bed to hold his hand while he changes a valve.'

'Now look here, old boy.' The Adjutant levered a piece of meat out from between two teeth and ate it. 'You know as well as I do that young Cleaver's got the best technical qualifications of anyone in the whole unit. It's not his fault he's been stuck on office work ever since he came to us. There's a fellow that'd smarten up that bunch of goons and long-haired bloody mathematical wizards they call a line-maintenance section. As it is, the NCOs don't chase the blokes and Dally isn't interested in chasing the NCOs. Isn't interested in anything but his bloody circuit diagrams and test-frames and what-have-you.'

To cover his irritation, Thurston summoned the Mess corporal, who stood by the wall in a posture that compromised between that of an attendant waiter and the regulation stand-at-ease position. The Adjutant had schooled him in Mess procedure, though not in Mess etiquette. 'Gin and lime, please, Gordon . . . Just as well in a way he is interested in line apparatus, isn't it, Bill? We'd have looked pretty silly without him during the move out of Normandy and across France. He worked as hard as any two of the rest of us. And as well.'

'He got his bouquet from the Colonel, didn't he? I don't grudge him that, I admit he did good work then. Not as good as some of his chaps, probably, but still, he served his turn. Yes, that's exactly it, Tom, he's served his—'

'According to Major Rylands he was the linchpin of the whole issue,' Thurston said, lighting a cigarette with fingers that were starting to tremble. 'And I'm prepared to take his word for it. The war isn't over yet, you know. Christ knows what may happen in the spring. If Dally isn't around to hold the line-maintenance end up for Rylands, the whole unit might end up in the shit with the Staff jumping on its back. Cleaver might be all right, I agree. We just can't afford to take the risk.'

This was an unusually long speech for anyone below the rank of major to make in the Adjutant's presence. Temporarily gagged by a mouthful of stew, that officer was eating as fast as he could and shaking his forefinger to indicate that he would as soon as possible propose some decisive amendment to what he had just been told. With his other hand he scratched the crown of his glossy black head, looking momentarily like a tick-tack man working through his lunch-break. He said indistinctly: 'You're on to the crux of the whole thing, old boy. Rylands is the root of all the trouble. Bad example at the top, do you see?' Swallowing, he went on: 'If the second-in-command goes round looking like a shithouse detail and calling the blokes by their Christian names, what can you expect? You can't get away from it, familiarity breeds contempt. Trouble with him is he thinks he's still working in the Post Office.'

A hot foam of anger seemed to fizz up in Thurston's chest. 'Major Rylands is the only field officer in this entire unit who knows his job. It is due to him and Dally, plus Sergeant Beech and the lineman-mechs, that our line communications have worked so smoothly during this campaign. To them and to no one else. If they can go on doing that they can walk about with bare arses for all I care.'

The Adjutant frowned at Thurston. After running his tongue round his upper teeth, he said: 'You seem to forget, Tom, that I'm responsible for the discipline of officers in this unit.' He paused to let the other reflect on the personal implications of this, then nodded to where Corporal Gordon was approaching with Thurston's drink.

As he signed the chit, Thurston was thinking that Gordon had probably been listening to the conversation from the passage. If so, he would probably discuss it with Hill, the Colonel's batman, who would probably report it to his master. It was often said, especially by Lieutenant Dalessio, the 'Dally' now under discussion, that the Colonel's chief contact with his unit was through the rumours and allegations Hill and, to a less extent, the Adjutant took to him. A tweak of disquiet made Thurston drink deeply and resolve to say no more for a bit.

The Adjutant was brushing crumbs off his battledress, which was of the greenish hue current in the Canadian Army. This little affectation, like the gamboge gloves and the bamboo walking-stick, perhaps suited a man who had helped to advertise men's clothes in civilian life. He went on to say in his rapid quacking monotone: 'I'd advise you, Tom, not to stick your neck out too far in supporting a man who's going to be out of this unit on his ear before very long.'

'Rylands, you mean?'

'No no no. Unfortunately not. But Dally's going.'

'That's gen, is it?'

'Not yet, but it will be.'

'I don't follow you.'

The Adjutant looked up in Gordon's direction, then leaned forward across the table to Thurston. 'It only needs one more thing,' he said quietly, 'to turn the scale. The CO's been watching Dally for some time, on my suggestion. I know the old man pretty well, as you know, after being in his Company for three years at North Midland Command. He's waiting to make up his mind, do you see? If Dally puts up a black in the near future – a real black – that'll be enough for the CO. Cleaver'll get his chance at last.'

'Suppose Dally doesn't put up a black?'

'He will.'

'He hasn't yet, you know. The terminal equipment's all on the top line, and Dally knows it inside out.'

'I'm not talking about that kind of a black. I'm talking about the administrative and disciplinary side. Those vehicles of his are in a shocking condition. I thought of working a snap 406 inspection on one of them, but that wouldn't look too good. Too much like discrimination. But there'll be something. Just give me time.'

Thurston thought of saying that those vehicles, though covered with months-old mud and otherwise offensive to the inspecting eye, were in good running order, thanks to the efficiency of the section's transport corporal. Instead, he let his mind wander back to one of the many stories of the Colonel's spell as a company commander in England. Three weeks running he had presented his weekly prize of £1 for the smartest vehicle to the driver of an obsolete wireless-truck immobilized for lack of spare parts. The Company Sergeant-Major had won a bet about it.

'We'll have some fun then, Tom old boy,' the Adjutant was saying in as festive a tone as his voice allowed. He was unaware that Thurston disliked him. His own feelings towards Thurston were a mixture of respect and patronage: respect for Thurston's Oxford degree and accent, job at a minor public school, and efficiency as a non-technical officer; patronage for his practice of reading literary magazines and for his vaguely scholarly manner and appearance. The affinity between Thurston's unmilitary look and the more frankly ragamuffin demeanour of Dalessio could hardly explain, the Adjutant wonderingly felt, the otherwise unaccountable tendency of the one to defend the other. It was true that they'd known each other at the officers' training unit at Catterick, but what could that have to do with it? The Adjutant was unaccustomed to having his opinions contested and he now voiced the slight bafflement that had been growing on him for the last few minutes. 'It rather beats me,' he said, 'why you're taking this line about friend Dally. You're not at all thick with him. In fact he seems to needle you whenever he speaks to you. My impression is, old boy, for what it's worth, you've got no bloody use for him at all. And yet you stick up for him. Why?'

Thurston amazed him by saying coldly: 'I don't see why the fact that a man's an Italian should be held against him when he does his job as well as anyone in the sodding Army.'

'Just a minute, Tom,' the Adjutant said, taking a cigarette from his silver case, given him by his mistress in Brussels. 'That's being a bit unfair, you know. You ever heard me say a word about Dalessio being an Eyeteye? Never. You were the one who brought it up. It makes no difference to me if a fellow's father's been interned, provided—'

'Uncle.'

'All right, uncle, then. As I say, that's no affair of mine. Presumably he's okay from that point of view or he'd never have got here. And that's all there is to it as far as I'm concerned. I'm not holding it against him, not for a moment. I don't quite know where you picked up that impression, old boy.'

Thurston shook his head, blushing slightly. 'Sorry, Bill,' he said. 'I must have got it mixed. It used to get on my wick at Catterick, the way some of the blokes took it out of him about his pal Musso and so on. I suppose it must be through that somehow, in a way, I keep feeling people have got it in for him on that score. Sorry.' He was not sorry. He knew quite certainly that his charge was well-founded, and that the other's silence about Dalessio's descent was a matter of circumspection only. If anyone in the Mess admired Mussolini, Thurston suspected, it was the Adjutant, although he kept quiet about that as well. It was tempting to dig at his prejudices on these and other questions, but Thurston did his best never to succumb to that temptation. The Adjutant's displeasure was always strongly urged and sometimes, rumour said, followed up by retaliatory persecution. Enough, dangerously much, had already been said in Dalessio's defence.

The Adjutant's manner had grown genial again and, with a muttered apology, he now offered Thurston a cigarette. 'What about another of those?' he asked, pointing his head at Thurston's glass.

'Thank you, I will, but I must be off in a minute. We're opening that teleprinter to the Poles at twenty-hundred and I want to see it's working.'

Two more officers now entered the Mess dining-room. They were Captain Bentham, a forty-year-old Regular soldier who had been a company sergeant-major in India at the outbreak of war, and Captain Rowney, who besides being in charge of the unit's administration was also the Mess's catering officer. Rowney nodded to Thurston and grinned at the Adjutant, whose Canadian battle-dress he had been responsible for securing. He himself was wearing a sheepskin jacket, made on the Belgian black market. 'Hallo, William,' he said. 'Won the war yet?' Although he was a great chum of the Adjutant's, some of his remarks to him, Thurston had noticed, carried a curious vein of satire. Bentham sat stolidly down a couple of places along the table, running his hands over his thin grey hair.

'Tom and I have been doing a little plotting,' the Adjutant said. 'We've decided a certain officer's career with this unit needs terminating.'

Bentham glanced up casually and caught Thurston's eye. This, coming on top of the Adjutant's misrepresentation of the recent discussion, made Thurston feel slightly uncomfortable. That was ludicrous, because he had long ago written Bentham off as of no particular account, as the most uninteresting type of Regular Army ex-ranker, good only at cable-laying, supervising cable-laying and looking after the men who did the actual cable-laying. Despite this, Thurston found himself saying: 'It wasn't quite like that', but at that moment Rowney asked the Adjutant a question and the protest, mild as it was, went unheard.

'Your friend Dally, of course,' the Adjutant answered Rowney.

'Why, what's he been up to?' Bentham asked in his slow Yorkshire voice. 'Having his hair cut?'

There was a general laugh, then a token silence while Gordon laid plates of stew in front of the new arrivals. His inquiry whether the Adjutant wanted any rice pudding was met with a facetious and impracticable instruction for the disposal of that foodstuff by an often-quoted route. 'Can't you do better than that, Jack?' the Adjutant asked Rowney. 'Third night we've had Chinese wedding-cake this week.'

'Sorry, William. My Belgian friend's had a little misunderstanding with the civvy police. I'm still looking round for another pal with the right views on how the officers of a liberating army should be fed. Just possess your soul in patience.'

'What's this about Dally?' Bentham persisted. 'If there's a move to give him a wash and a change of clothes, count me in.'

Thurston got up before the topic could be reopened. 'By the way, Jack,' he said to Rowney, 'young Malone asked me to remind you that he still hasn't had those cigarettes for the blokes he's lent to Special Wireless.'

Rowney sighed. 'Tell him it's not my pigeon, will you, Thomas? I've been into it all with him. They're under Special Wireless for everything now.'

'Not NAAFI rations. He told me you'd agreed to supply them.'

'Up until last week. They're off my hands now.'

'Oh no they're not,' Thurston said nastily. 'According to Malone they still haven't had last week's.'

'Well, tell him . . .'

'Look, Jack, you tell him. It's nothing to do with me, is it?'

Rowney stared at him. 'All right, Thomas,' he said, abruptly diving his fork into his stew. 'I'll tell him.'

Dodging the hanging lamp-shade, which at its lowest point was no more than five feet from the floor, Thurston hurried out, his greatcoat over his arm.

'What's eating our intellectual friend?' Rowney asked.

The Adjutant rubbed his blue chin. 'Don't know quite. He was behaving rather oddly before you blokes came in. He's getting too sort of wrapped up in himself. Needs shaking up.' He was just deciding, having previously decided against it, to inflict some small but salutary injustice on Thurston through the medium of unit orders. He might compel the various sections to start hand-ing in their various stores records for check, beginning with Thurston's section and stopping after it. Nice, but perhaps a bit too drastic. What about pinching his jeep for some tiresome extra duty? That might be just the thing.

'If you ask me,' Bentham was saying, 'he's too bloody stuck-up by half. Wants a lesson of some kind, he does.'

'You're going too far there, Ben,' the Adjutant said decisively. He disliked having Bentham in the Officers' Mess, declaring its tone to be thereby lowered, and often said he thought the old boy would be much happier back in the Sergeants' Mess with people of his own type. 'Tom Thurston's about the only chap round here you can carry on a reasonably intelligent discussion with.'

Bentham, unabashed, broke off a piece of bread and ran it round his plate in a way that Thurston and the Adjutant were, unknown to each other, united in finding unpleasant. 'What's all this about a plot about Dally?' he asked.

II

'You got that, Reg?' Dalessio asked. 'If you get any more interfer-ence on this circuit, put it back on plain speech straight away.

Then they can see how they like that. I don't believe for a bloody moment the line's been relaid for a single bastard yard. Still, it's being ceased in a week or two, and it never was of the slightest importance, so there's no real worry. Now, what about the gallant Poles?' He spoke with a strong Glamorganshire accent diversified by an occasional Italian vowel.

'They're still on here,' Reg, the lineman-mechanic, said, gesturing towards the test teleprinter. 'Want to see 'em?'

'Yes, please. It's nearly time to switch 'em through to the teleprinter room. We'll get that done before I go.'

Reg bent to the keyboard of the machine and typed:

HOW U GETTING ON THERE READING ME OK KKKK

There was a humming pause while Reg scratched his armpit and said: 'Gone for a piss, I expect . . . Ah, here he is.' In typical but inextinguishably eerie fashion the teleprinter took on a life of its own, performed a carriage-return, moved the glossy white paper up a couple of lines, and typed:

4 CHRISTS SAKE QUIT BOTHERING ME NOT 2000 HRS YET KKK

Dalessio, grinning to himself, shoved Reg out of the way and typed:

CHIEF SIGNAL OFFICER BRITISH LIBERATION ARMY ERE WATCH YR LANGUAGE MY MAN KKKK

The distant operator typed:

U GO AND SCREW YRSELF JACK SORRY I MEAN SIR

At this Dalessio went into roars of laughter, digging his knuckle into one deep eye-socket and throwing back his large dark head. It was exactly the kind of joke he liked best. He rotated a little in the narrow aisle between the banks of apparatus and test-panels, still laughing, while Reg watched him with a slight smile. At last Dalessio recovered and shouldered his way down to the phone at the other end of the vehicle.

'Give me the teleprinter room, please. What? Who? All right,

I'll speak to him . . . Terminal Equipment, Dalessio here. Yes. Oh, really? It hasn't?' His voice changed completely, became that of a slightly unbalanced uncle commiserating with a disappointed child: 'Now isn't that just too bad? Well, I do think that's hard lines. Just when you were all excited about it, too, eh?' Over his shoulder he squealed to Reg, in soprano parody of Thurston's educated tones: 'Captain Thurston is tewwibly gwieved that he hasn't got his pwinter to the Poles yet. He's afwaid we've got some howwid scheme on over heah to depwive him of it . . . All right, Thurston, I'll come over. Yes, now.'

Reg smiled again and put a cigarette in his mouth, striking the match, from long habit, on the metal 'No Smoking' notice tacked up over the ventilator.

'Give me one of those, Reg, I want to cool my nerves before I go into the beauty-parlour across the way. Thanks. Now listen: switch the Poles through to the teleprinter room at one minute to eight exactly, so that there's working communication at eight but not before. Do Thurston good to bite his nails for a few minutes. Put it through on number . . .' – his glance and fore-finger went momentarily to a test-frame across the aisle – 'number six. That's just been rewired. Ring up Teleprinters and tell 'em, will you? See you before I go off.'

It was dark and cold outside and Dalessio shivered on his way over to the Signal Office. He tripped up on the cable which ran shin-high between a line of blue-and-white posts outside the entrance, and applied an unclean expression to the Adjutant, who had had this amenity provided in an attempt to dignify the working area. Inside the crowded, brilliantly lighted office, he was half-asphyxiated by the smoke from the stove and half-deafened by the thumping of date-stamps, the ringing of telephones, the enraged bark of one sergeant and the loud, trem-ulous singing of the other. A red-headed man was rushing about bawling 'Emergency Ops for 17 Corps' in the accents of County Cork. Nobody took any notice of him: they had all dealt with far too many Emergency Ops messages in the last eight months.

*

Thurston was in his office, a small room partitioned off from the main one. The unit was occupying what had once been a Belgian military school and later an SS training establishment. This building had obviously formed part of the original barrack area, and Thurston often wondered what whim of the Adjutant's had located the offices and stores down here and the men's living-quarters in former offices and stores. The cubicle where Thurston spent so much of his time had no doubt been the abode of the cadet, and then *Unteroffizier*, in charge of the barrack-room. He was fond of imagining the heavily built Walloons and high-cheeked Prussians who had slept in here, and had insisted on preserving as a historical document the chalked *Wir kommen zurück* on the plank wall. Like his predecessors, he fancied, he felt cut off from all the life going on just outside the partition, somehow isolated. 'Alone, withouten any company,' he used to quote to himself. He would laugh then, sometimes, and go on to think of the unique lavatory at the far end of the building, where the defecator was required to plant his feet on two metal plates, grasp two handles, and curve his body into the shape of a bow over a kind of trough.

He was not laughing now. His phone conversation with Dalessio had convinced him, even more thoroughly than phone conversations with Dalessio commonly did, that the other despised him for his lack of technical knowledge and took advantage of it to irritate and humiliate him. He tried to reread a letter from one of the two married women in England with whom, besides his wife, he was corresponding, but the thought of seeing Dalessio still troubled him.

Actually seeing Dalessio troubled him even more. Not for the first time it occurred to him that Dalessio's long, matted hair, grease-spotted, cylindrical trouser-legs and ill-fitting battledress blouse were designed as an offensive burlesque of his own neat but irremediably civilian appearance. He was smoking, too, and Thurston himself was punctilious in observing inside his office the rule that prohibited smoking on duty until ten at night, but it was no use telling him to put it out. Dalessio, he felt, never obeyed orders unless it suited him. 'Hallo, Thurston,' he said amiably. 'Not still having a baby about the Poles, I hope?'

'I don't think I ever was, was I? I just wanted to make sure what the position was.'

'Oh, you wanted to make sure of that, did you? All right, then. It's quite simple. Physically, the circuit remains unchanged, of course. But, as you know, we have ways of providing extra circuits by means of electrical apparatus, notably by utilizing the electron-radiating properties of the thermionic valve, or vacuum-tube. If a signal is applied to the grid . . .'

Thurston's phone rang and he picked it up gratefully. 'Signal-master?' said the voice of Brigadier the Lord Fawcett, the largest and sharpest thorn in the side of the entire Signals unit. 'I want a special dispatch-rider to go to Brussels for me. Will you send him round to my office for briefing in ten minutes?'

Thurston considered. Apart from its being over a hundred miles to Brussels, he suspected that the story told by previous special DRs who had been given this job was probably quite true: the purpose of the trip was to take in the Brigadier's soiled laundry and bring back the clean stuff, plus any wines, spirits and cigars that the Brigadier's Brussels agent, an RASC colonel at the headquarters of the reserve Army Corps, might have got together for him. But he could hardly ask the Lord Fawcett to confirm this. Why was it that his army career seemed littered with such problems? 'The regular DR run goes out at oh-five-hundred, sir,' he said in a conciliatory tone. 'Would that do instead, perhaps?'

'No, it certainly would not do instead. You have a man available, I take it?'

'Oh yes, sir.' This was true. It was also true that the departure of this man with the dirty washing would necessitate another, who might have been driving all day, being got out of the section billet and condemned at best to a night on the Signal Office floor, more likely to a run half across Belgium in the small hours with a genuine message of some kind. 'Yes, we have a man.'

'Well, I'm afraid in that case I don't see your difficulty. Get him round to me right away, will you?'

'Very good, sir.' There was never anything one could do.

'Who was that?' Dalessio asked when Thurston had rung off.

'Brigadier Fawcett,' Thurston said unguardedly. But Dally probably didn't know about the laundry rumour. He had little to do with the dispatch-rider sections.

'Oh, the washerwoman's friend. I heard a bit about that from Beech. Not on the old game again, is he? Sounded as if he wanted a special DR to me.'

'Yes, he did.' Thurston raised his voice: 'Prosser!'

'Sir!' came from outside the partition.

'Ask Sergeant Baker to come and see me, will you?'

'Sir.'

Dalessio's large pale face became serious. He pulled at his moustache. Eventually he said: 'You're letting him have one, are you?' If asked his opinion of Thurston, he would have described him as a plausible bastard. His acquiescence in such matters as this, Dalessio would have added, was bloody typical.

'I can't do anything else.'

'I would. There's nothing to it. Get God's Adjutant on the blower and complain. He's an ignorant bugger, we know, but I bet he'd take this up.'

Thurston had tried this, only to be informed at length that the job of Signals was to give service to the Staff. Before he could tell Dalessio about it, Baker, the DR sergeant, arrived to be acquainted with the Lord Fawcett's desires. Thurston thought he detected a glance of protest and commiseration pass between the other two men. When Baker had gone, he turned on Dalessio almost savagely and said: 'Now look, Dally, leaving aside the properties of the thermionic bleeding valve, would you kindly put me in the picture about this teleprinter to the Poles? Is it working or isn't it? Quite a bit of stuff has piled up for them and I've been holding it in the hope the line'll be through on time.'

'No harm in hoping,' Dalessio said. 'I hope it'll be working all right, too.' He dropped his fag-end on the swept floor and trod on it.

'Is it working or is it not?' Thurston asked very loudly. His eyes wandered up and down the other's fat body, remembering how it had looked in a pair of shorts, doing physical training at the officers' training unit. It had proved incapable of the simplest tasks laid upon it, crumpling feebly in the forward-roll exercise, hanging like a crucified sack from the wall-bars, climbing by slow and ugly degrees over the vaulting-horse. Perhaps its owner had simply not felt like exerting it. That would have been bloody typical.

While Dalessio smiled at him, a knock came at the plywood door Thurston had had made for his cubicle. In response to the latter's bellow, the red-headed man came in. 'Sergeant Fleming sent to tell you, sir,' he said, 'we're just after getting them Polish fellows on the printer. You'll be wanting me to start sending off the messages we have for them, will you, sir?'

Both Thurston and Dalessio looked up at the travelling-clock that stood on a high shelf in the corner. It said eight o'clock.

III

'That's just about all, gentlemen,' the Colonel said. 'Except for one last point. Now that our difficulties from the point of view of communication have been removed, and the whole show's going quite smoothly, there are other aspects of our work which need attention. This unit has certain traditions I want kept up. One of them, of course, is an absolutely hundred-per-cent degree of efficiency in all matters affecting the disposal of Signals traffic, from the time the In-Clerk signs for a message from the Staff to the time we get . . .'

He means the Out-Clerk, Thurston thought to himself. The little room where the officers, warrant-officers and senior NCOs of the unit held their conferences was unheated, and the Colonel was wearing his knee-length sheepskin coat, another piece of merchandise supplied through the good offices of Jack Rowney in exchange, perhaps, for a few gallons of petrol or a couple of hundred cigarettes; Malone's men's cigarettes, probably. The coat, added to the CO's platinum-blond hair and moustache, increased his resemblance to a polar bear. Thurston was in a good mood, having just received the letter which finally buttoned up arrangements for his forthcoming leave: four days with Denise in Oxford, and then a nice little run up to Town for five days with Margot. Just the job. He began composing a nature note on the polar bear: 'This animal, although of poor intelligence, possesses considerable cunning of a low order. It displays the utmost ferocity when menaced in any way. It shows fantastic patience in pursuit of its prey, and a vindictiveness which . . .'

The Colonel was talking now about another tradition of his unit, its almost unparalleled soldier-like quality, its demonstration of the verity that a Signals formation *of any kind* was not a collection of down-at-heel scientists and long-haired mathematical wizards. Thurston reflected it was not for nothing that the Adjutant so frequently described himself as the Colonel's staff officer. Yes, there he was, Arctic fox or, if they had them, Arctic jackal, smiling in proprietary fashion at his chief's oratory. What a bunch they all were. Most of the higher-ranking ones had been lower-ranking officers in the Territorial Army during the thirties, the Colonel, for instance, a captain, the Adjutant a second-lieutenant. The war had given them responsibility and quick promotion, and their continued enjoyment of such privileges rested not on their own abilities, but on those of people who had arrived in the unit by a different route: Post Office engineers whipped in with a commission, older Regular soldiers promoted from the ranks, officers who had been the conscripts of 1940 and 1941. Yes, what a bunch. Thurston remembered the parting words of a former sergeant of his who had been posted home a few months previously: 'Now I'm going I suppose I can say what I shouldn't. You never had a dog's bloody chance in this lot unless you'd been at North Midland Command with the Adj. and the CO. And we all know it's the same in that Mess of yours. If you'd been in the TA like them you were a blue-eyed boy, otherwise you were done for from the start. It's all right, sir, everybody knows it. No need to deny it.'

The exception to the rule, presumably, was Cleaver, now making what was no doubt a shorthand transcript of the Colonel's harangue. Thurston hated him as the Adjutant's blue-eyed boy and also for his silky fair hair, his Hitler Youth appearance and his thunderous laugh. His glance moved to Bentham, also busily writing. Bentham, too, fitted into the picture, as much as the Adjutant would let him, which was odd when compared with the attitude of other Regulars in the Mess. But Bentham had less individuality than they.

'So what I propose,' the Colonel said, 'is this. Beginning next week the Adjutant and I will be making a series of snap inspections of section barrack-rooms. Now I don't expect anything in the nature of spit-and-polish, of course. Just ordinary soldierly cleanliness and tidiness is all I want.'

In other words, just ordinary spit-and-polish, Thurston thought, making a note for his sergeant on his pad just below the polar-bear *vignette*. He glanced up and saw Dalessio licking the flap of an envelope; it was his invariable practice to write letters during the Colonel's addresses, when once the serious business of line-communications had been got through. Had he heard what had just been said? It was unlikely.

The conference broke up soon afterwards and in the Mess ante-room, where a few officers had gathered for a drink before the evening meal, Thurston was confronted by an exuberant Adjutant who at once bought him a drink. 'Well, Tom,' he said, 'I reckon that fixes things up nice and neat.'

'I don't follow you, Bill.'

'Step number one in cooking your friend Dally's goose. Step number two will be on Monday, oh-nine-thirty hours, when I take the Colonel round the line-maintenance billet. You know what we'll find there, don't you?'

Thurston stared blankly at the Adjutant, whose eyes were sparkling like those of a child who has been promised a treat. 'I still don't get you, Bill.'

'Use your loaf, Tommy. Dally's blokes' boudoir, can't you imagine what it'll be like? There'll be dirt enough in there to raise a crop of potatoes, fag-ends and pee-buckets all over the shop and the rest of it. The Colonel will eat Dally for his lunch when he sees it.'

'Dally's got three days to get it cleaned up, though.'

'He would have if he paid attention to what his Commanding Officer says. But I know bloody well he was writing a letter when that warning was given. Serves the bastard right, do you see? He'll be off to the mysterious East before you can turn round.'

'How much does the Colonel know about this?'

'What I've told him.'

'You don't really think it'll work, do you?'

'I know the old man. You don't, if you'll excuse my saying so.'

'It's a lousy trick and you know it, Bill,' Thurston said violently. 'I think it's completely bloody.'

'Not at all. An officer who's bolshie enough to ignore a CO's order deserves all he gets,' the Adjutant said, looking sententious. 'Coming in?'

Still fuming, Thurston allowed himself to be led into the dining-room. The massive green-tiled stove was working well and the room was warm and cheerful. The house had belonged to the commandant of the Belgian military school. Its solid furniture and tenebrous landscape pictures had survived German occupation, though there was a large burn in the carpet that had been imputed, perhaps rightly, to the festivities of the *Schutz Staffel*. Jack Rowney, by importing photographs of popular entertainers, half-naked young women and the Commander-in-Chief, had done his best to document the Colonel's thesis that the Officers' Mess was also their home. The Adjutant, in excellent spirits, his hand on Thurston's shoulder, sent Corporal Gordon running for a bottle of burgundy. Then, before they sat down, he looked very closely at Thurston.

'Oh, and by the way, old boy,' he said, a note of menace intensifying the quack in his voice, 'you wouldn't think of tipping your friend Dally the wink about this little treat we've got lined up for him, would you? If you do, I'll have your guts for garters.'

Laughing heartily, he dug Thurston in the ribs and added: 'Your leave's due at the end of the month, isn't it? Better watch out you don't make yourself indispensable here. We might not be able to let you go, do you see?'

IV

Early on Monday Thurston was walking up from the Signal Office towards the area where the men's barrack-rooms were. He was going to find his batman and arrange to be driven some twenty miles to the department of the Advocate-General's branch which handled divorce. The divorce in question was not his own, which would have to wait until after the war, but that of his section cook, whose wife had developed an immoderate fondness for RAF and USAAF personnel.

Thurston was thinking less about the cook's wife than about the fateful inspection, scheduled to take place any minute now. He realized he had timed things badly, but his trip had only just become possible and he hoped to be out of the area before the Colonel and the Adjutant finished their task. He was keen to do this because the sight of a triumphant Adjutant would be more than he could stand, especially since his conscience was very uneasy about the whole affair. There were all sorts of reasons why he should have tipped Dalessio off about the inspection. The worst of it was, as he had realized in bed last night, when it was too late to do anything about it, that his irritation with Dalessio over the matter of the Polish teleprinter had been a prime cause of his keeping his mouth shut. He remembered actually thinking more than once that a thorough shaking-up would do Dalessio no harm, and that perhaps the son of an Italian café-proprietor in Cascade, Glamorganshire, had certain disqualifications for the role of British regimental officer. He twisted up his face when he thought of this and started wondering just why it was that the Adjutant was persecuting Dalessio. Perhaps the latter's original offence had been his habit of doing bird-warbles while the Adjutant and Rowney listened to broadcast performances of *The Warsaw Concerto*, the Intermezzo from *Cavalleria Rusticana*, and other sub-classics dear to their hearts. Cheeping, trilling and twittering, occasionally gargling like a seagull, Dalessio had been told to shut up or get out and had done neither.

Thurston's way took him past the door of the notorious line-maintenance billet. There seemed to be nobody about. Then he was startled by the sudden manifestation of two soldiers carrying brooms and a bucket. One of them had once been in his section and had been transferred early that year to one of the cable sections, he had forgotten which one. 'Good-morning, Maclean,' he said.

The man addressed came sketchily to attention. 'Morning, sir.'

'Getting on all right in No. I Company?'

'Yes, thank you, sir, I like it fine.'

'Good. What are you fellows up to so early in the morning?'

They looked at each other and the other man said: 'Cleaning up, sir. Fatigue party, sir.'

'I see; right, carry on.'

Thurston soon found his batman, who agreed with some reluctance to the proposed trip and said he would see if he could get the jeep down to the Signal Office in ten minutes. The jeep was a bone of contention between Thurston and his batman, and the batman always won, in the sense that never in his life had he permitted Thurston to drive the jeep in his absence. He was within his rights, but Thurston often wished, as now, that he could be allowed a treat occasionally. He wished it more strongly when a jeep with no exhaust and with seven men in it came bouncing down the track from the No. I Company billet area. They were laughing and two of them were pretending to fight. The driver was a lance-corporal.

Suddenly the laughing and fighting stopped and the men assumed an unnatural sobriety. The reason for this was provided by the immediate emergence into view of the Colonel and the Adjutant, moving across Thurston's front.

They saw him at once; he hastily saluted and the Adjutant, as usual, returned the salute. His gaze met Thurston's under lowered brows and his lips were gathered in the fiercest scowl they were capable of.

Thurston waited till they were out of sight and hurried to the door of the line-maintenance billet. The place was deserted. Except in illustrations to Army manuals and the like, he had never seen such perfection of order and cleanliness. It was obviously the result of hours of devoted labour.

He leant against the door-post and began to laugh.

V

'I gather the plot against our pal Dally misfired somewhat,' Bentham said in the Mess dining-room later that day.

Thurston looked up rather wearily. His jeep had broken down on the way back from the divorce expert and his return had been delayed for some hours. He had made part of the journey on the back of a motor-bike. Further, he had just read a unit order requiring him to make the jeep available at the Orderly Room the next morning. It wasn't his turn yet. The Adjutant had struck again.

'You know, I'm quite pleased,' Bentham went on, lighting a cigarette and moving towards the stove where Thurston stood.

'Oh, so am I.'

'You are? Now that's rather interesting. Surprising, even. I should have thought you'd be downcast.'

Something in his tone made Thurston glance at him sharply and put down the unit order. Bentham was standing with his feet apart in an intent attitude. 'Why should you think that, Ben?'

'I'll tell you. Glad of the opportunity. First of all I'll tell you why it misfired, if you don't already know. Because I tipped Dally off. Lent him some of my blokes and all, to get the place spick and span.'

Thurston nodded, thinking of the two men he had seen outside the billet that morning. 'I see.'

'You do, do you? Good. Now I'll tell you why I did it. First of all, the Army's not the place for this kind of plotting and scheming. The job's too important. Secondly, I did it because I don't like seeing an able man taken down by a bunch of ignorant jumped-up so-called bloody gentlemen from the Territorial Army. Not that I hold any brief for Dalessio outside his technical abilities. As you know, I'm a Regular soldier and I disapprove most strongly of anything damn slovenly. It's part of my nature now and I don't mind either. But one glance at the Adj.'s face when he was telling me the form for this morning and I knew where my duty lay. I hope I always do. I do my best to play it his way as a rule for the sake of peace and quiet. But this business was different. Wasn't it?'

Thurston had lowered his gaze. 'Yes, Ben.'

'It came as a bit of a shock to me, you know, to find that Dalessio needed tipping off.'

'How do you mean?'

'I mean that I'd have expected someone else to have told him already. I only heard about this last night. I was the only one here later on and I suppose the Adj. felt he had to tell someone. I should have thought by that time someone else would have let the cat out of the bag to Dally. You, for instance. You were in on this from the start, weren't you?'

Thurston said nothing.

'I've no doubt you have your excuses for not letting on. In spite of the fact that I've always understood you were the great one for pouring scorn on the Adj. and Rowney and Cleaver and the rest of that crowd. Yes, you could talk about them till you were black in the face, but when it came to doing something, talking where it would do some good, you kept your mouth shut. And, if I remember rightly, you were the one who used to stick up for Dally when the others were laying into him behind his back. You know what I think? I don't think you care tuppence. You don't care beyond talking, any road. I think you're really quite sold on the Adj.'s crowd, never mind what you say about them. Chew that over. And chew this over and all: I think you're

Court of Inquiry

I

'You free for a bit this afternoon, Jock?' Major Raleigh asked me in the Mess ante-room one lunch-time in 1944.

'I think so, Major,' I said. 'Provided I can get away about half-three. I've got some line-tests laid on for then. What do you want me for, anyway?'

'Here, let me top that up for you, old boy.' Raleigh seized a passing second-lieutenant by the elbow. 'Ken, run and get my batman to bring me one of my bottles of Scotch, will you? Oh, and incidentally what's become of your vehicle tool-kit deficiency return? It was supposed to be on my desk by ten-hundred this morning. Explanation?'

During this and what followed it, I first briefly congratulated myself on being directly responsible to the CO (the most incurious officer in the whole unit) rather than coming under Raleigh's command. Then I wondered what was in store for me after lunch. Perhaps a visit to another binoculars establishment or camera warehouse the major had discovered. My alleged technical proficiency had made me in some demand for such expeditions. Finally I looked about me. The Mess occupied a Belgian provincial hotel and this was its lounge, a square room lined with burst leather-padded benches. Officers sat on them reading magazines. Only the fact that two or three of them were also drinking stopped the place looking like a barber's waiting-room. Outside it was raining a little.

The major returned, smiling deprecatingly and resembling more than ever a moustached choirboy in battledress. 'Sorry about that,' he said, 'but you've got to keep them on their toes. Now about this business this afternoon. Young Archer's made another nonsense.'

'What's he done this time?'

'Lost a charging-engine. Left it behind on the last move, and naturally when he sent a party back the natives had removed it. Or so the story goes. I reckon that sergeant of his – Parnell, isn't it? – held a wayside auction and flogged it for a case of brandy. Anyway, it's gone.'

'Wait a minute, Major – wouldn't it have been one of those wee 1,260-watt affairs that take about a fortnight to charge half a dozen batteries? The ones nobody ever uses?'

'I wouldn't go all the way with you there, old boy.' The major rarely went all the way with anyone anywhere. Very often he went no distance at all.

'Aren't they obsolete?' I persisted. 'And wouldn't I be right in thinking they're surplus too?'

'That's not the point. This one was on young Archer's charge. The Quartermaster has his signature. Ah, here we are. Give me your glass, Jock.'

'Thanks . . . Well, where do I come into this, sir? Do I hold Archer for you while you beat him up, or what?'

The major smiled again, fixedly this time. 'Good idea. Seriously, though, I've had just about enough of young Archer. I want you to serve on the Court of Inquiry with me and Jack Rowney, if you will. In my office. I'll take you over after lunch.'

The major's modes of operation within his Company were often inventive to the point of romanticism. But even for him this was a far-fetched creation. 'Court of Inquiry? But couldn't we get this thing written off? There's surely no need . . .'

'I'd get someone else if I could, but everybody's got their hands full except you.' He looked me in the eye, and since I knew him well I could see he was wondering whether to add something like: 'How nice it must feel to be a mathematical wizard and live a life of leisure.' Instead, he waved to someone behind me, called: 'Hallo, Bill, you old chiseller', and went to greet the Adjutant, just arrived, presumably, on a goodwill mission from Unit HQ. There was much I wanted to ask Raleigh, but now it would have to keep.

II

Lunch in the heavily panelled dining-room was served by three Belgian waitresses wearing grey dresses and starched aprons. Their ugliness was too extreme to be an effect of chance. Perhaps they had been selected by a burgomagisterial committee as proof against the most licentious of soldiery. Such efforts would have been wasted. Libido burnt feebly in Raleigh's domain.

The meal was stew and diced vegetables followed by duff full of grape-pips. While he ate it the Adjutant, resplendent in a new Canadian battledress, chaffed Raleigh in the quacking voice which Archer was so good at imitating. I thought about Archer and one or two of his nonsenses.

The trailer nonsense had been a good instance of the bad luck he seemed to attract. The trailer had had a puncture on a long road convoy led by him and, since trailers carried no spare wheel, had clearly been unable to proceed farther. But if General Coles, commanding the 11th/17th Army Corps Group, was going to be able to communicate with his lower formations that evening it was as clearly essential that the convoy should proceed farther, and soon. With rather uncharacteristic acumen, Archer had had the trailer unloaded and then jacked up with both its wheels removed, reasoning that it would take very energetic intervention to steal the thing in that state. But someone did.

Then there had been the telephone-exchange-vehicle nonsense. On another convoy Archer had gone off without it, an action threatening similarly grave disservice to General Coles. Fortunately one of my sergeants, happening to watch Archer's wagon-train lumbering out, had gone and kicked out of bed the driver of the exchange vehicle, promising violence if his wheels were not turning inside ten minutes. A message by motor-bike to the head of the convoy, recommending a short halt, had done the rest. Taxing Archer with this afterwards, I wrung from him the admission that the dipsomaniacal Sergeant Parnell had been the culprit. He had been ordered to warn all drivers overnight, but half a bottle of calvados, plus the thought of the other half waiting in his tent, had impaired his efficiency.

'Why don't you sack that horrible lush of yours?' I had asked Archer in exasperation. 'You must expect things like that to happen while he's around. Raleigh would get him posted for you like a shot.'

'I can't do that,' Archer had moaned, accentuating his habitual lost look. 'Couldn't run the section without him.'

'To hell, man; better have no sergeant at all than him. All he ever does is talk about India and cock things up.'

'I'm not competent, Jock. He knows how to handle the blokes, you see.'

That was typical. Archer was no less competent, or no more incompetent, than most of us, though with Raleigh, the Adjutant and Captain Rowney (the second-in-command of the Company) taking turns to dispute this with him, his chronic lack of confidence was hardly surprising. And it was obvious to me that his men loathed their sergeant, whereas Archer himself, thanks merely to his undeviating politeness to them on all occasions, was the only one of their immediate superiors whom they had any time for. Without their desire to give him personal support in return, anything might have happened every other day to General Coles's communications, even, conceivably, to the campaign as a whole. According to Raleigh and the Adjutant, that was perhaps the most wonderful thing of all about Signals: junior officers got as much responsibility as the red-tab boys. But not as much pay, I used to mutter, nor as much power.

III

The afternoon had turned out fine, and I said as much to the Adjutant as, his goodwill mission evidently completed, he passed me on the wooden veranda of the hotel and got into his jeep without a word. Soon Raleigh, carrying a short leather-covered cane and a pair of string-and-leather gloves, turned up and walked me across the cobbled street to his office, pausing only to exhort a driver, supine under the differential of a three-tonner, to get his hair cut.

Raleigh's office had the distinction of being housed in an office. Pitted gilt lettering on the window advertised an anonymous society of mutual assurances. Archer had told me the other day how moved he had been, arriving there to be handed some distasteful errand or comradely rebuke, at the thought of the previous occupants in session, grouped blindfolded round a baize-covered table telling one another what good chaps they were.

He was in the outer room of the place now, sitting silently with the appalling Parnell among the clerks and orderlies. He looked more lost than usual, and younger than his twenty-one years, much too young to be deemed a competent officer. He was yawning a lot. I went up to him when the sergeant clerk called the major over to sign something.

'Look, Frank,' I said in an undertone: 'don't worry about this. This Court has no standing at all. Raleigh hasn't the powers to convene it; the Company's not on detachment. It's a complete farce – just a bit of sabre-rattling.'

'Yes, I know,' he said. 'Can I see you afterwards, Jock?'

'I'll come over to your section.' The line-tests could wait.

I went into the inner room, a long low affair lit by a single window and an unshaded bulb that pulsed slowly. Rowney stood up and swept me a bow. 'Ah, Captain D. A. Watson, Royal Signals, in person,' he fluted. 'Nice of you to look us up.'

'I always like to see how you administrators live.'

'Better than you long-haired scientists, I'll be bound.'

'Materially, perhaps. Spiritually, no.' It was hard not to talk like this to Rowney.

'Och aye, mon, ye're maybe nae sae far frae the truth.'

'Shall we get on, chaps?' the major asked in his on-parade

voice. 'Don't want to be all night over this.' He opened a file and nodded to me. 'Get Parnell in, will you?'

I got Parnell in. He smelt hardly at all of drink. He proceeded to give an oral rendering of his earlier written report: Raleigh had passed me a copy. At the relevant time he, Parnell, had been explaining the convoy's route to the drivers. Then he had got into the cab of his usual lorry (the one carrying the cookhouse stuff, no doubt). Then they had moved off. Soon after arrival at the other end, Mr Archer had said the charging-engine was missing and he, Parnell, must go back for it. Going back for it and returning empty-handed had taken eleven hours. In reply to questions, Parnell said yes, he had looked in the right place; no, nobody had been hanging about there; no, neither he nor, as far as he knew, anyone else had been detailed to look after the charging-engine; and yes, he would wait outside.

Archer came in and probably did his best to salute the Court smartly. The effort forced you to notice how badly he did it. He started on a rigmarole similar to Parnell's, then stopped abruptly and gazed at the major. 'Look, sir,' he said, biting his lips. 'Can I put this quite simply?'

Raleigh frowned. 'How do you mean, Frank?'

'I mean I lost the charging-engine and that's all there is to it. I should have made sure it was put on board and didn't. I just forgot. I should have gone round afterwards and had a look to make sure we'd left nothing behind. But I forgot. It's as simple as that. Just a plain, straightforward case of negligence and in-efficiency. And all I can say is I'm very sorry.'

Rowney started to ask a question, but the major restrained him. 'Go on, Frank,' he said softly.

Archer seemed to be trembling. He said: 'What makes me so ashamed is that I've let the Company down. Completely. And I don't see what I can do about it. There just isn't any way of putting it right. I don't know what to do. It's no use saying I'm sorry, I know that. I'll pay for the thing, if you like. So much a month. Would that help at all? God, I am a fool.'

By this time he was shaking a good deal and throwing his

hands about. I wondered very much whether he was going to cry. When he paused, blushing violently, I glanced at the other members of the Court. The head of the second-in-command was bent over the paper-fastener he was playing with, but Raleigh was staring hard at Archer, and on his face was a blush that seemed to answer Archer's own. At that moment they looked, despite Raleigh's farcical moustache, equally young and very alike. I felt my eyes widen. Was that it? Did Raleigh enjoy humiliating Archer for looking young and unsure of himself because he too at one time had been humiliated for the same reason? Hardly, for Raleigh was not enjoying himself now; of that I was certain.

Still holding his gaze, Archer burst out: 'I'm so sorry to have let you down personally, Major Raleigh. That's what gets me, failing in my duty by you, sir. When you've always been so decent to me about everything, and backed me up, and . . . and encouraged me.'

This last, at any rate, was a flagrant lie. Had it not been, Archer would not have been where he was now. And surely he must know he had lied.

The major turned his head away. 'Any questions, Jack?'

'No thank you, Major.'

'You, Jock?'

'No, sir.'

The major nodded. With his head still averted, he said: 'All right, thank you, Frank. Hang on a moment outside, will you? You can tell Parnell to get back to the section.'

Archer saluted and was gone.

'Well, thanks a million for inviting me along to your little show, Major,' Rowney said, stretching. 'Plenty of the old drama, what? Strong supporting cast. And very ably produced, if I may say so.'

Ignoring him, Raleigh turned to me. 'Well, Jock, what do you think?'

'About what exactly, sir?'

'Come on, man, we want to get this thing wrapped up. What finding? You're the junior member and you give your views first.'

I gave the more militarily relevant of my views and Rowney did the same. Within the next twenty seconds the Court had found that engine, charging, 1,260-watt, one, on charge to Lieutenant F. N. Archer, Royal Signals, had been lost by that officer in circumstances indicating negligence. Lieutenant F. N. Archer, Royal Signals, was hereby reprimanded. So that was that.

After an expressionless Archer had been acquainted with the findings and had left, I stopped at the door to chat to Rowney. I had never much cared for him but I was grateful to him this afternoon for having, in his own way, given his opinion of the major's little show. Out of the corner of my eye I saw Raleigh crumple up the Court of Inquiry documents and stuff them into his trouser-pocket.

Outside in the thin sunshine the three of us halted for a moment before dispersing. Raleigh's face took on a summarizing expression, with raised eyebrows and lifted lower lip. 'If only he'd pull himself together,' he said. 'But . . .'

IV

In Archer's section office and store, surrounded by piles of camouflage nets and anti-gas clothing, I apologized to him for having been a member of the Court. He sat inattentively on a crate containing a spare teleprinter, finally rousing himself to take a cigarette off me and to say: 'Funny thing about that charging-engine, you know. One of the things about it was that it wouldn't go. It never had gone in living memory. And then the tool-kit was missing. And no spare parts. And it was obsolete anyway, so it was no use indenting for spares. So it never would have gone.'

'Did you tell Raleigh that?'

'Yes. He said it was irrelevant.'

'I see.'

'Another funny thing was that the Quartermaster's got one nobody wants in his store. Surplus. In running order. With tools. And a complete set of spares. The QM offered it me.'

'Did Raleigh say that was irrelevant, too?'

'Yes. It wasn't the one I'd lost, you see. Oh, thanks very much, Corporal Martin, that's extremely kind of you.'

This was said to a member of Archer's section who had carried in a mug of tea for him, though not, I noticed aggrievedly, one for me.

Somewhere overhead aircraft could be heard flying eastward. Archer sipped his tea for some time. Then he said: 'Not a bad act I put on, I thought, in front of that rag-time bloody Court of Inquiry. Sorry, I know you couldn't help being on it.'

'An act, then, was it?'

'Of course, you owl. You didn't need to tell me the thing had no standing. But I had to pretend that I thought it had, don't you see? – and behave like a hysterical schoolgirl.'

Archer was a good mimic, I reflected, but it was perhaps questionable whether any amount of ordinary acting talent could have produced the blushes I had seen. On the other hand, I had no way of knowing how deeply he had thrown himself into the part.

'That was what Raleigh wanted,' he went on. 'If I'd stood up for my rights or anything, he'd just have decided to step up his little war of nerves in other ways. As it was I think I even made him feel he'd gone too far. That crack about him always backing me up was rich, I thought. Well, we live and learn.'

Archer no longer looked lost. Nor did he look particularly young. It was true, I thought, that the Army would lick anyone into shape. You could even say that it made a man of you.

I Spy Strangers

I

'Doing what's right, that's going to be the keynote of our policy. Honouring our obligations. Loyalty before self-interest. None of this letting our friends down when we think it's going to serve our turn. Not that it ever does in the end, of course, that type of thing. We can all see that from what happened pre-war. It was greed and selfishness got us into that mess. Anyway, coming down to details a bit now. First, Europe.'

The Foreign Secretary, a tall young man whose schoolmasterly and rather slovenly air did not rob him of a certain impressiveness, glanced over at the tanned, neatly moustached face of the Opposition's spokesman on Defence questions. It was from this quarter that real difficulty was to be expected, not from the Foreign Affairs spokesman, let alone from the Leader of the Opposition. For a moment the Foreign Secretary quailed. More than one member of the Government, he knew, found his policies absurd or extravagant rather than extremist and would gladly see him humiliated. He knew too that other, less overtly political reasons for this attitude were widespread on both sides of the House (and in the Visitors' Gallery). The temptation to play safe was strong. But he must resist it. He could not have it said that he had covered up his real programme with comfortable platitude. That was what They had always done.

'In Europe,' he went steadily on, 'we're going to go all out for co-operation and friendship with the Soviet Union. France too, naturally, but the state France is in these days, it'll be a long time before she's ready to play her full part in world affairs. It's obvious the lead's got to come from ourselves and the Russians. So first of all we have a system of guarantees of small countries, done between us. That is, Britain and the Soviet Union get together and say they'll clobber anyone who tries to walk into Austria and Czechoslovakia and Poland and Greece and Albania and all those places. And really clobber him, not just notes and protests and sanctions. We're not going to have it like it was last time.

'Then there's self-determination. That means everybody's got to have their own country and their own government. Nobody under foreign domination. Now I'll just take one example and show the type of thing I have in mind.'

He took his one example. It was Poland, not because he thought it was an example, good or bad, of anything in particular, but because he had not long ago read a short book on recent Polish history and, as was his habit, made notes on it. These supplied him now with many an unfamiliar name and obscure fact, made him sound like a bit of an expert on Poland, and by implication, he hoped, on politics in general. After an account of post-1918 events in Eastern Europe, he leant heavily on Poland's outmoded system of land tenure, the anti-democratic utterances of its government in exile and the Warsaw workers' resistance in 1939 and since.

He had got a lot of this off by heart and was able to look round the debating chamber. Two Opposition back-benchers were ostentatiously playing cards, conversations were muttering away here and there, and the Chancellor of the Exchequer was apparently asleep, but on the whole there seemed to be the right kind of semi-attentiveness. At least two people were taking everything in. They were the Speaker, whom the Foreign Secretary instinctively distrusted but of whose basic progressivism there could be little real doubt, and the Parliamentary Under-Secretary to the Home Office, whose brilliant brown eyes stared disconcertingly into his.

Did anything ever happen as it should? For months he had been wishing with all his heart that the Under-Secretary would look at him like that one day. But now that it seemed to have come about he felt none of the sudden joy and confidence he had expected. All he got was a jolt in the nerves which caused his mind to skip a groove or two, so that he found himself implying pretty unambiguously, in the next sentence he uttered, that the building of the Roznów Dam had been an act of irresponsible provocation justifying to the hilt the Russian invasion of Finland.

This evidently went unnoticed. The Foreign Secretary, judging his audience to be adequately softened up by abstruse information, modulated to an account, statistically supported, of German atrocities in Poland. This led to a more lyrical passage on the theme of Russo-Polish brotherhood in arms, followed by a carefully worded suggestion that Russia had earned the right to get things set up her way at her end of Europe. Next, a designedly short paragraph on the Americans, in which protestations of admiring gratitude – meant to fool nobody – introduced the message that to have fought for the liberation of a continent brought with it no automatic right to a say in its future, and that the sooner the Yanks realized this and cleared off back to their own half of the world the better for everyone.

There was some show of applause here on both sides of the House, and a voice from the Visitors' Gallery was heard to say that the fellow was talking a bit of sense at last. Mildly encouraged, trying not to look at the Under-Secretary to the Home Office, the Foreign Secretary turned to a fresh page of his notes. 'Next, the Middle East,' he said.

Immediate uproar broke out in all parts of the chamber. Those who had managed without apparent protest to sit through a deluge of information about the Silesian coalfields found they could not contemplate further lessons on the break-up of the Ottoman Empire or, it might be, the average weekly take-home pay of the Egyptian *fellaheen*. The Prime Minister felt it his duty to intervene. 'Turn it up, Hargy,' he called. 'You've had nearly twenty minutes now. Give the other lot a go, eh?'

The Foreign Secretary addressed the Speaker. 'What do you say, Mr Archer?'

'Well,' – the Speaker glanced to and fro – 'I think we might split this up a bit, don't you? Sort of debate parts of it at a time? How much more stuff have you got there?'

'About as much again, sir.'

There was a general groan and some shouts of 'Shame!'

'Order, order,' the Speaker said, blushing slightly. 'I think if you don't mind, Hargreaves, we might hold the rest of your speech for now. Let's hear from Sergeant – sorry: I now call upon the Leader of the Opposition.'

This personage, the left breast of whose uniform bore several campaign-medal ribbons, turned and exchanged energetic whispers with his colleagues. After a time he stopped shaking his head violently and started nodding it feebly.

Like many another political leader, he owed his position less to talent or even ambition than to a group of deficiencies: lack of general unpopularity, of immoderate enthusiasms, of firm views about anything. Sergeant Fleming helped his officers without taking their part in their absence, fiddled the stores inventory but not the leave roster, never stood the Company Quartermaster-Sergeant more than one extra drink an evening, helped to carry his passed-out mates to their billets and then dropped them on the floor. A natural middle-of-the-road man, Fleming, and equally naturally a Tory through and through, or perhaps just through. Nobody had thought of questioning his nomination as titular head of the alternative to a Government that extended, Popular Front fashion, from the Trotskyist at the Colonial Office to the Moral Rearmament International Christian Democrat who had found himself Chancellor of the Duchy of Lancaster.

Fleming's head was nodding faster now, though no less feebly, in fact slightly more so. He got up and said loudly and indistinctly: 'Well, we've heard what my learned friend, that is the Foreign Secretary, what he's had to say about what he thinks ought to be done about foreign countries and that. And I must say I've never heard such a load of rubbish in all my born days. It beats me that a so-called educated man with all his intelligence can talk all that rubbish. What do we care about all these Poles and French? They let us down, didn't they? No, we've got to look after ourselves because there's nobody else will. Break them all up into small states so's they can't start anything, that's the only way. Eh? All right, Bert. Well, I'm going to give you our military expert now because you've got to keep the peace, haven't you? That's the first thing, so I'll hand you over now to Sergeant Doll.'

The military expert's military aspect was half misleading. He was in the Army all right, but the shape and condition of his moustache, the unnecessary presence round his waist of a splendidly furbished webbing belt, the very knot of his khaki necktie suggested the Officers' Mess at some exclusive armoured-car regiment of incessantly invoked lancer or hussar ancestry, rather than the Orderly Room at an unemployed half-unit of the Royal Corps of Signals. Doll's extreme efficiency behind the sergeant's desk in that Orderly Room was perhaps what had led him, in compensation, to adopt this heavily martial persona. If so, he would only have been acting out on an individual and more symbolic scale the compulsion (born of the inferiority feelings common to all technical troops) that had afflicted his superiors during the period of training in England. All present could very well remember the cross-country runs, the musketry competitions, the three-day infantry-tactics schemes with smoke-bombs and a real barrage, the twelve-mile route-marches in respirators which had seemed in retrospect to show such a curious power of inverted prophecy when the unit finally completed its role in the European theatre of war without having had to walk a step or fire a shot.

One of the most convinced proponents of these early rehearsals for death or glory was at the moment sitting in the Visitors' Gallery with a hard expression on his soft face. He was Major R. W. Raleigh, the commander of a communications company until just after the German surrender, and now, the bulk of the unit having departed to help furnish signal facilities at the Potsdam Conference, the overlord of a sort of dispirited rump. This, originally comprising most of his old company with the addition of a spare section from the cable-laying company, had been swollen by successive injections administered by higher authority. In the chaos of disbandments, postings, re-formations and moves to the United Kingdom that characterized the aftermath of the campaign, a command like the major's represented a handy point of stabilization, a nucleus for any sort of drifting particle.

Expansion, once begun, had been rapid. Daily erosions took place as a corporal with one set of qualifications or three signalmen with another suffered removal for eventual use in the Far East, but these were far more than redressed by reinforcements. At one time or another, and with or without warning, there had arrived a further cable-laying section that had proved superfluous at Potsdam, most of the small but variegated Signals formation lately serving a now demolished independent parachute regiment, half a Base company without any officers or sergeants, an entire technical-maintenance section without any transport or stores, and two or three dozen teleprinter-operators, lineman-mechanics, drivers, electricians and fitters who had turned up individually or in little groups. All this amounted to a ration strength of something like twelve officers and four hundred other ranks, a total quite impressive enough to justify such gestures as renaming the original company office the Orderly Room and starting to refer to Sergeant Doll, the chief clerk in that office, as the Orderly Room Sergeant.

The major thought of Doll as a useful lad, and never more so than this evening. A certain amount of undisciplined behaviour, of affected intellectual nonsense, even of actual hints of disloyalty to the country – these were to be expected of a mock parliament, but there was surely no need for the thing to turn out quite so mock as it had. The blokes seemed to think that they could simply get up and say whatever they liked. Where that sort of attitude got you had been made all too clear at the previous sitting, when the bunch of jokers who called themselves the Government had brought in their Nationalization Bill. This meant, apparently, that they were in favour of collaring the coalmines, the steel industry, transport, public services – everything that created wealth and employment – and running them as they saw fit. That could never happen in the real world, in England, but the major could not agree with his friends in the Officers' Mess that the passing of that Bill merely showed how idiotic the whole issue had become – he wished he could. No, it was far more serious than that: the indication of a really ugly mood. He had too much sense of responsibility not to have come along tonight to keep an eye on things, use his influence to stop them getting out of hand. He hoped he would not have to intervene. It would not be necessary if Doll did his stuff properly, and Doll surely would. Reliable fellow, Doll, even if he was a bit of a puzzle. That perpetual parade-ground appearance and manner – what was it all in aid of?

Whatever the complications of Doll's internal drives, he was not a middle-of-the-road man; indeed, to extend the image a trifle, he was brushing up against the wall on the right-hand side. In the melodious voice that had served him so well as Complaints Supervisor at a large store in Leeds, he was saying: 'I shan't waste much time in destroying the dangerous nonsense we've just been exposed to. Russia has always been an aggressive power and always will be unless we stop her. All that restrained the Reds until 1939 was weakness. Then they went for the Baltic republics, Poland, Finland, plus various Balkan adventures. Their only interest in self-determination is to prevent it. Desertions to the Nazis included . . . I beg your pardon?'

'Facts!' the Foreign Secretary was shouting above the Speaker's half-hearted appeals for order. 'This is all just . . . insinuation. You haven't—'

'Facts?' The spokesman on Defence questions brought out his own notebook, then went on as mellifluously as before: 'All right, facts. From *The Times* of June 29th. Czechoslovakia signed Ruthenia over to Russia. Why? Because the Czechs wanted to get rid of it? From a BBC broadcast this morning. Russia is putting pressure on Turkey to revise their Black Sea Straits treaty and cede two territories to her. Why? Because the Turks are planning to blockade her? From another broadcast. Three hundred more Poles shot by the order of People's—'

'They were traitors, collaborators, there've been—'

'I've no doubt many of them were. But we shall never know now, shall we? These people should have been tried by an international court, as we've said we—'

'It was the heat of the moment. You always get—'

'As I started to tell you, these were executions carried out under sentences passed by People's Courts, there wasn't just a mob blazing away in the streets. But I really must appeal to you, Mr Speaker, to quell these interruptions. I managed to keep quiet while all that Red propaganda was going on, so I don't see why—'

'All right, Sergeant Doll. Hargreaves, I must warn you to keep quiet.' There was reluctance and a half-buried sympathy in the Speaker's tone.

'Sorry, sir. But I've simply got to ask him about the Polish elections. Surely that proves—'

'*Order*, Hargreaves. You'll have to shut up or leave.'

'Yes, sir.'

The House resettled itself rather sulkily, feeling, and muttering, that it was always the bloody same: the moment you got a decent row going, some pernickety sod piped up with some moan about order. Might as well be sitting in the billet reading last week's paper.

'Thank you, Mr Speaker.' Doll stared across at Hargreaves. 'As a matter of fact I welcome the opportunity of saying something about those elections. I find it rather odd that the Reds should be so keen to get those elections held at this stage, with the country still in turmoil – but then it'll be all right really, won't it? – with the Reds everywhere to see fair play. No undemocratic interference from us or the French or the Yanks that might result in free elections, because the wrong people might get elected then, mightn't they? Can't have that, can we? Comrade Stalin wouldn't like that.

'I should like to round off this question with a few words on the Warsaw rising and the Reds' unfortunate inability to come to the aid of their Polish brothers in arms. In the spring of this year—'

Hargreaves had lost all the poise that might have been expected of a Foreign Secretary, even a mock one. He leant forward on the heavy, scarred wooden bench and put his head in his hands. If only he knew more and could think faster; if only he had at his side, as living proof that Doll was wrong, one or other of the fine men and women he knew on his local Labour Party branch committee, people who had grown up in the service of Socialism and given it all their spare energy, fighting in Spain, leading hunger marches, canvassing in hopelessly impregnable Tory strongholds . . . He tried not to think of all that going to waste, failing ever to find its way to power. His almost continuous excitement over the results of the British General Election, due to be announced the following week, froze momentarily into despair. Contrary to what everyone thought, he had never been a member of the Communist Party. He was suspicious of the one-party system and his doubts about the Russian labour camps still lingered. But if Doll's ideas carried the day at home there was only one logical step to take. Hargreaves was enough of a Marxist to recognize a situation in which the Left must combine against the main enemy. To have taken this half-decision brought him no relief: on tonight's showing he was politically useless.

His obvious dejection was not lost on Major Raleigh, whose soft face had softened somewhat since Doll began to put things in the right perspective and who was now leaning back in his chair in search of what degree of comfort it could provide. This was not great. Like everything else in the room it seemed to have been made without reference to human use. Typical German unimaginativeness, the major thought to himself. The small oblong windows, through which a strong late-evening sun was pouring, were set too high in the wall to be properly seen out of, certainly by most of the children who until recently had attended prayers here, sung Nazi songs or whatever it was they did in their school hall. Two rows of flat-topped desks had been dragged out of an adjacent store-room to form the Government and Opposition front benches. It would have taken a long-torsoed boy or girl to work at one with any ease or even see fairly over it, and the design demonstrably called for a far shorter-legged man than the average mock parliamentarian currently in occupation.

The major brooded for a time upon Hargreaves and the many things that could be done with or to him to make him less all-embracingly unsatisfactory – failing which, some positive enactment of how the world in general felt about him would do him good. The things available to the major ranged from giving Hargreaves an extra duty for being unshaven (any and every day would do) to getting him transferred elsewhere. An influential contact in the relevant department at General HQ was in the habit of seeing to it that, to a large extent, the major was able to decide who should and who should not be posted out of his command. There was only one place where, after a brief break in the United Kingdom, Hargreaves would finally be sent: a very hot and distant place, full of stuff which would interest him and which, as a budding expert on world affairs, he could not afford not to know about.

In one of his rare moments of self-contemplation, brought on by slight uneasiness over the impending Election result, the major had started wondering about the morality of dispatching jungle-ward anybody under his authority who had happened to annoy him. The moment had sped harmlessly by when he remembered that, to an experienced and conscientious officer such as he trusted he was, men who annoyed him were certain to be, corresponded one hundred per cent with, men who were bad soldiers. It did not worry him that he was thus filling the relevant units of South-East Asia Command with drunks, incompetents, homosexuals, Communists, ration-vendors and madmen. His first duty was to the formation he led.

Thoughts of the Japanese campaign naturally led him to consider another person who was going the right way about getting to it soon. Lieutenant F. N. Archer, sometime defendant in a celebrated unconstitutional Court of Inquiry staged by the major in an only half-successful attempt to humiliate him, was now scowling openly at what Doll was saying. Archer sat in a tall ecclesiastical-looking throne affair, much carved with Gothic lettering, at the far end of the room from the Visitors' Gallery. This was no gallery, but a simple row of hard chairs at floor level. The real gallery over the oak doorway had not suited the major, who still resented Archer's original attempt to make him and his friends sit up there as if they were nothing to do with the proceedings. It had been just like Archer not to see that it was absurd to try and reproduce the House of Commons set-up in details like that. Not seeing the obvious was his speciality, as his regimental work showed. To have appointed him Speaker of this fandango had probably been a mistake, but then he was the one who was always showing off his political knowledge in the Mess. A fat lot that had amounted to.

His voice sounding hollow in the barely furnished room, Doll said: 'But before that we must immediately negotiate a peace with Japan, while she still has some sort of military machine left. We're going to need every ship and plane and man they have. A settlement wouldn't be difficult. They're talking about peace already. Nobody really cares who owns those islands – it's the bases that count. And with a common enemy that'd soon sort itself out.'

'What about the Chinese?' the Postmaster-General asked. He was a corporal of dispatch-riders from the parachute formation, one of the few recent arrivals who had taken part in the parliament.

Doll never smiled, but cordiality enhanced his tones when he answered: 'An excellent question. I think the Japs with their reduced bargaining-power could probably be bullied into making enough concessions to the Chinks to keep them quiet. Certainly the Yanks have got quite enough cash to bribe the Nationalist Chinks – Chiang's lot – into selling their little yellow souls. The Red Chinks are more of a problem, though they won't amount to much for a good while yet. I think there's a fair chance they could be bought off too, into some sort of tacit neutrality anyway.

'But the real problem is Europe. The thing there is to advance until we're stopped. We stop wherever they start shooting. And they won't do that for a bit. We push into Czechoslovakia and

Hungary and the Balkans and southern Poland if we can get there, until we're stopped. Then we dig in. They can't have troops everywhere. Later on we straighten the line by agreement with the Reds. It's our only chance of saving any of these people – to fight on our side later, if necessary.

'We'll need troops for that, of course. To dig in and stay there. Demobilization must be halted at once. Twenty-eight days' leave in the UK for everybody we can spare, then back on the job. No Yanks are going home if I have anything to do with it; they're all needed here. Re-form the French, Dutch, Belgian and Italian armies. And the Germans, as many of those boys as we can get. It does seem a pity we spent so much energy killing so many of them, doesn't it? When if we'd gone in with them when they asked us in 1941 we'd have smashed the Reds between us by now? But we'll leave that for the time being. We'll have to put the Nazi Party back on its feet, by the way. They understand these things. Perhaps old Adolf will turn up from wherever he is and give us a hand. We could use him.

'Well, that's about it. Keep them nattering away in Potsdam as long as possible and move like hell meanwhile. I think it would probably work. Everybody's exhausted, but our manpower and resources are superior. What we almost certainly haven't got is the will. That's their strong suit. In conclusion, let me just say formally that in foreign affairs the first policy of my party is resistance to Communism.'

Doll sat down, having finished his speech, a rare achievement in this chamber. There was a lot of applause, most of it based on close attention to what had been said. Nodding his head to the pair of gloomy subalterns who sat beside him, the major joined judicially in. He knew he was supposed to be impartial, but really there could be no question but that the whole thing was on the right lines, except perhaps for the bit about the Nazi Party, which was premature to say the least. His speculations why Doll had never put in for a commission were interrupted by the Foreign Secretary, who clattered to his feet and cleared his throat in a long bellow. Hargreaves's normally mottled face was flushed;

parts of his scrubby hair stuck out horizontally; his chest rose and fell.

'Could I ask first of all,' he said in a trembling voice, 'if the Honourable Member imagines that any British Government would put the policy he outlines, put into effect the policy he outlines?'

Doll's stare was not unfriendly. 'Oh no. That's to say almost certainly not. They'd be turned out as soon as the electorate realized what they'd let themselves in for. You'd be asking people to admit in effect that they'd been fighting on the wrong side, you see, and having their relatives killed doing it. And they're tired too. No, I'd say the chances—'

'Then what . . . what the hell . . . ? I mean what's the point of—?'

'The point? The point of what we're doing as I see it is to work out what we think we *should* do, not what the Government we elect *probably will* do. If we're all just playing a guessing game, then I think I'm with you. You'll very likely get what you want, especially if the country's fool enough to elect those Socialist prigs. I only hope you enjoy it when you find out what it's really like.'

'Mr Speaker, sir,' Hargreaves cried, and he was looking directly at Archer, 'I never thought to sit in this House, which is a, which exists only with the traditions of that other House across the sea, sir, and hear an Honourable Member admit to an admiration for the Nazi Party, which has been responsible for so many dreadful crimes, and which, the German Army I mean, we've been fighting it all these years and now I hear this said, or perhaps he now wishes to—'

'I didn't admit to an admiration for the Nazi Party, and I would never do so. Their racial policy was against reason and their appeal was based on mass hysteria. No, I was only arguing that in a desperate situation like ours you need all the allies you can get, especially if they can organize and fight. That we all know the Nazis can do.'

'No wonder you want the Nazis. You're an aggressor, you

want to aggress – you want to attack the Russians. The people who've died in their millions to stop the Nazis from conquering the world – honestly, how insane can you—'

The Foreign Secretary's voice tailed off. The House was perfectly silent, crossing its fingers with the wish that no pernickety sod was going to invoke order. Doll said efficiently: 'The Nazis could never have conquered the world. There were too few of them and they were confined to one country. The Reds are an international conspiracy. And my proposals were entirely defensive. What interests me is resistance to Communism, as I said, not an assault on it. It's too early for that, or too late. There's only been one assault on it in our lifetime, and it failed because we were too stupid to join in. And now perhaps somebody else might care to—'

'Fascist!' Hargreaves screamed. 'The strong arm, that's the thing for you, isn't it? The jackboot. The good old truncheon. I know your sort, Doll. There are people like you in England, all over, in the bloody Empire, Africa and India, smooth as buggery in the club with the old brandy and soda and then off to break a strike or flog a wog or . . . You're all the same. And everybody who clapped you . . .' His unblinking glance swept the chamber, meeting the major's eyes for a moment. 'Ought to be ashamed of yourselves. Black-and-Tan material. You're going to lose. You're on the side of death. History'll get you. Auden warned you but you never listened. I won't even sit in the same room with you.'

Sincere emotion enforces a hearing. Hargreaves had almost reached the impressive exit doorway – no more than twenty years old but, to an English eye, redolent of weighty Teutonic medievalism – before comment and protest got properly going. Doll smoothed his abundant straight dark hair. Archer and the Parliamentary Under-Secretary to the Home Office gazed with similar expressions after the retreating Hargreaves. The major blew his nose and tucked the pale tan silk handkerchief into the sleeve of his battledress blouse. His soft face concealed emotion at the hardly won memory (he did not care to blur with too much detail his faculty for making quick decisions) that Archer was Hargreaves's section officer and, as such, responsible for everything he did.

II

'Anything special for me this morning, Wilf?' Major Raleigh hung up his service-dress hat – which, in defiance of his own edict, he regularly wore with battledress – on the fist-sized bronze knob of the bookcase door. Behind the glass of this, apart from a couple of dozen battered books in a foreign language or two, there huddled a heap of painted china vases and ewers which the major thought might be eighteenth century or nineteenth century or one of those. He had collected them from various houses and shops in the area and sometimes wondered what to do with them.

Captain Cleaver looked listlessly at a pad on his table. 'I don't think so, Major. There's the pay to collect.'

'Get one of the cable wallahs to go. Time they did something to earn their living.'

'Well, it's a trip, you know, Major.'

'So much the better.'

'No, I was thinking somebody might like to go. Get out of the place for a bit.'

'Oh, I see what you mean. Go yourself if you like, Wilf.'

'Well, actually I was hoping to look in at the Officers' Shop if you're not going to need me here. That's in the opposite direction to the cashier.'

'Ask that parachute chap, then, Pinch or Finch or whatever his name is. He's been looking a bit down in the mouth.'

'Winch. Yes, he has, hasn't he? He must feel a bit of a fish out of water here. Nothing going on. It must have been a bit different at Arnhem. All that excitement. Pretty hectic too, though. I expect he misses that, don't you?'

'What?' The major, at his in-tray, stared up over his reading-glasses. They made him look ineffectively studious, like a neglected schoolboy at a crammer's. 'Misses what?'

'You know, the excitement and the big bangs and so on at Arnhem. I was asking you if you thought he was missing it.'

'Who?'

'Winch, the parachute chap.'

'How the hell should I know what he's missing and what he isn't missing? And he wasn't at Arnhem, I asked him. Got taken off the drop at the last minute because of dysentery.'

'I understood him to say—'

'He wasn't on the Normandy drop, either.'

'Well, he wouldn't have been, would he? Normandy was Sixth Airborne. Arnhem was First.'

'Yes. Look, Wilf, if you're going to the Officers' Shop there are a couple of things you might pick up for me, if you would.'

'Certainly, Major, of course.' Cleaver turned to a fresh page of his pad, pleased at the chance of writing something down, and poised his pencil devotedly. 'Now then, what can I do for you?'

'Half a dozen handkerchiefs, the silk ones. Don't seem to be able to get anything ironed round here. Three pairs of the light-weight socks, size eight shoe. Not the elastic tops. If there's only the elastic tops don't get anything. Ties? No, I'm all right for those.'

The major appeared to fall into a muse. Cleaver said: 'Anything else, Major?'

'Hold on, I'm thinking . . . Those American shirts. Has he got any left, do you know?'

'Well, he's probably got some more in by this time. He said he was getting some more in.'

'Make sure they're the same. The same as I'm wearing now. See? . . . You're not looking.'

'I am, honestly, sir. I know the sort.'

'Make sure the collar's the same. Get me three of them. Fifteen and a half neck.'

'Right.'

'Just a moment.' The major fondled his throat, his blue eyes bulging as he tried to see what he was doing. 'Better say sixteen to be on the safe side. I'll settle up with you when you see what you've got, okay?'

'Right, Major. Oh, by the way, I meant to tell you—'

'What?'

'A message came over the blower from Movement Control in Hildesfeld. Just an advance warning – there'll be a teleprint through this afternoon with all the griff. A platoon of the Montgomeryshire Light Infantry are moving into the area some time tomorrow and we're to help them find accommodation. They were supposed to be doing guard duty at one of the DP camps, but it closed down a couple of days ago and so there's nowhere for them to—'

'But it's not our responsibility to fix them up. They're not Signals.' Raleigh spoke with an anxious severity, as if, conceivably, the platoon referred to might turn out to be the one in which someone very dangerous to him was serving, someone who had seen him cheating at picquet or torturing a prisoner.

'I know, but that's not what they're on about. These people will come under the Admin Company in the ordinary way. It's just that – well, the Staff Captain in Hildesfeld seemed to think that with our knowledge of the area we could be pretty useful to these MLI types. Know where to look and save them time. Just lend them an officer and a sergeant for a day or so. Nobody at Movement Control who'd do and if there were they couldn't spare him. They're run off their feet there.'

The major hardly heard the last part of this. In the weeks since the war ended, even more since the larger part of the unit had gone to Potsdam, he had been possessed and tormented by dreams of triumph, renown or at least advancement. One of these, which he never visualized with full conscious attention, was about a local Nazi uprising crushed by him in a single prompt and ruthless blow. Another, disguised as an unuttered joke, involved the removal with ignominy of the CO as a chief executive of communications at Potsdam and the immediate substitution of himself: 'Where's Raleigh? Get hold of Raleigh.

There's only one man for this job and that's Dick Raleigh.'

Dreams three and four engaged him more continuously, if less profoundly. Three he had taken what steps he could to bring to life. In the last month he had written three demi-official memoranda to the Signals general at Army Group headquarters. Their theme was that, if the war against Japan lasted long enough, there would probably be a role in it for a new full-dress Headquarters Signals unit, and that the body of troops at present under his command, admittedly miscellaneous but in a high state of training, could with advantage be used as the basis of such a unit. He himself, he had pleaded, could ask for nothing better than to stay on in uniform past the date of his expected release, indeed indefinitely, if he could be allowed to serve as its leader.

The first memorandum had been acknowledged with the utmost formality, the others not at all. As each day brought no word from Army Group HQ, and as news of Japanese reverses mounted, the major fell back increasingly on his fourth dream. This had been put into his head by the compulsions of military geography. The medium-sized village in which he and his men were living had turned out to lie within administrative reach of a smallish but important railhead – the one at Hildesfeld. The Movement Control people there were faced with the task of propelling personnel westward about three times faster than their resources allowed. The accumulating residue had to be put somewhere. The major's village and its environs were an obvious lodgment for it. The major had taken it upon himself to provide communications between the railhead and the tankless tank troops, the gunless artillery sections, the reconnaissance detachments with nothing in Europe left to reconnoitre – all those whom destiny or administrative whim had transmitted in this general direction.

If this situation continued, authority would have to recognize it. A different type of man from the major might have noticed an analogy with the experiences of an ex-colonial territory on the threshold of statehood. As things were he simply saw himself as an Area Commandant with a lieutenant-colonelcy to match.

Only one officer of this rank was known to be living hereabouts, a youthful Engineer on twenty-four-hour warning of departure who was rumoured to divide his time between drinking schnapps in a farmhouse bedroom and driving round the countryside looking for more, this at a speed which suggested that death might remove him before officialdom could. Of the five or six local majors, inquiry showed that Raleigh was senior to three and had been around the place longer than any. 'Lieut-Col. R. W. Raleigh, R Sigs' sounded authentic. So did 'Winkworth (West) Conservative Association – *Chairman*: Colonel Richard W. Raleigh'.

'All right, Wilf,' the major said. 'I'll take care of it. Was there anything else?'

'About the Shop again, sir. I take it it would be all right to get a few things for one or two of the blokes while I'm there?'

The major frowned. It was his major's frown, his responsibility invoking frown, his slackness-detecting frown, his extra-duty-donating frown. He kept it on full for a while before he said: 'I'm not sure that's a very good idea.'

'Oh, I don't see why not. Things are pretty relaxed these days. We're not at war any more, after all. I can't see it doing anybody much harm.'

'I wouldn't go all the way with you there, old boy. While the blokes have got so much time on their hands it's particularly important to maintain discipline. It doesn't help at all, throwing shoes and ties and what-not around indiscriminately. This is an Officers' Shop we're talking about, not a natty gents' tailoring establishment. Why do you think officers and men are required to dress differently? To emphasize the difference in their status, of course. That's quite fundamental.'

'I know, Major' – Cleaver was being uncharacteristically persistent – 'but it's going on all over the place, you see. Only yesterday I saw a couple of the lads on the switchboard wearing those jeep coats, the sort with the—'

'They're in Archer's lot; I've already had a word with him about it. There's a great deal too much of this all-chums-together spirit around these days and I don't like it. It isn't . . . healthy. Anyway, who were you thinking of getting stuff for?'

'Well, evidently Doll could do with a couple of shirts, and the Quartermaster-Sergeant was talking about a few pairs of shoes – he didn't say who he wanted them for – and then my batman was asking—'

The major's frown, which had almost cleared, came back again, but with a difference that indicated that thought of some description was going on behind it. 'That's rather different. Doll knows this sort of thing is a privilege and he's not the kind of fellow to abuse it. The QMS has done a first-class job for everybody at a very difficult time,' – and, the major might have added, a five-star *cordon bleu* crossed-knife-and-fork-in-the-Michelin-guide-type job for himself out of the petrol-hunger of a chain of civilians that stretched back as far as Arromanches on the Norman coast – 'and if he needs a pair of shoes or two I don't think it's really up to us to question it. As regards your batman – well, I regard that as a personal matter between the two of you. Batmen have always had these little perks – it's a tradition. Yes, that's all right, Wilf.'

'Thanks, Major.'

'You did quite right to tell me, though,' Raleigh said emphatically, leaving the other in no doubt about its being quite wrong not to tell him in the future, and picked up a sheaf of vehicle returns. He knew full well what was on them, for the transport situation, like much else, had remained static for weeks, but the small effort involved in putting common knowledge into due form helped to keep the sections on their toes, or at any rate off their backsides.

Cleaver cranked his telephone and after a moment said: 'Parachute Section, please . . . What? When was this? I see. Is anyone working on it? Well, let me know the moment it's back, will you? – I say, Major.'

Raleigh looked up as if he had been deep in the vehicle returns for a day or so. 'What is it?'

'The line to the parachute people's out. Looks as if I'll have to go and tell Winch myself.'

'Winch?'

'About the pay. We decided—'

'Yes, yes. Get Doll to send someone over. It's only a few hundred yards.'

While Cleaver again cranked his phone and spoke, the major turned over his in-tray a second time, then got going on his own phone. 'Give me the Signalmaster . . . Signalmaster? Signals Command Group here, Major Raleigh. Who is that?'

'Archer, sir.'

'Frank, what's happened to the morning summary of communications? It's supposed to be on my desk at nine o'clock.'

Seated at his trestle table in the commodious and airy barn that housed the Signal Office, Archer blushed. 'I sent it across, sir. Nearly two hours ago.'

This inadvertent reminder of how long after nine o'clock the major had presumptively begun his morning's work did not go down well. 'I don't care how long ago you think you sent it across, Frank, it isn't here.'

'There's only one thing on it, sir – the line to Para-Sec is down; otherwise—'

'I know that. That's not the point. You'd better have a look round there and then come over and talk to me about it. I want a word with you anyway.'

Sighing, Archer got to his feet and stretched. Inactivity reigned about him. A single teleprinter clattered away in one corner. A bespectacled corporal read a paperback novel in front of the wood-and-canvas rack in which transmitted messages were filed. The rack had been cleared at midnight and now carried half a dozen exiguous batches of flimsy. The two counter-clerks were playing chess while the orderly, an aged and delinquent Highland infantryman, watched them in wonder. The locations clerk was busy with his eraser, removing what must have been one of the last official traces of yet another defunct unit.

Archer raised his voice. 'Hargreaves!'

Peering anxiously, laboriously pinching out a cigarette, Hargreaves hurried in from the open air. His battledress blouse, instead of lying open at the top to reveal a collar and tie, was buttoned up and hooked at the throat; he must have been one of the last men in the British Army to avail himself of the recent sartorial concession. No doubt the older style made fewer demands on his time and energy. 'Yes, Mr Archer?' he said.

'You took the summary of communications across to Command Group, didn't you?'

'The what, Mr Archer?'

'That thing I gave you to take over to the major's office, you took it, didn't you?'

'Oh yes. Captain Cleaver was there and I gave it to him.'

'You're sure?'

'Oh absolutely, Mr Archer.'

'You'd swear to that?' Archer smiled conspiratorially. 'They're trying to make out over there that I never sent it. You'd stand by me if it came to a court-martial, wouldn't you?'

Hargreaves looked worried. 'I don't quite understand, Mr Archer, but if there's any trouble you can count on me to—'

'Never mind, Hargreaves, I was only pulling your leg . . . Good show you put up last night at the parliament, by the way – I was meaning to tell you.'

'Oh, thank you very much, Mr Archer, how kind of you . . . You don't think perhaps it was a bit . . . extreme? You know, at the end.'

'Not a bit, you were quite justified. These people need to be talked to straight once in a while. You keep at it. Oh, and I thought that bit about Auden came in very well. I didn't know you were a fan of his.'

'I've just read a few of his things, sir.'

'I see.' Archer became conscious that he had been smiling rather a lot. 'Right, that's all, Hargreaves, thank you.'

'Thank you, sir.'

On Archer's table lay a letter he had been writing to a friend of his in Oxford, one who, like most of his contemporaries, was medically unfit for military service – a doubly fortunate short-coming in the present case, for one of this friend's several neuroses forbade him to be ordered about. The letter was full of undetailed assertions of hatred and misery, unsolicited news about what Archer's two girl-friends in England had been writing to him, and inquiries about issues of jazz records. He put on top of it the Signalmaster's Diary – its sole entry for the morning read *0840 On duty F. N. Archer Lt* – and told Sergeant Parnell, the superintendent, where he was going. Then he donned his ridiculous khaki beret and left.

Outside, the sunlight was intense. Hargreaves was standing in the shade, leaning against the corner timber of the barn and talking to a switchboard-operator called Hammond, who among other things was Parliamentary Under-Secretary to the Home Office. He gave Archer an inquisitive brown-eyed glance.

Archer went down the yard, at one side of which a dispatch-rider was dozing on a heap of straw, and crossed the cobbled street to the school building. He was thinking that the oddest thing about the major, or about himself, was that Raleigh's behaviour was getting funnier all the time without arousing any laughter in him, Archer. Take Raleigh's unconcealed delight whenever a new formation moved into the area and thus gave him another place to have a line run to and a telephone installed at, an amenity much resented by its beneficiaries, who would usually have spent most of the war too near a telephone and asked for nothing better than to remain incommunicable. The major had almost got drunk – he never did quite – on the strength of having foisted a special dispatch run and *a wireless link* upon a Displaced Persons Area Authority on the verge of closure. He seemed very near believing that stuff like this represented a serious and adequate role for a group that had provided half the communications of an Army Corps Group headquarters at war; he no longer excused the farce of having a Signal Office here at all by saying (untruly) that it kept the lads busy.

The same shift of attitude had taken place over his road. This boulevard through the camp area, too short to matter except in terms of the energy its construction absorbed and totally un-necessary anyway because of the dry summer, was about to be extended to other parts of the major's tribal domain. Archer foresaw himself doing further stints of uninformed supervision, watching the hard-core and rubble go down, scouring the village for more wheelbarrows, driving out to the Engineers detachment to borrow yet more. Hitler had been funny too, but you had had to live in Valparaiso or somewhere to be able to laugh at him with conviction.

A flight of green-painted wooden steps led up the side of the school. Sergeant Doll was sitting on them, evidently improving his tan. With the affability of a pub landlord at the entry of a notable big spender, he called from a distance: 'Good-morning to you, Mr Archer, and how are you this fine morning, sir?'

'Oh, fed up,' Archer said unguardedly.

'Well, I'm not, sir, I don't mind telling you.' Doll made no move to get up and let Archer pass. 'I've got plenty to eat and a decent bed and no work and nothing to spend my pay on and nobody to bother me. I'm winning, sir.'

'Yes, you are, aren't you?' Archer, whose head was on a lower level than Doll's, noticed that the other seemed to have no hairs whatsoever in his nose. This had the effect of making his moustache appear, if not actually false, at any rate an isolated phenomenon.

'That was a nice little spot of bother at the old House of Commons last night, sir, wasn't it? Of course that fellow Hargreaves, he's unbalanced, isn't he? A lot of these Reds are, you know. There must be something in that particular philosophy that sort of attracts such people. He must be a perfect little darling to have in the section, Master Hargreaves. I don't know how you put up with him, sir, honestly I don't. I'd have got rid of him many moons ago.'

'Oh, he's not as bad as all that. He is an educated man, after all.'

'That makes it twenty times worse, sir, in my view. The corruption of the best is worst, I remember reading that somewhere. You'd be the one who'd know where it comes from, I expect, sir, wouldn't you?'

Archer looked up sharply, but Doll's eye was as bland as ever. 'It's Latin,' Archer said. 'I think.'

'No doubt, sir. It's really a pity Hargreaves made an exhibition of himself like that. Damaged his own case, I thought. Don't you agree, sir?'

There was a pause while Archer recalled what was perhaps his sole intelligently self-interested action since joining the Company: putting a half-bottle of whisky on Doll's desk last Christmas Eve. Ever since then the major, who tended to make a confidant of Doll, had found that his little surprises for Archer, in the shape of unheralded inspections of the Signal Office and the like, had an odd way of turning out not to be surprises after all. Rather late in the day, Archer was discovering a related principle, that the Army afforded unique scope for vindictiveness and that disagreement on apparently neutral matters often provoked such a reaction. He knew now that the Adjutant of the unit, who had of course gone to Potsdam with the others, had been that sort of person, selecting junior officers for troublesome duties less by caprice than by remembering who had most recently contested his opinion in the Mess, even if the subject had been literature or the weather. Sometimes a tendency to confuse names (surprising in so incessant an advocate of attention to detail) gave his selections an involuntary impartiality. After thinking about it for two years, Archer was nearly sure that a historic mission to collect a new type of line-transmission apparatus, entailing a journey three-quarters of the way across England and back in January and two successive nights in an unheated railway carriage, had fallen to his share because a second-lieutenant called Belcher, whom Archer hoped he did not in the least resemble, had a day or two earlier contradicted the Adjutant about *Alice in Wonderland*. But as the Adjutant got to know his subalterns better, such miscarriages of injustice had become rarer, not that this change had been to Archer's advantage.

Although Archer had never made any progress in finding out what Doll was like, he judged it unwise to risk diminishing the effect of that half-bottle by saying what he really felt about

Hargreaves's outburst and thence, inevitably, what he felt about Doll's politics. The major's régime was doubtless drawing to a close, but its last days might well be marked by a fury of moral violence. Archer could not afford to irritate a friend at court, or anywhere else for that matter. He said decisively: 'Yes, he did go too far, much too far. I think he feels a bit cheap about it today. You weren't annoyed, I hope?'

'Oh no, sir, my back is broad. As I say, all he did was help my side. That Government'll fall soon, you mark my words. You were wanting to see the major, sir, were you?'

'Yes, I thought I might look in.'

'He's got Captain Cleaver with him at the moment . . . Ah, here is the captain now.'

Doll got up as Cleaver emerged from the doorway and descended the steps. Archer grinned at him; Cleaver was the one officer in the detachment whom he regarded with nothing but contempt – groomed for stardom by the Adjutant and finally rejected on the grounds of technical incompetence: a tremendous achievement. He had got his captaincy, though. 'Hallo, Wilf,' Archer said.

'Oh, hallo,' Cleaver said, getting into his tone surprise at being so familiarly addressed. He carried gloves and a short cane and looked more than ever like a British officer as pictured in a German army manual. 'The major's waiting for you.'

The major was looking out of the window. A cow wearing a large floppy hat had just run along part of his road (known to everyone but himself as Raleigh's Alley) and then turned off to flee up the lane past the wireless section's billet. From somewhere near at hand a loud silly laugh had floated into the air. Whether this was associated with the cow or not, the two manifestations combined to pique and depress the major. They formed for him a symbol of anarchy mounting, of discipline and seriousness and purpose melting away. He felt there was some connection here with the chance of a Labour victory at the polls. Apart from a few negligible wild men like Hargreaves and Archer, he had never met anyone who confessed to having cast his proxy vote for

Labour. On a recent visit to the Mess at Hildesfeld he had made a point of questioning his hosts on the matter and had heard the same story. His wife's letters said that nobody knew of anybody in the whole town who was a Labour supporter and that everybody felt very sorry for poor Mr Jack, the Labour candidate. And yet the major was uneasy. Something monstrous and indefinable was growing in strength, something hostile to his accent and taste in clothes and modest directorship and ambitions for his sons and redbrick house at Purley with its back-garden tennis-court.

Somebody tapped on the door. The major called 'Yes?' and started speaking the moment Archer began crossing the threshold – a valuable foil, this, to his normal keep-'em-waiting procedure. 'Now, Frank, where's the summary of communications?'

Archer walked over to Cleaver's table and instantly picked up a duplicated form in pale-blue ink with manuscript additions. 'Here it is, sir.'

The major took it and went back to his seat. On the whole, he seemed mollified rather than the contrary. 'About this parliament business, Frank. I'm not at all happy about it.'

'I'm sorry to hear that, sir.'

'I'm seriously thinking of closing it down.'

'Surely there's no need for that?'

'That disgusting display of Hargreaves's last night. Couldn't you have prevented it? After all, as Speaker you must have some . . . And as an officer, you—'

'I don't think that anything but force would have—'

'Worst thing in the world for discipline. If the blokes get the idea that they can simply—'

'Oh, I don't agree at all, sir.'

The major's eyes narrowed. 'What?'

'It's a chance for them to let off steam, you see. They're off parade – rank doesn't count in there. Everyone accepts that. I mentioned last night to Doll just now and he obviously didn't resent it.'

'That's not the point. And if rank doesn't count, why aren't officers and WOs allowed to take full part, instead of having to sit out like that? I let you have your way there, since you were organizing the thing, but I never followed your argument.'

'Well, sir, rank doesn't count there really, but chaps may think it does. They might feel chary of giving, er, let's say Wilf Cleaver a proper hammering when they wouldn't if it was a corporal from another section, or even their own.'

'Mm. I don't think the blokes are quite as stupid as you make out.'

Archer shrugged.

'Tell me, Frank, I've often wondered: why do you hang on to Hargreaves when you've had so many chances to get rid of him? Does the section no good all round, having a type like that in it. Bad for morale.'

'I just feel . . . he's more or less settled in there. He's not much liked, but at least he's tolerated. Anywhere else he'd probably have a much thinner time.'

'But good God man, a Signals section doesn't exist to give a home to stray dogs and to wet-nurse people. It's supposed to be an efficient unit in a war machine.'

'Hargreaves can't do the Allied cause much harm now.'

'Perhaps I'd better remind you, Frank, that we're all still in uniform and that our country is still at war. We're not on holiday.'

Standing before the major's table, Archer shrugged again and put his hands on his hips. His eyes fell on a framed text that said: *Ich will mich freuen des Herrn und frölich sein in Gott.*

'Confidentially now, old boy, what's the matter with Hargreaves? Basically the matter?'

'That's very simple, sir. He doesn't like the Army.'

The major laughed through his nose. 'I should imagine very few of us would sooner be here than anywhere else. If a man isn't a cretin he knows it's a question of getting a job done. A very important job, I take it you agree?'

'Oh yes, sir. And Hargreaves is clear on that too. But it isn't being in the Army that gets him down. It's the Army.'

'I'm afraid you're being too subtle for me, Frank.'

'Well, as far as I can make him out – he's not an easy man to talk to, but the way he sees it, people have been nasty to him in the Army in a way they wouldn't be in civilian life. The Army puts power into the hands of chaps who've never had it before, not that sort of power, and they use it to inflict injustices on other chaps whom they happen to dislike for personal reasons. That's the way the Army works. According to Hargreaves.'

'Don't stand like that, Frank,' Raleigh said, and waited until Archer had removed his hands from his hips and put them behind his back. 'Well, whatever friend Hargreaves feels about being in the Army, you can tell him from me to pull himself together. So far I've tried to keep the original Company in one piece as far as possible. When postings come through I've been seeing to it that they've got passed on to these new arrivals. But there's always plenty of call for blokes with Hargreaves's qualifications, or lack of them rather, and I can get him out of the way any time I want to. If there's one more bit of nonsense from him I'll see he's on the first available boat for Burma. Is that clear?'

'Yes, sir. I'll tell him.'

'And what's going on between him and young Hammond?'

'Going on? Nothing that I know of. They are friends. Hammond's about the only chap Hargreaves talks to.'

'Is that all he does to him? Talk?'

'I don't know what you're driving at, sir.'

'Oh yes you do, Frank, don't you try and bullshit me. There's something pretty unsavoury about that friendship, as you call it, if half I hear is true.'

'I'll go and fetch Hargreaves and Hammond now, sir, if you like, and you can fetch whoever's been telling you this and get him to repeat it in front of them. And me too, of course, as their Section Officer.'

'There's no need to take that tone, old boy. I'm simply telling you as a friend to be on your guard. You don't want a scandal in the section, do you? Hammond's a good lad and I shouldn't like him to get into any sort of trouble. If things turn out the way they might I'd consider him favourably for lance-corporal. Well,

I suppose you'd better be getting back to the Signal Office. Sorry to have kept you, but this Hargreaves business has been on my mind rather.'

'Yes, sir.'

'Oh, before you go, Frank, any news of *Journey's End*?'

'The librarian chap in Hildesfeld says he'll do his best, but it's been out of print for years. The British Drama League in England are on the job now, apparently.'

'Good. I hope it comes through. It would be fun to have a shot at putting it on. Do you know it at all?'

'I'm afraid not, sir.'

'It's good stuff, you know, Frank. You'd like it. The best thing on the first war by far. Really gets the spirit of the trenches, the feel of what it was like.'

III

Major Raleigh stood on the steps of the farmhouse where the Officers' Mess was, trying to smell the lilac bushes. He was having a hard time of it. Competing smells included the one from the cookhouse bonfire, a mixture of rum and hot cardboard; the one from the henhouse where the Mess's looted chickens lived; the one from the piggery; the one from nowhere and everywhere that was apparently endemic to continental farmyards, about midway between that of a brewery and that of burning cheese-rind. As one of his own wireless operators might have tried to tune out interference, the major stooped and laid his soft nose alongside one of the pale clusters. It tickled, but he got something.

The voice of Cleaver spoke behind him. 'Are you all right, Major?'

'Of course I'm all right,' Raleigh said, wheeling round as he came upright.

'I'm sorry, I thought you were ill.'

'Well I'm not. Are you ready?'

'Yes, Major. Nobody else seems to want to come.'

'Did you ask them?'

'Yes, Major.'

'All of them?'

'Yes, Major.'

'It's a pity some of them couldn't have taken the trouble to come along,' Raleigh said, voicing a desire for his brother-officers' company that was to cool sharply within the hour. 'All right, Wilf, let's get moving. We're late already.'

The two got into the major's car, a saloon with faded checkerboard painting on the radiator and a cracked mica windscreen. Its only superiority over the major's jeep lay in the latter vehicle's having reached the stage of needing to carry a can of petrol, a can of oil and a large can of water whenever it went anywhere. And this thing was a piece of loot, too. While he pulled at the starter and the motor lurched over, Raleigh imagined his friends at Potsdam, each in a Mercedes with the back full of cameras, watches, automatic pistols, pairs of binoculars, crates of champagne and vodka and American whiskey, haunches of venison . . . Girls did not appear on the major's list; he considered that side of life much overrated. Before the car came shudderingly to life he had time for a surge of feeling, equally compounded of envy and righteous indignation, at the memory of a current rumour about a large RAF Signals unit which, ordered to return to England with all its stores and transport, and thus secure against Customs inspection, had stuffed every cranny with cameras, watches, automatic pistols – perhaps girls.

They moved out of the yard, with a grinding bump when one of the rear mudguards, worse adjusted than its fellow, met the edge of the road surface. The sun was setting over the fields of rye or oats or barley or perhaps just wheat and there was arguably a fair amount of tranquillity and such about, but the major was beyond its reach. As he frequently said, it was people that interested him. The people interesting him at the moment were still the ones he knew at Potsdam. 'Funny to think of them all up there,' he said. 'Bill and the CO and Jack Rowney and Tom

Thurston and all that crowd. And Rylands and Ben and Dalessio and Jock Watson. Wonder what they're all up to. Parties with the Russians and the Yanks and God knows what. All the big brass-hats around. The Jerries too. And . . .' – the major tried briefly to visualize what more might be on view there than other soldiers – 'everything. Of course I realize we couldn't all have gone, but I do wish—'

'The CO and the Adjutant tended to pick the crowd who'd been with them at North Midland Command.'

'Yes, I know they did.' A military Calvinist who had had demonstrated to him his own non-membership of the elect, Raleigh spoke in a neutral tone. 'Not altogether, though. They took Dalessio with them.'

'I wonder why.'

'Rylands seemed to think Dalessio was indispensable,' the major said. Then, quite as if he realized that this was not the most tactful thing to say to a man whom all sorts of pressure had failed to get into Dalessio's job, he added: 'I wouldn't go all the way with him there.'

'I hear Bill and Jack and Tom are all majors now.'

'Yes. I'm particularly pleased Tom got his crown. He didn't fit in quite at first, I thought – bit of an awkward cuss. But some time last winter he pulled himself together and started doing a first-class job. Co-operated for all he was worth.'

The car laboured up an incline past the burnt-out wreck of a civilian lorry, relic of the celebrations on VE night. The cuff of a *Wehrmacht* jacket, charred and faded, hung out of the remains of the cab. Raleigh was about to comment adversely on this memorial of indiscipline, or of high spirits, but changed his mind and said abruptly: 'I'd give anything to be at Potsdam.'

'I'd have thought we were better off here, Major, with the Staff off our backs at last after two years.'

'They're doing a job there, that's the difference. I suppose . . . I suppose I might still get the chance of taking the Company to the Far East. Depends how the war goes, partly.' The major was thinking as usual in terms of a Headquarters Signals unit, not of a mere company, and of a lieutenant-colonelcy, but he was too shy to tell Cleaver this.

'I didn't realize you were as keen on the Army as all that, sir,' Cleaver said carefully.

'Well, I've been doing a lot of thinking these last few weeks, Wilf. Serious thinking. First real chance I've had since 1939. I worked it out that I've spent half my adult life in the Army. Pretty shaking thought, that. I've got used to being in uniform. Hardly remember what it was like in Civvy Street. And from the way things are going it looks as if I might not care for it when I arrive there. If these Socialists get in—'

'I shouldn't worry too much, Major. However badly it turns out there's sure to be scope for, well, initiative and quick thinking and all the rest of it.'

'I hope you're right.'

The major parked the car in the Signal Office yard between an iron canister full of broken glass and a disused boiler stuffed with torn sheets. The two officers crossed the road to the school building and entered the hall.

Parliament was in session. As Raleigh led the way to the Visitors' Gallery, his shoes thudding on the greasy bare boards, an instrument-mechanic on the Government side was saying: 'We're going to build a decent Britain. Fair shares for all and free schools and doctoring and hospitals and no class distinction. The old school tie and the old-boy network aren't going to work any more. To make sure of that we're going to abolish the public schools and Oxford and Cambridge, or at any rate change them so that anybody who's got the brains can go to them, and we're going to either abolish the House of Lords or make it a thing you vote on, just like the House of Commons. It's undemocratic any other way. Some of us want to abolish the Royal Family for the same reason, but we're not decided about that. Personally I think that if you scrap titles and the Honours List and all that carry-on, then you can leave the King and Queen to stew in their own juice.'

The major's mouth tightened. So far he had refrained from

interjecting more than a sentence or two into these debates, but after what he had just heard, and in this evening's intensified mood of discontent, he knew he would be failing in his duty to all sorts of entities – to common sense, to discipline both military and civil, to England, yes, and to the King, why be ashamed of it? – if he refrained from extensive comment. His eye met that of Cleaver, who looked away instantly. The major waited impatiently for the Home Secretary or whatever he was to finish.

Interest in the parliament had fallen off from the moment of its inception. Deliveries of newspapers and magazines had recently improved in speed and quantity and the major suspected that access to civilian drink had likewise improved; he must get his batman to keep his ears open. Less than half the original members were in their seats tonight. The Opposition front bench lacked its Leader and its spokesman on Defence questions: Doll had declared himself finally disgusted with his fellow-MPs' frivolity – 'I think it's ridiculous spending a lot of your time and thought preparing stuff for a load of apes, sir, don't you?' The ministerial bench was even more thinly held, with the Lord Privy Seal (if the truth were known) risking court-martial by thoroughly fraternizing with a nurse from the civilian hospital in Hildesfeld, the Chancellor of the Exchequer asleep on his bed with a three-day-old *Daily Express* over him, the Prime Minister himself with two of his mates from the Sergeants' Mess attacking something they vaguely thought of as gin in something they even more vaguely thought of as a pub on the far side of the railway yard. But the Foreign Secretary was in his seat, and the young man the major very precisely thought of as that official's boyfriend was in his.

The Home Secretary might have been thought to be drawing to a close, although, as the major reminded himself, you could never tell about that or *anything else* with fellows as unused as this to public speaking or indeed to *anything else* even remotely to do with the highly responsible and specialized and difficult task of running a modern industrial state. 'You heard the other week about how we're going to give the Empire back to the blokes that live there,' the Home Secretary was saying: 'well, we're going to do the same thing, so to speak, with Great Britain itself. The country belongs to the ordinary working bloke and by Christ he's going to be running things from now on. No messing.'

The major brushed his moustache with his knuckle and looked at the cracked and scaled maps which, in the absence of anything else that might blot out some of the clay-coloured plaster, somebody had pulled out of a cupboard and hung up. What a mess Europe had evidently been in in 1555, with all those hundreds of little countries, quite different from today, and how big Naples and Venice had been then. The major remembered enough German to wonder how there could ever have been *two* Sicilies. And again, who was Van Diemen and how had he filled in his time in Tasmania?

'Good enough, then,' the Home Secretary said. 'There are just three principles involved here: liberty, equality and fraternity. You'll remember that that's what the French Revolution was about. Well, we're not going to have a revolution about it, that's not the way we do things in England, not violent revolutions anyway, with barricades and shooting and so on and so forth. But there's going to be a revolution nevertheless and nobody's going to stop us.'

He sat down amid varied applause from his own side. The major looked at the Speaker for the first time and raised a finger in assumed humility. Archer seemed to pretend not to have seen him at first, then, having looked round the chamber, caught his eye and nodded to him.

'I shan't keep you long,' the major said as he rose to his feet. 'But there are just one or two points I feel I ought to put to you, if I may. We're all equal here – we're all members for Arromanches and Bayeux and Amiens and Brussels and Mechelen and Tilburg and Münster and Rheine and all the rest of the bloody places, and we can talk to each other as gentlemen. We've been through the whole thing together. And the first thing I want to say to you is this. Everybody's done a first-class job, you have and I hope we have as far as it was possible to us, and of course the fighting troops, nobody can say what they went through . . . Anyway, sitting here tonight it just occurred to me that it would be an awful pity if we were to let one another down by forgetting the things that have made it all possible, the teamwork and sense of responsibility, and behind that the way of life we've been fighting for. We've always been a pretty good-natured lot, we British, and the fellow up here' – he raised his hand to shoulder level – 'and the fellows down there' – he extended his arm downwards with the hand still spread – 'have always got on pretty well together. Each has had his job to do—'

Hargreaves stood up and said: 'I spy strangers.' He spoke loudly but unemotionally, as if promulgating his occupation rather than delivering a challenge.

The major stopped speaking immediately and looked towards the Speaker with an expression of courteous bafflement.

The Speaker's expression was of incredulous horror. He said: 'Er . . . Hargreaves . . . can't we . . . ?'

'I spy strangers,' Hargreaves repeated a little louder, gazing into space.

'Could I ask you to clarify that, Mr Speaker, sir?' the major asked good-humouredly.

Archer replied as if the words were being wrung out of him. 'I was reading . . . it's a formula calling for the expulsion of unauthorized persons from the debating chamber. The idea was—'

'Unauthorized persons?' Smiling, the major glanced from face to face. 'But surely—'

'The thing is that officially only Members of Parliament are allowed to be present,' Archer said, more steadily than before. 'Anybody else is here on sufferance. *I spy strangers* is the way of saying you want to cancel that sufferance, so to speak.'

Raleigh still smiled. 'Are you ordering me to withdraw, Mr Speaker?'

'I'm telling you what the book says.'

In the pause that followed, the major again looked round the

House, but nobody returned his look. He went on trying to think of something to say until it became clear to him that there was nothing to say. With a glance at Cleaver, who quickly rose and followed him, Major Raleigh withdrew.

Outside in the darkness he said: 'You drive, Wilf, will you? I want to think.'

'Are you all right, Major?'

'Wilf, if you ask me if I'm all right once more, I'll . . . Anyway don't. Just shut up.'

'Yes, sir.'

IV

'Well, you must be pretty pleased, Mr Archer, I expect, at the way things have gone.'

'Yes, I must admit I am, Sergeant. Such a thumping majority, too.'

'Yes, that did rather take me by surprise. I expected it to be a much closer run thing than this. Of course, being wise after the event, it's not difficult to see what happened. The Service vote did it. The lads have been in uniform all these years and they've had enough. Voting Labour's a protest. It's a way of saying you're browned off and want to go home.'

'Oh, there's a lot more to it than that, I'm quite sure. People are browned off *with* something, or rather somebody, a lot of somebodies. They're protesting *against*—'

'Well, you and I are never going to see eye to eye there, sir, are we? – not even if we discuss it all night. We might as well accept it.'

'Will you join me in a glass of whisky, Sergeant? If it doesn't seem too like drowning your sorrows while I celebrate.'

'Thank you, sir, I will. You've certainly got something to celebrate, and everybody else seems to be doing it, so I don't see why I shouldn't join in.'

Doll and Archer sat in the little sitting-room – all painted screens and wax fruit and clocks under glass domes – of the farmhouse that contained the Officers' Mess. Outside, a widespread uproar was distantly audible: shouts, the revving of jeep and motor-cycle engines, the braying of a trombone that was being blown through rather than played. Ten minutes ago what sounded very much like a long burst of light-machine-gun fire had come from the direction of the Signal Office. There was no reason to suppose that all this was a demonstration of Socialist triumph over cowed and silent Tories. Whether or not Doll was right about the motives which had prompted the return of a Labour Government in Great Britain, the local reaction to it tonight was largely non-political in temper.

'They're keeping hard at it,' Doll said, pointing out of the open window to a sudden burst of flame somewhere across the road. It was brighter than the now hour-old bonfire in the billet area. A few figures could be seen in the light of the new conflagration, reeling in and out of the darkness like pantomime drunks. 'Funny how nobody seems to be interfering. The major's right about one thing, anyway. Discipline's going. Ah, thank you, sir.' He raised one of the glasses of whisky which the Mess corporal had brought in response to Archer's bellow. 'Well. A solemn moment. What shall it be? I give you England, Mr Archer.'

'England.' Not your England, Archer said to himself, not the petrol-flogging CQMS's England, not the Major's England or Cleaver's England or the Adjutant's or the Colonel's or Jack Rowney's or Tom Thurston's England, but to a certain extent Hargreaves's England and absolutely my England, full of girls and drinks and jazz and books and decent houses and decent jobs and being your own boss. He said in a friendly tone: 'I wonder whether England's going to turn out the way you'd like her to.'

'Oh, I've no doubt she won't, sir. But that's not really going to concern me much. I shan't be there, you see. Emigration's the thing for me, as soon as I can fix it up.'

'Really? Where are you thinking of? Canada? Australia?'

'I think Africa, Mr Archer. A place where there's room for

initiative and where a determined man can still make his way. Kenya, perhaps, or one of the Rhodesias. There's some scope there. No, I've been thinking about it for a long time and today's news really decided me. Taken a load off my mind, in a way. Funny thing, I should be feeling depressed, with the Socialists getting in, but I don't at all. Quite the contrary, in fact.' Doll drained his glass.

'How about another of those?'

'No, thank you, sir, I really should be getting along and seeing the major. It's what I came for, after all.'

'I'll take you up.'

'There is just one point you might be able to help me with first, sir, if you would.' Doll opened the buff file-cover he had brought with him. 'This posting advice. I expect you know how the major's got all that organized. He can send who he likes. Well, he's asked to provide eight bodies of various kinds. All Signal Office Personnel. They'll be entraining for the UK in a couple of days, twenty-eight days' leave, then the boat for Burma. I should imagine they'll all be joining the same unit out there. Now the major's been in a funny mood recently. Sort of withdrawn. Normally he'd nominate all these bodies personally, but this morning he gave me three names and told me to fill in the others myself. Not like him at all. Anyway, I was just wondering if there's anybody in your section you'd care to lose. Apart from Hargreaves, that is. He was one of the major's three, as you probably know.'

'Yes, he did mention it to me. Tell me, Sergeant Doll, is there a vacancy for a switchboard-operator on that list?'

'There is, sir. Two, in fact.'

'Mm. It's tempting, but I'm afraid—'

'Perhaps it'll help you to make up your mind, Mr Archer, if I tell you now that I wasn't going to bother the major with signing the order himself. He's got enough on his mind already. And of course any officer's signature would do. Yours, for instance, sir.'

Archer hesitated. 'He's bound to see the file copy.'

'Yes, sir, but that won't be until tomorrow morning, will it?

And I was thinking of dropping the top copy off for transmission at the Signal Office tonight when I go back down. Get it out of the way.'

'He could cancel it and send an amended list.'

'Oh, do you think that's likely, sir? Major Raleigh wants to be thought of as someone who can take a quick decision and stick to it. It's like a moral code with him.'

'A good point, Sergeant. Very well, then. I think I'll nominate Signalman Hammond.'

'14156755 Signalman Hammond, J. R., SBO DII?' Doll ran his fingertip along a line of typing. 'Anybody else? Right. Now, if you'd just sign here, sir . . . Thank you. I suppose you'll be off yourself soon, Mr Archer, won't you, after what you were telling me?'

'I imagine so. Well, you won't be needing the major after all now, I suppose.'

'Oh yes I will, sir. That was just a routine matter. Something far more important has come up. There's a signal here from War Office telling 424 Wireless Section, 502 Line Section and 287 DR Section to stand by to move on twenty-four hours' notice. Half the Company. They've obviously decided we're to be broken up.'

'That's important all right,' Archer said. 'To the major more than anyone else, probably.'

'My feeling exactly, sir. That was why I thought it couldn't wait till the morning. I reckoned I had to let him know about it tonight.' Doll's eyes grew distant.

'He'd set his heart on taking the Company out East.'

'Oh, don't I know it, Mr Archer. That's the end of that ambition. I wonder what the next pipe-dream will be.' Suddenly getting to his feet, Doll roamed about the room with his hands in his pockets, an uncharacteristic bodily movement. 'It may surprise you to learn, sir,' he said cordially, 'that I'm by way of being a bit of an angler. Been at it since I was a boy. Well now, it used to surprise me very much at first how badly I got on with other anglers. Jealousy rather than congratulations if you managed to pull off something a bit out of the ordinary. No end of disagreements over red hackles and what-not. And a lot of boredom too. Now in one way you wouldn't expect that, sir, would you? You'd expect people who'd got interests in common to get on better with one another than the average, not worse. But when you come to think about it it's not so odd. Someone who's a bit like yourself can rub you up the wrong way worse than a chap who's totally different. Well, there's one obvious instance. I bet a lot of the lads in this Company hate their officers and NCOs a sight worse than they ever hated Jerry. They know them, you see.

'You'll have to forgive me for reciting you a sermon, Mr Archer, but this is a point about human nature that's always interested me. And it has got an application. I take it I wouldn't be intruding on your mental privacy, so to speak, sir, if I hazarded a guess that you regard myself and the major as pretty much birds of a feather?'

'I think that's fair enough.'

'Thank you, sir. In that case it may surprise you to learn that I can't think of anybody whom I despise as thoroughly as I despise the major. I know you hate him yourself or I wouldn't risk telling you this. You'll be leaving us soon anyway.'

Archer's puzzlement, which had been growing for the last five minutes, changed direction. 'But I've got personal reasons.'

'I too. Though they're quite different from yours. He's so sure he's better. But in fact he's shoddy material. Third rate. Not to be depended on. In many parts of the world over the next few years an important battle's going to be fought – largely against the ideas that you yourself stand for, sir, if I may say so with all respect. The major's going to be worse than useless to us there. To me and the people who think as I do. He's soft. He'll break. I can see him standing as a Labour candidate in ten years' time if the wind's still blowing that way. No principle. That's the one thing I can't forgive.'

Partly to throw off complacency at being taken into a fascist's confidence, Archer stood up briskly and said: 'I'll take you up to the major now.'

'Right, sir. I wish I'd been there to see him thrown out of that last parliament. Good for Hargreaves. And you yourself too, sir, of course.'

The muffled bang of an exploding petrol-tank reached them as they climbed the steep narrow stairs to the main ante-room. This had been created by the folding-back of folding doors between two former bedrooms and the importation of furniture from all over the house and elsewhere. Outside it was a tiny landing hedged by slender carved banisters. Archer left Doll here and went in

The major was sitting in half of the curious high-backed double armchair, a favourite of his despite its clear resemblance to part of a railway-carriage seat. Probably he found it suited his characteristic activity, the having of a word, whether denunciatory or conspiratorial, with someone. He had been having one now, an earnest one accompanied by gesture, with the young and usually solitary lieutenant-colonel of Engineers whose thirst for schnapps had established him as a local personality. In his hand at the moment was a glass not of schnapps but of the Mess's whisky, a glass which, appearance suggested, had been emptied and refilled several times that evening. The colonel was rather elaborately accoutred with belt, holster, revolver and lanyard. Both he and the major, who likewise seemed to have taken drink, were dramatically illuminated by a many-tiered candelabrum that made great use of frosted glass.

Raleigh had interrupted his confidential word with the colonel to have a more public one with the Mess corporal, who was saying: 'About forty, I should say, sir. Well dressed. Quite respectable.'

'And where's this picture she says she wants?'

'It was in her bedroom when it was her bedroom, sir.'

'But it isn't her bedroom any more. The house isn't hers either, it's been requisitioned. It belongs to me. No, she can't have her picture. I don't care whether she painted it herself or not, she can't have it. Go and tell her so, will you?'

When he saw that Archer was near, the major turned his back

as far as was possible without actually kneeling on his seat. The emotion he felt for the ex-Speaker of the now officially dissolved parliament was not military disapprobation nor yet personal anger, but sadness at the other's withholding of loyalty. All this and much more had been gone into at length the morning after Hargreaves had spied strangers. Archer had protested, with every appearance of sincerity, that the strangers could have been suffered to remain if anybody had thought to put forward a simple motion proposing this, and that nothing but general ignorance of procedure had brought about their exit. Raleigh paid no heed. In the course of a sad and objective appraisal of Archer's disloyalty he had recounted rumours about Archer's private life which, if repeated before witnesses and if the law of slander had run in the Army, might have been the occasion of awards in damages sufficient to buy and sell the contents of the Officers' Shop. Then, still avowing sadness, the major had announced that his duty to the Company forbade the retention in its ranks of anybody so provenly disloyal. In other words, it was Burma for Archer as soon as the major's pal at HQ could fix it. After that, the major had sadly shouted at Archer to get out of his sight.

Archer had, and as far as possible had stayed there. But now he had to get back into it for a moment. To facilitate this he leant against the sideboard (could it have been made of ebony?) and faced the couple in the double armchair.

The RE colonel, whose name was Davison, was not the kind of man to appeal to Raleigh. He was what Raleigh was fond of calling a disorganized sort of chap, meaning someone whose character had not been stripped down like a racing-car until nothing but more or less military components remained. But it was his policy to encourage colonels and such to be around. Colonel Davison, once acquainted with the volume and regularity of the Mess's liquor supply, had needed no encouragement. At the moment he was saying in his public-school voice (another selling-point for the major): 'But as I keep telling you, that's why the Army's so good. Because nobody could take the bloody nonsense seriously.'

The major came back with something inaudible to Archer, probably that he couldn't go all the way with the colonel there.

'Well, nobody with any sense, then,' Davison said. 'And that saves an awful lot of worry. Means you can start laughing.'

Again the major could not be heard, but this time he went on much longer. Davison listened, nodding steadily, his eyes on his glass, which he was rotating on the knee of his crossed leg. Archer's attention wandered. It came to rest on Cleaver, who was half-lying on a purple sofa reading an unexpurgated edition of *Lady Chatterley's Lover*. Archer had had a go at that too. General opinion in the Mess was that it ranked about halfway in the little library the batmen had been assiduously building up ever since the Company entered urban France: not so good as, say, Frank Harris's *My Life and Loves*, but clearly better than the available non-fictional treatments of these themes, vital books by Scotsmen with titles like *Married Happiness*. Cleaver laughed silently to himself, then looked quickly and furtively round without catching Archer's eye.

'It's all a joke,' Davison said loudly. 'The whole thing.'

The major saw Archer. 'Yes?'

'Sergeant Doll would like to see you, sir. He's just outside.'

When Raleigh had gone, Davison patted the space beside him. 'Come and sit down, laddie.'

'Thank you, sir.'

'Sir. Sir sir sir. Sir sir sir sir sir sir sir. Ha.'

From the way Davison swayed about in his seat as he said this, Archer concluded that he was not just drunk, but very drunk. 'Nice little place we've got here, don't you think?'

'Oh, delightful. Delightful. Your poor major's upset. Have you been being nasty to him? Have a drink. Corporal! More whisky needed here. Crash priority.'

'I'm never nasty to majors,' Archer said.

'Aren't you? I am. All the time. One of the consummations. Compensations. What do you do in Civvy Street, laddie?' The colonel was perhaps five years older than Archer.

'I don't do anything. Not yet. I was a student.'

'Jolly good luck to you. I'm an electrical engineer. So of course they put me on bridges. But it's all experience. A very good preparation, the Army.'

'For what?'

'Everything.'

As they received their drinks, Archer became aware that an altercation was going on just outside the room, with raised voices and what sounded like part of a human frame bouncing off the door. Was Doll fighting Raleigh?

'Just about everything. You'll have learnt a lot in the last few years which will stand you in good stead when you get into the great world.'

Archer's mouth opened. 'You mean that this is what *life* is like.'

'Roughly.'

Doll called from the doorway. 'Would you come, Mr Archer, quickly?'

Archer hurried over, followed by Davison, who said: 'If there's anything to see I'm going to see it.'

Four men confronted one another in the confined space at the stairhead: Hargreaves, Sergeant Fleming, Doll and Raleigh. Whatever he might have been doing a moment earlier, Hargreaves was doing nothing now except being held from behind by Fleming and denounced by Raleigh. Doll stood to one side, his file under his arm.

'I didn't know anything like this was going to happen, sir,' Fleming shouted to Archer. 'He just said very quiet he'd like to see the major if he was free, to apologize to him about the parliament, and I said couldn't it wait till the morning, and he said, still very quiet, his conscience was—'

'You dare come here and say that to me,' Raleigh shouted through this. His soft face had a glistening flush. 'You dirty little homo. Can't leave a decent lad alone. Rotten to the core. I know what goes on in that billet of yours. I'm going to take you off that draft and have you court-martialled for . . . for filth. There are plenty of people who'd be only too glad—'

Cleaver stepped forward and caught him by the arm. 'Shut up, major. Pipe down, you bloody fool. Come back in here, for Christ's sake.'

The major shook off Cleaver's hand. The movement brought him face to face with Archer. A theatrical sneer twisted Raleigh's soft features. 'And as for you . . . Tarred with the same brush. An officer. Selected for his qualities of leadership. That's good. I like that.'

There was a pause. The moment it was over Archer realized that he should have used it either to help Fleming get Hargreaves down the stairs or help Cleaver get Raleigh back into the ante-room. He could even have told the major just a little of what he thought of him. But he spent the time quailing under the major's stare.

Panting a little, Raleigh took up a fighting stance in front of Hargreaves. At the same time Colonel Davison spoke from the edge of the group. 'That'll do, everybody.' Fleming's expression made Archer turn quickly. He saw with incredulity that Davison was leaning against the door-jamb and levelling his drawn revolver in Raleigh's general direction.

'Often wanted to use this,' Davison said. He was thin and very tall. 'Properly, I mean. Not just on pigeons. Well, better late than never.'

'Put that away, Colonel,' Cleaver said.

Davison grinned. 'Sounds as if I'm exposing myself. But I know what you mean. My turn now. Who's gonna make me?'

'Let's be sensible.'

At this, Davison collapsed in laughter. 'One up to you, by God. Funny, isn't it? – always turns out like this if you try to do anything. Chaps saying let's be sensible. Let's be that whatever we do. Oh, my Christ.'

Still laughing, he staggered through the group and ended up by the banisters, laboriously trying to fit his revolver back into its holster. The major swung back towards Hargreaves. After-wards opinion was divided on whether he was really going to hit him, but Doll evidently thought so, for he bounded forward and shouldered the major aside. Raleigh collided hard with

Davison, whose attention was distracted by his revolver and holster and who at once, with a single cracking of wood, fell through the banisters and down into the tiled hall. He landed with another cracking sound which made the backs of Archer's thighs turn cold. Doll ran down the stairs, closely followed by Cleaver. Hargreaves said: 'I'm sorry, Mr Archer.'

V

'Cup of tea for you, sir. And the newspapers.'

'Thank you. Did you get on to the hospital?' Major Raleigh spoke almost without inflection, as he usually did these days.

'Yes, sir. Progress maintained. Too early yet to say when he'll be up and about again, but the concussion's definitely not as bad as they thought at first and the arm's coming along as well as can be expected after a complicated fracture.'

Outside, heavy transport could be heard toiling in low gear. 'What's that row?'

'That's 424 Wireless forming up to move out, sir. They're due at the railhead at fifteen-hundred hours.'

'I know.'

'Are you going down to see them off, sir?'

'No.'

'Oh, by the way, Colonel Davison sent you a message, sir.'

'Did he?'

'Yes, he did, sir. Thanks for the party and he hopes he wasn't a nuisance.'

The major screwed up his soft face as a motor-bike revved up in the road below. 'Shut the window, will you, Doll?'

'Right, sir.' The operation completed, Doll turned round and leant against the sill. 'Well, we've all been very lucky, sir, really, haven't we? Things might have turned out much more serious. By the way, I thought you were very wise not to go on with that idea of yours of having Hargreaves court-martialled. Very wise indeed, sir.'

'When I want your opinion of my decisions, Doll, I'll ask for it.' This tripped less well off the major's tongue than it might have done at another time. Only Colonel Davison's accident had prevented that last encounter with Hargreaves from degenerating into a serious breach of order. The persistence of this thought bothered Raleigh. He said wearily: 'And while you're here I'd like you to tell me in detail how Hammond got on to that list with Hargreaves.'

'I've nothing to add to my previous account, sir, but still. You asked me to complete the list at my discretion, right? So seeing Hargreaves's name there, and knowing that Hammond was his mate, I put him down too. We've always done that sort of thing.'

'Is that all you knew?'

'Why, of course, sir. What else is there to know?'

'How did Archer come to sign that message?'

'Well, again as before, sir, Mr Archer happened to call in at the Orderly Room and I asked him, as I might have asked any officer who was available. There were one or two things piled up and I wanted to get them off.'

'Did Mr Archer read it through before he signed it?'

'I really couldn't say, sir. Quite likely he had enough confidence in me not to bother. You've often done the same yourself, sir, and believe me I very much appreciate the implied compliment.'

'Are you telling me the truth, Doll?'

'Mr Archer will confirm every word I've said, sir, as far as it concerns him.'

The major sighed heavily. 'I suppose that's that.'

'I suppose so, sir. Actually it's a pity we've lost Hammond, a very pleasant young fellow I agree, but it's not going to make much difference, sir, is it? There'd have been nothing for him to do here after the Signal Office closes down next week. I don't suppose any of us will be together much longer. Captain Cleaver and Mr Archer and the others on twenty-four-hour warning. You'll be all on your own here before very long, sir.'

'I'm looking forward to it.'

Doll almost smiled. 'Of course, it's Mr Archer who's come best out of this. Dodging the Far East after all. What a bit of luck that was, eh, sir?'

Something close to attention entered the major's manner. 'Dodging the Far East?'

'Oh, no doubt about it, sir. Even if he goes tomorrow it'll take him ten days to get home, the way things are. Then he'll go on twenty-eight days' leave, which'll bring him to the first week in September. And with his release due a month at most after that it wouldn't be worth anybody's while to put him on a boat. No, he's—'

'Doll, I don't know what you're talking about.'

'Really, sir? I'm awfully sorry, I was sure Mr Archer would have told you long ago. When was he telling me about it, now? Yes, I can remember exactly – it was the earlier part of the evening on which Colonel Davison met with his accident. Mr Archer and I went on to discuss the Election results – that's right – and then we—'

'All right, I don't want the story of your life. I asked you to tell me—'

'Do forgive me, sir – I've got this bad habit of letting my tongue run away with me, I know. It's just that the events of that evening are so indelibly impressed on my memory, sir, if you know what I—Yes, sir. Well, Mr Archer showed me a letter from the head of his college in Oxford, the Master I think he called himself. It said they were arranging his release from the Army and reckoned he'd be out in good time to go into the college when the term begins, which I gather is about the 10th of October, though no doubt you could put me right there.'

'But he's only been in for three or four years. You and I and most of the blokes have been in for six.'

'Seven in my case, sir; you'll recall that I was one of the 1938 militiamen. Yes, I know it seems strange, Mr Archer getting out so soon, but apparently this is something called the Class "B" Scheme – we had a memo about it a couple of weeks ago which I'll look out for you if you're interested.'

'Don't bother.'

'How funny Mr Archer hasn't told you yet. I expect he's wait-ing for a suitable opportunity, sir, don't you?'

'Get out and leave me in peace.'

'Glad to, sir.'

Left in peace, the major sat on at his almost-empty table. The bulk of 424 Wireless Station was evidently moving out on to the main road along Raleigh's Alley, making full use of that thor-oughfare for the first and last time. The major's eye missed a letter from the British Drama League saying that *Journey's End* was not available. It caught an order informing him that with effect from two days' time the area of which he had hoped to become chieftain would be known as No. 9 Independent Transit Area and would fall under the command of a full colonel despatched from HQ. He picked up a newspaper headlined *IT'S NO JOKE-IO TO LIVE IN TOKYO: 600 Super-Forts Blast Jap Heartland* and put it down again. The other paper contained a large Election supplement. He summoned the resolution to study the details of what he had so far been able to take in only as an appalling generality. Turning to an inner page, he read:

WINKWORTH (WEST)

R. Jack (Lab)	28,740
Maj.-Gen. P. O. de C. Biggs-Courtenay, DSO (C)	9,011

Lab majority 19,729

LABOUR GAIN FROM CONSERVATIVE

1935: Maj.-Gen. P. O. de C. Biggs-Courtenay, DSO (C) 19,495; W. Mott (Lab) 9,319: C majority 10,176

The major dropped his head into his hands. This, he supposed, was the bottom. And yet he felt a stirring of hope. Having sunk to the lowest depths his nature was capable of, he could not help seeing the future as some sort of upward path. Nobody and nothing in his immediate environment gave him the smallest reason for confidence. Doll, Cleaver, Hammond, Davison, Archer (whom he had tried so hard to train up as a conscientious officer), the Company, the Signal Office, chances of leadership – all in their different ways had turned out to be not worth depending on. But the world was wide. Bad things could happen and it all went on as before. The thought of his friends in Potsdam filled him with encouragement now, not envy. Much of what he believed in must survive.

And the guarantee of that was England. England had been up against it in 1940, in 1914 and no doubt earlier, with the Napoleon business and so on. She had weathered every storm, she had never gone under. All that was needed was faith. Despite everything that Hargreaves and Archer and the rest of them might do, England would muddle through somehow.

Moral Fibre

'Hallo,' I said. 'Who are you?' I said it to a child of about three who was pottering about on the half landing between the ground floor of the house, where some people called Davies lived, and the first floor, where I and my wife and children lived. The child now before me was not one of mine. He looked old-fashioned in some way, probably because instead of ordinary children's clothes he wore scaled-down versions of grown-up clothes, including miniature black lace-up boots. His eyes were alarmed or vacant, their roundness repeated in the rim of the amber-coloured dummy he was sucking. As I approached he ran incompetently away up the further flight. I'd tried to speak heart-ily to him, but most likely had only sounded accusing. Accusing was how I often felt in those days, especially after a morning duty in the Library Reference Room, being talked to most of the way by my colleague, Ieuan Jenkins, and about his wife's head-aches too.

I mounted in my turn and entered the kitchen, where my own wife, called Jean, was straining some potatoes into the wash-hand basin that did, but only just did, as a sink. 'Hallo, darling,' she said. 'How were the borrowers this morning, then?'

'They were readers this morning, not borrowers,' I said, kiss-ing her.

'Aw, same thing.'

'Yes, that's right. They were as usual, I'm sorry to say. Who was that extraordinary child I saw on the stairs?'

'Ssshh . . . Must have been one of Betty's. She had to bring them with her.' Jean pointed towards the sitting-room, where clicks and thumps suggesting domestic work could be heard.

'Betty's?' I whispered. 'What's going on?'

'She's just finishing up in there. Betty Arnulfsen. You remember, the girl Mair Webster was going to fix us up with. You know.'

'Oh, the delinquent. I'd forgotten all about it.'

'She's coming to lunch.'

'Betty Arnulfsen?'

'No, Mair, dull.'

'Oh, Christ.'

'Now, don't be nasty, John. She's been very kind to us. Just because she's a bit boring, that doesn't mean she . . .'

'*Just* because. A *bit* boring. If it were only that. The woman's a menace, a threat to Western values. Terrifying to think of her being a social worker. All that awful knowing-best stuff, being quite sure what's good for people and not standing any nonsense and making them knuckle under and going round saying how she fully appreciates the seriousness and importance of her job, as if that made it all right. They bloody well ought to come and ask me before they let anybody be a social worker.'

'Then there wouldn't be any. You can take these plates in. She'll be here any minute.'

It was all most interesting, and in a way that things that happened to me hardly ever were. Mair Webster, who knew us because her husband was a senior colleague of mine on the staff of the Aberdarcy (Central) Public Library, had brought off what must have seemed to her a smart double coup by providing, as the twice-a-week domestic help we craved, one of the fallen women with whom her municipal duties brought her into contact. It had turned out that the woman in question wasn't really fallen, just rather inadmissibly inclined from the perpendicular. She'd had an illegitimate child or two and had recently or some time ago neglected or abandoned it or them – Mair had a gift of unmemorability normally reserved for far less emphatic characters – but that was all over now and the girl was taking proper care of her young, encouraged by her newly acquired husband, a Norwegian merchant seaman and a 'pretty good type'

according to Mair, who went on about it as if she'd masterminded
the whole thing. Perhaps she had. Anyway, meeting Betty Arnulfsen was bound to be edifying, however imperfectly fallen she
might be.

In the sitting-room, which doubled as dining-room and
lunching-room when people like Mair were about, a smallish
dark girl of nineteen or twenty was rearranging rugs and pushing
chairs back into position. At my entry the child I'd seen earlier
tottered behind the tall boxlike couch, where another of the same
size was already lurking. Of this supplementary child I could
make out nothing for certain, apart from a frizzy but sparse head
of ginger hair. The girl had looked up at me and then quickly
and shyly away again.

'Good morning,' I said, in the sort of tone officials visiting
things are fond of and good at. I seemed not to have chosen this
tone. It wasn't my day for tones.

'Morning, Mr Lewis,' she muttered, going on with her work.
'Miserable old weather.'

This notification, although accurate enough as far as it went,
drew no reply. I fussed round the gate-leg table for a bit, fiddling
with plates and cutlery and stealthily watching Betty Arnulfsen.
Her straight black hair was ribboned in place by what looked
like the belt of an old floral-pattern dress. In her plain skirt and
jumper and with her meek expression she had the air of an
underpaid shopgirl or bullied supply teacher. She wore no make-
up. Altogether she wasn't my idea of a delinquent, but then few
people are my idea of anything.

There was a ring at the front-door bell, a favourite barking-
trigger of the dog that lived downstairs. On my wife's orders I
went and let in Mair Webster, whose speed off the verbal mark
proved to be at its famed best. By the time we reached the kitchen
I already had a sound general grasp of the events of her morning.
These included a bawling-out of the Assistant Child Care Officer
down at the Town Hall, and a longer, fiercer, more categorical
bawling-out of the foster-mother of one of 'her' babies. 'Is Betty
here?' she added without pause. 'Hallo, Jean dear, sorry I'm late,

been dreadfully pushed this morning, everybody screaming for help. How's Betty getting on? Where is she? I just want to have a word with her a minute.'

I was close enough behind Mair to see the children returning to defensive positions behind the couch and Betty looking harried. It was my first view of her in full face and I thought her quite pretty, but pale and washed out. I also noticed that the ginger-haired child was sucking a dummy similar to that of its fellow.

'Ah, good morning, Betty,' Mair said bluffly. 'How are you getting on? Do you like working for Mrs Lewis?'

'Aw, all right.'

Mair's lion-like face took on the aspect of the king of beasts trying to outstare its tamer. 'I think you know my name, don't you, Betty? It's polite to use it, you know.'

At this I went out into the kitchen again, but not quickly enough to avoid hearing Betty saying, 'Sorry, Mrs Webster', and, as I shut the door behind me, Mair saying, 'That's more like it, isn't it, Betty?'

'What's the matter with you?' Jean asked me.

I stopped stage-whispering obscenities and spoke some instead, using them to point or fill out a report of the recent exchange. In a moment the sitting-room door was reopened, catching me in mid-scatalogism, and Mair's voice asked my wife to come in 'a minute'. At the ensuing conference, I was told later, Betty's willingness, industry and general efficiency as a domestic help were probed and a favourable account of them given. Meanwhile I put to myself the question whether the removal of all social workers, preferably by execution squads, wouldn't do everyone a power of good. You had to do some-thing about ill-treated, etc., children all right, but you could see to that without behaving like a sort of revivalist military police-man.

The meeting next door broke up. Betty and her children were hurried out of the place, the former carrying a tattered parcel my wife had furtively thrust into her hands. I found out after-wards that among other things it contained a tweed skirt of Jean's

I particularly liked her in and my own favourite socks. This was charity run riot.

At lunch, Mair said efficiently: 'The trouble with girls like that is that they've got no moral fibre.'

'How do you mean?' I asked.

'I mean this, John. They've no will of their own, you see. They just drift. Line of least resistance all the time. Now Betty didn't really want to abandon those twins of hers – she was quite a good mother to them, apparently, when she was living with her parents and going out to work at this café. Then she went to a dance and met this dirty swine of a crane driver and he persuaded her to go and live with him – he's got a wife and child himself, a real beauty, he is – and he wouldn't take the twins, so she just went off and left them and let her parents look after them. Then the swine went off with another woman and Betty's father wouldn't have her back in the house. Said he'd forgiven her once when she had the twins when she was sixteen and he wasn't going to forgive her again. He's strong chapel, you see, believes in sinners being cast into the outer darkness, you know the kind of thing. It's a tragic story, isn't it?'

'Yes,' I said, and went on to talk about the conflict between generations, I think it was. Mair's technique when others ventured beyond a couple of sentences was to start nodding, stepping up the tempo as long as they continued. When her face was practically juddering with nods I gave in.

'Well,' she went on in a satisfied tone, 'going back to where I was just now, Betty's father got into such a rage with her that he threw the twins out as well, and she got her job back at the café, which wasn't really a good thing because it's not a very desirable place, but at least it meant that there was some money coming in, but she couldn't take the twins to work with her, so she parked them with the woman she was renting her room from. Then she, the woman, went out for the evening one time when she was working late, Betty I mean, and the twins were left unattended and they ran out into the street and wandered about and a police-man found them and that's how we got brought into it. They were in a dreadful state, poor little dabs, half in rags and – quite filthy. I had the devil's own job stopping them being taken into care, I can tell you. You see, while Betty was with her parents in a decent home she looked after them all right, but on her own, with bad examples all round her, she just let things slide. No moral fibre there, I'm afraid. Well, I fixed her up at the day nursery – didn't know there were such things, she said, but I told her she'd just been too lazy to inquire – and after that things jogged along until this Norwegian came into the café for a cup of tea and saw Betty and bob's your uncle.'

'Hasn't the Norwegian got to go back to Norway ever?' Jean asked, her eyes on the forkful of fish that had been oscillating for some minutes between Mair's plate and her mouth.

'He's going over for a few weeks soon, he says. He's got a job at a chandler's in Ogmore Street – it's run by Norwegians, like a lot of them. Decent people. They've been married six weeks now, him and Betty, and he's very fond of the twins and keeps her up to the mark about them, and of course I give her a good pep talk every so often.'

'Of course,' I said.

'One job I had to do was take her out of that café. Lot of undesirables hang round the place, you know. A girl like Betty, quite pretty and none too bright, she'd have been just their meat. It's something to have kept her out of their clutches. Oh, yes, I'm quite proud of myself in a way.'

One Sunday afternoon a couple of months later I was dozing in front of the fire – Jean had taken the kids out for a walk with a pal of hers and the pal's kids – when the doorbell rang. Wondering if the caller mightn't at last be some beautiful borrower come to avow her love, I hurried downstairs. The person on the doorstep was certainly a woman and probably on the right side of thirty, but she wasn't beautiful. Nor – I'd have taken any odds – was she a borrower, not with that transparent mac, that vehement eye shadow, that squall of scent. 'Good afternoon,' I said.

The woman smiled, fluttering her Prussian-blue eyelids. 'You remember me, don't you, Mr Lewis? Betty Arnulfsen.'

I felt my own eyes dilate. 'Why, of course,' I said genially. 'How are you, Betty? Do come in.'

'Aw, all right, thank you. Thanks.'

'Haven't seen you for a long time.' Not for several weeks, in fact. She'd turned up three more times to do our chores and then that had suddenly been that. Application to Mair Webster had produced an evasive answer – an extreme and, as I now saw it, suspicious rarity.

'I was just passing by, see, so I thought I'd drop in and see how you was all getting along, like.'

'Good. It's very nice to see you again. Well, what have you been doing with yourself?'

It could have been more delicately put, for somebody, whether herself or not, had plainly been doing a good deal with Betty one way and another. As we stood confronted by the sitting-room fire I saw that her hair, which had been of a squaw-like sleekness, now looked like some kind of petrified black froth, and that her face was puffy underneath the yellowish coating of make-up. At the same time she'd altogether lost her hounded look: she seemed sure of herself, even full of fun. She wore a tight lilac costume with purple stripes on it and carried a long-handled umbrella that had elaborate designs on the plastic.

'Aw, I been doing lots of things,' she said in answer to my question. 'Having a bit of a good time for a change. Soon got brassed off with that old cow Webster telling me what I must do and what I mustn't do. I been keeping out of her way, going to live my own life for a change, see? I got a bit of money now. Here, have a fag.'

'No, thanks, I don't smoke.'

'Go on, it'll do you good, man.'

'No, honestly, I never do.'

'I can tell you're one of the careful ones.' She laughed quite a bit at this stroke, giving me a chance to notice the purplish inner portions of her lips where the lipstick had worn away or not reached. With a kind of indulgent contempt, she went on: 'And how you been keeping? Still working down that old library?'

'Oh, yes, I feel I ought to give them a hand occasionally.'

'Don't you get brassed off with it now and then?'

'Yes, I do, but I keep going. Can't afford to weaken.'

'That's the boy. Got to keep the dough coming in, haven't you?'

'Well, it helps, you know.'

'What you pulling in down there? Never mind, don't suppose you want to say. What you get up to after work?'

'Nothing out of the ordinary.'

'What you do, then, when you goes out for a night? Where do you go?'

'Oh, just here and there. I sometimes have a few along at the corner, at the General Picton.'

'I expect you got your own mates.' Her cigarette had gone out and she relit it. She wasn't really at home with it: smoking was something she was still in the process of taking up. After spitting out a shred of tobacco, she said: 'Never go round the pubs in Ogmore Street, do you?'

'Not as a rule, no.'

(Ogmore Street leads into the docks, and on these and associated grounds is usually steered well clear of during the hours of darkness by persons of refinement and discrimination.)

'We gets up to some games down Ogmore Street. We haves the time of our bloody lives, we do.'

'I bet you do.'

'Yeah,' she said with great conviction. 'Jean gone out, have she?'

'Just taken the kids for a breath of fresh air. I don't suppose she'll be long.'

'Ah. They all right, the kids?'

'Pretty fair. What are you up to yourself these days?'

She gave a great yell of laughter. 'That's a question, that is. What don't I bloody get up to? What am I up to, eh? That's a good one.' Then her manner grew seriously informative. 'I got in with the business girls now, see?'

'Oh, really?' A momentary vision of Betty drinking morning coffee at the Kardomah with a group of secretaries and shorthand typists was briefly presented to me, before being penetrated by her true meaning. 'Er . . . good fun?'

'It's all right, you know. Got its points, like. See what I got here.' She opened her handbag, a shiny plastic affair in a pink pastel shade, and, after I'd sat there wondering for a moment or two, drew out a roll of crumpled pound notes bound with an elastic band. 'Take you a long time to pull in this much down the library, wouldn't it?'

'Oh, no doubt about that.'

'We goes with the boys round the docks and the sailors when they comes off the ships. They're the best. They wants a bit of fun and they don't care what they pays for it. They got plenty of dough, see? They goes on the bloody binge down there. Lots of Norgies we gets. I like the Norgies.'

'Oh, yes, your husband's one, isn't he?'

This second deviation from the path of true tact was as little heeded as the first. 'That's right. He've gone back to Norway now.'

'For good?'

'No, don't think so. Father in trouble or something. Reckon he'll fetch up again some time.'

'How are the twins?' The domestic note, once struck, might be a handy one to prolong. What was the time? Where was Jean? Would she bring her red-faced English oh-I-say-darling pal back with her? Why not?

'They're okay. I got someone looking after them okay. These Norgies are dead funny, though. Makes me die. The Welsh boys, now, they likes me with my vest on, don't want it no other way, but the Norgies don't care for that, they wants everything off, and they don't like it outside, they always goes home with you for it. They likes to take their time, like. You know Joe Leyshon?'

'I've heard of him. Used to be in the fight game, didn't he?'

'He runs a lot of the girls down Ogmore Street, but I won't let him run me. He wants to run me, but I don't like him. Some of his mates is dead funny, though. We broke into a shop the other night over Cwmharan way. Didn't get anything much, few fags and things, but we had a laugh. Mad buggers, they are. We goes down the Albany mostly. You know the Albany? It's all right. You ought to come down there one night and have a couple of drinks and a bit of fun. What about it? I'm going down there tonight.'

'Well, I don't want to come barging in . . .'

'Go on, I'd show you around, you wouldn't come to no harm, I promise you. They're all right there, really. I'd see you had a good time. You could tell Jean you was out with your mates, see?'

'It's very kind of you, Betty, but honestly I don't think I could. I'm pretty well fixed up here, you know what I mean, and so I don't . . .'

'I tell you one thing, John.'

'What's that?'

'You're afraid to go with me.'

So many factors amalgamated to put this beyond serious dispute that reply was difficult. 'Oh, I wouldn't say that,' I said after a moment, trying to ram jocoseness into tone and manner. 'No, I wouldn't say that at all.'

Betty evidently saw through this. She said: 'You are. You're afraid.'

'It isn't that exactly. It's just that I try to stick to my wife as far as possible,' I told her, certain that I sounded like some ferret-faced Christian lance-corporal in a barrack-room discussion.

'Yeah, I know, you'd fold up if you hadn't got her to cling on to. You hangs around all the bloody time.' Contempt had returned to her voice, edged this time with bitterness, but she showed none of either when she went on to add: 'You're a good boy.'

'I wouldn't say – I don't know. Betty, you mustn't mind me saying this, but isn't it rather risky to go round breaking into places with these pals of yours? Aren't you afraid of getting caught?'

'Aw, short life and a merry one's what I say. It's worth it for a bit of excitement. Don't get much chance of a thrill these days, eh?'

'Well, it's up to you, but you don't want to get – you know – sent down, do you? The twins wouldn't have . . .'

'Don't preach, now. I gets brassed off with bloody preaching.'

'I'm sorry, I didn't mean to sound like that.'

'Okay.' She smiled.

In the succeeding silence a door boomed shut below. The slapping gait of my daughter Eira became audible, overlaid and in part obscured by the characteristic bellowing squeal of her younger brother. Both sounds began to ascend the stairs.

'Jean back, eh?' Betty got to her feet. 'I better be going.'

'Oh, don't go, stay and have a cup of tea with us.'

'I better not.'

Eira ran into the room, stopping short when she saw Betty and then moving towards the fire by a circuitous route, hugging the wall and the couch. 'Put my coat off,' she said to me distantly.

'Hallo,' Betty said with an elaborate rising inflection. 'Hallo. And whose little girl are you? Let auntie take your coat off, then. Come on, flower. That's right. Had a lovely run, have you? Did you see any bunnies? How you've grown. And you're bold as ever, I declare. Yes, you are. You're bold, very very bold. Yes, you are. You're very very brazen by there.'

Jean came in with the baby. 'Well, hallo, Betty,' she said, grinning. 'Nice to see you. Christ, shut up, can't you?' This last was addressed to the baby, who seemed almost, but not quite, worn out with mortal pain.

'Sorry I couldn't come along that Tuesday like we said, Mrs Lewis, but the twins was poorly and I couldn't fix it to let you know.'

'That's all right, Betty. I'll put the kettle on.'

'Let me take the baby for you.'

'Oh, thanks a lot. John, you might have kept the fire up.'

'Sorry, dear.' I picked up the coal scuttle, which was one of the obliquely truncated-cone type. It proved to weigh less than it should, less than a coal scuttle with any coal in it could. I could hardly remember ever having made up the fire without encountering, at the very outset, a light coal scuttle.

During a long, foul-mouthed ardour in the coal cupboard under the stairs, I thought first how funny it was that a fallen woman – really fallen now, right smack over full length – should talk to a child in just the same style as the perpendicularly upright went in for. But then presumably there were parts of the fallen that were bound to remain unfallen, quite important parts too. This brought up the whole mystery of prostituted existence: not what happened to your womanhood or your springs of emotion or your chances of getting clued up on the splendours and miseries of the flesh – screw all that – but what it was like to be a prostitute during the times when you weren't actually behaving like one, when you were in mufti: on a bus, cooking the baked beans, doing the ironing, going shopping, chatting to a neighbour, buying the Christmas presents. It must be like going round ordinarily and all the time you were a spy or a parson or a leading authority on Rilke, things which you surely often forgot about being. Anyway, to judge by the representative upstairs, being a prostitute was something you could be done a power of good by, and without having to be horrible first, either. As regards not having to get horrible later on, that too could no doubt be arranged, especially if you could keep out of the way of the various sets of men in white coats who, according to report, tended to close in on you after a few years in the game. That was a nasty prospect all right, and resembled many a kindred nastiness thought up by the Godhead in seeming a disproportionate penalty for rather obscure offences. Still, that minor cavil about the grand design had been answered long ago, hadn't it? Yes, more answers than one had been offered.

A little coal, too little to be worth expelling, had entered my shoe. I bore the scuttle upstairs to find Jean and Eira in the kitchen and Betty still holding the baby. Her demeanour had quietened and she was more like the Betty I had first met when she said: 'You won't tell Jean all what I been saying, will you?'

'Of course I won't.'

'And you won't tell that old Webster I been up?'

'Christ, no. What do you think I am?'

'She's a cow.'

'Oh, she's a cow all right.'

Betty nodded slowly, frowning, half-heartedly jogging the baby on her knee. Then she said: 'She's a real cow.'

This refinement upon the original concept made me laugh. Betty joined in. We laughed together for some time, so that Eira came in from the kitchen to see what the joke was.

'I don't mind telling you I was very depressed about that girl at one time,' Mair Webster said. 'Quite frankly I thought we might be going to lose her. It upset me a good deal, one way and another. Once her husband was out of the way for a couple of months, as soon as his back was turned she just took the line of least resistance. Her old cronies at the café, you see, she took up with them again, and got things fixed up with another of them there with minding each other's children while the other one was off after the men, turn and turn about and sharing the same flat, or couple of rooms rather, the most sordid den you could possibly imagine, I'm not exaggerating, I promise you. Well, I soon got Betty and the twins out of that hell hole and fixed them up in a decent place, good enough for the time being, anyway, until Arnulfsen got back from Norway. They've quite a nice little flat now – well, you'll be able to judge, John. It's nothing very grand, of course, but it's a darned sight better than what people like that are used to. Oh, thank you, Jean dear.'

'Everything looks pretty bright then, doesn't it?' my wife asked, pouring coffee. 'Troubles seem to be over.' Her manner showed a relief that I guessed to be partly personal. The strain of not telling Mair about Betty's earlier visit hadn't been lightly borne.

'I don't think I should say that exactly,' Mair said. 'Arnulfsen's forgiven her all right, and she's trying to make a go of it, quite seriously, I can tell. But they keep being bothered by the crowd she used to be in with before, girls who used to be in the same gang looking her up, and once they even had a lascar trying to force his way in; wanted to renew old acquaintance and got her address from the café, I suppose. There've been one or two things like that. And then some of the neighbours have got to hear about Betty's past and they keep teasing her about it, call out in the street after her. Chapel spirit gone sour, you see. It makes Arnulfsen pretty wild.'

While Jean expressed her indignation, I was wondering fairly hard how I was going to 'be able to judge' the Arnulfsens' flat. Was I in some way committed to a tea party there, or what? An answer couldn't be long delayed, for Mair was draining her cup and rising. 'Come along,' she said to me. 'We've not got too much time.'

'Time for what, Mair? I'm sorry . . .'

She threw me a momentary leonine glare before dipping to pick up her handbag. When she spoke, it was with an incredulity to which those accustomed to plan for others must often be subject. Since what she had lined up for me was necessitated both by logic and by natural law, how could I conceivably not know what it was? 'But surely you're coming along to Betty's with me? I'm only popping in to see how she is. Then I can drop you at the library by two-fifteen. Cheerio, Jean dear. Thank you for a lovely lunch. We must fix up a coffee date for next week. I'll give John a ring, if I can manage to pick a time when he's at the seat of custom.'

Wiggling her eyebrows at me to enjoin silence, Jean went into a vivacious speech which lasted more or less until I was sitting in Mair's car next to its owner. Opened envelopes, typed lists, printed forms lay about us as at some perfunctory demonstration of bureaucracy at work. Jean continued her facial ballet until we left.

I knew Mair was going to tell me some more, or possibly run over a few familiar but essential points, about what being a social worker was like. She enjoyed getting me on my own and doing this because, it appeared, I was a man and, as such, easy to talk to. Sometimes her husband came into these conversations, but not often, and when he did it was likely to be as a feature of her exposition of what being married to a social worker's husband was like. I hoped we were going to get the practical today; some of Mair's case histories were of great anthropological interest, and those that weren't were still a lot better than the theoretical.

We got the theoretical, but crossed with the autobiographical, which helped a bit. What had first attracted her to the idea of social work? Ah, there were many answers to this conundrum, every one of them demanding careful or at any rate lengthy consideration. Mair had taken a course in psychology, so she knew all about the power impulse and its tendency to be present in those who made a living out of good works. Several of her colleagues were prone to this affliction, and she had even detected it in herself before now. That was where psychological training was so useful: you knew how to examine your own motives and to guard against unworthy ones. With that out of the way, she felt safe in asserting that it was the duty of the mature and responsible elements of the community to do what they could for their less gifted fellows. At one time the more conscientious kind of squire had stood in a similar relation to his tenants, the right-minded employer to his workmen and their families, but the rise of the oligopoly (Mair kept up with Labour Party research pamphlets) had put paid to all that. One of the many all-important tasks of our society was the training of specialists for functions which at one time had been discharged as by-products of other functions. A case very much in point here was provided by the constantly expanding duties of – well, Mair recognized the term *social workers*, but for her own part she preferred (having once attended a Social Science Summer School in Cardiff) to think of herself and her associates as *technicians in paternalism*.

When she brought that one out I had the infrequent experience of seeing her face express only a limited satisfaction with what she'd said. We penetrated farther into an uncongenial district. Then Mair added: 'Actually, John, I'm not altogether happy about that label.'

'You're not?'

'No, I'm not. It's a scientific term, of course, and so it's quite accurate in a way, but like all scientific terms it's incomplete, it doesn't really say enough, doesn't go far enough, leaves out a lot. It leaves out the thing that keeps us all going, sees us over the rough patches and stops us losing faith, which is the one thing we can't afford to do in our job. It's – well, I can't think of any better name for it than . . . idealism. You can laugh if you like –' she turned her profile far enough round to assure me that any such laughter had better remain internal – 'but that's what it is. Just a simple, old-fashioned urge to do good, not in a chapel way, naturally, but scientifically, because we know what we're doing, but that's the basis of the whole thing, no point in beating about the bush. I know that sort of talk makes you feel uncomfortable, but I believe in—'

Before she could mention calling a spade a spade, a mode of nomenclature she often recommended, I told her that that wasn't quite it, and went on: 'This isn't aimed at you, Mair, but I think doing good to people's rather a risky thing. You can lay up a lot of trouble, for yourself as well as the people who're being done good to. And it's so hard to be sure that the good you're trying to do really is good, the best thing for that person, and the justification of the whole business is a bit—'

'I'm in favour of taking risks. There's far too much playing safe these days, it's ruining the country, all this stick-in-the-mud attitude. I believe in taking off my coat and getting on with the job.'

'But, Mair, these are risks that involve other people. You're deciding what's best for them and then doing it, just like that. You don't give them a chance to—'

'If you'd done as much social work as I have, John, perhaps you'd have some idea of how many people there are in this world who are constitutionally incapable of knowing what's best for them. They're like children. You wouldn't let Eira be the judge of what was best for her, would you? You wouldn't let her put her hand in the fire to see if it was hot, would you?'

'No, of course not, but children aren't—'

'I know you think social work's something terribly complicated and difficult. Well, believe me, ninety or ninety-five per cent of the time it couldn't be simpler, at least making the right decision couldn't: getting it carried out is something else again, of course, but the actual decision's a piece of cake, because you're dealing with complete fools or complete swine or both. You'd think the same after a month in my job, I know you would.'

'I hope not.'

'Honestly, John, if people in general thought like you there wouldn't be any progress at all.'

'No, there wouldn't, would there?'

At this fundamental point Mair steered the car to the kerb and stopped it, not, it transpired, in order to fight me but because we'd arrived. Facing us when we got out was a meagre row of shops: a newsagent's with a lot of advertisements written on postcards, a barber-cum-tobacconist, an outfitter's whose window stock alone would have outfitted a hundred middle-aged ladies in wool from head to foot, and a place that had no doubt once been a shop in the full sense but was now whitewashed to above eye level. This last establishment had to one side of it a door, recently painted a British Railways brown, and a bell which Mair rang. Then she took me by the arm and drew me a yard or two along the pavement.

I said: 'What's this in aid of, then?' in what was supposed to be a bantering tone. Actually I was only half noticing; my mind was busy trying to decide what Mair's 'you'd think the same after a month in the job' thing had reminded me of.

'You don't want to be in front of the front door of a house like this when they open it.'

'Oh?' That was it: the veteran colonial administrator to the just-out-from-England colonial administrator. *We're all a bit pro-wog when we first get out here, my boy; it's only natural. Soon wears off, though, you'll find.* 'Why not?'

'Well, the door opening makes the draught rush through the house, and the draught carries the bugs with it. You don't want them to land on you.'

'You mean really bugs?' She had my full attention now.

'You don't want them to land on you.'

'Hallo, Mrs Webster, don't often see you up this way.'

'Oh, good afternoon, Emrys, how are you?' Mair turned animatedly towards the new arrival, a young police constable with a long, pale nose. 'Wife all right?'

'Well, no, she hasn't been too grand, actually. They had her back in for three days' observation the week before last, and the doctor said—' His voice became indistinguishable, chiefly because he was lowering its pitch, but also because he was removing its source in the direction of the shop that had committed itself so wholeheartedly to the woollen garment. Mair retreated with him, nodding a fair amount. I was still feeling impressed by her bit of know-how about the bugs. Real front-line stuff, that.

'Yes, who's here, please?' This came from the now open front door, at which a small red-haired, red-faced man was standing.

'My name's Lewis.'

'I don't know you. What you want here?'

I looked along the pavement to where Mair, nodding faster, was standing with her back to me. It must have had all the appearance of a furtive, sidelong, up-to-no-good look. Like a fool, I said: 'I'm a friend of your wife's.' As I said this, I smiled.

'Get out of here,' the red-haired man bawled. He wore a red shirt. 'Get out, you bastard.'

'Look, it's all right, there's no need to—'

'Get out quick, you bastard.' For the first time he saw Mair and the policeman, who were now approaching. 'Mrs Webster, hallo. And you, officer. Take away this bastard.'

'Now calm down, Bent, nothing to get excited about. Mr Lewis is with me. He and his wife have been very kind to Betty. He's come along with me to see how you all are. He's a friend of mine.'

'Sorry, Mrs Webster. Sorry, sir, very sorry.'

'That's all right, Bent, Mr Lewis doesn't mind. He knows you didn't mean anything. You just forget it. Now, can we come in?'

'Please, yes, come in.'

'Bye-bye, Emrys, give Maureen my love. Tell her I'll pop in to see her in a day or two. And don't you worry. She's a good strong girl and with the better weather coming she'll soon pull round, I guarantee.'

'Thank you very much, Mrs Webster. Goodbye now.'

Before he turned away I caught a glimpse of Emrys's face and was startled to see on it an expression of relief and gratitude, quite as if he'd just received an important reassurance of some kind. I followed Mair across the threshold, frowning and shaking my head at life's endless enigma.

Bugs or no bugs, the house revealed itself to me as not too bad. There were loose and cracked floorboards, but none missing, and no damp; the kitchen we penetrated to was dark all right, but it smelt no worse than stale; through its open door I could see a scullery with a row of clean cups hanging above the sink and a dishcloth spread over the taps to dry. One of the twins came into view in that quarter, took in the sight of visitors and doubled away again.

'Good afternoon, Betty,' Mair was saying in her hospital-rounds manner. 'My goodness, you have done well, haven't you? You really ought to be congratulated. You have made the place look nice.'

She went on like that while I glanced round the place. It did look nice enough as far as it went, but that wasn't at all far. Most noticeably, there was an absence of the unnecessary things, the ornaments, the photographs and pictures, the postcards on the mantelpiece that every home accumulates. It was as if the moving men had just dumped the furniture down, leaving the small stuff to be unpacked later, only in this case there was nothing to unpack. Curtains perhaps fell into the category of the unnecessary, even, with a small single window like this one, of the excessive. They were of Betty's favourite lilac shade, and ranks of mauve personages, with sword and fan, periwig and towering hair-do, were doing a minuet on them. At this sight I felt pity stirring. Get back, you brute, I said internally, giving it a mental kick on the snout. Then I felt angry with a whole lot of people, but without much prospect of working out just who.

Mair was nearing her peroration. I looked covertly at Betty. Although no longer tarted up, she hadn't recovered the quiet, youthful air she'd had when I first saw her. She wore a grey cardigan which seemed designed to accentuate the roundness of her shoulders. The circles under her eyes weren't the temporary kind. She was staring up at Mair with the sarcastic patience of someone listening to a shaky alibi. Bent Arnulfsen, after standing about uneasily for a time, went out into the scullery and I heard water plunging into a kettle. Still talking, the old moral commando moved to follow him. 'I just want to have a word with Bent a minute,' she said, and shut the door behind her.

'Well, how are things?' I asked.

Betty glanced at me without friendliness, then away. 'Okay,' she muttered, picking at a hole in the cover of her chair.

'Your husband seems a nice chap.'

'What you know about it, eh?'

'I'm only going on how he struck me.'

'Aw, he's okay, I suppose. He's a good boy.'

'There's a lot to be said for good boys.'

'Suppose so.'

'You seem to have settled down here nicely.'

'Yeah.'

'Jean and the children asked to be remembered to you, by the way.'

To shrug both her shoulders would have meant heaving herself up from the chair back, so she made do with just shrugging the uppermost one. It was clear to me that there was nothing left of the cordiality of our last meeting, and no wonder. A man who had seen her when she was free was the last kind of person on earth who should have been allowed to see her now she was tamed. And in any contact not made on terms of equality the speech of one party or the other will fall almost inevitably into the accents and idioms of patronage, as I'd just heard my own speech doing. Severity is actually more respectful. But that wouldn't do here. Would anything? I said: 'Do you ever miss the old life?'

'What you want to know for? What's it got to do with you?'

'Nothing. I was only asking.'

'Well, don't ask, see? Mind your own bloody business, see? What you want to come here for anyway?'

'I'm sorry, Betty. I just came to see how you were getting on.'

'Like old Webster, eh? Well I don't like people coming along to see how I'm getting on, see? I gets brassed off with it, see?'

As she got up from her chair to make her point more forcibly, the scullery door opened and Mair came back into the room. My sense of relief filled me with shame. Triumph swept over Betty's face at being about to do what she must have wanted to do for quite a time.

'Your husband certainly thinks the world of you, Betty,' Mair led off. 'He's been telling me—'

'Get out, you old cow,' Betty shouted, blinking fast. 'I doesn't want you here, see? I got enough to put up with with the bloody neighbours hanging over the fence and staring in the bloody windows and them buggers upstairs complaining. I got enough without you poking your bloody nose in, see? Just you piss off quick and leave me alone.'

'Please, my dear, be quiet.' Bent Arnulfsen had reappeared in the scullery doorway. In one hand he held a brown enamel teapot, in the other the hand of one of the twins. 'Mrs Webster is kind. And this gentleman.'

'You keep out of this, man. Go on, Webster, what you waiting for? I said get out, didn't I? Who do you think you are, that's what I'd like to know – poking your bloody nose in everywhere and telling every bugger what to do. You're beyond, you are, Webster. Bloody beyond. And as for you—' At the moment when Betty, who was now crying, turned to me, Mair looked at her wristwatch with a quick movement. 'Who asked you to come snooping in, that's what I'd like to know,' Betty started to say to me, but Mair cut in.

'I'm afraid we shan't be able to manage that cup of tea, Bent,' she said interestedly; 'I'd no idea the time was getting along like this. I must take Mr Lewis off to his place of work or I shall get into trouble. I'll be in next week as usual and I'm sure things will have settled down by then. Goodbye, Betty; don't upset yourself, there's a good girl. Goodbye, Bent.'

With another look at me, full of accusation, Betty blundered out into the scullery and banged the door. Later I thought how cruel it was that she'd been met by bland preoccupation instead of the distress or anger she'd longed to provoke, that her brave show of defiance must have seemed to her to have misfired. But at the time I only wanted to get out before she came back.

Brushing aside Bent Arnulfsen's halting apologies, Mair led me away. 'Astonishing how predictable these girls are,' she said as we drove off. 'I'd seen that little lot coming for some time. You usually get it sooner or later and afterwards you often find you get on better than you did before. Sort of clears the air in a way. Next week she'll be falling over herself and holding on to my hand and going on about "Oh, Mrs Webster, how could I have said what I did, what a pig I was to you, Mrs Webster, and you so kind", and not being able to do enough for me. Not that that phase lasts very long, either. No, there's no doubt about it, if you look for thanks in this job you're wasting your time and letting yourself in for a big disappointment. The approval of your conscience is all the reward you ever get.'

'Seen this?' my wife asked me later in the same year.

I took the local paper from her and read that Elizabeth Grace Arnulfsen (19) had been sentenced to two months' imprisonment for helping to burgle a café in Harrieston. (The two men who'd been with her got longer sentences.) Mrs Mair Webster, it was further reported, had spoken of her belief that Elizabeth Arnulfsen was weak-willed rather than vicious and had been led astray by undesirable companions. She said this out of her thorough knowledge of the girl's character, and had been thanked for saying it.

'Well, I hope Mair's satisfied,' I said, throwing the paper down.

'Don't be silly, you know she'll be very cut up. She's always done her best for Betty.'

'Her worst, you mean.'

'Don't talk so soft.'

'Betty only burgled that place to get her own back.'

'What, on Mair?'

'Yes, I should say it was chiefly on Mair. Not on society or any of that crap. As a method of not being the kind of person Mair wanted her to be.'

'Mm. Sounds more like just high spirits to me. And according to what you told me Betty'd been breaking into places quite a time back.'

'Not until Mair'd started licking her into shape.'

'You're exaggerating the whole thing, John. What should have happened according to you, anyway? Betty going on being a tart?'

'Why not?'

'What about the twins and this Bent bloke?'

'Yes. No, she shouldn't have gone on being a tart, or couldn't or something. Pity in a way, though. She was enjoying herself.'

'You don't know anything about it. I'm going to make supper.'

'I know how not to deal with people like Betty. Shall I give you a hand?'

'No, you make the cocoa after. How do you stop people being tarts? How would you do it if it was you?'

'Always assuming I thought I ought to try. It's all a mess. It all needs going into.'

'Who's going to go into it? You and Mair?'

'No, just me. What about that supper?'

I could picture Mair doing what she'd have called helping Betty through the ordeal, going to see her in prison, meeting her when she got out and at once settling down again to the by now surely hopeless task of inducing her to lead a normal life with her husband and children. And what would friend Lewis be up to while all this was going on? Getting boozed with his mates, having fantasies about some new beautiful borrower, binding about his extra evening duties in the summer and explaining to his wife that you couldn't have good social workers, because the only kind of chap who'd make a good one was also the kind of chap who'd refuse to be one. Of the two of us, it had to be admitted that on the face of it Mair had a claim to be considered the less disreputable character, up there in the firing line while cowards flinched and traitors sneered.

Once you got off the face of it, though, and got on to what Mair was actually doing up there in the firing line, the picture changed a bit, just as things like the Labour Party looked better from some way away than close to. This was a timely reflection, because I'd been almost starting to admire Mair rather, and admiring someone you think is horrible is horrible. It was true enough that you had to have social workers, in the same way that you had to have prison warders, local government officials, policemen, military policemen, nurses, parsons, scientists, mental-hospital attendants, politicians and – for the time being anyway, God forgive us all – hangmen. That didn't mean that you had to feel friendlily disposed towards any such person, bar the odd nurse perhaps, and then only on what you might call extrinsic grounds.

Actually, of course, it wasn't Mair I ought to have been cogitating about. Mair, with her creed of take-off-your-coat-and-get-on-with-it (and never mind what 'it' is), could be run out of town at any stage, if possible after being bound and gagged and forced to listen to a no-holds-barred denunciation of her by Betty. What if anything should or could be done about Betty, and who if anyone should or could do it and how – that was the real stuff. I was sorry to think how impossible it was for me to turn up at the gaol on the big day, holding a bunch of flowers and a new plastic umbrella.

All the Blood Within Me

That morning Alec Mackenzie had been unable to eat even his usual small breakfast, so when, some minutes out of Euston, coffee and light refreshments were announced, he went along to the dining-car. He felt that, in view of what lay ahead, he should have something inside him, however nasty it or the task of getting it down might prove. It was good, too, to quit the company of those sharing his compartment, a standard crew of secret agents for the bus companies: two sailors and a portable radio, an ever-toddling toddler, a man whose pipe whimpered and grumbled, an old woman with a hat who moved her lips as she read her library book and wet her fingers thoroughly before turning each page.

The first person he saw on entering the dining-car was Bob Anthony, wearing a suit that looked like woven vegetable soup and reading a newspaper with awful concentration. Alec found it hard not to dive back the way he had come, let alone stand his ground, but he knew that the two of them must have caught the train for the same reason and would have to meet sooner or later. Hoping only that it would be later, he did not resist when the steward put him in a chair facing Bob's, but at the opposite end of the car.

For twenty-four hours now his brain had behaved as if some terminal had come loose, deactivating half of it and letting the rest work only at low efficiency. Perhaps this was what people meant when they talked about moving round in a trance. The half-rural landscape, wheeling past the window in average September sunshine, had a flat, pointless quality. Alec felt a slight amazement that things like keeping out of Bob's way for a few extra minutes should still matter to him, and again that he should find himself making his customary weak and futile appeal for a pot of tea instead of the donkey-coloured mixture now being served under the name of coffee. Habit persisted when other things broke down. He drank coffee and ate biscuits.

The one look he had had at Bob had been quite enough to assure him that Bob's recent outbreak of affluence showed no sign of abating. Alec was well enough resigned to his own failure – bowing uncomplainingly to the inevitable was part of his code – but he had no intention of ceasing to be indignant at Bob's luck. A long period of floundering round the legal profession had been halted by two deaths. The first of these, brought on by an alcoholic seizure occurring slightly ahead of expectation, had had the effect of hauling Bob up a notch or two; the second, in which drink had played a more devious role as the agent of a fall downstairs, had made him virtual head of the firm, Bob having helped fate along, so to speak, by becoming friendly with the faller's widow. The depth of this friendship remained obscure, but it was certain that the second dead man's half-share in the business had passed under Bob's control and stayed there.

An approaching disturbance – the sound of a hip striking the corner of a laden table, the clash of crockery on a tray abruptly snatched from collision – warned Alec that Bob was on his way to join him. He looked up and saw that, apart from some lateral distortion caused by the movement of the train, the old stooping gait was the same as ever, not in the least scholarly, the tread of someone closing in on bodily enjoyment or the means to buy some.

'Hallo, Mac,' Bob said in his curt tone and fake-genteel accent, then at once set about making people move so that he could sit where he wanted, opposite Alec. When he had done this he swept the cloth with the edge of his newspaper and they looked at each other in a way they often did, Bob unconcernedly claiming superior sophistication, Alec on the defensive, ready, if challenged, to stress the importance of integrity. Then both turned blank and grim. Alec found nothing to say; his attention was like a weight too heavy to move from where it had landed, on Bob's suit. Why was he wearing it? He must have others. Where were they?

'Well, Mac, words aren't much use at a time like this, eh?'

'No. No, they're not.'

Bob signalled emphatically for more coffee. 'I'd have thought you'd have gone down there yesterday.'

'I didn't like to intrude.'

'Oh, but surely, I mean Jim would have been glad to have you there, old chap. After all, you're not exactly a stranger.'

'I worked it out that he'd sooner have been on his own. I know I would if it had been me.'

'That's where you go wrong, Mac, if I may say so. You're by way of being a reserved type, always have been. I'm not blaming you, heaven knows – you can't help the way you're made – but most people aren't like that, you see. They want their pals round them. I call that a normal human instinct. Tell me, are you still living at that place of yours in Ealing?'

'You asked me that the last time you saw me in the Lord Nelson. I haven't moved since then.'

'It would drive me crackers, quite frankly, being on my own twelve hours of the day. What do you do when you feel like nipping out and having a few?'

'I haven't got much cash for nipping out and having a few, so the question doesn't arise very often.'

'No, I see.' Bob seemed not to have noticed the bitterness which Alec had been unable to keep out of his voice. Not noticing things like that was no doubt useful to one who led Bob's kind of life. After gazing with apparent incredulity at the coffee with which their cups were now being refilled, he went on: 'What do you do of an evening then? You can't just—'

'Oh, I get a bit of bridge now and again, and there are one or two people I drop in on. There's a colleague of mine in the export department living just ten minutes' walk away. I usually have some grub with him and his wife Sunday midday and occasionally in the week.'

'Still go to your concerts?'

'Not so much now.'

Bob shook his head and drew in his breath. 'It wouldn't do for me, I must say.'

'Well, we're not all built the same, are we?'

'No, I like being in company.'

Alec knew how true this was. The advent of the partner's widow had done nothing to curb Bob's habit of suddenly appearing in the Lord Nelson, the pub near the Temple both men were apt to use at lunch-time, and plying some woman with large gin-and-frenches while Alec sat up at the bar with his light ale and veal-and-ham pie and salad. Every few minutes the other two would burst out laughing at some trivial phrase, or go off into face-to-face mumbling that sometimes led to more laughter, all eyes and teeth. He never knew how to behave during these interludes.

The train had stopped at a station. Bob glanced out of the window and dropped his voice slightly. 'I suppose it was another stroke, was it? Jim wasn't very clear on the phone.'

'Yes, it was a stroke all right. She died before they could get her to hospital.'

'Good way to go, I suppose. Better than poor old Harry. He was under drugs for almost a year, you know. It makes you wonder what sort of exit you'll have when it comes to your turn. Selfish, of course, but natural. Do you ever think about that, Mac? How you'll go?'

'Yes.'

'Still, there's no use getting morbid. Actually I should think of the two of us you'll last longest. You thin little wiry chaps take a devil of a lot of killing, in my experience. You're a bit younger than me anyway, aren't you?'

'I was sixty-four in June.'

'Not six months in it. We don't live to much of an age in our family. Harry was the same age as me when he snuffed it, and then poor Dora was barely fifty, and now here's Betty only sixty-seven; well, I say "only", that's not really old as things go nowadays, is it? Still, look at it another way and it's a lot of years. You must have known her since, what, 'thirty-two or -three?'

'The . . . I'm not sure of the date, but it was August Bank Holiday, 1929.'

'Here, that's pretty good card-index work, Mac. Well I'm blowed. How on earth do you remember it so exactly?'

'It was the day of the mixed doubles tournament at that tennis club near Balham we all used to belong to.' Alec began filling his pipe. 'I got brought in to run the show at the last minute. Until the Friday I didn't see how there could be a show, and what with the teas to arrange and one thing and another it'll be a long time before I forget that day, believe me.'

'Mm. It, er, turned out all right, did it?'

'Yes, Betty and Jim got into the semi-finals. Nobody knew if they were any good or not, with them just moving into the district. But then they took the first set 6–1, and everyone could see . . . well, as soon as Betty had made her first couple of shots, really. Her backhand was very strong, unusual in a woman. I didn't get a chance against them myself, because . . .'

As clearly as if he had just seen a photograph of it, Alec recalled one moment of that first day. Jim, his bald head gleaming in the sun, was standing up at the net; Betty had stepped forward from the baseline and, with as much control as power, was sending one of her backhand drives not more than an inch or two above the net and squarely between their two opponents, who formed the only blurred patches in the image. Although the farthest away, Betty's figure was well defined, the dark hair in a loose bob, the sturdy forearms and calves, the straight nose that gave her face such distinction, even the thinning of the lips in concentration and effort. Some details were wrong – Betty's pleated white skirt belonged not to that afternoon, Alec knew, but was part of a summer dress she had worn on a day trip to Brighton just before the war, and Jim had not been so bald so early. There was nothing to be done about it, though: while a part of his mind fumbled left-handedly to correct it, the picture stayed as it was. Just as well, perhaps, that it had not been given to human beings to visualize things at will.

Long before Alec was finally silent, Bob was glancing fitfully about, extending and shortening his body and neck like someone trying to see over a barrier that constantly varied in height. He was always having to have things: another round of drinks, the right time, a taxi, the menu, the bill, a word with old so-and-so before they settled down. While he twitched a nose rich in broken capillaries, he said inattentively: 'Of course, you were pretty attached to her, weren't you, Mac?'

'Yes, I was.'

'And so was she to you, old thing.' The distance between Bob's waist and chin grew sharply, as if a taxi-driver or possibly a racing tipster had flung himself down full length behind Alec's seat. 'She was always on about you, you know. Talking about you.'

'Really?'

'Oh yes. You had a lot of brains, according to her. Looked up to you, so she said. I'd like a miniature of brandy, please,' he added over Alec's shoulder. 'Wait a minute. Better make it two.'

Alec began wondering how to decline the offer of a miniature of brandy. He need not have worried, because when they came Bob put them both carefully away in the pockets of the woven-soup suit. He then tried to pay for Alec's coffee, but Alec prevented him.

'Ah, we're just coming in,' Bob said: 'there's that pickle-factory place. Appalling stink when the wind's in the right direction, makes you wonder what they put in the blessed stuff. How are you feeling, old chap?'

'Me? I'm perfectly all right.' The barrier in Alec's head had given no sign of breaking down in the last five minutes, which meant it might just possibly stay in position for the next three hours, or however long it was going to be before he could decently leave. If he could hold out until then, the truth about him and Betty would never be known to any outsider, especially Bob. The thought of their secret being turned over by that parvenu mind, frivolous, hard-headed and puritanical in turn, and never the right one at the right time, was unendurable.

Bob had got up and was looking at his watch. 'Good for you, Mac. Mm, late as per usual. I think we'd better go straight to the church. It might be the best thing in some ways.'

'Will you sit, please,' the clergyman directed. He was a bulky man of about fifty-five with white hair carefully combed and set. He had a thick voice, as if his throat were swollen. It went down a tone or two each time he told the congregation to change its posture. His way of doing this even when it was clearly unnecessary, and of giving every such syllable its full value, made up a good substitute for quite a long sentence about the decline of church-going, the consequent uncertainty and uneasiness felt by many people on such occasions as did bring them into the house of God, his own determination that there should be no confusion in his church about what some might think were small points of procedure, and the decline of church-going. Now, after making absolutely certain that everyone had done his bidding, he pronounced the dead woman's name in the manner of an operator beginning to read back a telegram.

'Elizabeth . . . Duerden,' he said, 'has brought us together here today by virtue of the fact that she has recently died. I need not tell you that the death of someone we love, or even the death of any human being, is the most serious and important event with which this life can confront us. I want for a short time, if I may, to look into this business of death, to suggest a little of what it is, and of what it is not. I believe that the loss which her . . . family has suffered is not absolute, that that thing exists which we so frequently name and seek and offer, so rarely define and obtain and give, that there is consolation, if only we know where to look for it. Where, then, are we to look?'

By now the man sounded as if he had been going on for hours and had more hours ahead of him. Some of the thickness, however, had left his voice when he continued: 'In another age than ours, we should find it natural to look in the first place to the thought that to be separated from the ones we love by the death of the body is not final. We should derive our consolation from knowing that no parting is for ever, that all losses will, in God's good time, be restored. But that would hardly do today, would it, thinking along those lines? It wouldn't do much for most of us today.'

Something so close to vigour had entered the speaker's tone in the last couple of sentences that they were like an interruption, from which he himself took a moment to recover. Then he went on as thickly as ever: 'But God's mercy has seen to it that we need not depend for our consolation upon any such belief. We find this out as soon as we can put aside something of our agony and shock and begin to ask ourselves what has happened. What has happened is manifestly that somebody has been taken from us and nothing will ever be the same again. But what has not happened? That person has not been eradicated from our hearts and minds, that person's life has not been cancelled out like a row of figures in a sum, that person's identity is not lost, and can never be lost . . . Elizabeth Duerden lives in those who knew her and loved her. The fact that she lived, and was Elizabeth Duerden and no one else, had a profound effect upon a number of people, a considerable effect upon many more people, a slight but never imperceptible effect upon innumerable people. There is nobody, there never has been anybody, of whom it can be said that the world would have been the same if they had never lived.'

He can string words together, Alec thought. Or whoever had written the stuff could. He looked round the church, anxious to impress on his memory this part, at least, of today. But it was a modern building, thirty years old at the most, with bright stained glass, a tiled floor, and woodwork that reminded him of the dining-room suites he saw in suburban shop windows: none of the air of antiquity that had always appealed to Betty.

The Gioberti family occupied the pew in front. The farthest away from him was Annette Gioberti, who turned her head now and gave him a faint smile. The bearer of this exotic name looked like a soberly but becomingly dressed English housewife in her middle thirties, which, as the daughter of Jim and Betty, was much what might have been expected of her. Jim had been against the marriage at first, saying among other things that, while he had no objection to Italians or half-Italians as such, he did not fancy having his grandchildren brought up as Roman Catholics. But Betty had soon laughed him out of that by asking him when he had last had anything to do with the Church of England, and had added that Frank Gioberti was a decent, hard-working lad who was obviously going to do everything in his power to make Annette happy – what more could they ask?

Alec had never known Betty to err in her judgements of people, and in this case she had turned out to be almost too literally accurate. From what she told Alec, whose direct contacts with the Giobertis were rare, there was plenty of money around in that household, and no shortage of affection, especially if you counted the more obvious kind of show of it – expensive presents on anniversaries as well as birthdays, and bunches of flowers being delivered unexpectedly. But as regards the finer things of life (Alec always wanted to smile at this favourite phrase of Betty's, so characteristic of her in its naïve sincerity) there was a complete gap: no books apart from trashy thrillers, no music except what the wireless and gramophone churned out, and no pictures at all; in fact Betty had given them a Medici print of a medieval Virgin and Child one Christmas, thinking it would appeal to Frank, and had come across it months later in a drawer in one of the children's bedrooms.

The part of Frank that could be seen above the back of the pew seemed to Alec to offer a good deal of information. The thick black hair was heavily greased; the neck bulged in a way that promised a roll of fat there in due course; the snowily white shirt-collar and the charcoal-grey suit material did somehow or other manage to suggest, not lack of taste exactly, but the attitude that money was more interesting. Still, one had to be tolerant. A man who owned however many laundries it was in the Deptford area could hardly be expected to have the time or the inclination to take up the French horn. It was only the children who might be the losers, especially since, in a materialistic age like the present one, the parent had a special responsibility for suggesting that there were some worthwhile things which nobody could be seen eating or drinking or smoking or wearing or driving or washing dishes in on TV commercials. And then people wondered why there was all this . . .

Alec pulled himself physically upright in his seat. It was almost frightening, the way the mind could so easily follow its well-worn tracks, even at times of unique stress. Habit again: nature's protection. He turned cold at the thought that today might pass him by altogether, that he might in some way miss experiencing it or beginning to understand it. The most abject and revealing loss of composure would be better than that. He started doing what he could never have predicted: trying to feel. 'A human being,' the clergyman was saying, 'is the sum of many qualities, and it is from what we see of these that we form our ideas of what everything in life is, of what life itself is.' No help there. Alec glanced over to the front pew across the aisle, where Jim and Bob sat together. With the Giobertis, this was all the family there was. Jim's brother, who had emigrated to Canada getting on for thirty years ago, had not received Jim's cable, or had not answered it, and it was now nearly twenty years – yes, twenty next April – since young Charlie, Annette's brother, had been killed in a motor-cycle accident in Alexandria, three weeks after getting his commission in the Royal Armoured Corps. Well, he had been spared all this.

Jim's face, half-turned towards the clergyman, looked quite relaxed, and he had seemed so in the brief moment at the church door when Alec had just had time to grasp his hand and murmur a few words, though his movements and reactions had been a little slower than usual. It had been the same, Alec remembered, the night the telegram about Charlie arrived. He had got there in the small hours – he had left his digs within a minute of getting Jim's phone call but the train had been held up by an air alert – to find Betty in a state of collapse, naturally, and Jim simply being Jim, only more so: calm, solid, desperately hurt but not defeated, saying little as always, showing a degree of strength that even Alec, who admired him more than any other man he had ever met, had not expected. Thank God that Jim, at least, was still here. Now that he was alone, Jim might well consider throwing in his lot with him, sharing some sort of household, even perhaps (Alec put this part of his thought aside for future reference) coming into the small glass-merchandising firm of Keith Mackenzie and Company in which Alec, upon his retirement next year, was planning to join his brother Iain. If that appealed to Jim, it would be a kind of continuation of the Trio – the name Alec used in his own mind for the unit the Duerdens and he had comprised for over thirty years. And it would be a fine memorial to Betty.

'And so to have lived in vain,' Alec heard the clergyman say, 'is inconceivable.' Even the thickest and most preternaturally apathetic voices have a directional component, and Alec became half-aware that this one was being beamed towards him. When a pause followed, he looked up and saw that the clergyman was indeed staring angrily into his face. After another second or two of ocular reprimand, the man spoke again. He was plainly drawing to a close, and now the hint of a new tone was heard, the detached disgust of a schoolmaster reading out to his class some shameful confidential document he has snatched from the hot hand of one of their number.

'Whence do we derive our ideas of what is most precious and admirable and lovable in human nature? Not from any inborn knowledge, but from what we see in those around us. To know somebody, and even more to know them with love, is constantly to be made aware of what human nature is and can be. To have known somebody with love is to be permanently illuminated with the human capacity for tenderness, for generosity, for gaiety, for disregard of self, for courage, for forgiveness, for intelligence, for compassion, for loyalty, for humility – and nobody has ever lived who has been unable to offer his fellow-creatures some one or other of these. And is this illumination an aspect of life, a side of life, a part of life? No, it is life itself, this learning what we are. And can death diminish that? No, death can do nothing with it, death even throws it into prominence, death is cheated. As death will always be cheated. Let us pray. Will you kneel, please.'

Alec knelt and tried to pray, but could not decide what to pray to. The principle for good he sometimes thought of as existing above and beyond everything, and which he had expected (wrongly) to become more real to him as he grew older, seemed to involve a way of looking at things that included a belief in Betty's having a future, and he could not see how she could have any. So he made some wishes about the past instead, that Betty had had a happy life and had not suffered when she was dying. He felt his mind slowing down and becoming a blank, and would have begun to forget where he was if it had not been for the diminishing footfalls that told him he was about to be left alone. He got quickly to his feet and hurried outside.

Jim was shaking hands with the last group of local people under the eye of the clergyman, whose manner now implied that he had been forced into his vestments as part of a practical joke and could see, for the moment, no dignified way of extricating himself. He looked bigger, too.

Alec felt impelled to speak to him: 'Thank you for your address, Vicar, I thought it was most—'

'Rector,' the other said, moving off.

'Right, let's get on, Mac,' Jim said. 'Who are you going up with?'

There were only two cars to be seen, one with Bob in it, the other full of Giobertis. 'Oh, don't worry about me,' Alec said rather wildly. 'I can walk. How do I get to the—?'

'Nonsense, hop in with me and Bob.'

'No, that's for the . . . I wouldn't want to—'

'Well then, go with Annette and Frank and the kids. These buses take five easily.'

'In here, Uncle Mac,' Annette called, and began making a place for him between herself and her husband. The two Gioberti girls occupied the folding seats: Sonia, a bespectacled blonde child of

seven or eight with, so far as could be made out, a perfectly spher-
ical head, and Elizabeth, a somewhat darker fourteen-year-old with
a figure which, Alec supposed, many grown women would envy.
As they moved off, she asked: 'Where did you leave the car, Pop?'

Frank answered in his strong cockney accent: 'Outside that
hotel where we're going to have lunch, the King's Head or whatever it's called. Tumbledown-looking joint.'

'Why couldn't we have gone up to the cemetery in our car?'

'Because we're going up in this one.'

'Why? Ours is much more comfortable.'

'I dare say it is, but we're going up in this one and that's an
end of it, see?'

'What are we going up to the cemetery for?' Sonia asked.

'To see Gran being buried.'

'It won't hurt her,' Sonia stated.

'Of course it won't hurt her, she's dead.'

'What are we going up to see her being buried for?'

'Because that's what we do.'

'Sonia, take your shoes off there,' Annette said.

'And shut up,' Frank added.

'How's Christopher?' Alec asked. 'Let's see, he must be nearly—'

'He was four in June.'

'Really? It seems only the other—'

'Auntie Gina's looking after him today,' Elizabeth said with a
hint of triumph. 'Over at Camberwell.'

To forestall another invitation to silence from Frank, Alec
looked out of the window. His eyes immediately fell on the little
coffee shop with green check curtains where, whenever he came
down for the weekend, he and Betty would spend an hour or so
on the Saturday morning before strolling along to the King's
Head to meet Jim after his morning of local activities – work for
the Ratepayers' Association or the Golf Club committee – and
relaxing over a couple of pink gins in the saloon bar, followed
by lunch under the low beamed ceiling of the dining-room. It
was at times like that that the Trio had really come into its
own again, and for days and weeks afterwards there would be

a lifting of the shadow that had fallen over Alec's life since 1945. With the war over, the Duerdens had decided to stay on in this part of Buckinghamshire, where they had come in 1941 as a temporary measure to avoid the bombing, and not return after all to their house in Clapham. Since he could not reciprocate their hospitality, Alec had had to confine himself to staying with them only half a dozen times a year at the outside, and had seen them hardly more often for a meal or a theatre in London. He supposed he ought to be thankful that the Trio had survived as well as it had, that it had ever been able to recapture the spirit of its heyday, those twelve happiest years of his life between 1929 and 1941 when the Duerdens and he had occupied houses facing the Common, not four hundred yards apart.

Alec's face was still turned towards the window, but he saw nothing of the neat residential area, its pavements decorated with a staked lime sapling every fifty feet, through which they were now passing. He was thinking of the moment when he had first named the Trio to himself. He and two or three other people (he forgot who) had taken their music round to the Duerdens' one Sunday evening and, after the coffee and tomato sandwiches, Jim had asked him to have a shot at the accompaniment of a duet they had bought recently. He had sat down at the piano, which had an excellent tone for an upright, and played the thing for them at sight, something of a feat with such bold, dramatic writing, full of shifting trills in both hands. It was 'Onaway, Awake, Beloved', a far more interesting setting than that in Coleridge-Taylor's *Hiawatha*, which he had always thought – secretly, for Betty delighted in it, and had met the composer once at a wedding in Croydon – a bit of a bore. Out of the corners of his eyes Alec had been able to see both Betty and Jim as they sang, and when, with his support, the two voices swept into

> Does not all the blood within me
> Leap to meet thee, leap to meet thee,
> As the springs to meet the sunshine,
> In the moon when nights are brightest?

he had felt his own blood leaping through him in a strange, pain-ful rhythm, as if he had stumbled on a mysterious secret. And so he had; he had discovered that there could be a relationship between three people for which none of the ordinary words – friendship, love, understanding, intimacy – would quite do. When the song finished there had been enthusiastic applause from the others, even from ten-year-old Charlie, who was staying up late as a special treat, and Alec's excitement had passed unnoticed.

The car stopped outside the cemetery. Although Alec had walked along most of the roads in the area many times in the last twenty years, the exterior of this place, and its whole loca-tion, were totally unfamiliar to him.

'Here we are,' Frank said. 'Want any help, Uncle Mac?'

'No thank you.'

He got out and began walking towards the graveside, remem-bering that, outside his family and their circle, Betty was the only person who had ever called him 'Alec', and she only for a brief period, perhaps a year after their first meeting. Then she had slipped into calling him 'Mac' as everyone else did, or rather as Jim in particular did. With that fine tact of hers, the finer for being unselfconscious, she had made it clear that there was not to be even the slightest and most nominal acknowledgement of what she felt for Alec, just as he had never by a single word acknowledged what he felt for her. The idea that two people could fall in love instantly and irrevocably and never mention it, let alone do anything about it, would have seemed incompre-hensible or lunatic to anybody but themselves, or rather, again, to anybody but themselves and Jim. For Jim had somehow made it clear to Alec that he knew, but without hurt or resentment; he knew, but he understood and forgave, and so made it possible for Alec to go on seeing them without losing his self-respect. It was silently agreed between the three of them that while she loved Jim no less, she loved Alec too with a different – he recoiled from the mental impertinence of wondering if it were a deeper – kind of love. Few women would have been capable of that, but love had been Betty's gift.

Alec answered an imaginary question about what he had done with his life by saying to himself that he had loved a fine woman and known a true friend. The love came first, as love must. By repeating this slowly he succeeded for a time in shutting out the presence of those standing near him and all but the first phrase of the dreadful words the clergyman was saying. Then Alec started noticing the coffin lying in the grave. It had been lowered by means of green straps that recalled to him, in their colour and texture, the webbing belt Charlie Duerden had worn with his uniform when they lunched at Simpson's together during one of the boy's leaves. A handful of earth was thrown on to the coffin. Alec realized that he had been very afraid of the hollow noise this might make, but it was all right, the soil was dry and chalky, without noticeable clods, and when the spades got to work it could, from the sound, have been anything at all being buried. There were the beginnings of movement away from the graveside; Alec sighed and raised his head, and the whole scene shone brightly in his eyes: the people with their varied complexions and hair, the grass, the privet hedges, the vases of red and blue flowers on the graves, the great pair of cypresses by the entrance, all slightly over-coloured like a picture postcard. In the middle of it all Alec saw the clergyman, looked squarely at him for the first time since leaving the church, and saw that the clergyman, as earlier, was looking at him.

The next moment after Alec felt he was going to cry he started crying; he could no more have prevented it than he could have prevented himself from gasping if a bucket of icy water had been thrown over him. How did it help the *dead* to have made the living aware of certain things? What good to anyone were *ideas* about lovable qualities? What use was it to *learn* about tenderness? What could you *do* when you were illuminated about human possibilities, except go round telling yourself how illuminated you were? What was *knowing* in aid of? And what was it to *have loved* someone?

'Here we go, old chap,' Bob's voice said. 'Just let's take a little stroll together. That's right, steady as she goes. I was wondering when you were going to crack. I was saying to myself, I wonder when old Mac's going to crack. That's your trouble, if I may say so, old stick: you keep things bottled up too much. Far better let 'em come out, like this. Well, you've picked the right time. Just a minute.'

Alec became aware of the curious hooting noise he was making, and pressed his hands over his mouth. 'Nuisance,' he said. 'Sorry.'

'Don't talk unmitigated piffle, old thing. Holler away for a couple of hours if you feel like it. *Get rid of it*. Emotion has got to come out. Sooner or later it's got to come out. That's human nature. Here. Go on, knock it back. Down in one. I'll join you if I may. I knew these little beggars would come in handy. Expensive way of buying booze, but still.'

'Thirty years for nothing,' Alec said, coughing. 'Wasted my time.'

'Oh no you haven't, Mac. People who've really done that don't mind. Here's the gate.'

'No, pipe down, I'm doing this,' Frank said loudly. 'Mrs Allen – another grapefruit juice? Sure you don't want anything stronger? Mrs Holmes, what about you? Are you quite sure? Mrs Higginbotham? Ah, that's more like it. Another for you, darling? Right. Now, Rector . . . large Scotch . . . Bob . . . large brandy and soda . . . Mr Walton?'

Mr Walton, the undertaker, said he would have a pint of black-and-tan with Guinness and best bitter. A tall, vigorous young man in his middle thirties, he had the look of a woodcutter or hedger momentarily in town to get his implements sharpened. Part of this look derived from his heavy tan, which had been acquired, so he explained earlier, during a recent five-week holiday on the Costa Brava. Alec found he could imagine Mr Walton paying for an extra lavish sea-food dinner with one-sixth, say, of the profit on a moderately lavish funeral.

The party, some fifteen strong, was sitting or standing about in the lounge of the King's Head. Alec had been relieved at this choice of venue, thinking that the saloon bar at the side of the building would have been too full of associations, but a glance inside soon after arrival had shown him that, since his last visit here, the room had been so remodelled that he had been unable even to locate the nook by the vanished fireplace where he and Betty and Jim had drunk their pink gins not five Saturdays ago. All the horse-brasses and sporting prints, the uneven dark wood-work and frosted-glass panels that had given the bar its character had been swept away, and the new bright plastics made it bare and unwelcoming. Alec recognized this as part of a pattern of change. The things with which his life had been furnished – the tennis club, the Liberal Association and its strong social side, keeping up with the new plays, music in the sense he understood it, even such numerically unimportant occasions as George V's funeral and George VI's coronation – were no longer there.

The young waiter in the smart white jacket carried his tray over to where Alec was standing in silence with Jim. 'I wanted to say how sorry I am, sir. We shall all miss Mrs Duerden coming in here. We all liked her very much.'

'Thank you, Fred, that's very nice of you. I think this is yours, Mac.'

Alec took the whisky and soda. He had asked Frank for a small one, but its quantity, combined with the darkness of its colour, suggested that it was not very small. This would be his third double, not counting the brandy at the cemetery. Taking a hearty swallow, he tried for a moment to work out how much it was going to cost him to buy a round, then gave up. He could manage it, but it was a good job he had had the foresight to cash that three-quid cheque last night at his local. Much more impor-tant was the question of saying something meaningful to Jim, which he had not managed to do so far. He tried again: 'I know this must seem like the end of everything, but it isn't really, you must believe that.'

'Isn't it? Must I? I'm seventy years old, Mac. What am I supposed to start doing at my age? It's just a matter of waiting now.'

'Well, of course, that's how it seems, but—'

'No, that's how it is. Probably in a few months, I don't know, it'll look different again, but how, I just can't—'

'You'll find so many things you want to do.'

'Look, you're not going to waffle about developing new interests, are you? Spare me that. Did I tell you that part-time job of mine with those varnish and stain people packs up at Christmas? What do I take up then? Chess?'

'There's bound to be something.' Alec was disconcerted by the violence of Jim's tone and manner. He repressed an impulse to glance over his shoulder. Before he left he would mention to his friend the possibility of their joining forces in London, but now was clearly not the time.

'Oh yes, I'm sure,' Jim said bitterly. 'Wherever you look there's something. Oh, are you off, Rector? Haven't you got time for another one?'

'Unfortunately not.' The clergyman spoke with feeling so intense as to be unidentifiable. 'I have to be getting along.'

'Well, you've been very kind and I'm most grateful.' Jim turned aside to say goodbye to one of the local couples.

The clergyman looked at Alec. 'Thank you for saying you liked my address,' he said, blankly this time. 'It's the one I . . . You're not family, are you?'

'No, just a friend.'

'It's the one I use for those who have become members of my flock retroactively, so to speak – a proportion that increases every year.'

'I see. It was you who—?'

The half-question hung in the air for a second or two while what was arguably a smile modified parts of the clergyman's face. 'Yes,' he said, 'alone and unaided I did it. But of course I was a much younger man then. Goodbye to you.'

Soon afterwards they went in to lunch, just the family and Alec, five adults and two children. They sat at the round table in the window well away from the alcove favoured by the Trio: another relief. Further, Alec considered, it looked as if he were going to get away with not having to go up to the house at all.

He wanted never to see it again, marked throughout as it was by Betty's personality – apart from such details as the oversized TV set Frank had had delivered on the Duerdens' fortieth wedding anniversary.

Their waiter offered his condolences, then the head waiter and the wine waiter; Frank caught the last named by the sleeve before he could move away and ordered another round of drinks and two bottles of hock off him. The manager came over and chatted for a couple of minutes. He was a new man and had not known the Duerdens well, but, without pushing himself forward, he spoke the language of decent feeling. 'I had hoped to get to the church this morning,' he said, 'but I just couldn't, with the Business Circle lunch and a christening party out of the blue. But I was thinking about you.' Before departing he added: 'Mrs Duerden'll be missed all over the town. It won't be the same place without her.'

This moved Alec in a gentle, unagonizing way. Betty would never have wanted to be thought one of the important people in the district, but she had been a well-liked queen of her modest bits of castle. Such reflections occupied him for most of the meal, which soon began to acquire some sort of festive air. A couple of stories from Frank about the difficulties of bringing the laundry business up to date contributed little, Alec considered, apart from additional light on the fellow's character. When Bob got going, however, with what he called some unofficial law reports, it had to be admitted that he cheered everybody up. Even Jim had to laugh a few times, and the two Gioberti girls, each clutching a glass of pop, seemed spellbound.

While Alec ordered a round of liqueurs, Frank leaned back and lit a cigarette. 'Fantastic really,' he said. 'Here we are, the lot of us, all having a good time, and two hours ago we were all, well, overwhelmed by grief. It just shows you, don't it? I mean it's natural, see? The church, the graveyard, the pub. Whoever it was thought up how to run funerals knew his job. I reckoned the service was real nice, didn't you, Ann?'

Annette kept her eyes on the table. 'Very nice,' she said.

'It was a bit, what shall I say? austere, that's the only criticism I got. Of course, you don't want to listen to us, we're Romans, we go for a bit of, you know, colour and ritual and ceremony and incense and all that jazz. When you're used to that type of thing the other stuff's bound to come a bit drab, see what I mean?'

'Yes, I do,' Alec said. 'But you've got to remember that's the way we run things.' He paused to pick up four of the half-dozen pieces of silver that remained of his two pound notes. 'We like our religion to be austere, as you call it.'

'Like I said, it's what you're used to.'

Alec's voice rose. 'And we don't like a lot of dressing-up and chanting and bowing and scraping and any tomfoolery of that kind. That's not what we want in this country. We'll do things the British way . . .'

'Who's we, Uncle Mac? Okay, Ann.'

'. . . which means we're not going to take very kindly, necessarily anyway, to any religion that's . . . and a lot of other things for that matter, that aren't—'

'That are foreign, that what you mean?'

'Yes, if you want to put it like that.'

'Well, you want to put it like that, anyway, don't you? It's all right, Ann, honest. Yeah, the Pope does live in Rome, no getting away from that. There's no end of foreign things in this country when you get down to it, like the wine we just drunk, and that cigar you're smoking. And lots of foreign people, too, one sort and another. In fact I remember in my far distant youth they were always going on at us about that – you know, how anyone could come here and carry on pretty well any way he liked, provided he behaved himself. They used to reckon it was one of the big—'

'It's no use telling old Mac any of that,' Bob put in, swivelling his glance round the table: 'he thinks the English are foreigners really, don't you, old chap? and the Welsh and the Irish too, of course, and the Highland Scotch, and he's not too happy about Edinburgh and Glasgow; in fact, unless you come from Peebles you're a black man as near as dammit, what?'

Everybody laughed loudly, including Elizabeth and Sonia. Alec joined in with the rest. He would not have wanted to withdraw anything he had said to Frank. There was far too much of this sentimentality about nowadays, the idea that you had to be twice as nice to Negroes and Jews and Indians and so on whatever they were like, which the better types among them must surely resent. And he felt that a little opposition from time to time would not do Frank any harm. All the same, Alec realized, he had gone rather far. No need to have got hot under the collar like that – it must have looked . . . Suddenly nauseated, he rubbed his hand across his forehead. He had drunk too much whisky on an empty stomach, and he ought to have remembered that white wine never agreed with him. The notion of a few minutes in the open air abruptly became irresistible.

At the side of the building there was a small walled yard, embellished with a few climbing plants, where people could sit and drink in the summer if they cared to fetch their own orders from the saloon bar. The chairs and tables had been removed, no doubt to protect against his own folly anyone whom the sunshine might have lured into the treacherous autumnal outdoors. Alec perched himself on a low brick wall and was clasping his hands round one knee, pipe in mouth, when he was joined by Annette, who must have followed him more or less straight from the dining-room. She remained standing, a rather dumpy figure without a trace of her mother's looks.

He took her expression for one of inquiry. 'I'm all right,' he said. 'It was a bit stuffy in there, wasn't it?'

'I didn't like what you said to Frank just now.'

'I know, I'm sorry, Annette, I didn't think.'

'You knew he was in the Army for six years and got captured in North Africa? That makes him as British as anyone else as far as I'm concerned. That and having a naturalized British father and a mother born British and being born in England himself. And who cares anyway? And do you know how many Catholics there are in England? And it was all Catholics here once, before they—'

'Annette, I really am sorry. I had no intention of—'

'He's the best husband and father anyone could wish for. Never looks at another woman even though I know he gets plenty of chances. And then he runs into this kind of muck. He gets it in business all the time. "Mister who? How do you spell that? Oh." You can tell what they're thinking, that's when they don't come out and say it. I get it too, you see. "How long's your husband been over here?" It makes me mad. She was always going on about it. Fine Liberal she was.'

'But she wouldn't ever have dreamt of—'

'You didn't know her. The way she used to go on about Elizabeth. That's a laugh, isn't it, "Elizabeth"? That was him – you don't think I'd have been the one who wanted to name—'

The sunlight suddenly grew more intense and Alec shaded his eyes with the hand that held the pipe. 'What? I don't quite——'

'Never mind. She's well developed for her age, I know, but these days a lot of them are, with the diet or whatever it is. She'd never let me alone about it – I'd see her watching the kid, sort of fascinated, and then when we were by ourselves she'd say, "She's so *big*, isn't she?" as if it was . . . nasty or disgusting or something. "She's so *big*," she'd say, as if I'd done it on purpose to spite her. And then she'd say, "Of course, these Italian girls, they're women at fourteen, aren't they? Like Jewesses." Her own granddaughter. Three-quarters English. I don't think she ever believed Frank isn't a Jew really and hadn't taken up being a Catholic as a sort of extra. She never liked him and she didn't mind showing it, either.'

'But Annette, it was your father who was against Frank if either of them was; I remember them arguing about it. He said—'

'You know what Dad's like, up in the air one minute and forgotten all about it the next, it's just his way. No, she was the one. It wasn't like her to come out and say anything; all smiles on the surface and needling away whenever she got the chance. She was the same with Sonia's eyesight and Chris crying too much according to her. I often say to myself the only grandchildren she'd really like would be if Charlie and I got together and had some. She gave him a hell of a time, I don't know whether you knew, wanting to know where he was and who he was with all the time. He got away overseas as soon as he could, poor old Charlie.'

Annette stopped, not looking at Alec, who hugged his knees tighter to prevent them from trembling. 'I didn't realize you hated her,' he said.

'I didn't hate her, Uncle Mac – been easier if I had, in a way. Oh, she was all right in lots of ways and she did enjoy a laugh. It was the way she wouldn't ever leave me and my marriage and my kids alone made me mad.' At the mention of anger, anger itself returned to her voice, which had softened in the last minute or so. 'She liked baby-sitting when she came to stay because that gave her a chance to snoop around. She kept you on a pretty good string, didn't she, too, all these years? I felt sorry for you. Dad told me about it once when they'd had one of their rows. He didn't really mind because it gave her a bit of a kick. Mind you, according to him she let it slip once she thought early on you were going to ask her to go off with you, but then you never did. Why not?'

'It wasn't that sort of love,' Alec said.

'No, I know the sort. That's the best sort, the sort you don't have to do anything about or get to know the person, and it was fine for her. The way she used to put on a big tolerant act Sunday mornings when we came back from Mass when we stayed with them. Tolerant.'

Alec thought he saw tears of rage and grief in her eyes. He got up and put his arm diffidently round her shoulders. She went on standing in the same position with her weight on both feet, not stiffening or drawing away, but not relaxing against him either. What she had said had affected him chiefly with apprehension that she might lose all self-control. Whether or not her view of her mother was true, or truer than his, he still felt as if he had spent thirty-two years preparing a gift that had had, and could conceivably have had, no recipient. In return for his trouble he retained, safe against total erosion, Betty's gift to him of a few ideas about what human nature was like; and the last two or three hours had taught him something of how envy and pride could appreciably distort his judgement of other people. All this amounted to more than a little, without being, of course, anywhere near enough. He dropped his arm to his side.

Annette said: 'We'd better be getting back in. I'm sorry I came out with some of that. I didn't want to hurt your feelings – it was just that—'

'We've all been under a great strain.'

'You come back with us, Uncle Mac, and have some supper, there's plenty of stuff in. Frank'll run you home.'

'That's very kind of you, but it's right across London, you know.'

'Doesn't matter. We ought to see more of you. Seems silly not to.'

'It's a pity it's such a long way.'

Dear Illusion

I

'He is good, is he?' asked Pat Bowes, turning the car out of the main shopping street of the town into a lane that gave a glimpse of distant greenery. 'I mean I know people go on about him, but who don't they go on about these days? But he's supposed to be good in the same way as, I don't know, Keats and Milton and Christ, you'll have to help me out, not Shakespeare, Gerald Manley Hopkins. Isn't he?'

'How do you know about Hopkins?'

'I did him at school. I thought he came on a bit strong myself; you know, working himself up over not a hell of a lot. But the master was all for him. Great genius type of thing. I hope this is right.'

'First left after the bridge.' Sue Macnamara glanced at the typewritten sheet with the name of a national newspaper at the head of it. 'Wind-pump on the left – that must be that thing. Then left again after two hundred yards. Yes, Milton would be putting him a bit too high, but he's up with Keats and Hopkins all right, or so they say.'

'So they say was what I said. What do you say yourself?'

'I don't say anything much. I don't know.'

'But that's the sort of thing you're paid to know, Macnamara. This must be the turning. You with a degree from Cambridge College and all.'

'The works of Edward Arthur Potter weren't in my syllabus, Bowes. Anyway, one big thing about those works is that they're damned difficult. I was brought up on stuff you could make a bit of head or tail of. I suspect Potter of not being as good as he looks or sounds, but only suspect. And the critics are no help. They nearly all think he's great, but then they nearly all think people I know are bloody awful are great too. Here we are.'

'Edward Arthur Potter.' Bowes pulled up the estate wagon outside a longish, low house of pale stone. 'That's a crappy name. Ted Potter's what he's called. Like that composer bloke, Richard Robert Rodney Robin Roger Ronald Rooney Bennett. He means Dick Bennett. You go and knock on the door while I start shifting the gear.'

Sue Macnamara, a long-legged girl of thirty, got down and opened a creaking iron gate in the middle of a fence made of tall loops of iron. There was strong July sunlight, a smell of already rotten fruit and the droning of unseen but what sounded like oversized insects. Nothing had been done about the grass and other vegetation in the short front garden for quite a time. Like the window-frames, the front door was painted a shade of light blue that somebody must have noticed a long way from this or any other part of Kent and decided was appropriate to a poet's cottage. It – the front door – opened before it could be knocked on and a little old man appeared.

'Miss Macnamara?'

'Mrs. Sorry, I should have . . . You must be Mr Potter.'

She spoke without conviction. The face that looked hard but rather uninterestedly into hers – largely a matter of silvery-rimmed glasses, broad pointed nose and deep under-lip, the whole squashed on to very little in the way of a neck – did almost nothing to evoke the two or three standard photographs of Edward Arthur Potter she was used to seeing. Not quite nothing, though: there was just about enough likeness to suggest some doddering uncle or remoter connection supported out of charity, even a half-brother born of a feeble-minded kitchen-maid near the end of the last century. But anyone like that would probably be called Potter too, Sue thought to herself without urgency, shaking a small thick hand and responding to a smile that showed a few widely separated teeth.

'Yes. Yes, that's right.' The reply showed apparent surprise, as at a lucky hit. 'I thought the paper said you were bringing someone else with you, Mrs Macnamara. A photographer.'

He stressed the last word on its first and third syllables, giving it a downward social shove thereby, ranging it alongside piano-tuner and picture-framer. A handy one to use on Bowes when the moment came, thought Sue. She said,

'Yes, he's coming now. Fetching his stuff from the car.'

'So he is. It's these glasses. I can't seem to find the other pair. Not that they're much help. I must go and see the optician again.'

Bowes came bustling up the flagged path, hung about the shoulders with cameras and light-meters and clutching among other things a tripod of metallic tubing. With his squat body, round pale face and habitually open mouth, he looked to Sue as little competent to be a photographer, even in the degraded sense of one who photographed, as Edward Arthur Potter looked like a poet. She would have denied that she was one of those who expected a poet to look like an actor, or even like the kind of person the kind of actor that came to mind habitually acted: peasant revolutionary, dedicated scientist, early Christian martyr. And she knew well enough that poets were not supposed to talk like actors, like actors when acting, at least. Nevertheless, this poet's total lack of physical poeticality was a let-down, along with his manner of speech: slow, faintly glutinous, and couched in a rustic cockney that got the worst of two semi-separable worlds. Sue missed the touch of the charlatan that, after six years of this sort of journalism for the papers and television, she had learnt to expect in people who had to any degree deserved their success: not counting actors and actresses, of course, who behaved like charlatans whether they were any good or not.

Some of this occurred to her later; for the moment, all was action of a limited sort. Introductions were made, and Bowes at once ordered Potter out of his own house into its back garden. He did this in a way that showed he thought he knew just how to get people to do what he wanted without their ever feeling any pressure. In the garden, or the fenced-off bit of field where nothing grew but grass, two or three fruit-trees well past the arboreal change of life and a few clumps of tattered dandelions, he started moving pieces of outdoor furniture and other objects about with a photographer's unconsidering roughness, not out of any apparent impatience but as if all private property not his own were public property. Sue used this (as it proved) considerable intermission to show what was a genuine acquaintance with some of Potter's work, mentioning a couple of individual poems. Potter showed mild and unfeigned surprise.

'I didn't think anybody really read me these days. Nobody under about sixty, anyway. When did you first come across "Drizzle and Thrush"?'

'When it first appeared. In the *New Statesman*, wasn't it?'

'Not just homework, then. Mind you, I'm all for homework. Did you like it?'

'I'm not sure.' Sue discarded without forethought the lying flattery she had been ready with.

'Neither am I, my dear, neither am I. That's the problem. My problem, I should say. Would you like some tea or something?'

'Not for me, thank you,' she said, wanting to avoid a second bout of delay before the interview could start. Then she caught a mental glimpse of an apple-cheeked, check-aproned wife buttering home-made scones in the kitchen. 'But if you and Mrs Potter were thinking of . . .'

'She's not here. My wife's . . . not here.'

He spoke with great but unspecific force, implying anything from violent death to a grossly whimsical sortie round the shops in the town. Sue, whose thorough self-briefing had indicated a Mrs Potter alive and in residence, responded with a dead bat.

'You're on your own for a little while, then.'

'Yes, I am, and a very unpleasant mode of existence it is too, I don't mind telling you. I avoid it whenever I can. But the woman who looks after my sister-in-law, who can't move, fell downstairs on Monday and broke both her legs, so I've had to let my wife go until such time as they can find someone else. That's why I'm glad you don't want any tea, because I'd have had to go and get it. In my experience, no kind of meal or refreshment is worth a single moment's preparation. On one's own part, that is.'

'What do you live on, then, when Mrs Potter's away?'

'Beer and cornflakes mostly. I don't take sugar on them, the cornflakes, so that's one bit of bother saved. Of course, there is opening the new packet. I can't see any way round that.'

Neither could Sue, but she was saved having to admit as much by the intervention of Bowes, who sat Potter down in one of Potter's garden chairs, a canvas-and-rusted-metal affair, in the manner of an army dentist with a battalion's worth of extractions and fillings before him. His thrusting of a light-meter to within an inch of Potter's face was also faintly dental, suggesting a dry run with syringe or drillhead. Sue found herself stationed in a similar chair near Potter at one of the comparatively few angles nobody would naturally choose for any sort of conversation. Not far off, Bowes had thrown together a sort of cairn of stuff he must have found lying about: a couple of metal drums that might once have held paraffin, some cardboard boxes, some flowerpots, some white-painted rocks fit for a past or future rock-garden, a primordial lawn-mower, a half-sized St Francis or related figure in dirty stone. Without any trouble, Sue could visualize the end-product of this arrangement as a fashionable back-to-front portrait, a sprawling, blurred mélange in the fore-ground with the tiny in-focus shape of Potter in the distance, plus, no doubt, about two-fifths of herself at the edge – whatever fraction would most bore and annoy the beholder. Right up the art editor's street, and Bowes would know it; but he was not the sort of photographer, nor the sort of man, to have two or three tries at something when two or three hundred would do. Here he was in his ritual dance, approaching, retreating, squatting, on tiptoe, clicking, winding on, now and then standing stockstill to gaze at Potter in evident consternation, only to go twitching back into the measure.

Sue had opened her notepad. 'Before we begin, Mr Potter, I

should tell you that you'll be sent a proof of the article in advance, so that you can make any alterations or cuts.'

'I say, that's jolly decent of you. Not many of you do that.'

'I think quite a lot of people are more forthcoming if they know they have that sort of control.'

'Enlightened self-interest, which is very enlightened. Right, then. I was born in Croydon, Surrey in 1899, and educated at the—'

'Excuse me, Mr Potter: I think I already have really all the obvious known facts about you, what with the Lacey-Jones book, and your publisher . . .'

'Good Lord.' He lifted his glasses above his eyebrows and looked at her as hard as he had done when they first met, but this time not uninterestedly. His eyes were light brown, with darker flecks. 'This is the first time one of you has ever . . . But then you're not really one of you, if I make myself clear. I should have seen that before.'

'Could we have the glasses up again, please?' said Bowes in a managerial tone, and fell to bobbing and straightening as he clicked his way round a semi-circle that brought his camera within a hand's breadth of Sue's ear. She said to Potter, who was still obediently holding his glasses up in the required position,

'Can you think while this sort of thing's going on?'

'I can think while any sort of thing's going on, in so far as I can think at all. I wrote my first poems while I was working in a timber yard. But you'll have read about all that. What there was of that, I mean.'

'Can I ask you about those first poems? And about what made you write them? I'm sorry, I know that's a damned silly question, but our readership's not of a very—'

'I think it's a fascinating question, not as regards me person-ally, but as regards all writers of poems. But before we get on to it, I'll save you the embarrassment of asking another question I'm sure you'll quite reasonably want to ask. I write with a pen or a pencil, or anything that makes marks, on any sort of paper. I expect if I had nothing but a blackboard and a piece of chalk

I could manage with them. Not a typewriter: I've nothing against the typewriter, I just can't use it, not even for the fair copies – I get my wife to do them, and then she sends them off to my agent without my looking at them again. She keeps a carbon for the files. She does all that, very nicely too.'

'I see. Why don't you look at the fair copies before they go off?'

'No point in it. I write very clearly and my wife's a very accurate typist.'

'So in a sense the first you see of the poem in its finished state is when it appears in print.'

Potter glanced over at Bowes, who was doing something technical to one of his cameras, or trying to. 'Well . . . it'd be truer to say that the last I see of it in its finished state is when I give the manuscript of it to my wife for her to type it out.'

'You mean you don't ever . . . you don't normally look at it when it's originally published? I suppose it is more satisfying to wait until you've got a whole collection in front of you, inside hard covers, properly done. The way they lay poems out in magazines and so on is often very . . . shoddy . . .'

'Some – some people probably do find a book of things they've written more satisfying than the separate bits typed out or in a magazine. I just find it more frightening.'

'Frightening?' Sue was nearly certain that Potter had never publicly talked to this effect before, but the rising excitement she felt (and tried to conceal) was more than journalistic. 'Why do you say that?'

'Seven books of my poems have been published, and they all cover, each one covers about five years' work. Seven fives are thirty-five: I started late. As you know, Mrs Macnamara, but that's by the way. One book is five years' work, and five years' work is roughly between fifty and sixty poems, and that's all. What I mean by that is that that's all I do in the five years that I count as doing anything. I worked in the timber yard and then in that factory office, and afterwards for those tinned-fruit people until I'd started making enough money from my poems to retire.

As you know. It was work, at the timber yard and the other places: somebody had to do it and I'm not despising it: but I don't count it. All I count is the books, and unless the books—'

'We'll take the break there,' said Bowes generously, coming down to a stooped position at the mid-point of the triangle formed by Potter, Sue and the heap of properties. 'Very good, both of you. Now you relax while I go and reload and do a bit of minor surgery on this bit of Jap ironmongery' – he waved an offending camera – 'out in the car. Rejoin us in a couple of minutes.'

When he had gone, Sue lit a cigarette and considered, as calmly as possible, how to lead Potter back and round and along and forward again to the point he had reached when interrupted. 'Could you tell me a little more about how you write? How a poem takes shape, or how you know when it has?'

'Lots of words and phrases go through a person's mind all the time without staying there. At least they do through mine. Then, every so often, without the person knowing why, one of the words or phrases, it just sticks there and won't go away. That's the beginning. I don't mean necessarily the beginning of the poem when you see it when you read it, but it can be, quite often it is, but it's your way into the poem, if that doesn't sound too silly. I mean it's the man who's writing the poem's way into his poem. Then a lot more words go on going through until another one gets caught, like in a net, and it sticks with the first ones because it belongs with them, you realize, or you realize later that it belongs with them. And so on. Do you fuck?'

'Yes, but only my husband,' said Sue with some approximation to the truth.

'That's a pity. I mean it's a pity for me, because I get so few chances these days: I can quite see it's a jolly good thing for you. And your husband. I'm in the same sort of position myself as a rule, but obviously a good deal less so, if that makes any sense, because I don't happen to be very attracted to women of sixty-eight. That's how old my wife is, you see. With her being away, and you being here anyhow, so to speak, I thought it would be

silly not to just ask. And then in the end it dawns on you that
there's no more to come, not this time, that's all there's going to
be of it. The thing's over and done with and finished. At that
point you write it down.'

It was not until now that Sue realized that, for the past quarter of a minute, Potter had been talking about his poetry again.
His question had taken her completely by surprise, a gigantic
achievement in the face of one so constantly asked if she fucked
(in those or other terms) as Sue Macnamara: no preliminary
switching-on of casualness, no quick range-estimating glance, no
perceptible inner shaping up or squaring of the shoulders, nothing. In the same way, her refusal had evoked not the least hint
of pique, mortification, retrospective embarrassment or – what
she had noticed as quite common among the over-fifties – ill-
dissimulated relief: all this gathered up in his not having bothered
to make anything whatever in the way of an as-I-was-saying
gesture before he went back to his previous theme, about which
something had better be said soon on her own part.

'I see. You always wait until the poem's complete in your mind
before you put anything on paper.'

'Normally. If I've got to go and get on a train or something
like that before it's finished, I write down as much as I've done
and then think about something else until I can have another go
at it. That seems to work.'

'Sorry about that,' said Bowes as he approached, expressing
sincere regret for having, however unavoidably, let the rest of
the company in for a stretch of utter idleness. He went into a
prowling circuit of the space where they sat, every few steps
snatching his camera up to eye-level, failing to take a photograph
and subsiding again: a more intrusive routine, if anything, than
the clicking and buzzing it replaced. But at least he was about,
and so might deter Potter from asking Sue just how it had come
to pass that she only fucked her husband, should it occur to
Potter to do so.

'When the poem's all there on paper, do you revise it much?'

'Not at all, ever. I don't even read it through. I give it straight to my wife to type, or if it's the middle of the night I leave it face down on my table until I can give it to her.'

'You were saying you didn't read it, any given poem, when it's typed or even when it comes out in a magazine. When do you read it?'

Potter moved the tip of his tongue to and fro between gaps in his teeth. 'I suppose I must have read all my poems at least once. But it's not a thing I dwell on, or enjoy at all. The early morning's the only time. Then I may pick up one of my books and read a few things. To remind myself I've done them, more than anything else. I keep a count of how many I've done. I've just finished number four hundred and twenty-three. I wrote it out just this morning, as a matter of fact.'

'What do you feel when you read one of your poems?'

'If I'm lucky, relief that it doesn't seem any worse than it seems. Often, I wonder what on earth I meant, but I don't try to remember. Or it just doesn't register in any way.'

'No pleasure? Pride in achievement?'

'Achievement? No, nothing like that.'

Having learnt how easily a revelation of real interest could stem the most torrential flow of confidences or confessions, Sue tried to keep up her bright, nurse-like tone. 'Another over-simplifying question, I'm afraid, Mr Potter: why do you write poetry?'

'No, I think it really is a simple question. Or perhaps I just mean the answer I personally would give's quite simple. I write poetry to be able to go on living at all. Well, not quite at all, but to function as a human being. I'm afraid that doesn't sound very simple now I've said it. I'll have to risk you putting me down as pompous and sorry for myself. When I was working in that timber yard, my life started being a burden to me. Not just the life in the yard, but the whole of my life. It happened quite suddenly and I'll never know why. Nothing had gone wrong; I was happily married, in a secure job and earning enough to keep the two of us in reasonable comfort – we've never had the luck to have any children, but it wasn't that either. I stopped being able to enjoy anything or see the point of anything. I felt bad from morning to night every day. Then, after about a month, some words came into my mind and straight away I felt a little better. I forget what they were, but they brought more words with them and they made me feel a little better still. By the time the words stopped coming I felt at peace. I wrote them down on the back of a delivery note – I do remember that – and it was only then I woke up to the fact that what I'd done was write a poem. The moment I'd finished writing the words down I started feeling bad again. Not as bad as just before the words started coming, but still bad. The next day I felt a little worse, and the day after that worse again, and so on for another three or four weeks until another lot of words started turning up. It's been like that ever since.'

'This feeling bad,' said Sue, telling herself that after all she was a journalist – 'can you describe it any more fully?'

'No. If I could I would, believe me. I don't know what the poems have to do with it, either. I tried once not writing the poem down, but all that happened then was that I forgot it and started feeling bad again, so the only net result was that I was a poem short. Of course, if you look at it in one way, it's all rather like that business they call occupational therapy, where people weave carpets to take their mind off themselves and their problems. The point there is that it doesn't make any difference to anybody whether the carpets are any good or not. I've been wondering for over thirty years, on and off, if it's the same with my poems.'

The placid, rather monotonous voice stopped as Bowes shoved his stocky bulk squarely between the other two and let off a long burst of click-and-buzz. He had been well within earshot for some time, but his assumption of his own total primacy over anybody interviewing or being interviewed had its helpful side: he was stone-deaf to all talk not directly about sex, cars or photography. Sue thought Potter might have guessed something of the sort. She used the couple of minutes' interval to complete, in her own semi-shorthand, a nearly verbatim account of what Potter had said in the last four or five. She was certain that the information in it had never been divulged before.

Clearly and succinctly, Bowes now intimated that they were all to move indoors, to where Potter worked. Potter said he worked nowhere in particular, or everywhere, though there was a little table where he occasionally wrote things down, and Bowes answered that that was what he had meant.

They entered a low-ceilinged room that quite a few people would have felt inclined to call a parlour. By a window giving on to the front garden there was a characterless table and a hard chair with a flattened cushion. On the table Sue saw a cheap scribbling pad, one of its sheets detached and showing evidence of writing on the side not in view: no doubt that morning's poem. Bowes at once set about assembling an indoor cairn on a larger, oval table: a biscuit-barrel and two empty decanters from the sideboard, ornamental mugs and pottery figures from the mantelshelf, a multi-tiered cake-stand complete. The general style of these, and of other objects in the room, was in a current fashion, but that would be coincidence; they must be survivals of what the Potters had bought when they were first married in 1924, or had come by from their parents. To judge from his behaviour, and the shakier evidence of his work, Potter was not a man to care for or notice what was around him.

Sue moved to a small bookcase that held the expected complete works in the expected new-looking condition, and a few dozen other volumes, mostly paperbacked and all, or all of those she could take in at a glance, by authors she had never heard of. Potter's reading habits were well enough known, but she judged that a short trot over familiar ground would give him time to adjust to the change of scene and, with luck, to prepare himself for further revelations.

'Do you read a lot, Mr Potter?' asked Sue, while Bowes began setting up his lights and reflectors.

'Not a lot, no. I've never really taken to it. Either it's in you or it isn't is how I'd put it, and it doesn't seem to be in me. Oh, I quite enjoy books about Poland and Samoa and places like that where I've never been, but that's about as far as it goes.'

'No poetry?'

'Yes, a little from time to time, just to see what other people are doing. I sometimes buy one of those anthologies.'

'Who do you like particularly?'

'Well, it's hard to say. The standard seems to be so high, it's amazing. Let's see, I like Christopher Logue, John Betjeman, Allen Ginsberg, Philip Roth, Basil Bunting, John Berryman, Roy Fuller, John Lennon, Sylvia Plath, Fats Larwood, Robert Lowell . . . And Ezra Pound and W. H. Auden, of course. But, as I say, so many people are good.'

'But surely—' Sue cut herself off, realizing she could not say any of the seven or eight things she wanted to say. 'Surely you prefer some of those names to others?'

'Not . . . not really.'

'I see. Have you any, what our readers would call hobbies?'

'You mean how do I spend my time. I do quite a lot of walking; there's still some country left round here. I have to answer quite a few letters, and then my agent rings me up. And in the evenings my wife and I play halma or something, or we watch television.'

'In the chair, please, Mr Potter,' said Bowes opportunely, setting off the equivalent of a smallish, slow-burning phosphorus bomb. 'That's lovely. Doing very well.'

Potter sat on for a few moments, seeming to shrink a little physically in the glare. Then he said, 'As I was telling you, Mrs Macnamara, I keep wondering about those poems of mine. The people who weave those carpets have had other things in their lives. They've done other things. They've been builders or lawyers or sailors or mothers or lorry-drivers or something. Or they've told jokes very well or got drunk a lot or . . . had a lot of women or played tennis or travelled or helped other people. I couldn't have done some of those things and I didn't want to do any of the others. I've never done anything but write poems. So if the poems are no good my life's been wasted.'

'Oh, but everybody agrees they're good. I was reading—'

'Not everybody. I don't agree for one. I don't say I disagree, but I don't agree. And unless I'm very much mistaken, neither do you.'

Sue could find nothing to say. She flinched at a sudden click-accompanied movement of Bowes behind her shoulder.

'Good.' Potter nodded approvingly. 'Well, my dear, I was afraid all that was going to sound pompous, and it has. And not only sounded pompous. I think I must have got more conceited as I've grown older. It's conceited of me to wonder whether I'm anything more than somebody who's been lucky enough to be able to make up his own occupational therapy without any help from outside. But it's a bad bargain no matter how you look at it.'

'Could I have you writing, please?' ordered Bowes from the shadows.

'Of course,' said Potter, taking out a felt-tipped pen and doodling quite convincingly on his pad. 'It's a bad bargain even if the poems are good. Whatever that may mean. From my point of view, nothing at all could compensate for getting on for forty years of feeling bad with a couple of days of not feeling so bad and ten minutes of feeling all right thrown in about once a month. There's a very good young doctor in the town here who took over not so long ago from the fellow I've always had. He reads a bit of poetry and he says he likes what I write. I've told him a lot of what I've told you. He takes my point about occupational therapy and he says I sort of psychoanalyse myself through my work so that I can carry on. But I'm fed up with carrying on. He's got every pill under the sun in that surgery of his, and he says he could probably find one that would make me feel all right most of the time, but it would probably, at least as probably, stop me wanting to write poems, or having to write poems. I've been holding out against that for about six months. Conceit again, I suppose. But I've decided I'm too old to be conceited any more. I'd like to feel all right for the rest of my life and never mind the poetry. So I'm stopping it, the poetry. In fact I have stopped. This one this morning was the last. Tomorrow morning I'll be off to see that doctor and he'll start me on what he calls a course. I'm really quite excited about it.'

'Now I'd like you looking as if you're looking for inspiration,' said Bowes.

Potter raised his head and eyes to the ceiling less like a looker for inspiration than a man inwardly calling for celestial vengeance on some other party.

'Can I print that?' Sue recognized that the question she had been trying to frame, about why she was being told all this, had been answered. 'About your giving up poetry?'

'Oh, certainly. After all, this is an interview.'

'You realize it's news?'

'News? Well, some very funny things seem to be news these days, don't they? Do you want to telephone your editor?'

'No thank you,' she said, having, as he spoke, faced and solved a dilemma: whether to approach as soon as possible the parent newspaper for whose colour magazine she regularly wrote and had come here today, or to say nothing and allow her report of the interview, adorned with Bowes's efforts, to appear as planned in (perhaps) four months' time. If Potter told his piece of news to the representative of some other journal in the meanwhile, a lot of people would be cross with her, and her article, with its climactic point already common knowledge, might suffer severe cuts or even not appear at all. But that was just as likely to be its fate if she took the first of the two courses open to her, and she recoiled from the prospect of seeing an abbreviated, garbled and vulgarized version of her material under some such heading as 'Veteran Bard Lays Down Pen'. It must be the second alternative, then, with the comforting thought that, since nobody on the magazine was inquisitive enough to read copy on the look-out for possible news items, or indeed for almost any other reason, the laying-down of the pen might very well rest securely in its context until her publication day.

'Is there going to be much more of this?' asked Potter, who was still looking, in fact glaring by now, high over Sue's head. 'I'm afraid I find it rather tiring.'

'How many more, Pat?'

'Nearly there. Another couple.'

That meant a dozen or so, but a quick dozen. For the second

time in five minutes, Sue searched for a remark. Finally she said,

'You must think of the thousands and thousands of people to whom you've given pleasure.'

'Yes, I do try to sometimes. It's true I get a lot of letters saying some very nice things, and believe me I'm not at all ungrateful, but—'

'Could you relax and look out of the window as if you're thinking?'

'I'll do my best,' said Potter, setting a new lower limit to the amount of dryness the tone of a human voice could carry without its being altogether imperceptible. 'But, as I was going to say, I have wondered if the pleasure people say I've given them mightn't have prevented them from coming by some much higher kind of pleasure from other writers of poetry who really are good. I expect all this pop music prevents some youngsters from ever appreciating Brahms or Elgar.'

'You must know that's not a fair comparison, Mr Potter. And I don't think it's true anyway, your example.'

'Perhaps it isn't, my example. There's no way of knowing.'

'Right, that's it,' said Bowes. 'I've got some first-class ones there. Thank you for being so patient, Mr Potter. I can tell you're a pro at this job.'

The lights went and for a second or two the room seemed dark; then Sue saw it was only late afternoon outside. Bowes started disassembling his equipment while Potter, on his feet, stuck his hands in his pockets and stared at the floor. Sue waited until Bowes had gone out to the car and then said:

'I don't want to poke my nose in, but what are you having for your dinner tonight?'

'Cornflakes and a couple of sardines, I thought. And a bottle of light ale.'

'But that's not enough. You must have a proper meal. Something hot.'

'I can't be bothered.'

'May I see your kitchen?'

'Yes, it's just . . . through the . . . in here.'

In one corner of the small room was a tiny larder containing a good deal of tinned and cartoned food and very little fresh food. Sue made a selection from the tins, found two Spanish onions that seemed to have started to lose weight, decided that some cold boiled potatoes must be harmless despite their appearance, and looked round for a frying-pan.

'What are you doing?' asked Potter as if the preparation of a meal were genuinely strange and wonderful to him.

'Do you like corned-beef hash?'

'I like all food, but I don't see—'

'I'll just have a word with Mr Bowes.'

The word, or words, told Bowes that Potter wanted to add some information in total confidence. Tractable as ever outside the photographic sphere, Bowes at once said he would go and have a pint at a pub he had noticed a couple of hundred yards back down the road, and that Sue could join him there at any time she might fancy.

Back in the kitchen, Sue found Potter standing, presumably by chance, exactly beneath a well-patronized fly-paper that hung from the ceiling. He said,

'I don't want you to go to any trouble on my account.'

'It's very little trouble.' She set about peeling and slicing the onions. 'It's a small return for all the help you've given Mr Bowes and me. Now I'm going to cook this to the point where all you have to do is warm it up before you eat it. Can I trust you to do that?'

'Yes. Yes, I'll do that.'

Nothing more was said for some minutes, while she went on with her work. Then he asked abruptly,

'Would you consider staying on here a little while and sharing the corned-beef hash with me?'

'I'd like to, Mr Potter, but I'm afraid I've—'

'No, of course, yes, I quite see.'

The immediacy of his interruption showed her in the plainest terms that he had taken her to be simply blocking off the possibility of a return to the question he had put to her in the garden.

She turned away from the gas stove, went over and took him by the hand.

'I shall have to go quite soon, Mr Potter,' she said slowly, 'because I have to be back in London in time for my husband to take me to the theatre. Do you see now?'

He nodded, not perfunctorily, and moved towards the window. She worked on through another pause, which again he broke.

'Mrs Macnamara, I want to ask you a fact, but you must understand I need it just as a fact, nothing more. What's your Christian name?'

'Susan, but I'm always called Sue.'

'Is that s, u, e?'

'Yes.'

'Thank you.'

He left the room and stayed away until the hash was nearly ready. When he came back he was carrying a sheet, now folded in two, of the paper she had seen on his table.

'I think you'll know what this is, Mrs Macnamara. I'd like you to accept it as a very small mark of my esteem, and as a way of saying thank you for being so sympathetic and understanding.' (A careful rehearsal of this in the parlour was not very difficult to imagine.) 'Please don't look at it until you've left here,' he went on, holding the paper out to her. 'There are no surprises, but I'd just rather you didn't.'

'You've made a copy of it, have you?'

'No. I never do that.'

'But what about your wife typing it out? I can't walk away with a unique copy. Suppose I lost it? And what about publication?'

'I don't suppose you'll lose it. If you really want to, perhaps you could type it out one day and send a copy to my agent' – whom he named – 'and a carbon here. Addressed to my wife. Please take it.'

She took the sheet, faintly warm from his hand. 'I don't know what to say.'

'There's nothing that needs to be said. I've thanked you with that and you've thanked me by making me this splendid meal. Is it done? How do I heat it up?'

'Ten minutes on a half gas'll be enough.'

'Just as it is. I see. Now I mustn't keep you from your husband; I expect you're late already. Where's that young man got to?'

'He's waiting in the pub.'

'Good, so you'll be able to get back to London all right. It's been a great pleasure meeting you, Mrs Macnamara. Goodbye.'

'Goodbye, Mr Potter,' she said as they shook hands on the doorstep.

At the gate she looked back, but the door had already shut. Four telegraph poles away in the direction of the town Bowes's car was parked by an inn-sign. She began to walk slowly down the road towards it, wishing she had been able to think of some leave-taking message to Potter that would not have been either sickly or stilted, deciding to write him a letter the next day, then taking the sheet of paper from her handbag and unfolding it. The writing was in soft pencil, clear and commonplace. It read:

UNBORN

From summer evenings, gazing
heartrise always ahead, there,
book and dream,
                            reaching out,
ten miles of fields of raw daffodils
streets engines advertisement hoardings
all raw,
            myself raw,
                        but certain.

Swept now, swept
                book
                dream
                field
                street

engines cheerfully off or rusted
hoardings ablaze or demolished
nobody there
                    Not unfound
not unreached, unborn
                              unfated

Dear illusion with the bright hair
all swept aired lit plain known listed

swept

At the foot were a couple of lines in the same hand, written upside down. She turned the sheet round and read,

To Sue Macnamara with the kindest regards possible
                              from Ted Potter

That last was the product of something like ten minutes' thought, she said to herself, and written upside down to avert the risk of reading a single word of the poem.

II

The poem stayed in Sue's mind for the rest of the evening and, though diminishingly, much longer, both as a poem and as an amalgam of less clearly definable things: a piece of self-revelation that might fall anywhere between compressed but pondered auto-biography and record of a passing mood, a gift to herself offered out of considered or unconsidered politeness, desire to return a favour that might or might not have seemed unimportant. Typing it out next morning inevitably forced her to read it as a poem a good deal more closely than (she admitted to herself) she had ever read a Potter poem before.

It was probably this closeness that made its theme effortlessly plain to her – and this, in turn, suggested an unpalatable reason for Potter's success with critics and public: he wrote in a way that looked and felt modern, or at any rate post-Georgian, but with a certain amount of effort could be paraphrased into something quite innocuously traditional, even romantic. And the reader's self-satisfaction at having made his way through apparent obscurity could easily be transmuted into affection for poem and poet.

In 'Unborn', at any rate, Potter, or some version of Potter, was just saying that an ideal he had pursued since youth had turned out to be not unrealized but unrealizable, because its object had never existed. What that object might have seemed to be was less plain: 'dear' along with 'bright hair' certainly suggested a woman – or a man, though nothing in his other works, or in gossip, or in what she had seen of him bore out that interpretation, which she discarded promptly and for good. But then, the brief and unspecific image of the 'dear illusion' might so easily refer not to a person at all, but to some abstraction dimly seen as a person, and almost any abstraction of the nicer sort would fit: love, happiness, beauty, joy, adventure, self-respect, self-mastery, self-sufficiency, God . . .

With the typing done and checked against the original, Sue knew 'Unborn' well, and the knowledge was, again, unpalatable. For a moment she felt cross with it: taken out of its drunkard's or dotard's telegraphese and put into plain English, conventionally assembled instead of sprawling hither and thither over the page, it would have shown itself up, she suspected, as being not only traditional but trite. And in what sense might (or could) the daffodils be raw? And were the hoardings ablaze with colour or literally on fire? And were there not too many '-ings' in the first half-dozen lines, and had 'hair' been intended to rhyme with 'there' in an otherwise rhymeless poem, and however that might be was it anything better than slack to let 'aired' in so soon afterwards? And '*heart*rise' (what a word, anyway) taken with '*ahead*' was somehow . . . Was just the sort of thing poets got rid of in revision.

Sue felt bad about raising these objections, even though she would always keep them to herself, which made it odder that the nearest imaginable comparison to how she felt was, it turned out, how she would feel if she were to show up a child's ignorance publicly. Had Potter not given her the manuscript there would have been no issue, but he had, and she had met him and listened to him, and so the poem took on the quality of a friend's muffled cry of distress without, unfortunately, ceasing to be a poem in its own right and demanding to be read as one. The only course was to try to forget its text while remembering its existence. She locked it away in a desk drawer among other keepsakes, wrote covering letters to go with the copies for Potter's agent and Mrs Potter, and then settled down to write to Potter himself. This final task proved less disagreeable than she had feared: she was thankful to be able to say with truth that she had been moved both by the gift and by reading what she had been given.

The following month, she sent Potter a proof of her piece. It came back unamended with a short handwritten note complimenting her on her accuracy – 'though you make me sound more clear-headed than I am sure I can have been' – and adding that the corned-beef hash had been delicious. About the same time, 'Unborn' was published in the *Listener*; she did not read it. After several more months, more than she had been led to expect in the first place but fewer than she had in fact expected, the magazine printed her article; she did not read that either, merely scanning it for cuts and mutilations, a virtually separate activity in somebody of her experience. There were, for once, no cuts. Bowes had, as always, produced pictures that were technically excellent and artistically sub-modish, though there was one indoor shot of Potter at his table that recalled him sharply: well enough, anyhow, for the fuzzy-edged bulk of an Edwardian tea-caddy, looming in the extreme foreground, to seem no worse than irrelevant. The news – it was news, since he had revealed nothing of it in the interim – the news of Potter's decision to put away his pen drew no public attention at the time. Those to whom it might have seemed important either ignored the interview altogether or failed to extricate such a disclosure from its context of travel advertisements and illustrated recipes.

Something else Sue omitted to read, or to reread, during this period was any of Potter's other poems. She shied away from the strong possibility of finding that she felt as uneasy about them as she had about 'Unborn'. In the winter, the magazine sent her to South America to do a series on what it called the cultural life of the chief cities there. With her went not Bowes, but a photographer of the alternative sort, the sort that took at most one photograph of every subject, and she slept with him a certain amount. Potter began to fade from her mind. Then, almost exactly a year after she had been to see him, she came across his name in an arts-page headline in a Sunday paper.

Edward Arthur Potter (she read), who according to rumour (in plain language, according to an authentic statement in another journal, she thought to herself) had taken a vow of poetic silence, must have gone back on it, for his publishers were to bring out in the coming autumn a collection of his recent verse. There seemed to be hopes of some commemorative event – an official dinner, an award – that might go a little way to offset the shameful lack of attention so far paid a man described as arguably Britain's greatest living bard. The report closed with a passage of largely directionless rancour about the neglect of Potter in particular and almost everybody else in general.

The news pleased and worried Sue. Potter deserved recognition as a – well, at least as someone who had devoted the better part of his life to writing poetry, even if, or even though, recognition of the sort in view might not appeal to him much. On the other hand, it did seem very likely that the pills from the hand of the young doctor had failed to do their job, that Potter was back on his self-administered version of occupational therapy and that he was again spending nearly all his time feeling bad.

Worry about others' concerns, like pleasure on their account, needs regular renewal if it is not to fall away; the summer brought Sue fresh assignments and a falling-away of her worry and pleasure in the case of Potter's prospective award/dinner. But, in due time, award/dinner became award-dinner in a real sense. A body claiming, in its title, to superintend our culture announced that

Edward Arthur Potter was shortly to receive a special prize of £1,000 to mark the publication of his latest book, *Off*, and to attest to his status as premier lyrist in the English language. The cheque, together with an ornamental certificate designed by a leading designer, would be handed over in the course of a function at a Regent Street restaurant famous until only a few years back for its food and service. A week after seeing this report, Sue got an invitation to the award-dinner. Stapled to a corner of the lavish card was a strip of flimsy which bore, in smudged carbon, a bald statement to the effect that this favour had come her way at Mr Potter's personal request – thus conveying, with masterly economy, the organizers' helplessness in the circumstances to prohibit the attendance of somebody they themselves would never have dreamt of asking along.

On the night, Sue left her husband contentedly watching television and appeared at the restaurant, the main bar of which turned out to be given over to the Potter occasion. She had arrived early, but there was already a fair-sized group round the man of the hour. Experience of such gatherings suggested her first move: getting one drink down her and another into her hand. There were plenty of recognizable faces, perhaps too many, not more than half of them belonging to the world of letters in even the most charitably extended sense of the phrase. A sports commentator, a girl who made boots, a television bishop in mufti, a man who not long before had covered half a mile of cliff near Dover with paint of various colours – all sorts of people who surely could not be famous just because of what they did, who did nothing else but what they did and who were famous all the same. Not only that: when she began her career, what had slightly astonished Sue at affairs of this sort was the number of old contemptibles, of those whose claim to fame, if any, dated so far into the past that they could more than safely be dropped. Tonight she was struck by the number and contemptibility of new contemptibles, persons categorically unfit (on all but the most trend-crazed reckoning) to be invited along to see Potter honoured. Thirty-three next year, she said to herself.

Having beaten off an embryonic pass by an elderly small boy who turned out to be a concrete poet, Sue made her way over to a couple of journalist acquaintances. The Press had come along all right. So had its visual auxiliaries: cameras flashed every few seconds. Somebody who ought to have been flashing away with the very, very best of them, but who did no more than drink and chat, was Pat Bowes, to whom Sue turned. He kissed her genially and said,

'You're looking smashing, Macnamara. Great lot here tonight, aren't they?'

'You look all right too, Bowes. Where's your camera?'

'At home. I'm here because I'm so distinguished, not to work. Mr Potter's personal request.'

'Me too. No notebook, thank God.'

'Nice of the old lad to ask me along. I mean it's obvious why he got hold of you, with you making that hit with him, but he needn't have asked me.'

'Well, you were nice to him the day we went there.'

'No I wasn't, love. I'm always a right bugger with my sitters, you know that. No, he asked me because he didn't like to think of me probably finding out you'd been here and thinking he hadn't bothered to remember me. I call that really nice.'

Sue nodded.

'What I don't understand is about this book. He told you he'd packed it all in. End of the road kind of style. He didn't strike me as the sort of bloke who'd change his mind about a thing as important to him as that.'

'Nor me. I don't know what's happened.'

'We won't find out tonight. The chances of a quiet confidential word with the guest of honour are, I would say, remote in the extreme. Not because of him – he'd much rather have a good natter with you than talk to all these important sods, but they've brought him here and they'll hang on to him. Anyway. Have the mag been on to you about Peduzzi?'

'No, what about him?'

'They will. Famed Macnamara–Bowes team spotlight yet

another feature of the cultural scene. A pretty far-bloody-flung feature too. He's filming in Ceylon till the end of the month, they said, then a short stop-over in Italy before he takes off I forget where. I'd sooner do him in Ceylon myself, of course. Could you work it?'

'How long would it take?'

'I'd say five days minimum all in. He isn't sitting on his arse in Colombo, you see. There'd be ox-cart stuff before we could get to him.'

'I'll check and let you know.'

A vague plum-in-throat bawling emerged from the ambient uproar and resolved itself into, 'Mrs Macnamara, please. Mr Bowes, please.'

'Christ, we're being paged,' said Bowes. 'Butlered, rather.'

'Mr Potter,' said the functionary, looking from one to the other with open incredulity, 'would be obliged if you would join him for a few minutes.'

Her first real look at Potter that evening showed a small neat dinner-jacketed figure without any of the soup-stains or shave-traces that might have been expected; she guessed the reason when she recognized his agent close to his side. There were a great many introductions, starting with the cultural bureaucrat in overall charge and the leading literary critic booked for the main speech – more leading, this one, than the leading designer of the certificate (who was also about the place) in the proportion of a knighthood to an OBE. There would have been still more introductions if Potter had not cut them off by taking a long time over saying how glad he was to see Sue and Bowes again.

'Is Mrs Potter here this evening?' asked Sue.

'I'm afraid she's not in the best of health.'

'Sorry to hear that,' said Bowes.

Potter moved closer to Sue and said quietly, 'In fact there's absolutely nothing wrong with her. I just thought it would be better if she stayed away. You'll probably see what I mean by the time the evening's over. It's not her sort of thing at all.'

'No, well . . .'

'Have you seen my book yet, Mrs Macnamara? Have you, Mr Bowes? No, not a great many people have, outside the committee and so on. But there's a copy for everybody beside their place at dinner for them to take home, if they still want to after they've heard me speak. Anyway, I hope they give it a glance. I shall be most interested to hear what people think of it, more interested than with any of my previous books.'

There was a nervous jocularity in his tone and manner that Sue found mildly strange, until she noticed the glass of whisky in his hand and reflected that, for him, large parts of the evening would be an ordeal, and of an unfamiliar kind. Then he said to her, again in an undertone:

'Would you have a quick drink with me afterwards, Mrs Macnamara? Upstairs, in a little place called the Essex Room. I've spoken to one of these chaps about it. We'll be breaking up quite early.'

'Thank you, Mr Potter, I'd love to.'

'Good . . . Mr Bowes, I'm afraid I never thanked you for taking such magnificent photographs. I was going to write to you, but then I got bogged down with one thing and another, and then it seemed too late.'

'Don't worry about that. Glad you liked them.'

Here a Cabinet minister interposed himself between Sue and Potter, of whom she saw nothing further until the party, two hundred or more strong, was settling itself down at the couple of dozen large tables in the dining-room, a slow and lubberly process. Potter was among bureaucrats and critics and other poets and their wives halfway across the room from Sue. The first course, already in position, was pieces of tinned grapefruit apparently strung together on fine thread and adorned with a tattered cherry. She picked up the copy of *Off* that indeed lay by her plate and began, without eagerness, to glance through it.

The poems, she saw quite soon, did not really look like Potter poems, which, within wide limits, had always had a characteristic shape on the page, sprawling and staccato at the same time. The new ones did not much look like one another, either. From glancing through, she turned to reading. On an early page she found a piece in heroic couplets after the manner of Dryden – a long way after, she found, because it turned out to convey no meaning whatever at any point, could have been thrown off, dashed down as fast as his hand would travel over the paper by someone solely concerned with filling up iambic pentameters that rhymed. Beside it, 'Unborn' was a model of sober clarity. But 'Unborn' was not beside it, in the sense that it was not (she double-checked) in the book. Had it been one of a number of rejects, part of the whey thrown out when the cream was skimmed off for a new volume? In their interview, Potter had implied clearly that he reprinted in hard covers everything he wrote. Well, he might have omitted the poem in deference to a desire on his wife's part not to see the immortalization of that rival-figure, the bright charmer with the . . . Sue tried to remember: dear charmer with the bright hair – no, not charmer. Dear something, though.

At this point she found that somebody had taken her grapefruit away and put some fish where it had been, while somebody else (probably) had poured her some wine. She tried to eat and easily succeeded in drinking. She also thought. This was made a little easier for her by her absorption until just now in *Off*: her neighbours' attention had been pre-empted by their further neighbours, and throughout the meal she got away with saying almost nothing, either to the disc-jockey on her left or to the plain, horse-oriented jockey on her right. From time to time she looked at *Off* again. One poem, or 'poem', she encountered ran:

Man through different shell all over turns into sea swelling birth comes light through different man all over light shell into sea. Rock waits noon out of sky by tree same turns into rock by noon out of sky underneath tree out of same rock. Woman keeps flower beside leaves every time towards fruited earth keeps leaves every time towards flower fruited woman turns into earth beside leaves. Shell all over man waits rock out of noon towards earth every time beside woman. Man woman earth.

She found this about as digestible as the overcooked but luke-warm chicken *à la Kiev* that followed the fish. A glance over at Potter suggested that he was listening closely to whatever a bureaucrat or critic might have been telling him. Was he really listening, closely or not? Sue felt with uneasy certainty that there was something wrong or odd or out of place here. Where was here? In *Off*, to start with. For a final sample, she opened the book at its last page, and read,

> I slash the formless web of hate,
>   I plumb the worked-out mine of love;
> My wrist receives the birds that sate
>   Their lust engendered from above.

> While rosy sunsets lurch and fade
>   Across the endless strife of seed,
> The debt of living must be paid
>   To creditors who starve in need.

Whatever else that was or was not, it was not the voice of Potter as it had always been. Well, what of it? He was experi-menting, looking for a new style; unusual and admirable at his time of life. Sue held on to that while the meal came to an end and the speeches got under way. The first of these began with a not very closely compressed account of the recent doings of the cultural body, retailed on a note of open and personal self-congratulation. Towards the end it bore round to the subject of poetry, and finally mentioned the name of Edward Arthur Potter. After a couple of entr'actes featuring minor characters, which brought the audience even nearer to the purpose of tonight's occasion, the leading critic started his discourse.

Sue had to admit he did his job well. Long stretches of what he said rose appreciably above the general level – that of an academic lecture in ancient Sumerian – reached by his predeces-sors. He showed familiarity with Potter's work and what must have seemed to everybody there, except perhaps Potter himself, a genuine love of it. He started his peroration by saying,

'I should like everybody to notice three things about this volume. First, its title, *Off*. Does this mean that Edward Arthur Potter is off, about to quit the scene and be heard from no more? All of us here, and millions more in the English-speaking world and outside it, hope that this is untrue, and that his unique lyric genius, which has spoken so eloquently for nearly forty years, will continue to delight us for a long time to come. Secondly . . .'

There was a great deal of applause. Sue was good at distinguishing between the polite variety of this, however conscientious it might be, and the enthusiastic. What she heard was unmistakably of the second sort. Potter or his work, however curiously mutated in the process, had reached out beyond the small circle of poetry-readers and the rather larger one of poetry-lovers. She hoped he was pleased.

'Secondly,' went on the leading critic, 'I ask you to look at the dedication. "To all those who have encouraged me to continue in my work as poet." That, I think, is a reminder many of us need, a reminder of the essential loneliness of the creative artist and of his dependence on the understanding and support of his public. We, representatives of our honoured guest's public, have in the past been shamefully negligent in showing that understanding and proclaiming that support. I hope very much that tonight's words and deeds will go some little way to atone for our neglect.

'Lastly, the content of *Off*, the poems that have been given us. They speak for themselves and need none of my poor help and all I will dare to do, on behalf of us all, is to salute in them, as in the whole of this great English poet's work, the uniqueness of vision, the distinctive and utterly individual tone of voice that characterize the heart and mind of Edward Arthur Potter. Mr Potter, it is my—'

The ovation, which was what it turned out to be, went on for two and a quarter minutes by Sue's watch. Its earlier moments accompanied the offer and acceptance of certificate and cheque, prolonged for the benefit of the photographers, and similarly prolonged handshakes involving Potter and several of those near him. After that, he stood with his knuckles on the table and his face lowered. Finally, he said in his thick, rather slow rustic cockney,

'My lords, ladies and gentlemen. I'm going to make a short speech, even shorter than the one I'd prepared, because what Sir – Sir Robert has just said fits in so well with what I want to say. As regards those three things he wanted you to notice.

'The title. It isn't really complete. There ought to be another word in front of it. Something – off. A verb in I believe it's called the imperative. It's not my style to come out with the one I'm thinking of in public, but the whole phrase means, Go away. Clear off would be nearly good enough.

'Then the dedication. With respect, Sir Robert wasn't quite right in saying I've been neglected. If only I had been. Right from the start some people have been kind, or what they must have thought was kind, writing nice articles and sending me nice letters. If I had been neglected, I probably wouldn't have wasted my time for thirty-eight years writing what's supposed to be poetry; I'd have looked round for some other way of coping with the state of mind that made me write those things. That's why I'm telling everybody who's ever encouraged me to clear off.'

Potter was speaking now into a silence so total that the sound of individual vehicles in the street outside could be clearly heard. He went tranquilly on:

'Then the third thing, the poems in the book. I wrote them all in a day, just putting down whatever came into my head in any style I thought of, and pretty well everybody thinks they're good, the committee and all sorts of critics and other poets I had proof copies sent to. Or they said they thought they were good. But they aren't good. How can they be? I ought to know, didn't I? Well, that's rather awkward, because if people think they are good, and what's more good in the same way as my previous poems, which fairly beats me, I must say – in that case they don't know what they're talking about and never have known. And in *that* case, this diploma thing here is worthless, or even a bit of a cheat. You'd think it was a bit of a cheat if, well, if a lot of

Eskimos said somebody was a very good cricketer, and we were all supposed to take them seriously. I know I would, anyhow.'

Potter's glance moved in Sue's direction, as if searching for her. She felt frightened and hoped nothing worse was to come. He picked up the certificate and the cheque and held them out in front of him, causing a fresh flurry among the photographers while everybody else sat quiet and still.

'By rights I ought to tear up the diploma, but someone's obviously been to a lot of trouble over it and I shouldn't like to hurt his feelings, so I'll just leave it here. I can't do that with the cheque, because it's a bad thing to leave cheques lying about, so that I will tear up.' He tore it up. 'I don't need the money anyway. That's all. Except I don't want anyone to feel I'm telling him to clear off personally or in any bitter way. It's just a sort of general attitude. Goodbye.'

He was out through the doorway in five or six seconds, yards ahead of the first reporter. Sue was quick off the mark too, but by the time she reached the vestibule she was among thirty or forty vocally bewildered people looking for a vanished Potter. But then, round the corner, she asked the lift attendant for the Essex Room. The man looked at her carefully.

'What name, please, madam?'

'Sue Macnamara.'

'Mrs Macnamara?'

'Yes.'

It was rather like that on the fourth floor, where a door was unlocked from the inside at the news that Mrs Macnamara was outside. Potter surprised Sue afresh by the smartness of his appearance. He said,

'Splendid. What would you like to drink?'

'Could I have a whisky and water?'

'A large tumbler of whisky and water and a bottle of light ale, please.' He relocked the door. 'I thought if you didn't want all the whisky you could always leave some.'

'Aren't you going to have any cornflakes?'

He laughed heartily, showing most of the teeth he had. His

manner in general had already struck her as much more confident now than at their previous meeting, almost jaunty. They sat down in a corner on padded straight chairs, face to face across a low table.

'Fancy you remembering that,' he said. 'But then you've got a good memory for all sorts of things. Well, this disappearing act is a bit of fun, isn't it? It's amazing what a few five-pound notes will do. Now we'd better get on. There are some things I want to ask you, and tell you, and we mustn't be too long, because poor Charles, that's my agent, he'll be in rather a state, I've no doubt. It's the first time I've ever done a thing like this, disappear, I mean. Well, and tell people to clear off in public into the bargain. Was that all right, by the way? That was one of the things I wanted to ask you.'

'The clear-off treatment? It was very effective, I thought, judging by the general reaction.'

'Good, but I really meant I hope it wasn't too offensive. You know, wounding. Malicious and all that.'

'I don't think so. You made it clear you hadn't got it in for anyone in particular.'

'Oh, that came over all right, did it? That's a relief. Tell me, my dear, did you find time to look inside that silly old book they were making such a fuss about?'

'Yes, I read some of it.'

'Nothing in it, is there?'

'The last poem made sense of a sort, or the last bit of it.'

'Ah, it's easy enough to make sense of a sort if you don't care what sort. But the book . . . It is rubbish, isn't it?'

'I thought so, yes.'

'I'll take your word for it.' He sighed and smiled. 'That's the most important thing of the lot. Imagine what it would have been like to find you could only write stuff that was any good when you were trying to write rubbish. What a lot of silly donkeys they are, though. Fancy that Sir Robert fellow going on about my individual tone of voice. When I'd purposely made every poem different from the rest of me and different from each other, too.

And he's quite clever, you know, that's what frightens me. I've talked to him several times and he's really a very interesting man. But they're all the same. It does seem a pity. Ah, here we are.'

A minute later, locked in once more, they were drinking their drinks.

'What was I saying?' asked Potter.

'About them all being the same.'

'I should have said nearly all of them. There are just a few people, none of them very well known I'm told, who've always said I'm no good. When the publishers and everybody were sending proofs and advance copies round, asking all these critics and so forth for their comments, I made jolly sure those ones, the anti-me ones, all got a copy. Two of them answered, saying politely they were afraid the thing didn't seem to them to merit any special recognition or something. The others didn't answer at all. Another form of politeness. That was a sort of check. If any of them had said it was any good when I knew it wasn't, then they might have been wrong when they said my other stuff was no good. But they didn't. It all fits together. Yes, I think I've proved as conclusively as it can be proved that I've never been any good.'

This was said in the same cheerful tone as before. Sue tried to think instead of merely feel. It took a few seconds.

'But, Mr Potter, that's not the sort of thing that ever can be proved.'

'Not like in geometry, no. Just a very strong presumption. Quite strong enough for me.'

'But . . . you may still be good even though . . .'

'You mean God or somebody may think I'm good. I'd certainly respect his opinion. But he's not letting on, is he?'

'You'll be remembered. Your work will live on. You've been too famous and highly thought of for it not to.'

'When I was a boy there was a very famous man who wrote tragedies in verse. They were very successful – produced by Beerbohm Tree and so on. And he was very highly thought of, too. The critics compared him with Sophocles and Shakespeare. He died during the war, the first war that is, just after I left school.

He was called Stephen Phillips. Ever heard of him?'

Sue shook her head.

'Neither had Sir Robert when I asked him. And he was born in the year Phillips died. Now isn't that a funny coincidence?'

Both were silent for a time. Then she said,

'Why did you put on this show tonight?'

'That's a good question – I quite see I could have conducted my test and then just privately refused the award. I suppose it was conceited of me. But it was fun. And I felt like getting a bit of my own back on some of the people who'd conned and flattered me into wasting all those years. And then – this is probably silly, but I might be remembered for a little while just because of this show. Potter? Oh yes, wasn't he that lousy old poet who got together a lot of people who'd said he was good and told them to clear off? A sort of footnote in literary history. Perhaps poor old Phillips might not be completely forgotten if he'd climbed up on the stage at the end of the first night of his *Paolo and Francesca* and told the audience to go and fuck themselves.'

'Yes. Do you want me to report this? Some of it? It could go in our daily.'

'I really don't mind either way. Would you like to report it?'

'I don't think so, Mr Potter.'

'Don't then. I wasn't telling you with that in mind. I just wanted to tell someone who'd see what I meant. No, more than that. I wanted to tell you.'

'Thank you. How have you been feeling since we met before? You said you were going to—'

'Oh yes. You know, it worked like a charm. The very first lot of pills he tried on me. You can probably see. No more feeling bad. No more wanting to write poems, either. But that's all right, isn't it, in the circumstances? But what the pills didn't take away was this curiosity about whether . . .'

Somebody knocked on the door and rattled its handle. A worried voice called,

'Ted? Ted, are you in there?'

'Hang on, Charles, will you? I'll be out in just a minute.' Potter lowered his voice again. 'He must have used ten-pound notes. Or his intelligence and energy. He's got plenty of all three.'

'They might not have read the book, just going by all your previous—'

'None of them? It's unlikely.'

'Or they might have thought this book was no good and not wanted to hurt your feelings, not wanted to stop you getting the award which they might have thought you'd earned with your previous work.'

'All of them? All saying how it continued the great Potter tradition? Holding a secret mass meeting to agree on a Potter policy? Sir Robert for one would never dream of stooping to anything like that. He's got far too much integrity. What he hasn't got is the ability to tell the difference between a good poem and a bad one. Or even between one kind of bad poem and another. I don't know, perhaps that's harder. Yes. I think in my heart of hearts I must have known I was no good. Otherwise why wouldn't I read my poems when I'd finished them? I'd have read them over and over again very carefully, to try and decide. And of course, I'd decided on the title and dedication of this lot before anybody else had ever seen it.'

'You'll feel differently about this tomorrow. You've given yourself a shock by this test thing of yours.'

They got to their feet as she spoke. Without drawing close to her he rested his hand on her shoulder, having to reach up slightly to do so.

'Do I look shocked? Tonight was just setting the seal on it. I've known the result of the test for weeks now. Don't worry about me, Mrs Macnamara. As I told you, I never feel bad about anything. Not any more.'

III

'Why did he do it, do you reckon?' asked Pat Bowes.

'I don't know. Are we going to make this plane?'

'On our heads. Quit fussing, Macnamara.'

'There's all this stuff of yours . . .'

'So there's all this stuff of mine. Somebody'll have to help me with it. There are men at the airport who earn their livings helping people with stuff.'

Bowes's car, which had a certain amount of Sue's stuff in it as well as a lot of his, hurried westwards down Cromwell Road.

'You're not going to get me off Potter, love. You were one of the last two or three people to talk to him. He must have said something. Or would you rather not talk about it? In which case tell me to shut my jumbo trap.'

'No, I don't mind. I'd have thought it was obvious enough anyway. He felt he'd found out he was no good.'

'That wouldn't make me knock myself off. I know, I'm an insensitive bastard, but there must have been more to it than that.'

'I don't think so. He'd made one gesture, telling his public to go and screw themselves, but that wasn't enough. He wanted to apologize.'

'Apologize? For being just a wee bit offensive to a lot of stuffed shirts who aren't even—'

'No, for being a bad poet, for having spent most of his life doing nothing but write bad poetry, or poetry he thought he'd proved was bad, and wasting everybody's time. He wanted to show he minded. More than about anything else, more than about his wife, which was why he did it in a way that couldn't possibly be mistaken for an accident.'

'Bit rough on the old girl, that part of it.'

'Very. It's the only part of it I don't sympathize with him about, but I can understand. Bad poets mind about poetry just as much as good poets. At least as much.'

'I don't see why it should be at least as much, but you'd know, I suppose. Well, it was a nasty shock. I thought he was a nice old buffer. It's a shame being nice doesn't mean you're good. When I think of some of the talented sons of bitches I've run into . . .'

'I know.'

'You seem to have got on to a lot about him nobody else has. I reckon I read pretty well every word the papers had to say, and there was nothing anywhere near this apologizing stuff of yours, or minding about poetry. You ought to write it up some time.'

Immediately on getting home on the night of the award, Sue had written out everything she remembered – a very large proportion – of her last conversation with Potter. The account was now locked up in her keepsake drawer, with the manuscript of 'Unborn' clipped to it. Certainly she ought to write it up some time; not yet, not until after Mrs Potter was dead. By then, perhaps, it might be possible to see how to write it up, or write it: how best to serve Potter's memory, how to interpret his intention in telling her what he had told her that night. For the present, she felt like somebody ineptly clutching a token of quite obscure significance, a gift with no recipient.

Sue and Bowes continued on their journey in the direction of Peduzzi, who at that moment, it being evening in Ceylon, was sitting in a hut drinking a sort of beer and congratulating himself on the (in fact both pretentious and technically incompetent) piece of film he had shot that day.

Something Strange

Something strange happened every day. It might happen during the morning, while the two men were taking their readings and observations and the two women busy with the domestic routine: the big faces had come during the morning. Or, as with the little faces and the coloured fires, the strange thing would happen in the afternoon, in the middle of Bruno's maintenance programme and Clovis's transmission to Base, Lia's rounds of the garden and Myri's work on her story. The evening was often undisturbed, the night less often.

They all understood that ordinary temporal expressions had no meaning for people confined indefinitely, as they were, to a motionless steel sphere hanging in a region of space so empty that the light of the nearest star took some hundreds of years to reach them. The Standing Orders devised by Base, however, recommended that they adopt a twenty-four-hour unit of time, as was the rule on the Earth they had not seen for many months. The arrangement suited them well: their work, recreation and rest seemed to fall naturally into the periods provided. It was only the prospect of year after year of the same routine, stretching farther into the future than they could see, that was a source of strain.

Bruno commented on this to Clovis after a morning spent repairing a fault in the spectrum analyser they used for investigating and classifying the nearer stars. They were sitting at the main observation port in the lounge, drinking the midday cocktail and waiting for the women to join them.

'I'd say we stood up to it extremely well,' Clovis said in answer to Bruno. 'Perhaps too well.'

Bruno hunched his fat figure upright. 'How do you mean?'

'We may be hindering our chances of being relieved.'

'Base has never said a word about our relief.'

'Exactly. With half a million stations to staff, it'll be a long time before they get round to one like this, where everything runs smoothly. You and I are a perfect team, and you have Lia and I have Myri, and they're all right together – no real conflict at all. Hence no reason for a relief.'

Myri had heard all this as she laid the table in the alcove. She wondered how Clovis could not know that Bruno wanted to have her instead of Lia, or perhaps as well as Lia. If Clovis did know, and was teasing Bruno, then that would be a silly thing to do, because Bruno was not a pleasant man. With his thick neck and pale fat face he would not be pleasant to be had by, either, quite unlike Clovis, who was no taller but whose straight, hard body and soft skin were always pleasant. He could not think as well as Bruno, but on the other hand many of the things Bruno thought were not pleasant. She poured herself a drink and went over to them.

Bruno had said something about it being a pity they could not fake their personnel report by inventing a few quarrels, and Clovis had immediately agreed that that was impossible. She kissed him and sat down at his side. 'What do you think about the idea of being relieved?' he asked her.

'I never think about it.'

'Quite right,' Bruno said, grinning. 'You're doing very nicely here. Fairly nicely, anyway.'

'What are you getting at?' Clovis asked him with a different kind of grin.

'It's not a very complete life, is it? For any of us. I could do with a change, anyway. A different kind of job, something that isn't testing and using and repairing apparatus. We do seem to have a lot of repairing to do, don't we? That analyser breaks down almost every day. And yet—'

His voice tailed off and he looked out of the port, as if to assure himself that all that lay beyond it was the familiar starscape of points and smudges of light.

'And yet what?' Clovis asked, irritably this time.

'I was thinking that we really ought to be thankful for having plenty to do. There's the routine, and the fruits and vegetables to look after, and Myri's story . . . How's that going, by the way? Won't you read us some of it? This evening, perhaps?'

'Not until it's finished, if you don't mind.'

'Oh, but I do mind. It's part of our duty to entertain one another. And I'm very interested in it personally.'

'Why?'

'Because you're an interesting girl. Bright brown eyes and a healthy glowing skin – how do you manage it after all this time in space? And you've more energy than any of us.'

Myri said nothing. Bruno was good at making remarks there was nothing to say to.

'What's it about, this story of yours?' he pursued. 'At least you can tell us that.'

'I have told you. It's about normal life. Life on Earth before there were any space stations, lots of different people doing different things, not this—'

'That's normal life, is it, different people doing different things? I can't wait to hear what the things are. Who's the hero, Myri? Our dear Clovis?'

Myri put her hand on Clovis's shoulder. 'No more, please, Bruno. Let's go back to your point about the routine. I couldn't understand why you left out the most important part, the part that keeps us busiest of all.'

'Ah, the strange happenings.' Bruno dipped his head in a characteristic gesture, half laugh, half nervous tremor. 'And the hours we spend discussing them. Oh yes. How could I have failed to mention all that?'

'If you've got any sense you'll go on not mentioning it,' Clovis snapped. 'We're all fed up with the whole business.'

'You may be, but I'm not. I want to discuss it. So does Myri, don't you, Myri?'

'I do think perhaps it's time we made another attempt to find a pattern,' Myri said. This was a case of Bruno not being pleasant but being right.

'Oh, not again.' Clovis bounded up and went over to the drinks table. 'Ah, hallo, Lia,' he said to the tall, thin, blonde woman who had just entered with a tray of cold dishes. 'Let me get you a drink. Bruno and Myri are getting philosophical – looking for patterns. What do you think? I'll tell you what I think. I think we're doing enough already. I think patterns are Base's job.'

'We can make it ours, too,' Bruno said. 'You agree, Lia?'

'Of course,' Lia said in the deep voice that seemed to Myri to carry so much more firmness and individuality in its tone than any of its owner's words or actions.

'Very well. You can stay out of this if you like, Clovis. We start from the fact that what we see and hear need not be illusions, although they may be.'

'At least that they're illusions that any human being might have, they're not special to us, as we know from Base's reports of what happens to other stations.'

'Correct, Myri. In any event, illusions or not, they are being directed at us by an intelligence and for a purpose.'

'We don't know that,' Myri objected. 'They may be natural phenomena, or the by-product of some intelligent activity not directed at us.'

'Correct again, but let us reserve these less probable possibilities until later. Now, as a sample, consider the last week's strange happenings. I'll fetch the log so that there can be no dispute.'

'I wish you'd stop it,' Clovis said when Bruno had gone out to the apparatus room. 'It's a waste of time.'

'Time's the only thing we're not short of.'

'I'm not short of anything,' he said, touching her thigh. 'Come with me for a little while.'

'Later.'

'Lia always goes with Bruno when he asks her.'

'Oh yes, but that's my choice,' Lia said. 'She doesn't want to now. Wait until she wants to.'

'I don't like waiting.'

'Waiting can make it better.'

'Here we are,' Bruno said briskly, returning. 'Right . . . Monday. *Within a few seconds the sphere became encased in a thick brownish damp substance that tests revealed to be both impermeable and infinitely thick. No action by the staff suggested itself. After three hours and eleven minutes the substance disappeared.* It's the *infinitely thick* thing that's interesting. That must have been an illusion, or something would have happened to all the other stations at the same time, not to speak of the stars and planets. A total or partial illusion, then. Agreed?'

'Go on.'

'Tuesday. *Metallic object of size comparable to that of the sphere approaching on collision course at 500 kilometres per second. No countermeasures available. Object appeared instantaneously at 35 million kilometres' distance and disappeared instantaneously at 1,500 kilometres.* What about that?'

'We've had ones like that before,' Lia put in. 'Only this was the longest time it's taken to approach and the nearest it's come before disappearing.'

'Incomprehensible or illusion,' Myri suggested.

'Yes, I think that's the best we can do at the moment. Wednesday: a very trivial one, not worth discussing. *A being apparently constructed entirely of bone approached the main port and made beckoning motions.* Whoever's doing this must be running out of ideas. Thursday. *All bodies external to the sphere vanished to all instruments simultaneously, reappearing to all instruments simultaneously two hours later.* That's not a new one either, I seem to remember. Illusion? Good. Friday. *Beings resembling terrestrial reptiles covered the sphere, fighting ceaselessly and eating portions of one another. Loud rustling and slithering sounds.* The sounds at least must have been an illusion, with no air out there, and I never heard of a reptile that didn't breathe. The same sort of thing applies to yesterday's performance. *Human screams of pain and extreme astonishment approaching and receding. No visual or other accompaniment.*' He paused and looked round at them. 'Well? Any uniformities suggest themselves?'

'No,' Clovis said, helping himself to salad, for they sat now at the lunch table. 'And I defy any human brain to devise any. The whole thing's arbitrary.'

'On the contrary, the very next happening – today's when it comes – might reveal an unmistakable pattern.'

'The one to concentrate on,' Myri said, 'is the approaching object. Why did it vanish before striking the sphere?'

Bruno stared at her. 'It had to, if it was an illusion.'

'Not at all. Why couldn't we have had an illusion of the sphere being struck? And supposing it wasn't an illusion?'

'Next time there's an object, perhaps it will strike,' Lia said.

Clovis laughed. 'That's a good one. What would happen if it did, I wonder? And it wasn't an illusion?'

They all looked at Bruno for an answer. After a moment or two, he said: 'I presume the sphere would shatter and we'd all be thrown into space. I simply can't imagine what that would be like. We should be . . . Never to see one another again, or anybody or anything else, to be nothing more than a senseless lump floating in space for ever. The chances of—'

'It would be worth something to be rid of your conversation,' Clovis said, amiable now that Bruno was discomfited. 'Let's be practical for a change. How long will it take you to run off your analyses this afternoon? There's a lot of stuff to go out to Base and I shan't be able to give you a hand.'

'An hour, perhaps, after I've run the final tests.'

'Why run tests at all? She was lined up perfectly when we finished this morning.'

'Fortunately.'

'Fortunately indeed. One more variable and we might have found it impossible.'

'Yes,' Bruno said abstractedly. Then he got to his feet so abruptly that the other three started. 'But we didn't, did we? There wasn't one more variable, was there? It didn't quite happen, you see, the thing we couldn't handle.'

Nobody spoke.

'Excuse me, I must be by myself.'

'If Bruno keeps this up,' Clovis said to the two women, 'Base will send up a relief sooner than we think.'

Myri tried to drive the thought of Bruno's unusual behaviour out of her head when, half an hour later, she sat down to work on her story. The expression on his face as he left the table had been one she could not name. Excitement? Dislike? Surprise? That was the nearest – a kind of persistent surprise. Well, he was certain, being Bruno, to set about explaining it at dinner. She wished he were more pleasant, because he did think well.

Finally expelling the image of Bruno's face, she began rereading the page of manuscript she had been working on when the screams had interrupted her the previous afternoon. It was part of a difficult scene, one in which a woman met by chance a man who had been having her ten years earlier, with the complication that she was at the time in the company of the man who was currently having her. The scene was an eating alcove in a large city.

'Go away,' Volsci said, 'or I'll hit you.'

Norbu smiled in a not-pleasant way. 'What good would that do? Irmy likes me better than she likes you. You are more pleasant, no doubt, but she likes me better. She remembers me having her ten years ago more clearly than she remembers you having her last night. I am good at thinking, which is better than any amount of being pleasant.'

'She's having her meal with me,' Volsci said, pointing to the cold food and drinks in front of them. 'Aren't you, Irmy?'

'Yes, Irmy,' Norbu said. 'You must choose. If you can't let both of us have you, you must say which of us you like better.'

Irmy looked from one man to the other. There was so much difference between them that she could hardly begin to choose: the one more pleasant, the other better at thinking, the one slim, the other plump. She decided being pleasant was better. It was more important and more significant – better in every

way that made a real difference. She said: 'I'll have Volsci.'
Norbu looked surprised and sorry. 'I think you're wrong.'
'You might as well go now,' Volsci said. 'Ila will be waiting.'
'Yes,' Norbu said. He looked extremely sorry now.
Irmy felt quite sorry too. 'Goodbye, Norbu,' she said.

Myri smiled to herself. It was good, even better than she had remembered – there was no point in being modest inside one's own mind. She must be a real writer in spite of Bruno's scoffing, or how could she have invented these characters, who were so utterly unlike anybody she knew, and then put them into a situation that was so completely outside her experience? The only thing she was not sure about was whether she might not have overplayed the part about feeling or dwelt on it at too great length. Perhaps *extremely sorry* was a little heavy; she replaced it by *sorrier than before*. Excellent: now there was just the right touch of restraint in the middle of all the feeling. She decided she could finish off the scene in a few lines.

'Probably see you at some cocktail hour,' Volsci said, she wrote, then looked up with a frown as the buzzer sounded at her door. She crossed her tiny wedge-shaped room – its rear wall was part of the outer wall of the sphere, but it had no port – threw the lock and found Bruno on the threshold. He was breathing fast, as if he had been hurrying or lifting a heavy weight, and she saw with distaste that there were drops of sweat on his thick skin. He pushed past her and sat down on her bed, his mouth open.

'What is it?' she asked, displeased. The afternoon was a private time unless some other arrangement were made at lunch.

'I don't know what it is. I think I must be ill.'

'Ill? But you can't be. Only people on Earth get ill. Nobody on a station is ever ill: Base told us that. Illness is caused by—'

'I don't think I believe some of the things that Base says.'

'But who can we believe if we don't believe Base?'

Bruno evidently did not hear her question. He said: 'I had to come to you – Lia's no good for this. Please let me stay with you, I've got so much to say.'

'It's no use, Bruno. Clovis is the one who has me. I thought you understood that I didn't—'

'That's not what I mean,' he said impatiently. 'Where I need you is in thinking. Though that's connected with the other, the having. I don't expect you to see that. I've only just begun to see it myself.'

Myri could make nothing of this last part. 'Thinking? Thinking about what?'

He bit his lip and shut his eyes for a moment. 'Listen to this,' he said. 'It was the analyser that set my mind going. Almost every other day it breaks down. And the computer, the counters, the repellers, the scanners and the rest of them – they're always breaking down too, and so are their power supplies. But not the purifier or the fluid-reconstitutor or the fruit and vegetable growers or the heaters or the main power source. Why not?'

'Well, they're less complicated. How can a fruit grower go wrong? A chemical tank and a water tank is all there is to it. You ask Lia about that.'

'All right. Try answering this, then. The strange happenings. If they're illusions, why are they always outside the sphere? Why are there never any inside?'

'Perhaps there are,' Myri said.

'Don't. I don't want that. I shouldn't like that. I want everything in here to be real. Are you real? I must believe you are.'

'Of course I'm real.' She was now thoroughly puzzled.

'And it makes a difference, doesn't it? It's very important that you and everything else should be real, everything in the sphere. But tell me: whatever's arranging these happenings must be pretty powerful if it can fool our instruments and our senses so completely and consistently, and yet it can't do anything – anything we recognize as strange, that is – inside this puny little steel skin. Why not?'

'Presumably it has its limitations. We should be pleased.'

'Yes. All right, next point. You remember the time I tried to sit up in the lounge after midnight and stay awake?'

'That was silly. Nobody can stay awake after midnight. Standing Orders were quite clear on that point.'

'Yes, they were, weren't they?' Bruno seemed to be trying to grin. 'Do you remember my telling you how I couldn't account for being in my own bed as usual when the music woke us – you remember the big music? And – this is what I'm really after – do you remember how we all agreed at breakfast that life in space must have conditioned us in such a way that falling asleep at a fixed time had become an automatic mechanism? You remember that?'

'Naturally I do.'

'Right. Two questions, then. Does that strike you as a likely explanation? That sort of complete self-conditioning in all four of us after . . . just a number of months?'

'Not when you put it like that.'

'But we all agreed on it, didn't we? Without hesitation.'

Myri, leaning against a side wall, fidgeted. He was being not pleasant in a new way, one that made her want to stop him talking even while he was thinking at his best. 'What's your other question, Bruno?' Her voice sounded unusual to her.

'Ah, you're feeling it too, are you?'

'I don't know what you mean.'

'I think you will in a minute. Try my other question. The night of the music was a long time ago, soon after we arrived here, but you remember it clearly. So do I. And yet when I try to remember what I was doing only a couple of months earlier, on Earth, finishing up my life there, getting ready for this, it's just a vague blur. Nothing stands out.'

'It's all so remote.'

'Maybe. But I remember the trip clearly enough, don't you?'

Myri caught her breath. I feel surprised, she told herself. Or something like that. I feel the way Bruno looked when he left the lunch table. She said nothing.

'You're feeling it now all right, aren't you?' He was watching her closely with his narrow eyes. 'Let me try to describe it. A surprise that goes on and on. Puzzlement. Symptoms of physical exertion or strain. And above all a . . . a sort of discomfort, only in the mind. Like having a sharp object pressed against a tender part of your body, except that it is in your mind.'

'What are you talking about?'

'A difficulty of vocabulary.'

The loudspeaker above the door clicked on and Clovis's voice said: 'Attention. Strange happening. Assemble in the lounge at once. Strange happening.'

Myri and Bruno stopped staring at each other and hurried out along the narrow corridor. Clovis and Lia were already in the lounge, looking out of the port.

Apparently only a few feet beyond the steelhard glass, and illuminated from some invisible source, were two floating figures. The detail was excellent, and the four inside the sphere could distinguish without difficulty every fold in the naked skin of the two caricatures of humanity presented, it seemed, for their thorough inspection, a presumption given added weight by the slow rotation of the pair that enabled their every portion to be scrutinized. Except for a scrubby growth at the base of the skull, they were hairless. The limbs were foreshortened, lacking the normal narrowing at the joints, and the bellies protuberant. One had male characteristics, the other female, yet in neither case were these complete. From each open, wet, quivering toothless mouth there came a loud, clearly audible yelling, higher in pitch than any those in the sphere could have produced, and of an unfamiliar emotional range.

'Well, I wonder how long this will last,' Clovis said.

'Is it worth trying the repellers on them?' Lia asked. 'What does the radar say? Does it see them?'

'I'll go and have a look.'

Bruno turned his back on the port. 'I don't like them.'

'Why not?' Myri saw he was sweating again.

'They remind me of something.'

'What?'

'I'm trying to think.'

But although Bruno went on trying to think for the rest of that day, with such obvious seriousness that even Clovis did his best to help with suggestions, he was no nearer a solution when they parted, as was their habit, at five minutes to midnight. And when, several times in the next couple of days, Myri mentioned the afternoon of the caricatures to him, he showed little interest.

'Bruno, you are extraordinary,' she said one evening. 'What happened to those odd feelings of yours you were so eager to describe to me just before Clovis called us into the lounge?'

He shrugged his narrow shoulders in the almost girlish way he had. 'Oh, I don't know what could have got into me,' he said. 'I expect I was just angry with the confounded analyser and the way it kept breaking down. It's been much better recently.'

'And all that thinking you used to do.'

'That was a complete waste of time.'

'Surely not.'

'Yes, I agree with Clovis, let Base do all the thinking.'

Myri was disappointed. To hear Bruno resigning the task of thought seemed like the end of something. This feeling was powerfully underlined for her when, a little later, the announcement came over the loudspeaker in the lounge. Without any preamble at all, other than the usual click on, a strange voice said: 'Your attention, please. This is Base calling over your intercom.'

They all looked up in great surprise, especially Clovis, who said quickly to Bruno: 'Is that possible?'

'Oh yes, they've been experimenting,' Bruno replied as quickly.

'It is perhaps ironical,' the voice went on, 'that the first transmission we have been able to make to you by the present means is also the last you will receive by any. For some time the maintenance of space stations has been uneconomic, and the decision has just been taken to discontinue them altogether. You will therefore make no further reports of any kind, or rather you may of course continue to do so on the understanding that nobody will be listening. In many cases it has fortunately been found possible to arrange for the collection of station staffs and their return to Earth: in others, those involving a journey to the remoter parts of the galaxy, a prohibitive expenditure of time and effort would be entailed. I am sorry to have to tell you that your own station is one of these. Accordingly, you will never be relieved.

All of us here are confident that you will respond to this new situation with dignity and resource.

'Before we sever communication for the last time, I have one more point to make. It involves a revelation which may prove so unwelcome that only with the greatest reluctance can I bring myself to utter it. My colleagues, however, insisted that those in your predicament deserve, in your own interests, to hear the whole truth about it. I must tell you, then, that contrary to your earlier information we have had no reports from any other station whose content resembles in the slightest degree your accounts of the strange happenings you claim to have witnessed. The deception was considered necessary so that your morale might be maintained, but the time for deceptions is over. You are unique, and in the variety of mankind that is no small distinction. Be proud of it. Goodbye for ever.'

They sat without speaking until five minutes to midnight. Try as she would, Myri found it impossible to conceive their future, and the next morning she had no more success. That was as long as any of them had leisure to come to terms with their permanent isolation, for by midday a quite new phase of strange happenings had begun. Myri and Lia were preparing lunch in the kitchen when Myri, opening the cupboard where the dishes were kept, was confronted by a flattish, reddish creature with many legs and a pair of unequally sized pincers. She gave a gasp, almost a shriek, of astonishment.

'What is it?' Lia said, hurrying over, and then in a high voice: 'Is it alive?'

'It's moving. Call the men.'

Until the others came, Myri simply stared. She found her lower lip shaking in a curious way. *Inside* now, she kept thinking. Not just outside. *Inside.*

'Let's have a look,' Clovis said. 'I see. Pass me a knife or something.' He rapped at the creature, making a dry, bony sound. 'Well, it works for tactile and aural, as well as visual, anyway. A thorough illusion. If it is one.'

'It must be,' Bruno said. 'Don't you recognize it?'

'There is something familiar about it, I suppose.'

'You suppose? You mean you don't know a crab when you see one?'

'Oh, of course,' Clovis looked slightly sheepish. 'I remember now. A terrestrial animal, isn't it? Lives in the water. And so it must be an illusion. Crabs don't cross space as far as I know, and even if they could they'd have a tough time carving their way through the skin of the sphere.'

His sensible manner and tone helped Myri to get over her astonishment, and it was she who suggested that the crab be disposed of down the waste chute. At lunch, she said: 'It was a remarkably specific illusion, don't you think? I wonder how it was projected.'

'No point in wondering about that,' Bruno told her. 'How can we ever know? And what use would the knowledge be to us if we did know?'

'Knowing the truth has its own value.'

'I don't understand you.'

Lia came in with the coffee just then. 'The crab's back,' she said. 'Or there's another one there, I can't tell.'

More crabs, or simulacra thereof, appeared at intervals for the rest of the day, eleven of them in all. It seemed, as Clovis put it, that the illusion-producing technique had its limitations, inasmuch as none of them saw a crab actually materialize: the new arrival would be 'discovered' under a bed or behind a bank of apparatus. On the other hand, the depth of illusion produced was very great, as they all agreed when Myri, putting the eighth crab down the chute, was nipped in the finger, suffered pain and exuded a few drops of blood.

'Another new departure,' Clovis said. 'An illusory physical process brought about on the actual person of one of us. They're improving.'

Next morning there were the insects. The main apparatus room was found to be infested with what, again on Bruno's prompting, they recognized as cockroaches. By lunch-time there were moths and flying beetles in all the main rooms, and a number of large flies became noticeable towards the evening. The whole of their attention became concentrated upon avoiding these creatures as far as possible. The day passed without Clovis asking Myri to go with him. This had never happened before.

The following afternoon a fresh problem was raised by Lia's announcement that the garden now contained no fruits or vegetables – none, at any rate, that were accessible to her senses. In this the other three concurred. Clovis put the feelings of all of them when he said: 'If this is an illusion, it's as efficient as the reality, because fruits and vegetables you can never find are the same as no fruits and vegetables.'

The evening meal used up all the food they had. Soon after two o'clock in the morning Myri was aroused by Clovis's voice saying over the loudspeaker: 'Attention, everyone. Strange happening. Assemble in the lounge immediately.'

She was still on her way when she became aware of a new quality in the background of silence she had grown used to. It was a deeper silence, as if some sound at the very threshold of audibility had ceased. There were unfamiliar vibrations underfoot.

Clovis was standing by the port, gazing through it with interest. 'Look at this, Myri,' he said.

At a distance impossible to gauge, an oblong of light had become visible, a degree or so in breadth and perhaps two and a half times as high. The light was of comparable quality to that illuminating the inside of the sphere. Now and then it flickered.

'What is it?' Myri asked.

'I don't know, it's only just appeared.' The floor beneath them shuddered violently. 'That was what woke me, one of those tremors. Ah, here you are, Bruno. What do you make of it?'

Bruno's large eyes widened further, but he said nothing. A moment later Lia arrived and joined the silent group by the port. Another vibration shook the sphere. Some vessel in the kitchen fell to the floor and smashed. Then Myri said: 'I can see what looks like a flight of steps leading down from the lower edge of the light. Three or four of them, perhaps more.'

She had barely finished speaking when a shadow appeared before them, cast by the rectangle of light on to a surface none of them could identify. The shadow seemed to them of a stupefying vastness, but it was beyond question that of a man. A moment later the man came into view, outlined by the light, and descended the steps. Another moment or two and he was evidently a few feet from the port, looking in on them, their own lights bright on the upper half of him. He was a well-built man wearing a grey uniform jacket and a metal helmet. An object recognizable as a gun of some sort was slung over his shoulder. While he watched them, two other figures, similarly accoutred, came down the steps and joined him. There was a brief interval, then he moved out of view to their right, doing so with the demeanour of one walking on a level surface.

None of the four inside spoke or moved, not even at the sound of heavy bolts being drawn in the section of outer wall directly in front of them, not even when that entire section swung away from them like a door opening outwards and the three men stepped through into the sphere. Two of them had unslung the guns from their shoulders.

Myri remembered an occasion, weeks ago, when she had risen from a stooping position in the kitchen and struck her head violently on the bottom edge of a cupboard door Lia had happened to leave open. The feeling Myri now experienced was similar, except that she had no particular physical sensations. Another memory, a much fainter one, passed across the far background of her mind: somebody had once tried to explain to her the likeness between a certain mental state and the bodily sensation of discomfort, and she had not understood. The memory faded sharply.

The man they had first seen said: 'All roll up your sleeves.'

Clovis looked at him with less curiosity than he had been showing when Myri first joined him at the port, a few minutes earlier. 'You're an illusion,' he said.

'No I'm not. Roll up your sleeves, all of you.'

He watched them closely while they obeyed, becoming impatient at the slowness with which they moved. The other man whose gun was unslung, a younger man, said: 'Don't be hard on them, Allen. We've no idea what they've been through.'

'I'm not taking any chances,' Allen said. 'Not after that crowd in the trees. Now this is for your own good,' he went on, addressing the four. 'Keep quite still. All right, Douglas.'

The third man came forward, holding what Myri knew to be a hypodermic syringe. He took her firmly by her bare arm and gave her an injection. At once her feelings altered, in the sense that, although there was still discomfort in her mind, neither this nor anything else seemed to matter.

After a time she heard the young man say: 'You can roll your sleeves down now. You can be quite sure that nothing bad will happen to you.'

'Come with us,' Allen said.

Myri and the others followed the three men out of the sphere, across a gritty floor that might have been concrete and up the steps, a distance of perhaps thirty feet. They entered a corridor with artificial lighting and then a room into which the sun was streaming. There were twenty or thirty people in the room, some of them wearing the grey uniform. Now and then the walls shook as the sphere had done, but to the accompaniment of distant explosions. A faint shouting could also be heard from time to time.

Allen's voice said loudly: 'Let's try and get a bit of order going. Douglas, they'll be wanting you to deal with the people in the tank. They've been conditioned to believe they're congenitally aquatic, so you'd better give them a shot that'll knock them out straight away. Holmes is draining the tank now. Off you go. Now you, James, you watch this lot while I find out some more about them. I wish those psycho chaps would turn up – we're just working in the dark.' His voice moved further away. 'Sergeant – get these five out of here.'

'Where to, sir?'

'I don't mind where – just out of here. And watch them.'

'They've all been given shots, sir.'

'I know, but look at them, they're not human any more. And

it's no use talking to them, they've been deprived of language. That's how they got the way they are. Now get them out right away.'

Myri looked slowly at the young man who stood near them: James. 'Where are we?' she asked.

James hesitated. 'I was ordered to tell you nothing,' he said. 'You're supposed to wait for the psychological team to get to you and treat you.'

'Please.'

'All right. This much can't hurt you, I suppose. You four and a number of other groups have been the subject of various experiments. This building is part of Special Welfare Research Station No. 4. Or rather it was. The government that set it up no longer exists. It has been removed by the revolutionary army of which I'm a member. We had to shoot our way in here and there's fighting still going on.'

'Then we weren't in space at all.'

'No.'

'Why did they make us believe we were?'

'We don't know yet.'

'And how did they do it?'

'Some new form of deep-level hypnosis, it seems, probably renewed at regular intervals. Plus various apparatus for producing illusions. We're still working on that. Now, I think that's enough questions for the moment. The best thing you can do is sit down and rest.'

'Thank you. What's hypnosis?'

'Oh, of course they'd have removed knowledge of that. It'll all be explained to you later.'

'James, come and have a look at this, will you?' Allen's voice called. 'I can't make much of it.'

Myri followed James a little way. Among the clamour of voices, some speaking languages unfamiliar to her, others speaking none, she heard James ask: 'Is this the right file? Fear Elimination?'

'Must be,' Allen answered. 'Here's the last entry. *Removal of Bruno V and substitution of Bruno VI accomplished, together*

with memory-adjustment of other three subjects. Memo to Prep-
aration Centre: avoid repetition of Bruno V personality-type with
strong curiosity-drives. Started catching on to the set-up, eh?
Wonder what they did with him.'

'There's that psycho hospital across the way they're still investigating; perhaps he's in there.'

'With Brunos I to IV, no doubt. Never mind that for the
moment. Now. *Procedures: penultimate phase. Removal of all*
ultimate confidence: severance of communication, total denial
of prospective change, inculcation of "uniqueness" syndrome,
environment shown to be violable, unknowable crisis in prospect
(food deprivation). I can understand that last bit. They don't look
starved, though.'

'Perhaps they've only just started them on it.'

'We'll get them fed in a minute. Well, all this still beats me,
James. *Reactions. Little change. Responses poor. Accelerating*
impoverishment of emotional life and its vocabulary: compare
portion of novel written by Myri VII with contributions of pre-
decessors. Prognosis: further affective deterioration: catatonic
apathy: failure of experiment. That's a comfort, anyway. But
what has all this got to do with fear elimination?'

They stopped talking suddenly and Myri followed the direction of their gaze. A door had been opened and the man called
Douglas was supervising the entry of a number of others, each
supporting or carrying a human form wrapped in a blanket.

'This must be the lot from the tank,' Allen or James said.

Myri watched while those in the blankets were made as
comfortable as possible on benches or on the floor. One of them,
however, remained totally wrapped in his blanket and was paid
no attention.

'He's had it, has he?'

'Shock, I'm afraid.' Douglas's voice was unsteady. 'There was
nothing we could do. Perhaps we shouldn't have—'

Myri stooped and turned back the edge of the blanket. What
she saw was much stranger than anything she had experienced
in the sphere. 'What's the matter with him?' she asked James.

'Matter with him? You can die of shock, you know.'

'I can do what?'

Myri, staring at James, was aware that his face had become distorted by a mixture of expressions. One of them was understanding: all the others were painful to look at. They were renderings of what she herself was feeling. Her vision darkened and she ran from the room, back the way they had come, down the steps, across the floor, back into the sphere.

James was unfamiliar with the arrangement of the rooms there and did not reach her until she had picked up the manuscript of the novel, hugged it to her chest with crossed arms and fallen on to her bed, her knees drawn up as far as they would go, her head lowered as it had been before her birth, an event of which she knew nothing.

She was still in the same position when, days later, somebody sat heavily down beside her. 'Myri. You must know who this is. Open your eyes, Myri. Come out of there.'

After he had said this, in the same gentle voice, some hundreds of times, she did open her eyes a little. She was in a long, high room, and near her was a fat man with a pale skin. He reminded her of something to do with space and thinking. She screwed her eyes shut.

'Myri. I know you remember me. Open your eyes again.'

She kept them shut while he went on talking.

'Open your eyes. Straighten your body.'

She did not move.

'Straighten your body, Myri. I love you.'

Slowly her feet crept down the bed and her head lifted.

The 2003 Claret

'How long to go now?' the Director asked for the tenth time.

I compared the main laboratory chronometer with the dial on the TIOPEPE (Temporal Integrator, Ordinal Predictor and Electronic Propulsion Equipment). 'He should be taking the trance-pill in a few seconds, sir,' I said. 'Then there's only the two minutes for it to take effect, and we can bring him back.'

'Supposing he hasn't taken the pill?'

'I'm sure he'd survive the time-shift even if he were fully conscious, sir. It's instantaneous, after all.'

'I know, but being snatched back from fifty years in the future can't do a man's mind any good, can it? We just don't know what we're up against, Baker. I wish those blasted politicians had let us go slow on this project. But no, there mustn't be any delay or the Russians will have developed time-travel before the Atlantic Powers, so we bundle Simpson off to the year 2010 and if we lose him or he turns up a raving lunatic it's our fault.' The Director sat moodily down on a work-bench. 'What happens if he gets tight?'

'He won't have done that, sir. Simpson's one of the Knights of Bordeaux. They never get drunk – isn't it a rule of the society?'

'I believe so, yes.' The Director cheered up a little. 'He'll probably have a good deal to tell us, with any luck. The Douro growers are saying that last year was the best since 1945, you know, Baker. Imagine what that stuff must be like where Simpson is. Just one glass—'

'Did you actually tell Simpson to sample the wines in 2010?'

The Director coughed. 'Well, I did just make the suggestion to him. After all, part of our terms of reference was to report on social conditions, in addition to the political situation. And drinking habits are a pretty good guide to the social set-up, aren't they? Find out how people treat their port and you've found out a lot about the kind of people they are.'

'Something in that, sir.' I'm a beer man myself, which made me a bit of an outsider in the team. There were only the four of us in the lab that night – the VIPs and the press boys had been pushed into the Conference Room, thank heaven – and all the other three were wine-bibbers of one sort or another. The Director, as you will have gathered, was fanatical about port; Rabaiotti, my senior assistant, belonged to a big Chianti family; and Schneider, the medical chap, had written a book on hock. Simpson was reputedly on the way to becoming a sound judge of claret, though I had sometimes wondered whether perhaps tactical considerations played their part in his choice of hobby. Anyway, I considered I was lucky to have got the job of Chief Time-Engineer, against competition that included a force-field expert who doubled as an amateur of old Madeira and an electronics king named Gilbey – no relation, it turned out, but the Director couldn't have known that at the time.

'The receiver is tuned, Dr Baker.'

'Thank you, Dr Rabaiotti. Would you like to operate the recall switch, sir?'

'Why, that's extremely kind of you, Baker.' The Director was shaking with excitement. 'It's this one here, isn't it?' His hand brushed the trigger of a relay that would have sent Simpson shooting back to about the time of Victoria's accession. This may have been half-deliberate: the Director often got wistful about what pre-phylloxera stuff might or might not have tasted like.

'No, this one, sir. Just press it gently down.'

The switch clicked and instantly the figure of Simpson – tallish, forty-ish, baldish – appeared in the receiver. We all gave a shout of triumph and relief. Rabaiotti killed the power. Schneider hurried forward and there was tension again. 'I'd give a case of Dow 1919 to see him conscious and mentally sound,' the Director muttered at my side.

'Everything all right so far,' Schneider called. 'I've given him a shot that'll pull him round in a minute or two.'

We lit cigarettes. 'Pity conditions wouldn't allow of him bringing anything back,' the Director said. 'Just think of a forty-year-old 1970 all ready to drink. But I suppose it would have cost too much anyway. Next time we must find a better way of handling the currency problem. Very risky giving him raw gold to pawn. And we're restricted to a lump small enough not to arouse too much suspicion. Oh, well, he should have been able to afford a few glasses. I hope that champagne's all right, by the way?'

'Oh, yes, I put it in the molecular-motion-retarder myself, with the setting at point-three. It'll be nicely chilled by now.'

'Splendid. I do want the dear boy to get a decent livener inside him before he faces all those cameras and interviews. I should have preferred a dry port myself, or possibly a Bittall, but I know what the occasion demands, of course. It's a Lambert 1952 I've got for him. I don't understand these things myself, but the Director of Lunar Projectiles swears by it.'

'He's coming round now,' Schneider shouted, and we all pressed forward.

There was an intense silence while Simpson blinked at us, sat up and yawned. His face was absolutely impassive. Very slowly he scratched his ear. He looked like a man with a bad hangover.

'Well?' the Director demanded eagerly. 'What did you see?'

'Everything. At least, I saw enough.'

'Had there been a war? Is there going to be a war?'

'No. Russia joined the Western Customs Union in 1993, China some time after 2000. The RAF's due to be disbanded in a few months.'

Then everyone hurled questions at once: about flying saucers, the Royal Family, the sciences, the arts, interplanetary travel, climatic conditions in the Rheingau – all sorts of things. Simpson seemed not to hear. He just sat there with the same blank look on his face, wearily shaking his head.

'What's the matter?' I asked finally. 'What was wrong?'

After a moment, he said in a hollow voice, 'Better if there had been a war. In some ways. Yes. Much better.'

'What on earth do you mean?'

Simpson gave a deep sigh. Then, hesitantly, to a silent audience and with the bottle of champagne quite forgotten, he told the following story.

The landing went off perfectly. Hyde Park was the area selected, with a thousand-square-yard tolerance to prevent Simpson from materializing inside a wall or halfway into a passer-by. Nobody saw him arrive. He changed his gold into currency without difficulty, and in a few minutes was walking briskly down Piccadilly, looking into shop-windows, studying dress and behaviour, buying newspapers and magazines, and writing busily in his notebook. He had several fruitful conversations, representing himself according to plan as a native of Sydney. This brought him some commiseration, for England had just beaten Australia at Lord's by an innings and 411 runs. Yes, everything seemed normal so far.

His political report and much of his social report were complete by six-thirty, and his thoughts started turning to drink: after all, it was a positive duty. As he strolled up Shaftesbury Avenue he began looking out for drink advertisements. The beer ones had much in common with those of 1960, but were overshadowed in prominence by those recommending wines. MOUTON ROTH-SCHILD FOR POWER, BREEDING AND GRANDEUR, one said. ASK FOR OESTRICHER PFAFFENBERG – THE HOCK WITH THE CLEAN FINISH, enjoined another. MY GOLLY, MY ST GYOERGHY-HEGYI FURMINT, bawled a third. Well, practical experiment would soon establish what was what. Simpson slipped quietly through the doorway of an establishment clearly devoted to drink.

The interior was surprising. If some French provincial café had not been gutted of décor and furnishings to get this place up, then a good job of duplication had been done. Men in neat, sombre clothing sat at the tables talking in low tones, wine-glasses and wine-bottles before them, while aproned waiters moved silently about. One of them was decanting a red wine from a bottle that was thick with dust and cobwebs, watched critically by all the nearby drinkers. Simpson crept to a seat in an unfrequented part of the room.

A waiter approached. 'What can I bring you, monsieur?'

Here it must be explained that Simpson was not quite the claret-fancier the Director thought him. He enjoyed claret all right, but he also enjoyed other French wines, and German wines, and Italian wines, and Iberian wines, and Balkan wines, and fortified wines, and spirits, and liqueurs, and *apéritifs*, and cocktails, and draught beer, and bottled beer, and stout, and cider, and perry – all the way down to Fernet Branca. (There were some drinks he had never drunk – *arak*, *kava*, Gumpoldskirchner Rotgipfler, methylated spirits – but they were getting fewer all the time.) Anyway, feeling dehydrated after his walk round the streets, he unreflectingly ordered a pint of bitter.

'I'm sorry, monsieur, I don't understand. What is this bitter?'

'Bitter beer, ale; you know. Haven't you got any?'

'Beer, monsieur?' The waiter's voice rose in contempt. '*Beer*? I'm afraid you're in the wrong district for that.'

Several men turned round, nudged one another and stared at Simpson, who blushed and said, 'Well . . . a glass of wine, then.'

'France, Germany, Luxembourg, Austria . . .'

Simpson tried to think. 'A claret, please. Let's say – a nice St Emilion.'

'Château Le Couvent, Château Puyblanquet, Château Bellefore Belcier, Château Grand Corbin d'Espagne . . .'

'Oh . . . I leave it to you.'

'*Bien*, monsieur. And the year? Will you leave that to me too?'

'If you don't mind.'

The waiter swept away. Conscious that all eyes were upon him, Simpson tried to sink into his chair. Before he could compose himself, a middle-aged man from a nearby table had come over and sat down next to him. 'Well, who are you?' this man asked.

'A – a traveller. From Sydney.'

'These days that's no excuse for not knowing your wines,

friend. Some of them Rubicons and Malbecs are as firm and fully rounded as all bar the greatest Burgundies. And I found a Barossa Riesling on holiday this year that was pretty near as gay as a Kreuznacher Steinweg. You well up on the Barossas, friend?'

'No, not really, I'm afraid.'

'Thought not, somehow. Otherwise you wouldn't stalk in here and screech out for *beer*. Ger, ought to be ashamed of yourself, you ought.'

'I'm awfully sorry.'

'Should hope so and all. Now, I'm an honest working man, see? I'm a DRIP, I am.'

'A drip?'

'Domestic Reactor Installation Patentee. Don't they go in for them down under? Now you listen to me. When I come in here to meet my colleagues and crack a bottle or two after the daily round, I don't want my palate soured by some toff yelling out about beer, especially not when we got a really elegant Gevrey Chambertin or Chambolle Musigny or something of that in front of us. It's psychosomatic, like. Just the idea of beer's enough to cut off some of the subtler overtones, get me?'

'I'm sorry,' Simpson said again. 'I didn't realize. But tell me: don't you eat while you're drinking these wines?'

'What, and foul up the taste-buds with fat and sauces and muck? You got a nerve even mentioning food in a place like this. We're oenophiles in here, I'll have you know, not a bunch of pigs. Ah, here's your claret.' The stranger held the glass up to the light, then sniffed it delicately. 'Right, now let's see what you got to say about this. And get on with it.'

Simpson drank. It was the most wonderful wine he had ever known, with a strange warm after-taste that seemed to seep upwards and flood his olfactory centres. He sighed deeply. 'Superb,' he said at last

'Come on, come on, we want more than that; you got to do better than that. Give us a spot of imagery, kind of style, a reference to art, that type of stuff.'

'It's – I don't know – it's the richness of summer, all the glory of . . . of love and lyric poetry, a whole way of life, profound and . . . some great procession of—'

'Ah, you turn me up,' the man said violently. 'This is a 2003 Château La Bouygue, reconstituted pre-phylloxera of course. Now, light and free, not rich in association but perfectly assured without any insincerity, instrumental where the 'o1s are symphonic, the gentleness of a Braque rather than the bravura of a Matisse. That's as far as you can go with it. Love and lyric poetry indeed. I never heard such slop in my life. You aren't fit to come in here, friend. You get off out to one of the pubs with your boss-class pals, that's where you belong.'

Simpson threw down some coins and ran, a gust of ill-natured laughter sounding in his ears. He felt like walking the streets for the two hours in 2010 that still remained to him, but a nagging curiosity emboldened him to ask to be directed to a pub.

The place he finally made his way to was on the corner of a narrow street on the edge of Soho. It was a red-brick affair like a miniature grammar school or a suburban bank. As he approached, a bus drew up and a crowd of young people got off, chattering loudly to one another in what Simpson made out as a version of the upper-class tones current in his own time. He was more or less swept in through the front door of the pub, and had no time to puzzle out the significance of a notice above the entrance, painted by hand with what seemed deliberate inelegance, and bearing the legend: CRACKED UP BY THE WALLOP AND SCOFF MOB.

He found himself in a large, ill-lighted and crowded room of which the main feature was a long counter that ran from end to end zigzag-wise, as if to accommodate as many as possible of the tall stools that were closely packed along it. What were evidently glass sandwich cupboards stood every couple of feet along the red plastic top. A group of people, half-crowd, half-queue, was clustered round the entrance, and Simpson mingled with them. He noticed that most of the stools were occupied by persons drinking beer or some such liquid out of pint glasses and eating rolls or sandwiches. Conversations were bawling away around him.

'My dear, simply nobody goes to the Crown these days. Simon and I were given fresh crisps the last time we went.'

'It doesn't surprise me. We had some mustard that couldn't have been more than a day old.'

'The wallop's first-class down at the George, and as for the scoff – the bluest piece of ham you ever saw. A really memorable thrash. I'm getting the secretary of the Mob to crack them up in the next issue of the *Boozer Rag*.'

'Have you bagged stools, sir?'

'I beg your pardon?'

'Sorry, mate. Have you bagged, mate?'

'No, I'm afraid not. May I see the head potman?'

'I'll get him over directly, mate.'

'Shall we start thinking about what we're going to have? Pickled onions to start? With a glass of mild?'

'Nuts for me. Mixed and salted.'

'Right, that's three onions, one nuts. And then I can recommend the cheese rolls. They know me here and always see that I get the three-day-old, with plenty of rind.'

After some time, Simpson obtained a stool and ordered a pint of bitter from the grubby barmaid.

'Certainly, love. A fresh barrel has just come on.'

'Oh, I'll have mild instead, then.'

'By all means, love, if you wish for it. Your taste is your own. And what will you have in the way of scoff, love?'

'Oh, er – nothing to eat, thank you.'

'If I may say so, love, with all due respect, you might perhaps do better at the wine-bar if you don't wish for any scoff. We have standards to maintain here, love.'

'I'm awfully sorry. What . . . scoff do you recommend?'

'Our gherkins have frequently been cracked up, love. Not a dish is sold till it's two days old.'

'They sound delightful. One dish, please.'

'Very good, love. With cigarette-ash garnishings, of course.'

The beer came. It was horrible. The gherkins came. Simpson took no notice of them. Dazedly he watched and listened to those around him. A kind of ritual seemed to be being enacted by a group of four immediately next to him. The two couples raised their pints in concert, intoned the word 'Cheers' in a liturgical manner, poured a few drops on to the front of their greasy pull-overs, and sank their drinks in one swallow. Afterwards they all sighed loudly, wiped their mouths with their hands, banged the empty glasses down on the counter, and spoke in turn.

'Lovely drop of wallop.'

'First today.'

'I needed that.'

'Lays the dust.'

'You can't beat a decent pint.'

'Full of goodness.'

'Keeps your insides working.'

'It's a real drink.'

When this point was reached, all four shouted 'Let's have another' in unison, and were immediately served with fresh drinks and small plates of sandwiches. The bread on these was curled up at the corners, revealing purple strips of meat criss-crossed with gristle. One of the men felt the texture of the bread and nodded approvingly. 'I told you this place was good,' his friend said. Then the party got down to what was clearly the *pièce de résistance*, alternately biting at the sandwiches and taking pulls of beer, chewing the resulting mush with many a belch of appreciation. Simpson lowered his head into his hands. The talk went on.

'What's the fighting like here?'

'Oh, excellent. The governor of the boozer gets it under way at ten-thirty sharp, just outside on the corner. I did hear a whisper that he's going to allow broken bottles for the last five minutes tonight. The police should be with us by then. They're very keen round here.'

'At the Feathers, you know, they kick off at ten-fifteen inside the bar. Don't know whether I agree with that.'

'No. After all, it's only the finale of the evening.'

'Absolutely. Shouldn't make it too important.'

'Definitely not. Getting tight's the object of the exercise.'

'Quite. By the way, who's that fellow next to you?'

'No idea. Wine-bar type, if you ask me.'

'Hasn't touched his gherkins. Refused fresh bitter. Shouldn't be here at all.'

'Couldn't agree more. I mean, look at his clothes.'

'Wonder how long since they were slept in.'

'If they ever have been.'

'Disgusting.'

'And what would you like to follow, love?'

This last was the barmaid. Simpson raised his head and gave a long yell of fury, bewilderment, horror and protest. Then he ran from the room and went on running until he was back at the point where the TIOPEPE was to pick him up. With shaking fingers he put the trance-pill into his mouth.

The Director broke the silence that followed the end of Simpson's story. 'Well, it's a long time ahead, anyway,' he said with an attempt at cheerfulness.

'Is it?' Simpson shouted. 'Do you think that sort of situation develops in a couple of weeks? It's starting to happen already. Wine-snobbery spreading, more and more of this drinking what you ought to drink instead of what you like. Self-conscious insistence on the virtues of pubs and beer because the wrong people are beginning to drink wine. It'll be here in our time, don't you worry. You just wait.'

'Ah, now, Simpson, you're tired and overwrought. A glass of champagne will soon make you see things in a different light.'

'Slip away with me afterwards,' I murmured. 'We'll have a good go at the beer down in town.'

Simpson gave a long yell – much like the one, probably, he vented at the end of his visit to 2010. Springing to his feet, he rushed away down the lab to where Schneider kept the medical stores.

'What's he up to?' the Director puffed as we hurried in pursuit. 'Is he going to try and poison himself?'

'Not straight away, sir, I imagine.'

'How do you mean, Baker?'

'Look at that bottle he's got hold of, sir. Can't you see what it is?'

'But . . . I can't believe my eyes. Surely it's . . .'

'Yes, sir. Surgical spirit.'

The Friends of Plonk

The (technical) success of Simpson's trip to the year 2010 encouraged the authorities to have similar experiments conducted for a variety of time-objectives. Some curious and occasionally alarming pieces of information about the future came to our knowledge in this way; I'm thinking less of politics than of developments in the domain of drink.

For instance, let me take this opportunity of warning every youngster who likes any kind of draught beer and has a high life-expectancy to drink as much of the stuff as he can while he can, because they're going to stop making it in 2016. Again, just six months ago Simpson found that, in the world of 2045, alcoholic diseases as a whole accounted for almost exactly a third of all deaths, or nearly as many as transport accidents and suicide combined. This was universally put down to the marketing, from 2039 onwards, of wines and spirits free of all the congeneric elements that cause hangovers, and yet at the same time indistinguishable from the untreated liquors even under the most searching tests – a triumph of biochemitechnology man had been teasingly on the brink of since about the time I was downing my first pints of beer.

Anyway, by a lucky accident, the authorities suddenly became anxious to know the result of the 2048 Presidential election in America, and so Simpson was able to travel to that year and bring back news, not only of the successful Rosicrucian candidate's impending installation at the Black House, but also of the rigorous outlawing of the new drink process and everything connected with it. After one veiled reference to the matter in conversation, Simpson had considered himself lucky to escape undamaged from the bar of the Travellers' Club.

For a time, our section's exploration of the rather more distant future was blocked by a persistent fault in the TIOPEPE, whereby the projection circuits cut off at approximately 83.63 years in advance of time-present. Then, one day in 1974, an inspired guess of Rabaiotti's put things right, and within a week Simpson was off to 2145. We were all there in the lab as usual to see him back safely. After Schneider had given him the usual relaxing shots, Simpson came out with some grave news. A quarrel about spy-flights over the moons of Saturn had set Wales and Mars – the two major powers in the Inner Planets at that period – at each other's throats and precipitated a system-wide nuclear war in 2101. Half of Venus, and areas on Earth the size of Europe, had been virtually obliterated.

Rabaiotti was the first to speak when Simpson had stopped. 'Far enough off not to bother most of our great-grandchildren, anyway,' he said.

'That's true. But what a prospect.'

'I know,' I said.

'Well, no use glooming, Baker,' the Director said. 'Nothing we can do about it. We've got a full half-hour before the official conference – tell us what's happened to drink.'

Simpson rubbed his bald head and sighed. I noticed that his eyes were bloodshot, but then they nearly always were after one of these trips. A very conscientious alcohologist, old Simpson. 'You're not going to like it.'

We didn't.

Simpson's landing in 2145 had been a fair enough success, but there had been an unaccountable error in the ground-level esti-mates, conducted a week earlier by means of our latest brain-child, the TIAMARIA (Temporal Inspection Apparatus and Meteor-ological-Astronomical-Regional-Interrelation Assessor). This had allowed him to materialize twelve feet up in the air and given him a nasty fall – on to a flower-bed, by an unearned piece of luck, but shaking him severely. What followed shook him still further.

The nuclear war had set everything back so much that the reconstructed world he found himself in was little more unfamiliar than the ones he had found on earlier, shorter-range time-trips. His official report, disturbing as it was, proved easy enough to compile, and he had a couple of hours to spare before the TIOPEPE's field should snatch him back to the present. He selected a restaurant within easy range of his purse – the TIAMARIA's cameras, plus our counterfeiters in the Temporal Treasury, had taken care of the currency problem all right – found a vacant table, and asked for a drink before dinner.

'Certainly, sir,' the waiter said. 'The Martian manatee-milk is specially good today. Or there's a new delivery of Iapetan carnivorous-lemon juice, if you've a liking for the unusual. Very, uh, full-blooded, sir.'

Simpson swallowed. 'I'm sure,' he said, 'but I was thinking of something – you know – a little stronger?'

The waiter's manner suffered an abrupt change. 'Oh, you mean booze, do you?' he said coldly. 'Sometimes I wonder what this town's coming to, honest. All right, I'll see what I can do.'

The 'booze' arrived on a tin tray in three chunky cans arranged like equal slices of a round cake. The nearest one had the word BEAR crudely stamped on it. Simpson poured some muddy brown liquid from it into a glass. It tasted like last week's swipes topped up with a little industrial alcohol. Then he tried the can stamped BOOJLY. (We all agreed later that this must be a corruption of 'Beaujolais'.) That was like red ink topped up with a good deal of industrial alcohol. Lastly there was BANDY. Industrial alcohol topped up with a little cold tea.

Wondering dimly if some trick of the TIOPEPE had managed to move him back into some unfrequented corner of the 1960s, Simpson became aware that a man at the next table had been watching him closely. When their eyes met, the stranger came over and, with a word of apology, sat down opposite him. (It was extraordinary, Simpson was fond of remarking, how often people did just this sort of thing when he visited the future.)

'Do excuse me,' the man said politely, 'but from your expression just now I'd guess you're a conozer – am I right? Oh, my name's Piotr Davies, by the way, on leave from Greenland Fruiteries. You're not Earth-based, I take it?'

'Oh . . . no, I'm just in from Mercury. My first trip since I was a lad, in fact.' Simpson noticed that Piotr Davies's face was covered by a thick network of burst veins, and his nose carried the richest growth of grog-blossom Simpson had ever seen. (He avoided looking at the Director when he told us this.) 'Yes,' he struggled on after giving his name, 'I am a bit of a connoiss – conozer, I suppose. I do try to discriminate a little in my—'

'You've hit it,' Piotr Davies said excitedly. 'Discrimination. That's it, the very word. I knew I was right about you. Discrimination. And tradition. Well, you won't find much of either on Earth these days, I'm afraid. Nor on Mercury, from what I hear.'

'No – no, you certainly won't.'

'We conozers are having a hard time. The Planetary War, of course. And the Aftermath.' Davies paused, and seemed to be sizing up Simpson afresh. Then: 'Tell me, are you doing anything tonight? More or less right away?'

'Well, I have got an appointment I must keep in just under two hours, but until then I—'

'Perfect. Let's go.'

'But what about my dinner?'

'You won't want any after you've been where I'm going to take you.'

'But where are you—?'

'Somewhere absolutely made for a conozer like you. What a bit of luck you happened to run into me. I'll explain on the way.'

Outside, they boarded a sort of wheel-less taxicab and headed into what seemed to be a prosperous quarter. Davies's explanations were copious and complete; Simpson made full use of his supposed status as one long absent from the centre of things. It appeared that the Planetary War had destroyed every one of the vast, centralized, fully automated distilleries of strong liquors;

that bacteriological warfare had put paid to many crops, including vines, barley, hops and even sugar; that the fanatical religious
movements of the Aftermath, many of them with government
backing, had outlawed all drink for nearly twenty years. Simpson
shuddered at that news.

'And when people came to their senses,' Davies said glumly,
'it was too late. The knowledge had died. Oh, you can't kill a
process like distillation. Too fundamental. Or fermentation,
either. But the special processes, the extra ingredients, the skills,
the *tradition* – gone for ever. Whisky – what a rich, evocative
word. What can the stuff have tasted like? What little there is
about it in the surviving literature gives a very poor idea. Muzzle
– that was a white wine, we're pretty sure, from Germany, about
where the Great Crater is. Gin – a spirit flavoured with juniper,
we know that much. There isn't any juniper now, of course.

'So, what with one thing and another, drinking went out. Real,
civilized drinking, that is – I'm not talking about that stuff they
tried to give you back there. I and a few like-minded friends tried
to get some of the basic information together, but to no avail.
And then, quite by chance, one of us, an archaeologist, turned
up a primitive two-dimensional television film that dated back
almost two hundred years, giving a full description of some
ancient drinks and a portrayal of the habits that went with them
– all the details. The film was called 'The Down-and-Outs', which
is an archaic expression referring to people of limited prosperity,
but which we immediately understood as being satirically or
ironically intended in this instance. That period, you know, was
very strong on satire. Anyway, the eventual result of our friend's
discovery was . . . this.'

With something of a flourish, Davies drew a pasteboard card
from his pocket and passed it to Simpson. It read:

THE FRIENDS OF PLONK
Established 2139 for the drinking of
traditional liquors in traditional
dress and in traditional surroundings

Before Simpson could puzzle this out, his companion halted the taxi and a moment later was shepherding him through the portals of a large and magnificent mansion. At the far end of a thickly carpeted foyer was a steep, narrow staircase, which they descended. When they came to its foot, Davies reached into a cupboard and brought out what Simpson recognized as a trilby hat of the sort his father had used to wear, a cloth cap, a large piece of sacking and a tattered brown blanket. All four articles appeared to be covered with stains and dirt. At the same time Simpson became aware of a curious and unpleasant mixture of smells and a subdued grumbling of voices.

In silence, Davies handed him the cap and the blanket and himself donned the sacking, stole-fashion, and the trilby. Simpson followed his lead. Then Davies ushered him through a low doorway.

The room they entered was dimly lit by candles stuck into bottles, and it was a moment before Simpson could take in the scene. At first he felt pure astonishment. There was no trace here of the luxury he had glimpsed upstairs: the walls, of undressed stone, were grimy and damp, the floor was covered at random with sacks and decaying lumps of matting. A coke stove made the cellar stiflingly hot; the air swam with cigarette smoke; the atmosphere was thick and malodorous. Against one wall stood a trestle table piled with bottles and what looked like teacups. Among other items Simpson uncomprehendingly saw there were several loaves of bread, some bottles of milk, a pile of small circular tins and, off in a corner, an old-fashioned and rusty gas-cooker or its replica.

But his surprise and bewilderment turned to mild alarm when he surveyed the dozen or so men sitting about on packing-cases or broken chairs and squatting or sprawling on the floor, each wearing some sort of battered headgear and with a blanket or sack thrown round his shoulders. All of them were muttering unintelligibly, in some instances to a companion, more often just to themselves. Davies took Simpson's arm and led him to a splintery bench near the wall.

'These blankets and so on must have been a means of asserting the essential democracy of drink,' Davies whispered. 'Anyway, we're near the end of the purely ritualistic part now. Our film didn't make its full significance clear, but it was obviously a kind of self-preparation, perhaps even prayer. The rest of the proceedings will be much less formal. Ah . . .'

Two of the men had been muttering more loudly at each other and now closed physically, but their blows and struggles were symbolic, a mime, as in ballet or the Japanese theatre. Soon one of them had his adversary pinned to the floor and was raining token punches upon him. ('We're rather in the dark about this bit,' Davies murmured. 'Perhaps an enacted reference to the ancient role of drink as a sequel to physical exertion.') When the prostrate combatant had begun to feign unconsciousness, a loud and authoritative voice spoke.

'End of Part One.'

At once all was animation: everybody sprang up and threw off his borrowed garments, revealing himself as smartly clad in the formal dress of the era. Davies led Simpson up to the man who had made the announcement, probably a member of one of the professions and clearly the host of the occasion. His face was sprayed with broken veins to a degree that outdid Davies's.

'Delighted you can join us,' the host said when Simpson's presence had been explained. 'A privilege to have an Outworlder at one of our little gatherings. Now for our Part Two. Has Piotr explained to you about the ancient film that taught us so much? Well, its second and third sections were so badly damaged as to be almost useless to us. So what's to follow is no more than an imaginative reconstruction, I fear, but I think it can be said that we've interpreted the tradition with taste and reverence. Let's begin, shall we?'

He signed to an attendant standing at the table; the man began filling the teacups with a mixture of two liquids. One came out of something like a wine-bottle and was red, the other came out of something like a medicine bottle and was almost transparent, with a faint purplish tinge. Courteously passing Simpson the first of the cups, the host said: 'Please do us the honour of initiating the proceedings.'

Simpson drank. He felt as if someone had exploded a tear-gas shell in his throat and then sprayed his gullet with curry-powder. As his own coughings and weepings subsided he was surprised to find his companions similarly afflicted in turn as they drank.

'Interesting, isn't it?' the host asked, wheezing and staggering. 'A fine shock to the palate. One might perhaps say that it goes beyond the merely gustatory and olfactory to the purely tactile. Hardly a sensuous experience at all – ascetic, almost abstract. An invention of genius, don't you think?'

'What – what's the . . . ?'

'Red Biddy, my dear fellow,' Piotr Davies put in proudly. There was reverence in his voice when he added: 'Red wine and methylated spirits. Of course, we can't hope to reproduce the legendary Empire Burgundy characters that used to go into it, but our own humble Boojly isn't a bad substitute. Its role is purely ancillary, after all.'

'We like to use a straw after the first shock.' The host passed one to Simpson. 'I hope you approve of the teacups. A nice traditional touch, I think. And now, do make yourself comfortable. I must see to the plonk in person – one can't afford to take risks.'

Simpson sat down near Davies on a packing-case. He realized after a few moments that it was actually carved out of a single block of wood. Then he noticed that the dampness of the walls was maintained by tiny water-jets at intervals near the ceiling. Probably the sacks on the floor had been specially woven and then artificially aged. Pretending to suck at his straw, he said nervously to Davies: 'What exactly do you mean by plonk? In my time, people usually . . .' He broke off, fearful of having betrayed himself, but the man of the future had noticed nothing.

'Ah, you're in for a great experience, my dear friend, something unknown outside this room for countless decades. To our ancestors in the later twentieth century it may have been the stuff of daily life, but to us it's a pearl beyond price, a precious fragment salvaged from the wreck of history. Watch carefully – every bit of this is authentic.'

With smarting eyes, Simpson saw his host pull the crumb from a loaf and stuff it into the mouth of an enamel jug. Then, taking a candle from a nearby bottle, he put the flame to a disc-shaped cake of brownish substance that the attendant was holding between tongs. A flame arose; liquid dropped on to the bread and began to soak through into the jug; the assembled guests clapped and cheered. Another brownish cake was treated in the same way, then another. 'Shoe-polish,' Simpson said in a cracked voice.

'Exactly. We're on the dark tans this evening, with just a touch of ox-blood to give body. Makes a very big, round, pugnacious drink. By the way, that's processed bread he's using. Wholemeal's too permeable, we've found.'

Beaming, the host came over to Simpson with a half-filled cup, a breakfast cup this time. 'Down in one, my dear chap,' he said.

They were all watching; there was nothing for it. Simpson shut his eyes and drank. This time a hundred blunt dental drills seemed to be working at once on his nose and throat and mouth. Fluid sprang from all the mucous membranes in those areas. It was like having one's face pushed into a bath of acid. Simpson's shoulders sagged and his eyes filmed over.

'I'd say the light tans have got more bite,' a voice said near him. 'Especially on the gums.'

'Less of a follow-through, on the other hand.' There was the sound of swallowing and then a muffled scream. 'Were you here for the plain-tan tasting last month? Wonderful fire and vehemence. I was blind for the next four days.'

'I still say you can't beat a straight brown for all-round excoriation. Amazing results on the uvula and tonsils.'

'What's wrong with black?' This was a younger voice.

An embarrassed silence, tempered by a fit of coughing and a heartfelt moan from different parts of the circle, was ended by someone saying urbanely: 'Each to his taste, of course, and there is impact there, but I think experience shows that that sooty, oil-smoke quality is rather meretricious. Most of us find ourselves moving tanwards as we grow older.'

'Ah, good, he's . . . yes, he's using a tin of transparent in the next jug. Watch for the effect on the septum.'

Simpson lurched to his feet. 'I must be going,' he muttered. 'Important engagement.'

'What, you're not staying for the coal-gas in milk? Turns the brain to absolute jelly, you know.'

'Sorry . . . friend waiting for me.'

'Goodbye, then. Give our love to Mercury. Perhaps you'll be able to start a circle of the Friends of Plonk on your home planet. That would be a magnificent thought.'

'Magnificent,' the Director echoed bitterly. 'Just think of it. The idea of an atomic war's too much to take in, but those poor devils . . . Baker, we must prepare some information for Simpson to take on his next long-range trip, something that'll show them how to make a decent vodka or gin even if the vines have all gone.'

I was hardly listening. 'Aren't there some queer things about that world, sir? Shoe-polish in just the same variants that we know? Wholemeal bread when the crops are supposed to have —'

I was interrupted by a shout from the far end of the lab, where Rabaiotti had gone to check the TIAMARIA. He turned and came racing towards us, babbling at the top of his voice.

'Phase distortion, sir! Anomalous tracking on the output side! Completely new effect!'

'And the TIOPEPE's meshed with it, isn't it?' Schneider said.

'Of course!' I yelled. 'Simpson was on a different time-path, sir! An alternative probability, a parallel world. No wonder the ground-level estimate was off. This is amazing!'

'No nuclear war in our time-path – no certainty, anyway,' the Director sang, waving his arms.

'No destruction of the vines.'

'No Friends of Plonk.'

'All the same,' Simpson murmured to me as we strolled towards the Conference Room, 'in some ways they're better off than we are. At least the stuff they use is genuine. Nobody's going to doctor bloody shoe-polish to make it taste smoother or to preserve it or so that you'll mistake it for a more expensive brand. And it can only improve, what they drink.'

'Whereas we . . .'

'Yes. That draught beer you go on about isn't draught at all: it comes out of a giant steel bottle these days, because it's easier that way. And do you think the Germans are the greatest chemists in the world for nothing? Ask Schneider about the 1972 Moselles. And what do you imagine all those scientists are doing in Bordeaux?'

'There's Italy and Spain and Greece. They'll—'

'Not Italy any more. Ask Rabaiotti, or rather don't. Spain and Greece'll last longest, probably, but by 1980 you'll have to go to Albania if you want real wine. Provided the Chinese won't have started helping them to get the place modernized.'

'What are you going to do about it?'

'Switch to whisky. That's still real. In fact I'm going to take a bottle home tonight. Can you lend me twenty-five quid?'

Too Much Trouble

Until almost the other day, we on the time-travel project knew much more about the twenty-first century than about the remaining years of our own. Persistent instabilities in the TIOPEPE had had unpredictable and disturbing consequences whenever we set our objective any nearer than 1995. One such attempt had put Simpson down in what we afterwards computed to have been 8200 or so, where he had immediately found himself being chased across country by a number of creatures resembling giant vegetable marrows covered in scales and with half a dozen legs apiece, doubtless from some other planet, but he had had no leisure or desire to observe them closely, let alone set about looking for a drink. Our second attempt at a short-range projection, thanks to an unsuspected build-up of negative feedback, had landed the unlucky fellow back in the days of the Black Death, and resulted in a three months' quarantine inside the lab for the lot of us.

The period of confinement, however, meant that we got a lot of work done. Rabaiotti and I really settled down to the instability problem, and by the end of the three months had come up with an answer, a kind of elaborate anti-overshoot servomechanism now known as the TAITTINGER – Temporal Accuracy Injector and Time-Travel Indeterminacy Nullifier (General Electric and Rank). We duly reported our success to the authorities and sat back to await instructions, which promptly arrived.

On Easter Tuesday, 1975, we received orders to report on how far the occupation of Mars was going to have gone by 1983. Within twenty-four hours we had everything lined up and shot Simpson forward eight years to the day.

In all technical respects, the operation could not have gone off better. Simpson reappeared in the receiver exactly on schedule, alive and well. Or fairly well. He looked haggard and in the depths of gloom, though that was nothing out of the ordinary after a time-trip. What startled us was that he had clearly been in a fight, his face battered and his clothing torn and dirty. Schneider gave him a tranquillizing shot and started to clean him up.

'What happened, man?' the Director demanded. 'What did they do to you?'

'Oh, this,' Simpson said, indicating his face. 'That's nothing. It's what I saw and heard . . . Listen, all of you. We've got to sell up and buy an island somewhere. Somewhere they can't get at us.'

'You mean there's going to be an invasion or something?' Schneider asked.

Simpson shook his head slowly. 'Oh no. I'd have come across the results of anything like that in my trips to the 2000s, wouldn't I? No, it's just . . . the life we're going to be leading. So soon. Give me a drink. A strong one.'

Schneider frowned, but made no other objection when I poured a stiff shot from the medicine-cupboard brandy bottle and passed it to Simpson. He downed it in two gulps and, hesitantly at first, told us his tale.

At first sight, London seemed quite unchanged: demolition and construction works everywhere, vast unoccupied blocks already beginning to deteriorate, road repairs at hundred-metre intervals with their familiar two-man work-gangs, barely moving crowds overflowing the pavements, and the traffic averaging perhaps three kilometres an hour, little if at all lower than the 1975 rate. About half of it consisted of private cars towing trailers piled with coloured plastic bins or containers, which was a novelty, but Simpson let it lie for the moment, and concentrated on making his way from his arrival-point – a w.c. in the Oxford Circus public lavatory, pre-probed by the TIAMARIA and found vacant for the necessary few seconds – down Regent Street to Piccadilly Circus.

Arrived there on foot no more than half an hour later, he again found a very recognizable scene. The Eros statue had gone, and this gave him a brief pang, but it was unexpectedly reassuring to find the drop-outs still there (so to speak) in their hundreds on the main traffic island and the surrounding pavements, sleeping and meditating and taking trips, twanging their electric *rebahbs* – the Moorish thing had really caught on, then – and playing their transwristors, chanting their traditional slogans in tribute to the victories of Greater Vietnam and the glorious dead of the London School of Economics, no doubt fornicating here and there among the discarded hypodermics and the piles of leaflets, assaulting passers-by and fighting the occasional policeman. Several times, Simpson heard American accents among the main stream of pedestrians, and concluded that this had remained a major stop on the sight-seeing route between Buckingham Palace and the Tower of London.

Within twenty minutes he had reached St James's Square and was climbing the steps of the London Library, the facilities of which had proved invaluable on several of his previous, longer-range trips. But this time the doors were closed and the building was evidently deserted. This was a considerable set-back. In a fit of anxious irritation he thumped violently at the woodwork.

'Shut, mate,' called a cheerful voice behind him.

'So I see.' Simpson descended the steps and approached the speaker, a middle-aged man in overalls who, cigarette in mouth, was leaning against the door of a car parked at the kerb. 'Do you happen to know why?'

'Know why? You forgotten what day it is?'

'Wednesday. What about it?'

'What about it? It's *Easter* Wednesday. Don't expect anything to be open today, do you? Where've you been, anyhow?'

'Oh, abroad. Only got back this morning.'

'Where abroad? Same everywhere, I thought, bar Israel.'

'I've been in space too,' Simpson said, improvising hastily. 'You know, Mars and so on.'

'Oh, yeah.' The man lost interest at once.

'Do I understand you to say *everything*'s shut? All the libraries and reading-rooms, all that?'

'That's right. It's the Easter slack period, see. Good Wednesday
through to Easter Friday and then the weekend. As usual.'

Simpson was shocked and shaken. The ordinary six-day Easter
holiday, from Good Thursday to Easter Tuesday, was fair and
reasonable, but this was insane. 'So nothing'll be open before
Monday morning.'

'Tuesday afternoon. Chum, you really have been in space,
haven't you?'

'Sorry . . . Look, where can I buy a newspaper?'

'A *newspaper*?' The stranger reacted as if Simpson had inquired
about the purchase of an elephant. 'In the slack period?'

'Oh yes. So I'd have to wait for that until . . . today week.'

'You'd get a *News-Standard* then, yeah. If you want a daily
it'll be tomorrow week. It must be, let's see, the *Times-Guardian*'s
turn. That's right, it was the *Express-Telegraph* last week, the
week before Easter, rather.'

'Thanks,' Simpson said dully. He was striving to think how he
could gain access to some public source of information before
his time was up and he had to return. 'Er . . . I've got a report to
write for my firm. In a hurry. About, well, recent events. Is there
anywhere at all, any agency, any Government department,
research centre, emergency service that might . . . ?'

The man was staring at Simpson and smiling broadly, with
the expression of a contemporary garage mechanic, say, telling
a customer that the spare part for his car had not turned up, but
much intensified. It was obviously a rare and delicious experience
for him to have found somebody so well qualified to be informed
that he could not get what he wanted anywhere on Earth (and
no doubt on the planets, too). 'There's nothing, friend,' he said
finally. 'Nothing at all. Think yourself lucky you haven't got a
broken leg, eh?'

'And no drinks.' Simpson had thought aloud.

'Now drinks, that's a different matter,' the stranger said, his
manner growing perceptibly warmer. 'The pubs are open –

Sunday hours, of course. In fact, I was thinking of dropping in for a pint myself. There's a place just up there, before you get to Jermyn Street. Care to join me?'

Simpson accepted with some relief, an emotion that changed to alarm when he realized, a minute later, that the pub in question was one he often used himself. It would be highly embarrassing to meet the 1983 Simpson in there. Then reason returned: he had only to remember to steer clear of the area when this day came round for the second time in his life, and all, or at least that much, would be well.

He exchanged names with his companion, who was called Ernie Mullins and said he worked in a vegetable factory.

'Oh, really?' Simpson said. 'What, er, what side of it are you on?'

'Vending. Outlet apparatus inspector.'

'I see. Whereabouts is this?'

'South-West Area. Leatherhead. It's not much of a job I've got, but it means a big part of Fetch-and-Carry's off my mind.'

Simpson did not like to question such a clearly basic concept as Fetch-and-Carry. Instead, he asked: 'I suppose you get a fair amount of custom out there, these days?'

'Yes, pretty fair. On a full working day we get nearly two hundred thousand, which is over half a million in a full working week. A lot more than that before the slack periods, of course. And the second week in December's murder, when they're buying for all that time ahead.'

'That many customers in Leatherhead?' Simpson inquired with careful casualness.

'Well, there are six million people in the South-West Area now, don't forget. I think we're overloaded myself. People ought to have bigger deep-freezes, so they could stock up for three months instead of three weeks. But there's not the room. Here we are.'

They were about to enter the pub when its door was jerked open from the inside and three struggling men began to emerge. One of them (a powerful pig-faced character who turned out to be the landlord, and to whom Simpson took an instant dislike) was trying to expel another (a long-haired, heavily bearded person of about forty) with some assistance from the third (a near-replica of Ernie Mullins). All three were shouting angrily.

'Fascist bastard!' the bearded man yelled. 'Power-structure élitist!'

'Get bloody lost! Get back to your sit-in!' This was the landlord. 'You can't treat me like your Board of Governors!'

'You irrelevant authoritarian! You pathetic oligarch!'

'Can't you read?' the third man demanded, pointing to a sign above the doorway that proclaimed: NO STUDENTS ALOWED.

'Of course he can't read, Joe, don't make me laugh, he's a student, isn't he? Now, you, bugger off back to your boycott before I get cross! Ernie, give us a hand.'

Not very willingly, Ernie gave a hand, and in no time, still bawling accusations of Fascism, pathos and irrelevance, the bearded man was reeling off towards the square. Simpson was introduced to the landlord, who nodded and went back into his house, and to Joe, who shook hands amiably and suggested a pint on him.

The bar of the pub was superficially as Simpson remembered it, but he soon saw that the counter was lined with dispensing machines of various sorts, past which a thick queue was laboriously shuffling. He went along behind Joe and Ernie, and was eventually handed a large plastic beaker. When the time came, Joe put some coins into a slot on a machine marked BITTER, collected three small packets from an aperture in it, and handed one each to the other two. He led them past other machines labelled MILD, STOUT, SCOTCH, GIN, VODKER – from the last-named three, stubby pipes emerged – PORK PIE, SOSSIDGE, HAM SANGWIDGE and CRISPS. At the end of the counter, Joe took three smaller packets from a dispenser, doled out two of these as before, and nearly filled his beaker with what proved to be plain water. When the others had done the same, the trio moved away from the counter into the middle of a considerable crowd of drinkers, all standing: there was nowhere to sit down.

Joe and Ernie, followed by Simpson, dropped their larger packets unopened into their beakers. In a few seconds they had
dissolved, wrapping and all, producing a clear lightish-brown
liquid. The smaller packets went in similarly, and a foamy head
formed.

'Cheers,' Joe said.

'Let's be lucky,' Ernie said.

'All the best,' Simpson said tentatively.

This proved acceptable, and they drank. The 'bitter' was bland,
by no means unpalatable, and without either much resemblance
to the beer Simpson was used to or any particular character of
its own. (He told us it bore very much the same relation to our
bitter as powdered coffee to coffee.)

'Well, what do you think of it?' Ernie asked, but before Simpson could reply a sort of altercation had broken out at the bar.

'Do something about it, then!' an elderly man was repeatedly
shouting at the landlord, who after a time switched off the miniature television set he had been watching and waddled impatiently
up to the counter.

'Give over, can't you?' he said. 'What can I do?'

'Repair the bloody thing! I want vodka and I'm going to have
vodka!'

'Not this week you're not! The machine's broke and that's
that!'

'Replace the bloody unit, then!' the elderly man yelled. 'Or get
a mechanic on to it!'

'You off your rocker? What's a mechanic? And how can I
replace it now? Look, you take a gin on the house and pipe
down.'

This was evidently thought suitable, and the hubbub died
away. Simpson turned to his companions.

'Bad management, running out of vodka in the middle of a
holiday.'

'Oh, he's not run out,' Joe said. 'Just the dispensing unit gone.
Might happen to anybody.'

'You mean there's plenty of the stuff around, but it isn't coming

through to the tap? Well, why can't he take it from the bottle or
the tank or whatever it is? That wouldn't be any—'

'Too much trouble, mate. You can't expect him to do that.'

'Good God! He's got a pretty soft life, that landlord, hasn't
he?'

'Has he hell! Think of Fetch-and-Carry in a place like this.'

'Fetch-and-Carry?' Though he had heard the phrase already,
Simpson was now comparatively relaxed and off his guard, and
for a moment he revealed his total bewilderment.

Joe and Ernie looked at each other and seemed to make up
their minds. Ernie spoke.

'You've been inside, Simmy, haven't you? You can tell us.'

Simpson in his turn came to a decision. 'Yes.'

'Course you have. Nothing to be ashamed of. Goes on all the
time. The wife's brother, he was in eleven years. It's the strain,
see. Treat you all right, did they?'

'Not too bad.' (Neither then, nor later, did Simpson establish
what he had been inside, whether gaol or madhouse or some
new-fashioned place of confinement.)

'So they ought. Well, you'll be needing to know about Fetch-
and-Carry. Where are you going to live?'

'Oh . . . just round here.'

'Fine, you'll be South-West Area, then. The thing is, draw up
your week's timetable and stick to it. Mondays do your burnable
rubbish out at the Coulsdon dump. That'll take you the morning
and some of the afternoon. Fill in the rest of the time with your
shoes or the cleaners' or your fancy shopping. Tuesday take your
unburnables down to Mitcham, then fetch your meat from
Epsom or your fish from Weybridge or your booze from Ascot,
if you can afford any. Wednesdays you'll want to do the Post
Office, and that's where Joe comes in. He's in the S-W GPO at
Staines.'

'It's not such a bad trip as it sounds,' Joe said. 'We're pretty
organized there. Shouldn't take you more than a couple of hours
to sort out your mail and any telegrams, and then you can go
straight to your telephone period. I'll fix that for you.'

Simpson looked his incomprehension.

'It's easy enough. You go to your booth, see, and you take your incoming calls first is the best way to handle it. After that you make your outgoings.'

'What's happened to private phones?'

'Oh, that was all stopped. They were always going wrong, and more people kept wanting one, and it was too much trouble driving out just to do the one job. The big offices and that, they run their own booth systems. Under licence from us, of course.'

'Then . . . the whole system of services has packed up?'

'They're trying to do away with what's left of it, yeah.'

'Same with things like milk? Laundry? Newspapers?'

'Same with everything, Simmy, mate. Thursdays and Fridays, now, when they bring out the dailies, you'll find it's a good scheme to pick 'em up at the Area newsagent in Woking, between your calls at Leatherhead and Ascot, say, about one-thirty or two.'

'But, I mean, what about repairs and so on? You can't take a whole television set or washing machine back to the shop just because some tiny thing's gone wrong.'

'Oh, can't you? That's what a lot of the Fetch-and-Carry's about today. The places stay open over the slack, see, because they're all automated. The guv'nor here'll be off to Norwood with his vodka machine before he opens tomorrow. Not for repairs, though. Pick up a new one.'

'But that's completely uneconomic.'

'Maybe it is, but it's what you do. Only way you can save trouble.'

Simpson tried to think. 'So it comes to this. You do very little actual work, but you spend all your free time doing the things for yourself that it's too much trouble for other people to do for you.'

'You learn quick. That's just how it goes. Only way they can get you to take trouble. We caught on to it first – you know, the British. Then everywhere else went down the same road. We led the way there.'

'We would,' Simpson said through his teeth.

A silence fell between the three, though there was quite enough ambient noise from the other drinkers. Wearily, Simpson drained his beaker, and the smooth, denatured taste faded at once from his mouth. A thought struggled to the surface of his mind.

'Can you get wine these days?' he asked.

'Plenty,' Ernie said. 'Burgundy, claret, hock, all that. I don't go for it myself, but it's easy enough. You pick up your wine-cakes from Ascot, stick 'em in a jug when you get home, add water, and in five minutes—'

'Wine-cakes! *Christ!*'

'Keep your voice down, mate,' Joe advised, moving Simpson a little away from a couple of burly labouring types who had turned round with an unfriendly stare. 'There's alcohol in the things, same as in the beer-cakes. I don't know how they do it, but they do. You'll see. Come on, what about another? Forget our sorrows.'

'My turn,' Simpson said. 'No, Ernie, let me, I'd like to.'

'How are you for cash?'

Simpson produced his wallet, which was stuffed with pound notes unimprovably forged by our Temporal Treasury. 'That ought to be enough, oughtn't it?'

'Fine, but have you got change? Thirty pence a pint, it is.'

'Ninety altogether. I can give him a pound and get ten pence change.'

'Well . . . you can't, Simmy, sorry. Nobody gives change any more, except at the change shops. You got to have the exact money, because it's—'

'I know!' Simpson shrieked. This last, trivial revelation turned his mounting despair to fury. 'It's too much trouble! Too much trouble to hand over a coin! Too much bloody trouble! What's the matter with you all? Oh, you two are decent enough blokes, but you're spineless! You've given in to the system! You must fight it!'

He yelled more in the same strain, but could not afterwards remember just what. Indeed, the whole situation immediately became confused. He took a swingeing punch on the ear, probably from one of the labourers who had glared at him earlier, and staggered sideways into the throng away from Ernie and Joe, whom he saw no more. Further blows fell on him, accompanied by shouts of 'Student! Another bloody student! Let's do this one up proper!' The landlord arrived, not, it transpired, to separate the combatants, nor to throw Simpson out, but to join in beating him up.

Things were looking desperate, and Simpson was dimly relinquishing hopes of ever returning to 1975, when a new arrival, previously unseen, entered the fray on his side. With swift, well-aimed punches this person disposed of the immediate opposition and hauled Simpson out into the street. They ran. Guided by his rescuer, Simpson stumbled into an alley and found himself pushed behind a fire-escape. In the middle distance were sounds of a pursuit assembling.

'This is a cul-de-sac,' Simpson panted.

'That's why they won't look here yet,' the other man said, breathing easily.

'God, you're in good trim. Back there, the way you—'

'I ought to be. I've had eight years to train for this.'

The voice was eerily familiar. So – Simpson studied it for the first time – was the face. A little balder, a little redder, but . . .

'My God . . . it's you. I mean me.'

'If we stick to regarding each other as two different persons, which we are, we'll get on better,' Simpson II said, with the authority of one who has everything thought out in advance. 'We've got a moment's breather now. You'd better use it.'

'But how do I get back?' Simpson asked wildly, ignoring this advice.

'I'll show you. It's all lined up.'

'Why did they send you?'

'I was the only really fit man on the team,' (Simpson grinned at each of us in turn when he reached this part of his story) 'and we didn't dare tell anyone else. I knew the exact situation in the pub, too.'

'You took your time about coming.'

'Sorry. I had a long journey. And then there was traffic. Big meeting in Trafalgar Square about legalizing heroin.'

A straggle of men calling for student blood ran inefficiently past the open end of the alley. When the sounds had died away, Simpson II pulled Simpson out of cover and led him across to a dilapidated and empty garage.

'In here. Quick. Put this in your pocket.'

'What is it?'

'Full report on the occupation of Mars.'

'But . . .' It took Simpson, flustered as he was, a moment to remember what was his official reason for being there at all. Then he recoiled. 'But I can't transfer something from one time to another! They're always on about it, especially the Director. Danger of a paradox or a—'

Speaking with great emphasis, Simpson II swept this objection aside. (Simpson, now almost cheerful, insisted on reporting verbatim the terms in which he did so.) 'If you leave it behind, you'll have failed in your mission so totally that you'll never get a decent job again. And you're going to need that for the money. And since I've lived through what's going to happen to you after this, I know you're going to have taken it with you, so get on with it and stop arguing.'

'All right. Thanks.'

'A pleasure.'

Simpson was about to depart when he remembered something vital, and turned. 'Hey, before I go – is the drink situation really quite hopeless?'

'Put it this way,' Simpson II said in a hurry, 'the 1981 El Minya whites are almost . . .'

He broke off abruptly as shouts and running footfalls came into earshot again. Propelled by his rescuer, Simpson half-fell through the garage doorway and at once the TIOPEPE grabbed him.

'El Minya,' the Director said. 'Somewhere in Spain, no doubt. Never heard of it. Anyway, the Spanish white wines are all terrible, aren't they? Still, I suppose when there's nothing else . . .'

'They'd be in wine-cakes like the rest of the stuff.' Simpson's earlier gloom had returned in full.

Rabaiotti said nothing. I said nothing. Schneider had slipped away, perhaps to fetch the drinks we so sorely needed.

'Well,' the Director said, trying to strike a consoling note, 'it's just a phase, isn't it? That's the way to look at it. After all, everything was all right again in 2010 when you went there, Simpson. And the position couldn't have cured itself in a couple of months.'

'No, it might take twenty years. That's 1990. Say ten of those twenty years to get things back into reasonable shape. That's 2000. Say the 1983 situation had only been going in full for three years, which is pretty bloody optimistic. That's 1980. So from then until 2000 or so it'll be wine-cakes and beer-cakes. Oh, it'll look like a phase from 2050 all right. But what good's that?'

'There's spirits,' Rabaiotti muttered.

'I didn't taste those. I expect they'll make you drunk, though. Which is how I intend to be for the duration of the phase.'

The others nodded hopelessly. Then Schneider came tearing back into the lab, a large book held open in front of him.

'El Minya!' he screeched. 'El Minya!'

In a moment we were clustered round him. 'What is it? What have you—?'

'I knew I knew it! It was one of the German objectives in 1943. It's not in Spain, it's in Egypt. On the Nile. Here, look at the atlas. Don't you see? Israel! The only place where that Ernie chap said things were different!'

'But Israel only goes up to the Suez Canal in that part,' I objected.

'Now it does! *Now* it does! Just the other day there was a report that they were preparing to get on the march again. The finest agriculturalists in the world! Who can make the desert blossom like a rose! Or flourish like a vine!'

The Director looked round the circle, beaming. 'Saved, gentle-men! No wonder you, Simpson, or rather the other you, said you'd had a long journey. All the way from Jerusalem!'

Investing in Futures

'There's no risk involved and no one else I can send,' the Director said imploringly. 'Please help me, you four – we've been through a lot together, after all. I just have to know the answer about those damned vines. And you appreciate why.'

Our association had started back in the old days of the first temporal probes. Then, under a still-secret programme, the government had used our Unit to explore the nearer future and find answers to some of its more awkward problems. And we of the Unit, being all of us rather interested in the fortunes of our own chosen kind of alcoholic drink, had privately used those chances to explore the future of vintage port (the Director's obsession), my own humble draught beer, and so on with the rest of the team.

All that was over. The probes had long been stopped as uneconomic. The Unit was disbanded and the Director had for years been, officially, sadly, the ex-Director. But he had sounded quite as excited and secretive as his old self when, two days previously, he had telephoned me and asked me to get the others together at an obscure address in Soho. The four of us had turned up on the dot, all agog.

He had begun no less mysteriously by running over the known and abominated career of phylloxera XO, the deadly sub-species of vine-aphid first seen in the Bordeaux vineyards in 1984, classified and named in California three years later, rampaging everywhere by the end of the '80s and now, in 1993, the apparently invincible curse that had reduced world wine-production to 59% of 1986 levels. He continued with fresh data: using revolutionary forced-growth techniques, French agricultural scientists had succeeded in developing five new strains of vine, which early tests had shown to be resistant to all forms of phylloxera including the XO. But early tests were early tests: it would take ten years of growth in the soil, of successive harvest, of standing up to the assaults of the deadly little insects before any of the new strains could be pronounced proof against them and systematic replanting begun. Five special areas in Burgundy were ready for the ten-year trials. 'And that,' the Director had said with relish, 'is where we come in. Literally. Or to be even more precise, it's where you come in, Simpson.'

At that old Simpson, our traveller on previous time-trips, just gaped.

'Yes. You're off to the year 2003 as soon as we can arrange it. You'll bring back reports on all five of the experimental vineyards. Cuttings too if possible.'

'Against Temporal Regs, sir,' I objected. 'Inter-sectoral transfers are out.'

'I'm sorry, Baker, we'll have to overlook that. This whole thing is – well, not very official anyway, or even legal. But just consider. Frankly, I'm not a rich man. I doubt whether any of you are either – one doesn't get rich in this business. But anyone who knows the result of those long-term trials now, in 1993, is going to know something very valuable. Do you – if I may so express myself – read me?'

There was a new stir of interest. 'But how would anyone get there, sir?' I demurred. 'All the hardware was broken up ages ago.'

'That's where you're wrong. At least not all of it has proved impossible to reassemble. With a little goodwill. If all goes well we could share the cost, eh?'

'I'm ten years out of touch, sir.' This was Rabaiotti, my senior assistant.

'We're all getting on a bit, sir,' said Schneider, our former MO.

Which was when the Director came out with the appeal I quoted earlier, and after that it was just a question of detail.

When, the following week, we assembled in a sort of dungeon off Whitehall we found waiting for us the good old modified TALISKER (Temporal Accelerator with Latent-Indeterminacy Suppressor and Kinetic-Energy Recompensator) that had served us so well in the past – or should I say, in bygone futures? Rabaiotti fed the power, took a long look, ran his hands over the relay banks, nodded slowly at me and started punching co-ordinates. Schneider was passing his hand-scanner over Simpson. The Director called me over to meet a tall swarthy man whom he introduced as a friend of his, a Dr Hanif Khan.

I didn't know why, but I immediately felt there was something odd about Dr Khan, not suspect exactly, just odd, something too that was unknown to the Director. Before speaking Khan produced what looked like a small old-fashioned television set with attachments but which I recognized as one of the new boson microscopes.

"I'm a botanist specializing in vines,' Khan said. His manner was disarming enough. 'Used to be quite a tough job, you know. Not any more, thanks to this jigger. Quite frightening, what it can see. In fact nobody seems quite sure what it can't see. Anyway, one thing it will certainly be able to see is whatever we may want to know about what your chap brings back from, er, over the way. No problem.'

I nodded appreciatively.

'Well, Hanif,' the Director said, 'would you like to run your eye over our baby here? If you have any questions I'll no doubt prove incompetent to answer them.'

True enough. I made to go along but Khan politely held up his hand.

'You've plenty to see to, Dr Baker. I mustn't interfere with any of that.'

So I let them get on with it while I checked and rechecked the settings with Rabaiotti, sat Simpson on the stool and pressed the SEND/RETURN strap, a feature of the TALISKER that caused him to vanish and reappear in no time at all, though subjectively he had spent over four hours away. There was some dirt on his face and rather more on his clothes; otherwise he seemed none the worse. Schneider forbade contact until he had scanned him out, micro-scoured him and handed him a large Scotch and water. Then we crowded round and listened to his story.

The date keyed into the TALISKER was 15 July 2003, selected on the reasoning that after celebrating Bastille Day the day before many Frenchmen would be in a state of reduced curiosity and vigilance when Simpson turned up in their midst. As it happened nobody saw him arrive in a secluded hollow in the hills above Beaune. At once aware of the great surrounding silence, he checked his position and surveyed his route.

It was 4 p.m. and the sun was shining. The special vineyards lay grouped round a central research station seven kilometres to the south-west. He had plenty of time to make his way to that station and, in the character of a visiting oenologist from New South Wales, fix himself a brief tour of the vineyards. If unable to secure cuttings or in any other difficulty he was to conceal himself and operate after dark.

His journey would be made on foot. Temporal Regulations strongly disfavoured the use of futural transport and, after an encounter with a subway escalator in 2062, he had been happy to abide by them. With a last check of map and compass (stereo-map and lumen-compass, naturally) he set off in good spirits down the grassy slopes. Once or twice he took a deep breath. The air was strikingly pure, even for such a very remote spot as this appeared, though the bird population was plentiful and busy enough.

Simpson was a claret man and had often visited the Bordeaux villages and vineyards, and if he had known those of Burgundy even one-quarter as well he might have started to ask himself questions sooner than he did. As it was he went happily on until a glance at the map showed he should be near the main Beaune–Pommard road – no, wait: should have crossed it a hundred metres back. There was no such road on the ground, no road at all anywhere that he could see, though he had passed close to more than one earth track. What was to be seen of the work of man? From higher up he had spotted a couple of churches, a large house with towers at each end, the roofs of a small village, a windmill. From here a rutted path led past a crude wooden hut and out of sight. Poor crops of some unfamiliar cereal – millet, perhaps, or rye – covered part of the hillside. Nothing else.

He had decided that he must have crossed that road after all, that the mud-slide he remembered picking his way over had surely buried a long section of it, when he heard voices approaching round the bend of the path he was standing on. Without hesitation he ran for the shelter of a low bank topped with bushes and peered out from there. He could not have said what had induced him to hide.

In a moment a farm-cart of sorts drawn by a skinny horse rattled and jolted into view. A lank-haired fellow of about thirty held the reins and plied a whip, an older man sat beside him, another man and a woman lolled in the body of the cart among a load of swedes or other root-crop. The four were calling out roughly to one another in what Simpson, with his goodish but limited French, identified as an uncouth local dialect. All were deeply tanned, none wore anything much better than rags, and a strong animal odour drifted across as they went by. The impression they gave of brutal debasement was overpowering.

Before they were out of sight a dreadful suspicion from the back of Simpson's mind had hardened into certainty. Twice in 1991 the world had come near to war, first over the Khvoy incident, then again during the siege of Durban. The third crisis must have come and this time not gone away. What he had just been looking at was a group of the survivors, the pitiful remnants of humanity after the great catastrophe. But was such thorough-going degeneration possible in ten years or less? Had the TALISKER taken him further into the future than intended? Firmly he thrust away such futile guessing-games and concentrated his mind first on the Temporal Regulation requiring every mission to be carried out to the fullest extent possible, and then on what could still be in it for him. After a short rest and ten mg of paracynomyl he was on his way to the research station, or whatever might remain of it.

Nothing remained of it – at least, nothing he could discern under the thicket of brambles and briers that covered the site – but there were remnants of the surrounding vineyards, if the sickly stunted plants now growing there were truly such. But part of his task was to take cuttings and he proceeded to do so. Absorbed in this, he failed to heed the approach of the watchman. There was a struggle; he took a blow on the head and perhaps lost consciousness for a time. Anyhow he remembered nothing clearly till he was sitting on the bare stone floor of a large antiquated kitchen with an upper servant of some kind, as it might have been a steward, demanding to know who he was. (These and some later inferences were reached by Simpson or one or other of his audience as he told his tale.)

As soon as the steward saw Simpson's credentials his manner changed from irate suspicion to caution if not respect. He bustled off, returning with a man in his fifties who could be positively identified from his dress and tonsure as an ecclesiastic, a monk. But any hopes Simpson might have had of understanding treatment from a man of learning were soon dashed. The cleric studied the typewritten documents briefly and uneasily, darting similar glances at Simpson and his no doubt strange-seeming get-up. Finally he thrust the papers back at him, snapped an order to the steward in his odd sibilant patois and unceremoniously withdrew.

It was not much, but it was toleration. Simpson was placed near one end of a long oak table, brought water in response to his mimings and left free to take stock of his surroundings. Light came from a few stubby candles and a vast open fire above which joints of meat sizzled. The air was hot, smoky and heavy with cooking and other smells. Hams and other preserved eatables hung from the ceiling. There was a great coming and going of attendants with serving-dishes and general carry-on until the main business of getting the meal up to the monks' dining-hall was accomplished. At this stage of the game the steward, now

seen as a likeable character in a fine embroidered jacket, no doubt
a relic of happier times, settled himself next to Simpson and
genially indicated that he should help himself to food and drink.

There was no shortage of either: mutton, cold fowl, sausage,
coarse bread, butter, cheese, fresh berries, beer, red wine, all set
out at once and indiscriminately. As he had begun to guess with
the songbirds, Simpson saw while he piled his plate that whatever
had assailed humanity had not affected other forms of life.

Or had it? He was hungry and the ambient smells were so
heavy that his jaws had closed on a lump of mutton before he
was aware that it was putrid, turning rotten. The steward saw
his distress, nodded cheerfully and passed him a crock of salt.
Wary of giving offence, Simpson managed a couple of nauseating
mouthfuls. The fowl was a little better, if only because the gamey
reek seemed less incongruous; the seasoning of the sausage burnt
his tongue. The fruit was sour, the cheese quite frightening. Pushing aside the rancid butter he tried the bread, but it was full of
gritty residues. The watery beer at least offset some of the salt,
until after a few swallows its mawkish flavour became too much.
It was out of a pure sense of mission that he accepted a pot of
wine.

No use trying for the nose in this place. He took a sip, then
more. Often since that evening in the bowels of Whitehall Simpson has tried to describe that wine of which perhaps 50 ml passed
down his throat. It was not exactly that it was unlike any other
wine he had ever tasted, nor yet that it was finer, nobler: it was
greater in sheer size. If a Château Haut Brion at the top of its
form could be compared with a fragrance of Cathay, then what
he drank now was all the riches of the East. He lowered the cup
and gazed at the steward, who took it from him with a grimace
of apology and stirred into it watered honey and a spoonful of
some herbal infusion. With admirable fortitude he sampled the
result, and had some difficulty describing that too, though some
of the phrases he used were most evocative.

Wide-eyed, hand on stomach, Simpson lurched from the
kitchen to the accompaniment of good-natured jeers and shouts

of encouragement. But he was not really ill. Once in the open he completed the circuit in the bracelet on his wrist and the TALISKER had him safe and sound.

Dr Khan was twitching with excitement. He shook Simpson's hand a dozen times, almost snatched the vine cuttings from him and placed them in the field of his microscope. Its screen remained blank for nearly a minute while we all stared at it as if hypnotized. Then several rows of symbols flashed up together. Khan pressed buttons once, twice, got new answers and gave a great sigh. With a flourish he cleared the machine and, very much master of ceremonies, turned and faced his audience.

'What Dr Simpson has brought us,' Khan began, 'is something altogether more interesting and shall I say more *valuable* than the result of any immunological experiment. We have in our possession not the latest of vines but the first, not a mutation but the rootstock, the *Urrebe*. As confirmed just now by archaeo-botanical comparison, it is a living specimen of the extinct primeval vine-grape bearer, *vitis vinifera pristina*, of which more in a moment. First I have some explaining and apologizing to do, and first of all to you, sir.'

Here he bowed to the Director, who sent the rest of us a nervous smile.

'While you were most lucidly explaining to me the tuning of your temporal transmitter I was impertinent enough to distract your attention and change the setting in a most radical way. Yes, as he must already have begun to suspect, Dr Simpson has visited not the future but the past, the late fourteenth century I should judge – I wasn't too sure of the calibration. Dr Simpson, I do beg your pardon for my reckless and high-handed—'

The Director had turned the colour of a fine Travel rosé and was speechless, but Simpson had opened a transparent packet and taken out a small metal object which he passed up to Khan. 'I didn't only collect vines back there. That's the salt-spoon I was handed by the steward – or perhaps I should say the seneschal.'

Khan reactivated his appliance, inserted the spoon and lowered a bar. 'This may take a little longer. Er, as I say, I'm afraid I was really most rash.'

'It was worth it,' Simpson said. 'One thing – I don't understand why that monk reacted as he did. I see now he couldn't have read a word of my papers, but it was as if he was afraid of them.'

Rabaiotti grinned. 'Of course he was afraid of them. Documents in an unknown language produced by an unknown method? Think yourself lucky not to have been dragged out and burnt on the spot.'

'If it had been anywhere else but a monastery . . .'

'Everything one had ever thought about the Middle Ages, eh? Notably the horrid—'

A bleeper started up on the microscope and the screen illuminated itself. 'Compounded – in other words put together, made – AD 1325 plus or minus five,' Khan announced. 'Apparent age 19 plus or minus one. A little earlier than I estimated.'

'Nice to think it might have been 1346,' I said. 'Edward III and the Black Prince moving in to clobber the Frogs at Crécy. What if they'd been on the look-out for English spies?'

'Burgundy wasn't part of France then,' Schneider put in.

'Could we have some order, gentlemen?' the Director called. 'I'd like to hear more from Dr Khan about just how valuable this thing is.'

'Thank you, sir. Our discovery, our prize is reproducible and fructifiable or will be within a short time. Soon we shall be enjoying the wine that Dr Simpson's hosts found too feeble to drink unadulterated. And marketing the living vines that produce it.'

'Splendid, but for how long?' Rabaiotti asked. 'Why should we imagine that this *vitis pristina* will be any more proof against phylloxera than the vines we know?'

'Because of its natural defences,' Khan said earnestly. 'Those defences that human beings have almost as if deliberately destroyed with the very chemicals meant to improve them. Once, phylloxera vastatrix was an almost harmless little beast – almost, not quite. So he had to be sprayed out of existence and indeed he was ousted temporarily, only to return with greater strength against a weakened prey. And the next time was worse.

'The dates will show you. First organized spraying of French vines, 1803, under Chaptal, Napoleon's Minister of the Interior. First severe phylloxera damage, 1811–12. First toxic smoke attempts, 1859. New phylloxera penetration into Loire vineyards, 1865. And so on. That was my first clue. The medicine on which the disease flourished was progressively undermining the patient. And incidentally it seems the price the vines paid for sheer survival was loss of quality in the product. As always. There's not much meat on a mountain goat.

'So . . . soon, very soon, we here will collectively launch what will be nothing less than the wine of the century – the twenty-first century, that is, by courtesy of the fourteenth!'

It was quite soon, in 1997 to be exact, and I was there when the corks were pulled at the first tasting, and by universal consent the wine was absolutely horrible. It hadn't travelled, so to speak. But by then we, the six of us, had all cleaned up.

Hemingway in Space

The woman watched him and he made another sweep. There was nothing again but he knew one of them was around. It got so you always knew. After twenty years it got so you always knew when one of them was around.

'Anything?'

'Not yet.'

'I thought you could tell just where to find these things,' she said. 'I thought we hired you because you could take us straight to one of these things. I thought that was why we hired you.'

'Easy now, Martha,' the young fellow said. 'Nobody can find xeeb where there aren't any xeeb, not even Mr Hardacre. We'll come across one any minute now.'

She moved away from the three of them at the instrument panel and her thighs were arrogant under the tight space-jeans. You bitch, Philip Hardacre thought suddenly. You goddam, bored, boring, senseless bitch. He felt sorry for the young fellow. He was a pretty nice young fellow, and here he was married to this goddam senseless bitch, and it looked like he was too afraid of her to tell her to get the hell out, although you knew he wanted to.

'I feel him near,' the old Martian said, turning the bigger and more grizzled of his two heads towards Philip Hardacre. 'We shall see him soon now.'

The woman leaned against the ship's side and stared out the port. 'I can't think why you have to go hunting these monstrosities. Two days it's been since we left, and we could have been in Venusport all that while instead of cooped up in this steel jalopy a couple of light years from civilization. What's so good about getting a xeeb even if you do get one? What does it prove, getting a xeeb?'

'The xeeb is the largest life-form in this part of the galaxy.' The young fellow was a school professor or something like that, and you could tell it from the way he spoke. 'More than that, it's the only sentient creature living out here in free space, and it's ferocious; it's been known to take on a scout ship. It's the toughest damn thing there is. That's it, isn't it?'

'That's part of it,' Philip Hardacre said. There was that, although there was much more, the freedom out there and the stars against the black and the men small in their suits and afraid and yet not afraid and even the xeeb small in the vastness and the cool joy if the xeeb was a good one.

'He comes,' the old Martian said in his whistling tones, his smaller head bent toward the screen. 'See, lady.'

'I don't want to see,' she said, turning her back. It was a deadly insult under the ancient Martian code of honour, and she knew it and Philip Hardacre knew she knew it, and there was hate in his throat, but there was no time now for hate.

He got up from the panel. There was no doubt about it. An amateur could have taken the blip for an asteroid or another ship but after twenty years you knew immediately. 'Suit up,' he said. 'Spaceside in three minutes.'

He helped the young fellow with the helmet and what he had been dreading happened, the Martian had taken out his own suit and was stiffly putting his rear pair of legs into it. He went over to him and put his hand between the two necks in the traditional gesture of appeal. 'This is not your hunt, Ghlmu,' he said in the archaic Martian courtly tongue.

'I am still strong and he is big and he comes fast.'

'I know, but this is not your hunt. Old ones are hunted more than they hunt.'

'All my eyes are straight and all my hands are tight.'

'But they are slow and they must be quick. Once they were quick but now they are slow.'

'Har-dasha, it is thy comrade who asks thee.'

'My blood is yours as in all the years; it is only my thought that must seem cruel, old one. I will hunt without you.'

'Hunt well, Har-dasha, then. I await you always,' the old creature said, using the ritual formula of acquiescence.

'Are we going to shoot this goddam whale or not?' The woman's voice was shrill. 'Or are you and that thing going on whistling at each other all night?'

He turned on her savagely. 'You're out of this. You're staying right here where you belong. Put that blaster back on the rack and take off that space-suit and start making food. We'll be back in half an hour.'

'Don't you give me orders, you bum. I can shoot as well as any man and you won't stop me.'

'Around here I say what everybody does, and they do it.' Over her shoulder he could see the Martian hanging up his suit and his throat went dry. 'If you try to get in that airlock with us we head right back to Venus.'

'I'm sorry, Martha, you'll have to do as he says,' the young fellow said.

The two big Wyndham-Clarke blasters were ready primed and he set them both at maximum, while they stood in the airlock and waited for the air to go. Then the outer door slid into the wall and they were out there in the freedom and the vastness and the fear that was not fear. The stars were very cold and it was black between the stars. There were not many stars, and the black was vast where there were no stars. The stars and the black together were what gave the freedom. Without the stars or without the black there would not have been the freedom, only the vastness, but with the stars and the black you had the freedom as well as the vastness. The stars were few and the light from them was small and cold, and around them there was the black.

He spoke to the young fellow over the suit radio. 'Can you see him? Toward that big star with the small companion.'

'Where?'

'Look where I'm pointing. He hasn't spotted us yet.'

'How does he spot us?'

'Never mind that. Now, listen. Each swoop he makes, give him one shot. Just one. Then go forward on your suit jet as fast as you can. That confuses him more than lateral movement.'

'You told me.'

'I'm telling you again. One shot. He homes on your shot. Get ready; he's seen us; he's turning.'

The great beautiful phosphorescent shape narrowed as it came head-on to them, then appeared to swell. The xeeb was closing fast, as fast as any he'd known. It was a big, fast xeeb and likely to be a good one. He'd be able to tell for sure after the first swoop. He wanted the xeeb to be a good one for the young fellow's sake. He wanted the young fellow to have a good hunt with a good, big, fast xeeb.

'Fire in about fifteen seconds, then jet,' Philip Hardacre said. 'And you won't have too long before his next swoop, so be ready.'

The xeeb closed, and the young fellow's shot arc'd in. It was too early to be a good shot and it barely flicked the tail end. Philip Hardacre waited as long as he dared and fired toward the hump where the main ganglia were and jetted without waiting to see where he had hit.

It was a good xeeb all right. From the way its phosphorescence had started to pulsate you could tell it had been hit somewhere in the nervous system or what passed for that, but within seconds it had turned and begun another great beautiful graceful swoop on the two men. This time the young fellow held his fire a little longer and got in a good shot near the hump and jetted as he had been told. But then the xeeb dropped in the way they did once in a hundred times and xeeb and man were almost on each other. There was nothing for Philip Hardacre to do but empty his Wyndham-Clarke all at once in the hope that the loosing of so much energy would get the xeeb to change its mind and home on him instead. Then he was jetting forward at top speed and calling over the suit radio to make for the ship at once.

'It puffed something at me and I lost my blaster,' came the young fellow's voice.

'Make for the ship.'

'We won't get there, will we?'

'We can try. You may have damaged him enough with that last shot to slow him down or spoil his sense of direction,' Philip Hardacre said. He already knew that it was all over for them. The xeeb was only a few miles above them and beginning to turn for a fresh swoop, moving slower but not slow enough. The ship was above them too in the other direction. This was what you faced every time you hunted xeeb and when it happened at last it was just the end of the hunt and the end of the freedom and the vastness, and they would have had to end some time.

There was a long arc of light from the ship and the xeeb was suddenly brighter than ever before for an instant, and then the brightness went out and there was nothing there.

The Martian had fallen into a crouching position in the airlock and the third Wyndham-Clarke was still in his pincers. The two men waited for the outer door to close and the air to flood in.

'Why didn't he put on his suit?' said the young fellow.

'There wasn't time. He had about a minute to save us. A Martian suit takes much longer than that to put on.'

'What would have got him first, the cold?'

'Airlessness. They respire quickly. Five seconds at most. Just enough to aim and fire.' He was quick after all, Philip Hardacre thought.

Inside, the woman was waiting for them. 'What happened?'

'He's dead, of course. He got the xeeb.'

'Did he have to get himself killed doing it?'

'There was one weapon on board and one place to use it from,' Philip Hardacre said. Then his voice went quiet. 'Why are you still wearing your space-suit?'

'I wanted to get the feel of it. And you said to take it off.'

'Why couldn't you have taken the gun into the airlock?'

Her eyes went dull. 'I didn't know how the lock worked.'

'But Ghlmu did. He could have operated it from in here. And you can shoot, or so you said.'

'I'm sorry.'

'Sorry I like,' the young fellow said. He didn't sound like a school professor now, or afraid of her. 'Sorry brings back that old guy as alive as ever he was, doesn't it? Sorry is about the best I ever heard. And sorry is something else too. Sorry as all hell is how I feel when I drop you off in Venusport and take the shuttle to Earth by myself. You like Venusport, don't you? Well, here's your chance to get lost in it.'

Philip Hardacre finished composing the old Martian's limbs and appendages and muttered as much as he knew of the prescribed incantation. 'Forgive me,' he said.

'Get supper,' the young fellow said to the woman. 'Right away.'

'This was your hunt,' Philip Hardacre said to his friend's body.

Who or What Was It?

I want to tell you about a very odd experience I had a few months ago, not so as to entertain you, but because I think it raises some very basic questions about, you know, what life is all about and to what extent we run our own lives. Rather worrying questions. Anyway, what happened was this.

My wife and I had been staying the weekend with her uncle and aunt in Westmorland, near a place called Milnethorpe. Both of us, Jane and I that is, had things to do in London on the Monday morning, and it's a long drive from up there down to Barnet, where we live, even though a good half of it is on the M6. So I said, Look, don't let's break our necks trying to get home in the light (this was in August), let's take it easy and stop somewhere for dinner and reckon to get home about half-past ten or eleven. Jane said okay.

So we left Milnethorpe in the middle of the afternoon, took things fairly easily, and landed up about half-past seven or a quarter to eight at the . . . the place we'd picked out of one of the food guides before we started. I won't tell you the name of the place, because the people who run it wouldn't thank me if I did. Please don't go looking for it. I'd advise you not to.

Anyway, we parked the car in the yard and went inside. It was a nice-looking sort of place, pretty old, built a good time ago I mean, done up in a sensible sort of way, no muzak and no bloody silly blacked-out lighting, but no olde-worlde nonsense either.

Well, I got us both a drink in the bar and went off to see about a table for dinner. I soon found the right chap, and he said, Fine, table for two in half an hour, certainly sir, are you in the bar, I'll get someone to bring you the menu in a few minutes. Pleasant sort of chap, a bit young for the job.

I was just going off when a sort of paunchy business type came in and said something about, Mr Allington not in tonight? and the young fellow said No sir, he's taken the evening off. All right, never mind.

Well, I'll tell you why in a minute, but I turned back to the young fellow, said, Excuse me, but is your name Palmer? and he said Yes sir, and I said, Not David Palmer by any chance? and he said No sir, actually the name's George. I said, or rather burbled, A friend of mine was telling me about this place, said he'd stayed here, liked it very much, mentioned you, anyway I got half the name right, and Mr Allington is the proprietor, isn't he? That's correct, sir. See you later and all that.

I went straight back to the bar, went up to the barman and said, Fred? and he said Yes sir. I said, Fred Soames? and he said, Fred Browning, sir. I just said, Wrong Fred, not very polite, but it was all I could think of. I went over to where my wife was sitting and I'd hardly sat down before she asked, What's the matter?

What was the matter calls for a bit of explanation. In 1969 I published a novel called *The Green Man*, which was not only the title of the book but also the name of a sort of classy pub, or inn, where most of the action took place, very much the kind of establishment we were in that evening.

Now the landlord of the Green Man was called Allington, and his deputy was called David Palmer, and the barman was called Fred Soames. Allington is a very uncommon name – I wanted that for reasons nothing to do with this story. The other two aren't, but to have got Palmer and Fred right, so to speak, as well as Allington was a thumping great coincidence, staggering in fact. But I wasn't just staggered, I was very alarmed. Because the Green Man wasn't only the name of the pub in my book; it was also the name of a frightening creature, a sort of solid ghost conjured up out of tree-branches and leaves and so on that very nearly kills Allington and his young daughter. I didn't want to find I was right about that, too.

Jane was very sensible, as always. She said stranger coincidences had happened and still been just coincidences, and
mightn't I have come across an innkeeper called Allington somewhere, half forgotten about it and brought it up out of my
unconscious mind when I was looking for a name for an innkeeper
to put in the book, and now the real Allington's moved from
wherever I'd seen him before to this place. And Palmer and Fred
really are very common names. And I'd got the name of the pub
wrong. I'm still not telling you what it's called, but one of the
things it isn't called is the Green Man. And, my pub was in Hert-
fordshire and this place was . . . off the M6. All very reasonable
and reassuring.

Only I wasn't very reassured. I mean, I obviously couldn't just
leave it there. The thing to do was get hold of this chap Palmer
and see if there was, well, any more to come. Which was going
to be tricky if I wasn't going to look nosy or mad or something
else that would shut him up. Neither of us ate much dinner,
though there was nothing wrong with the food. We didn't say
much, either. I drank a fair amount.

Then halfway through, Palmer turned up to do his everything-
all-right routine, as I'd hoped he would, and as he would have
done in my book. I said yes, it was fine, thanks, and then I asked
him, I said we'd be very pleased if he'd join us for a brandy
afterwards if he'd got time, and he said he'd be delighted. Jolly
good, but I was still stuck with this problem of how to dress the
thing up.

Jane had said earlier on, why didn't I just tell the truth, and
I'd said, since Palmer hadn't reacted at all when I gave him my
name when I was booking the table – see what I mean? – he'd
only have my word for the whole story and might still think I
was off my rocker, and she said of course she'd back me up,
and I'd said he'd just think he'd got two loonies on his hands
instead of one. Anyway, *now* she said, *Some* people who've read
The Green Man must have mentioned it – fancy that, Mr
Palmer, you and Mr Allington and Fred are all in a book by
somebody called Kingsley Amis. Obvious enough when you

think of it, but like a lot of obvious things, you have got to think of it.

Well, that was the line I took when Palmer rolled up for his brandy, I'm me and I wrote this book and so on. Oh really? he said, more or less. I thought we were buggered, but then he said, Oh yes, now you mention it, I do remember some chap saying something like that, but it must have been two or three years ago – you know, as if that stopped it counting for much. I'm not much of a reader, you see, he said.

So. What about Mr Allington, I said, doesn't he read? Not what you'd call a reader, he said. Well, that was one down to me, or one up, depending on how you look at it, because *my* Allington was a tremendous reader, French poetry and all that. Still, the approach had worked after a fashion, and Palmer very decently put up with being cross-questioned on how far this place corresponded with my place, in the book.

Was Mrs Allington blonde? There wasn't a Mrs Allington any more; she'd died of leukemia quite a long time ago. Had he got his widowed father living here? (Allington's father, that is.) No, Mr Allington senior, and his wife, lived in Eastbourne. Was the house, the pub, haunted at all? Not as far as Palmer knew, and he'd been there three years. In fact, the place was only about two hundred years old, which completely clobbered a good half of my novel, where the ghosts had been hard at it more than a hundred years earlier still.

Nearly all of it was like that. Of course, there were some questions I couldn't ask, for one reason or another. For instance, was Allington a boozer, like my Allington, and even more so, had this Allington had a visit from God. In the book, God turns up in the form of a young man to give Allington some tips on how to deal with the ghosts, who he, God, thinks are a menace to him. No point in going any further into that part.

I said nearly all the answers Palmer gave me were straight negatives. One wasn't, or rather there were two points where I scored, so to speak. One was that Allington had a fifteen-year-old daughter called Marilyn living in the house. My Allington's daughter was thirteen and called Amy, but I'd come somewhere near the mark – too near for comfort.

The other thing was a bit harder to tie down. When I'm writing a novel, I very rarely have any sort of mental picture of any of the characters, what they actually look like. I think a lot of novelists would say the same. But, I don't know why, I'd had a very clear image of what my chap *David* Palmer looked like, and now I'd had a really good look at *George* Palmer, this one here, he was *nearly* the same as I'd imagined, not so tall, different nose, but still nearly the same. I didn't care for that.

Palmer, George Palmer, said he had things to see to and took off. I told Jane what I've just told you, about the resemblance. She said I could easily have imagined that, and I said I suppose I might. Anyway, she said, what do you think of it all?

I said it could still all be coincidence. What could it be if it isn't coincidence? she asked. I'd been wondering about that while we were talking to Palmer. Not an easy one. Feeling a complete bloody fool, I said I thought we could have strayed into some kind of parallel world that slightly resembles the world I made up, you know, like in a science-fiction story.

She didn't laugh or back away. She looked round and spotted a newspaper someone had left on one of the chairs. It was that day's *Sunday Telegraph*. She said, If where we are is a world that's parallel to the real world, it's bound to be different from the real world in all sorts of ways. Now you read most of the *Telegraph* this morning, the real *Telegraph*. Look at this one, she said, and see if it's any different. Well, I did, and it wasn't: same front page, same article on the trade unions by Perry, that's Peregrine Worsthorne, same readers' letters, same crossword down to the last clue. Well, that was a relief.

But I didn't stay relieved, because there was another coincidence shaping up. It was a hot night in August when all this happened – or did I mention that before? Anyway, it was. And Allington was out for the evening. It was on a hot night in August, after Allington had come back from an evening out, that the monster, the Green Man, finally takes shape and comes pounding up the road to tear young Amy Allington to pieces. That bit begins on page 225 in my book, if you're interested.

The other nasty little consideration was this. Unlike some novelists I could name, I invent all my characters, except for a few minor ones here and there. What I mean is, I don't go in for just renaming people I know and bunging them into a book. But of course, you can't help putting *something* of yourself into all your characters, even if it's only, well, a surly bus-conductor who only comes in for half a page.

Right, obviously, this comes up most of all with your heroes. Now none of my heroes, not even old Lucky Jim, are me, but they can't help having pretty fair chunks of me in them, some more than others. And Allington in that book was one of the some. I'm more like him than I'm like most of the others; in particular, I'm more like my Maurice Allington in my book than the real Allington, who by the way turned out to be called John, seemed (from what I'd heard) to be like my Maurice Allington. Sorry to be long-winded, but I want to get that quite clear.

So: if, by some fantastic chance, the Green Man, the monster, was going to turn up here, he, or it, seemed more likely to turn up tonight than most nights. And, furthermore, I seemed sort of better cast for the part of the young girl's father, who manages in the book to save her from the monster, than this young girl's father did. You see that.

I tried to explain all this to Jane. Evidently I got it across all right, because she said straight away, We'd better stay here tonight, then. If we can, I said, meaning if there was a room. Well, there was, and at the front of the house too, which was important, because in the book that's the side the monster appears on.

While one of the blokes was taking our stuff out of the car and upstairs, I said to Jane, I'm not going to be like a bloody fool in a ghost story who insists on seeing things through alone, not if I can help it – I'm going to give Bob Conquest a ring. Bob's an old chum of mine, and about the only one I felt I could ask to come belting up all this way (he lives in Battersea) for such a ridiculous reason. It was just after ten by this time, and the Green Man wasn't scheduled to put in an appearance till after one a.m., so Bob could make it all right if he started straight away. Fine, except his phone didn't answer; I tried twice.

Jane said, Get hold of Monkey; I'll speak to him. Monkey, otherwise known as Colin, is her brother; he lives with us in Barnet. Our number answered all right, but I got my son Philip, who was staying the weekend there. He said Monkey was out at a party, he didn't know where. So all I could do was the necessary but not at all helpful job of saying we wouldn't be home till the next morning. So that was that. I mean, I just couldn't start getting hold of George Palmer and asking him to sit up with us into the small hours in case a ghost came along. Could any of you? I should have said that Philip hasn't got a car.

Well, we stayed in the bar until it closed. I said to Jane at one point, You don't think I'm mad, do you? Or silly or anything? She said, On the contrary, I think you're being extremely practical and sensible. Well, thank God for that. Jane believes in ghosts, you see. My own position on that is exactly that of the man who said, I don't believe in ghosts, but I'm afraid of them.

Which brings me to one of the oddest things about this whole business. I'm a nervous type by nature, I never go in an aeroplane, I won't drive a car (Jane does the driving), I don't even much care for being alone in the house. But, ever since we'd decided to stay the night at this place, all the uneasiness and, let's face it, the considerable fear I'd started to feel as soon as these coincidences started coming up, it all just fell away. I felt quite confident, I felt I knew I'd be able to do whatever might be required of me.

There was one other thing to get settled. I said to Jane, we were in the bedroom by this time, I said, If he turns up, what am I going to use against him? You see, in the book, Maurice Allington has dug up a sort of magic object that sort of controls the Green Man. I hadn't. Jane saw what I was driving at. She said she'd thought of that, and took off and gave me the plain gold cross she wears round her neck, not for religious reasons, it was her grandmother's. That'll fix him, I thought, and as before I felt quite confident about it.

Well, after that we more or less sat and waited. At one point a car drove up and stopped in the car park. A man got out and went in the front door. It must have been Allington. I couldn't see much about him except he had the wrong colour hair, but when I looked at my watch it was eight minutes to midnight, the exact time when the Allington in the book got back after his evening out the night he coped with the creature. One more bit of . . . call it confirmation.

I opened our bedroom door and listened. Soon I heard foot-steps coming upstairs and going off towards the back of the house and then a door shutting, and then straight away the house seemed totally still. It can't have been much later that I said to Jane, Look, there's no point in me hanging round up here. He might be early, you never know. It's a warm night, I might as well go down there now. She said, Are you sure you don't want me to come with you? Absolutely sure, I said, I'll be fine. But I do want you to watch from the window here. Okay, she said. She wished me luck and we clung to each other for a bit, and then off I went.

I was glad I'd left plenty of time, because getting out of the place turned out to be far from straightforward. Everything seemed to be locked and the key taken away. Eventually I found a scullery door with the key still in the lock.

Outside it was quite bright, with a full moon or not far off, and a couple of fairly powerful lights at the corners of the house. It was a pretty lonely spot, with only two or three other houses in sight. I remember a car went by soon after I got out there, but it was the only one. There wasn't a breath of wind. I saw Jane at our window and waved, and she waved back.

The question was, where to wait. If what was going to happen – assuming something was – if it went like the book, then the young girl, the daughter, was going to come out of the house because she'd thought she'd heard her father calling her (another bit of magic), and then this Green Man creature was going to, from one direction or the other he was going to come running at her. I couldn't decide which was the more likely direction.

A bit of luck, near the front door there was one of those heavy wooden benches. I sat down on that and started keeping watch first one way, then the other, half a minute at a time. Normally, ten minutes of this would have driven me off my head with boredom, but that night somehow it was all right. Then, after some quite long time, I turned my head from right to left on schedule and there was a girl, standing a few yards away; she must have come round that side of the house. She was wearing light green pyjamas – wrong colour again. I was going to speak to her, but there was something about the way she was standing . . .

She wasn't looking at me, in fact I soon saw she wasn't looking at anything much. I waved my hand in front of her eyes, you know, the way they do in films when they think someone's been hypnotized or something. I felt a perfect idiot, but her eyes didn't move. Sleep-walking, presumably; not in the book. Do people walk in their sleep? Apparently not, they only pretend to, according to what a psychiatrist chum told me afterwards, but I hadn't heard that then. All I knew, or thought I knew, was this thing everybody's heard somewhere about it being dangerous to wake a sleepwalker.

So I just stayed close to the girl and went on keeping watch, and a bit more time went by, and then, sure enough, I heard, faintly but clearly, the sound I'd written about, the rustling, creaking sound of the movement of something made of tree-branches, twigs, and clusters of leaves. And there it was, about a hundred yards away, not really much like a man, coming up at a clumsy, jolting sort of jog-trot on the grass verge, and accelerating.

I knew what I had to do. I started walking to meet it, with the cross ready in my hand. (The girl hadn't moved at all.) When the thing was about twenty yards away I saw its face, which had fungus on it, and I heard another sound I'd written about coming from what I suppose you'd have to call its mouth, like the howling of wind through trees.

I stopped and steadied myself and threw the cross at it and it immediately vanished – immediately. That wasn't like the book, but I didn't stop to think about it. I didn't stop to look for the cross, either. When I turned back, the girl had gone. So much the better. I rushed back into the inn and up to the bedroom and knocked on the door – I'd told Jane to lock it after me.

There was a delay before she came and opened it. I could see she looked confused or something, but I didn't bother with that, because I could feel all the calm and confidence I'd had earlier, it was all just draining away from me. I sat her down on the bed and sat down myself on a chair and just rattled off what had happened as fast as I could. I must have forgotten she'd been meant to be watching.

By the time I'd finished I was shaking. So was Jane. She said, What made you change your mind? Change my mind? – what about? Going out there, she said; getting up again and going out. But, I said, I've been out there all the time. Oh no you haven't, she said, you came back up here after about twenty minutes, she said, and you told me the whole thing was silly and you were going to bed, which we both did. She seemed quite positive.

I was absolutely shattered. But it all really happened, I said, just the way I told you. It couldn't have, she said; you must have dreamed it. You certainly didn't throw the cross at anything, she said, because it's here, you gave it back to me when you came back the first time. And there it was, on the chain round her neck.

I broke down then. I'm not quite clear what I said or did. Jane got some sleeping pills down me and I went off in the end. I remember thinking rather wildly that somebody or other with a funny sense of humour had got me into exactly the same predicament, the same mess, as the hero of my book had been: seeing something that must have been supernatural and just not being believed. Because I knew I'd seen the whole thing; I knew it then and I still know it.

I woke up late, feeling terrible. Jane was sitting reading by the bed. She said, I've seen young Miss Allington. Your description of her fits and, she said, she used to walk in her sleep. I asked her how she'd found out and she said she just had; she's good at that kind of thing.

Anyway, I felt better straight away. I said it looked as if we'd neither of us been dreaming even if what I'd seen couldn't be reconciled with what she'd seen, and she agreed. After that we rather dropped the subject in a funny sort of way. We decided not to look for the cross I'd thrown at the Green Man. I said we wouldn't be able to find it. I didn't ask Jane whether she was thinking what I was thinking, that looking would be a waste of time because she was wearing it at that very moment. I'll come back to that point in a minute.

We packed up, made a couple of phone calls rearranging our appointments, paid the bill and drove off. We still didn't talk about the main issue. But then, as we were coming off the Mill Hill roundabout, that's only about ten minutes from home, Jane said, What do you think happened? – happened to sort of make it all happen?

I said, I think someone was needed there to destroy that monster. Which means I was guided there at that time, or perhaps the time could be adjusted, I said; I must have been, well, sent all that stuff about the Green Man and about Allington and the others.

To make sure you recognized the place when you got there and knew what to do, she said. Who did all the guiding and the sending and so on? she said. The same, the same chap who appeared in my book to tell Allington what he wanted done. Why couldn't he have fixed the monster himself? she said. There are limitations to his power. There can't be many, she said, if he can make the same object be in two places at the same time.

Yes, you see, she'd thought of that too. It's supposed to be a physical impossibility, isn't it? Anyway, I said probably the way he'd chosen had been more fun. More fun, Jane repeated. She looked very thoughtful.

As you'll have seen, there was one loose end, of a sort. Who or what was it that had taken on my shape to enter that bedroom, talk to Jane with my voice, and share her bed for at any rate a few minutes? She and I didn't discuss it for several days. Then one morning she asked me the question more or less as I've just put it.

Interesting point, I said; I don't know. It's more interesting than you think, she said; because when . . . whoever it was got into bed with me, he didn't just go to sleep.

I suppose I just looked at her. That's right, she said; I thought I'd better go and see John before I told you. (That's John Allison, our GP.)

It was negative, then, I said. Yes, Jane said.

Well, that's it. A relief, of course. But in one way, rather disappointing.

The Darkwater Hall Mystery

On consulting my notes, their paper grown yellow and their ink brown with the passage of almost forty years, I find it to have been in the closing days of July, 1885, that my friend Sherlock Holmes fell victim, more completely perhaps than at any other time, to the innate melancholy of his temperament. The circumstances were not propitious. London was stiflingly hot, without a drop of rain to lay the dust which, at intervals, a damp wind swept up Baker Street. The exertions caused Holmes by the affair of the Wallace-Bardwell portfolio, and the subsequent entrapment of the elusive Count Varga, had taken their toll of him. His grey eyes, always sharp and piercing, acquired a positively hectic brightness, and the thinness of his hawk-like nose seemed accentuated. He smoked incessantly, getting through an ounce or more of heavy shag tobacco in a single day.

As his depression became blacker, he would sit in his purple dressing-gown with his fiddle across his knee and draw from it strange harmonies, sometimes sonorous, sometimes puzzling, more often harsh and disagreeable. Strange too, and quite as disagreeable, were the odours given off by his chemical experiments; I did not inquire their purpose. When he brought out his hair-trigger pistol and proceeded to add elaborate serifs to the patriotic VR done in bullet-pocks in the wall opposite his armchair, my impatience and my concern together dictated action. Nothing short of a complete rest, in conditions of comfort and ease such as I could not possibly provide, would restore my friend to health. I moved swiftly; telegrams were exchanged; within little more than twelve hours Sherlock Holmes was on his way to Hurlstone in Sussex, the seat of that Reginald Musgrave whose family treasures he had so brilliantly rediscovered some five years earlier. Thus it was that events conspired to embroil me in what I must describe as a truly singular adventure.

It came about in the following fashion. That same afternoon, I had just returned from visiting a patient when the housekeeper announced the arrival of a Lady Fairfax. The name at once stirred something in my memory, but I had had no time to apprehend it before my visitor had crossed the threshold of the sitting-room. There entered a blonde young woman of the most unusual beauty and distinction of feature. I was at once aware in her of a discomposure obviously not at all derived from the sweltering weather, to which indeed her bearing proclaimed utter indifference. I encouraged this lovely but troubled creature to be seated and to divulge her purpose.

'It was Mr Sherlock Holmes whom I came to see, but I understand he has gone away and is not expected back for a fortnight,' she began.

'That is so.'

'Can he not be recalled?'

I shook my head. 'Quite out of the question.'

'But I come on a matter of the utmost urgency. A life is in danger.'

'Lady Fairfax,' said I, 'Holmes has been overworking and must have rest and a change of air. I speak not only as his friend but as his physician. I fear I cannot be influenced by any other consideration.'

The lady sighed and lowered her gaze into her lap. 'May I at least acquaint you with the main facts of the matter?'

'Do so by all means, if you feel it will be of service to you.'

'Very well. My husband is Sir Harry Fairfax, the sixth baronet, of Darkwater Hall in Wiltshire. In his capacity as a magistrate, he had brought before him last year a man known locally as Black Ralph. The charge was poaching. There was no doubt of his guilt; he had erred before in this way and in others, and my husband's sentence of twelve months in gaol was lenient to a degree. Now, Black Ralph is at liberty again, and word has reached our servants that he means to revenge himself on my husband – to kill him.'

'Kill him?' I ejaculated.

'Nothing less, Dr Watson,' said Lady Fairfax, clasping and unclasping her white-gloved hands as she spoke. 'My husband scouts these threats, calling Black Ralph a harmless rascal with a taste for rhetoric. But the fellow is no mere drunken reprobate such as one finds in every village; I have seen him and studied him, and I tell you he is malignant, and in all likelihood mentally deranged as well.'

I was at a loss. My visitor was by now extremely agitated, her vivid lips atremble and her fine blue eyes flashing fire. 'He sounds most menacing,' said I, 'and I understand your desire for assistance. I chance to know a certain Inspector Lestrade at Scotland Yard who would be happy to lend you all the aid he could.'

'Thank you, but my husband refuses to go to the police and has forbidden me to do so.'

'I see.'

'There must, however, be other consulting detectives in London whom I might approach. Perhaps you know of some of them?'

'Well,' said I after a short space, 'it's true that in the last year or so a number of – what shall I call them? – rivals of Sherlock Holmes have sprung up. But they're very slight and unsatisfactory fellows. I could not in honesty recommend a single one.'

There was a silence. The lady sighed once more and at last turned to me. 'Dr Watson, will *you* help me?'

I had half expected this preposterous suggestion, but was none the better armed against it when it came. 'I? I am quite unfit. I'm a simple medical man, Lady Fairfax, not a detective.'

'But you have worked with Mr Holmes on his previous cases. You are his close friend and associate. You must have learned a great deal from him.'

'I think I can say I know his methods, but there are aspects of his activities of which I am altogether ignorant.'

'That would not prevent you from talking to my husband,

from making him see the peril he faces. Nor from approaching Black Ralph, warning him, offering him money. Dr Watson, I know you think me overwrought, fanciful, perhaps even deluded. Is it not the case, that you think so?'

This was uncommonly and uncomfortably shrewd, not only as an observation, but also as a turn of tactics. I made some motion intended to be evasive.

'Thank you for being so honest,' was the smiling response. 'Now I may be all you suppose, but I lay no obligation upon you, and would two or three comfortable days out of London in this weather be so great a burden?'

Sherlock Holmes once observed that the fair sex was my department. I never fully took his meaning, but if it was to the effect that I enjoyed any ascendancy in that sphere, he misreckoned. Otherwise I should scarcely have found myself, the evening after the interview just described, alighting at a remote railway halt some miles from Westbury.

At once a tall, broad-shouldered man in black accosted me, mentioning my name in a foreign accent. He was an obvious Spaniard – by name Carlos, as I was later to learn – with the dignified deportment of that race and an address that contrived to be at once courteous and proud. Courtesy was to the fore while he introduced himself as butler to Sir Harry Fairfax and installed me and my luggage in the smart wagonette that waited in the station yard; and yet his sombre looks bespoke a temperament to which the keeping of pledges and the avenging of slights were of deadly concern. Not that I took much note at the time; I was pleasantly struck by the baronet's civility in sending an upper servant to meet me, and soothed by the unhurried drive through the leafy lanes, where, as the shadows lengthened, a cooling breeze blew. I looked forward, too, to renewing my acquaintance with the charming Lady Fairfax, and, with a lively quickening of curiosity, to uncovering whatever might be the nature of the threat to her husband.

The carriage mounted a crest in the road and these agreeable feelings were soon dissipated. We had come to the edge of the chalky upland that forms most of the county and entered a region of clay and rock. Some half a mile off stood a tall house of grey stone mantled with ivy and of a design that even at this distance seemed ill contrived. To one side of it lay a plantation of trees with foliage of a deep, almost bluish hue uncommon in England; on the other there wound a stream or small river. I knew at once that the house was our destination, and as soon as a curve in the stream brought the murky, weed-clogged flood close to the road, saw the force of its name. A moment later I was almost spilled from my seat by the wild shying of the pair of cobs that drew the wagonette. The cause was not far to seek – a human figure of indescribable menace lurking in the hedgerow. I caught a glimpse of a hairy fist shaken, of rotten teeth bared in a snarl, no more, but I would have been sure that it was Black Ralph I had seen even if the Spaniard's dark eye had not fixed me with a sufficiently eloquent look.

Darkwater Hall was no more prepossessing at close quarters. Weathering showed it to be not of recent erection, but its bulging windows and squat chimneys belonged to no period or style I had ever encountered. The interior was comparatively conventional. Carlos took me to a more than adequate bedroom and quickly fetched me ample hot water, so I was able to make a very tolerable change and go to greet my hosts in renewed spirits.

With his fresh complexion, steady eye and open, unassuming manner, Sir Harry Fairfax was one of the finest types of English country gentlemen. I judged him to be about thirty years old. His brother Miles resembled him in age and nothing else, a sallow, sneering young man probably addicted to cigarettes and strong waters. From neither brother did I obtain what I had hoped the meeting would furnish, some clue or indication, something that would force out of the subconsciousness of my mind whatever it was that had stirred there when I heard the name of Fairfax; reference books had proved useless. For the moment, the memory stayed buried.

As before, I had no time to ponder the point, for my hostess, in a gown of azure velvet that showed off the brilliance of her eyes, steered me towards the fifth member of the party. Him I identified as an Army man (from the set of his shoulders) who had served some years in the tropics (from his deep tan), but whose career had not prospered (from his disappointed air), and was somewhat tickled to hear him introduced as Captain Bradshaw of the Assam Light Horse. No one who had failed to gain his majority by the age of forty-five, which I estimated Bradshaw to have reached, could be called a successful soldier. I hid a smile at the thought of the 'Excellent, Watson!' which a well-known voice might have breathed into my ear, had its owner been present, and took to conversation.

'I was a sort of soldier myself when I was a youngster,' said I.

'Oh yes? Where did you serve?'

'Afghanistan.'

'You saw some action there, I take it.'

'Not the sort that a fighting soldier sees, but enough. I was wounded and at last invalided out.'

'What infernal luck.'

'You're on leave, no doubt.'

'Awaiting retirement,' said Bradshaw in a tone as dejected as his bearing.

Miles Fairfax now cocked his unkempt head at me. 'Welcome to Darkwater Hall, Dr Watson. Life here may strike you as a trifle dull and rustic after the bustle and polish of London, but believe me, it has its points of interest.'

'Indeed.'

'I presume you're a medical doctor, not one who professes law or divinity?'

'Medicine's my trade, yes.'

'Then the following fact, omitted by my brother when he introduced us, might amuse you. Although unlike in every possible way, he and I are twins.'

'That's not so surprising,' said I. 'Many pairs of twins are no more alike than ordinary brothers and sisters, and we know how they can differ.'

'Assuredly,' said he at his most sarcastic. 'Is it true, Doctor, that twins can be born several or even many hours apart?'

'It is.'

'Not so in our case – eh, Harry? Twenty minutes was all that separated our respective arrivals in this world. But it was enough.'

His sister-in-law put a gently restraining hand on his arm, but the fellow shook it off with a roughness that, had it been my place to do so, I should have considered correcting. I was now morally certain he was intoxicated.

'Yes,' he went on with a growl, 'twenty minutes settled the disposal of the baronetcy, the house, the estate, the money. God's will, what?'

'At least, Mr Fairfax,' said I, 'it's evident you're a good loser.'

That shot went home, and it silenced him for a while, but I was relieved when Carlos announced dinner, thus effecting a change of scene and mood. It proved to be a change not wholly for the better, in that the spacious room in which I now found myself was dominated by a most outlandish carving or relief occupying the section of wall above the fireplace. It was of some dark wood and I could not be sure what it portrayed, except that in one corner a human figure, half naked, was being bound to a post by others wearing hooded robes, while further off I thought I saw a scaffold. All in all, it made an unequivocally distasteful impression upon me. The fare, however, was palatable enough, and the service most adroit and pleasant, provided by Carlos and a young woman I learned was his wife, named Dolores. With her raven hair, creamy skin and deep brown eyes she was in striking contrast to her mistress, but female beauty takes many forms.

I was in the midst of recounting, at the baronet's invitation, the full facts of the strange affair at Stoke Moran, when Lady Fairfax gave an abrupt gasp and raised her hands to her throat. I followed her horrified gaze and spied, through a gap in the curtains, a face I had seen for a moment earlier that day, a face once more contorted with malice.

'Black Ralph! At the window!' I cried, and jumped up from

my chair. Bradshaw was already on his feet, standing between
the lady and the point where the intruder had appeared. Sir Harry
and I had left the house within seconds, but, though we searched
thoroughly the nearer part of the grounds, we returned empty-
handed, much to Miles's scoffing amusement. Some time later,
my host contrived to disengage me from the rest of the company,
having imputed to me a desire to be shown the contents of his
gun-room. He enjoyed some friendly amusement at my expense
when I cautioned him to stay away from the windows there until
I had drawn the curtains over them.

'Do you imagine that Black Ralph has come back with a
Gatling gun?' he asked with a smile.

'I imagine nothing, Sir Harry. I go by what I see and hear', and
I told him of my earlier sighting of that villainous creature.

He was quite unmoved, attributing these visitations to the idle
curiosity of a simpleton. 'I am at no risk, Doctor,' he ended firmly.

'Lady Fairfax thinks differently.'

'That's her way. She watches over me with a care that would
sometimes befit a mother more than a wife. Such matters will be
resolved with the arrival of our first child.'

'Is that happy event in positive prospect?'

'Not as yet.'

Rather abruptly, he thrust into my hands a pair of antique
duelling-pistols that had resided in a glass case, and inquired my
opinion of them. I made what reply I could, as also when he
passed me an early revolver from the time of Waterloo. After a
moment he began to speak of his brother.

'Visitors are always apt to bring out the worst in him. I fancy
he sees himself through their eyes and dislikes the sight. A man
with no occupation, no interest in country pursuits – except
shooting, at which he excels – and yet too indolent to make a
move. Poor, poor Miles, the prisoner of his own nature, as we
all are! And poor Bradshaw too.'

'How so?'

'Well, frankly, Watson – and in the circumstances there seems
little point in not being frank with you – Jack has been living

here largely on my charity. I offer it gladly as he served under my father, but it galls him. And beneath that quiet exterior, you know, there's a cauldron of feelings. Not a stable character, Jack's. It told against him in the regiment, so the dad said.'

In the pause that followed, I ran my eye over a weapon I recognized, one of the single-action Rossi-Charles rifles with the old aperture sight. Though inaccurate at anything of a range, they had been much prized at one time for never jamming and for their lightness and cheapness. I mentioned having come across them in Afghanistan and Sir Harry told me his father had picked this one up after Jellalabad. Forty years ago and more, I remember thinking to myself, and am still at a loss to say why I did – forty years ago, before I was born.

The rest of the evening passed pleasantly if inconclusively enough, and in due course the party dispersed. My bedroom was on the second floor, above which lay what I had taken to be a number of unoccupied or unused garrets and the like; I was slightly surprised, then, to hear, as I made ready to retire, the distinct sound of a door shutting somewhere above my head, and proceeded to listen with half an ear to a conversation of which I could at first make out nothing but that, of a small number of speakers, one or more was male and one or more female. My attention mounted as the voices grew in volume and feeling until, when it was plain that upstairs a tenacious woman faced an importunate man, I hung on every word, but no words were distinguishable, none save one, the interjection 'No!' thrice pronounced in feminine accents, and accompanied by what was beyond all doubt the defiant stamp of a feminine foot. This evidently settled the matter; the colloquy at once died down and soon ceased, the door opened and shut again, and in a few moments all was still.

The whole incident had not lasted a minute, and its meaning and importance were far from certain. Nevertheless, I found some difficulty in composing my mind for sleep. The man's voice I had been unable to identify; the woman's was quite positively that of Lady Fairfax. What, I asked myself, could have taken her at such an hour to a part of the house so remote from where her own quarters must be situated?

When sleep came it was deep and dreamless. Next morning, thoroughly refreshed, I had barely finished breakfast when the household exploded into sudden clamour. It appeared that the gun-room had been broken into by a window and the Rossi-Charles rifle and half a dozen rounds of its ammunition removed. Nothing else was missing, according to Carlos, who, I gathered, was in virtual charge of his master's modest armoury. Mindful of Sherlock Holmes's dictum, that there is no branch of detective science so important as the art of tracing footsteps, I fetched the large magnifying-glass I had had the forethought to bring with me and set to work on the approaches to the window. But circumstance was against me in the very particular in which it so often favoured my friend; the ground, baked hard by the hot summer, yielded no trace of what I sought. I returned to the gun-room to find an altercation in progress.

'It is indeed suspicious—' Sir Harry was saying.

'Suspicious!' his wife flashed at him. 'Might a bullet in your heart come near to furnishing a certainty?'

'In law it is no more than suspicious, and even a magistrate cannot have a man confined on such grounds. I have no charge to bring.'

Bradshaw, at the lady's other side, seemed disposed to agree, pointing out that there had been no witnesses to the burglary.

'Then,' came the ready rejoinder, 'Harry must be placed under guard, protected night and day.'

'I refuse to be made a prisoner in my own house, and out of doors the plan would be quite impracticable, eh, Jack?'

'I shouldn't care to undertake it myself with anything less than a full platoon,' declared the soldier.

'Then you must leave the Hall, go somewhere safe and secret until—'

'What, and give a rascal like Black Ralph the satisfaction of making me bolt like a rabbit? I'd sooner die.'

His sincerity was unmistakable, and made an impression on all his hearers, even his brother, who for the moment forgot to sneer, though he remembered soon enough when I took a hand in the conversation.

First explaining the absence of footsteps outside, I added, 'But I did find some fragments of glass on the soil, as we did on this side of the window.'

'Is that so surprising?' was the baronet's question.

I answered it with another. 'Is this door normally kept locked?'

'Why, yes, of course.'

'How many keys are there?'

'Two. I have one, Carlos the other.'

'Does he carry it with him at all times?'

'No, for the most part it's kept on a ring hanging up in his pantry.'

'And is that generally known in the household?'

'It might well be, yes.'

The younger twin said with a curl of his lip, 'Your reasoning is pellucidly clear, Dr Watson. Any of us, and Carlos besides, could have let himself in here, broken the window from *inside* in order to suggest an intruder from *outside*, and made off with the rifle. How exquisitely ingenious!'

'Mr Fairfax,' said I, summoning up as much reasonableness as I could, 'all I seek to do is to explore possibilities, however remote they may appear to be, and however absurd they may turn out in retrospect to have been.'

'As the great Sherlock Holmes would be seeking to do, were he here.'

'I am not too proud to learn from my betters,' I observed a little tartly as I drew Sir Harry aside.

Before I could speak, he said with some warmth, 'You don't seriously suppose, do you, Watson, that Carlos, or Jack Bradshaw, or my own brother would have stolen that weapon? For what conceivable motive?'

'Of course I don't suppose any such thing,' said I. 'This Black Ralph miscreant is obviously the culprit. No, I was merely—'

'Displaying your powers of observation?' he asked, his good humour at once restored.

'Very likely. Now you must tell me where to find the fellow. There's no time to be lost.'

'I beg you to be careful, Watson.'

'*You* are to be careful, Sir Harry. Keep to the house as far as you can. Take Bradshaw with you if you must venture out. Warn the servants.'

He promised to do as I said, and his directions conducted me straight to the noisome hovel which was Black Ralph's abode, but my journey was in vain. The slattern who answered my knock informed me that the man had left the previous day to visit his sister near Warminster and was not expected back for a week. I did not stay to puncture such an obvious tissue of falsehood. When an inquiry at the local tavern fell out equally fruitless, I returned to Darkwater Hall and addressed myself to questioning the servants, the source of the disquieting rumours that had reached Lady Fairfax in the first place.

My most puzzling informant was the girl Dolores, who fortunately spoke English well, though with a stronger accent than her husband. At first she had little to say, answering in curt monosyllables or merely shrugging her graceful shoulders by way of reply. But then, by luck or instinct, I ventured to ask what were her personal views of her employer. At once her dark eyes blazed and I caught a glimpse of splendid white teeth.

'He is cold!' she cried. 'He is a good man, this Sir Harry Fairfax, a fine English gentleman, but he is cold! His blood is like the blood of a fish!'

Making no move to restrain her, for we were out of hearing of the household at the time, I did no more than encourage her to explain herself.

'I cannot! How can I, to another Englishman?'

'Has he treated you unkindly?'

'Unkindly, never; I tell you he is a good man. But coldly, coldly!'

'In what way coldly?'

Again the girl did no more than shrug her shoulders. I sensed

I would get no further along this path and took a new approach by asking whether Carlos also held the opinion that Sir Harry was a good man.

'Yes, yes,' was the reply, accompanied by a toss of the head. 'I think so. Or perhaps I should better say that I hope so, I greatly hope so.'

'Why is that?'

But here once more I found there was no more progress to be made. I revolved in my mind this interview, together with other matters, through an agreeable luncheon and the earlier part of a confoundedly sultry afternoon. Half-past four found me in the drawing-room taking tea with my hostess.

'We won't wait for Harry,' said she. 'He often misses tea altogether.'

'Where is Sir Harry at this moment?'

'At the stables. He should be safe enough there.'

'I see there is a fourth cup.'

'In case Miles should decide to join us.'

'But you make no provision for Captain Bradshaw.'

'Ah, he never takes tea. Nothing must be allowed to interfere with his afternoon walk. Jack Bradshaw is a very serious man.'

'He is certainly very serious about you, Lady Fairfax.'

'What do you mean?'

'He's in love with you, as you know. I learned it last night, at dinner. You showed signs of strong fear; Bradshaw had not seen what it was that had frightened you, but he could tell its direction from your gaze, and at once – before I was on my feet, and I moved quickly – interposed himself between you and the source of danger. Such speed comes from instinct founded on deep emotion, not from the conscious part of the mind.'

The lady was not indignant, nor did she affect disbelief or surprise. I was sufficiently emboldened by this further evidence of her sagacity to inquire if I might go further in plain speaking.

'We shall make no progress if we allow ourselves to be circumscribed by false notions of delicacy,' she replied.

'Very well. Remember that I am discussing remote contingencies, nothing more. Now – if I wanted to procure Sir Harry's demise, when should I best make my attempt?'

'When his life had recently been threatened by a convicted felon.'

'Just so. What of my motive?'

'We know of one possibility, that your victim stands between you and the object of your passion. No doubt there are others.'

'Certainly. Perhaps I'm the prey of a special kind of envy, or a sense that Fortune has been unjust to me.'

'I follow you.'

'Or again I may feel that my honour has been slighted so grievously that only death can redress the wrong.'

'Do you call that plain speaking, Dr Watson?' was a question never answered, for at that moment the tea-cup in that graceful hand shattered into fragments and the crack of a rifle was heard from the nearer distance. Bidding Lady Fairfax lie down, I hastened out through the open French windows and searched the adjacent shrubbery, but with no result. On my return to the house, I found the baronet with his arms about his wife, who was decidedly less shocked than many young women would have been after such an experience. After satisfying myself that she needed none of my professional care, I searched for the bullet that had passed between us and eventually retrieved it from the corner where it had ricocheted after hitting the back wall. This contact had somewhat deformed it, but I was soon satisfied that it had come from the Rossi-Charles rifle.

By now, Miles Fairfax had arrived from his sitting-room on the first floor, unaware, on his account, of anything amiss until summoned by a servant. Had he not heard the shot? He had indeed heard *a* shot, but had taken it for one more of the hundreds fired in the vicinity every year for peaceful purposes. Bradshaw appeared a little later, back, he declared, from his walk, and evidently much agitated at the narrowness of Lady Fairfax's escape.

He clutched his forehead wildly. 'In Heaven's name, what lunatic would seek to harm so innocent a creature?' he cried.

'Oh, I think it must have been to me that harm was intended, Jack,' said Sir Harry. 'Consider where Watson was sitting. From any distance, it would have been perfectly possible to mistake him for me.'

'Harry,' said his wife in tones of resolve, 'there must be no shoot tomorrow. I forbid it.'

'What shoot is this?' I asked.

'A very modest affair, Doctor,' returned Sir Harry. 'We intend to do no more than clear some of the pigeons from the east wood. A few people from round about will be joining us.'

'And is your intention known in the district?'

'Well, it is our yearly custom. I suppose it must be known.'

'Don't go, dearest,' implored the lady. 'Let the others do as they please, but you remain behind.'

I took it upon myself to intervene. 'My dear Lady Fairfax,' said I, 'Sir Harry must be there. It's our best chance. We must bring Black Ralph into the open and end this menace. I will be responsible for your husband's safety.'

And, with the support of Bradshaw and, unexpectedly, that of Miles Fairfax, I carried the day. Later I made some preparations with which I will not weary the reader, and, in common with the rest of the household, retired early. I was drifting off to sleep when, just as on the previous night, I heard the door above me shut. In an instant I was fully awake. The voices began again, but with the immediate difference that the man was unmistakably Sir Harry Fairfax, speaking with a measured harshness that chilled the blood. I caught a phrase here and there – 'castigation of sin' and 'suffer condign punishment'. They were enough to recall to me what hitherto the name of Fairfax and the sight of the fiendish representation in the dining-room had failed to do. It had been an eighteenth-century occupant of that baronetcy, one Sir Thomas Fairfax, who had conducted nameless rites in this very house, subjecting his own wife to indignities which I cannot set down here. At that moment I heard from upstairs the voice of the present Lady Fairfax raised in piteous entreaty and then what could have been nothing but the savage crack of a whip. A stifled scream followed.

I could hesitate no longer. Lighting a candle, I took my revolver from its hiding-place at the bottom of my travelling-bag, threw on a dressing-gown and made for the upper storey. Within seconds I had found the room I sought and paused outside it before committing myself.

After a moment, Sir Harry's voice, its unnatural harshness intensified, spoke from beyond the closed door. 'Now, I say, you shall make an act of contrition!' There was another pause, and then the voice came again. 'Ah. So you remain, devil. You are incorporate with the body you inhabit. You and she are one flesh. Then as one flesh shall you suffer chastisement!'

With the whiplash ringing in my ears I burst in and confronted two figures garbed after the fashion of a hundred years before. Emily Fairfax wore a gown of black bombazine; he who must be her husband was unrecognizable by reason of the red velvet mask that, apart from eye-holes, covered all his face above the mouth. That mouth was now open in consternation.

'Enough, Fairfax, enough!' I cried. 'What is this hideous mummery? These, I suppose, were the practices of your accursed ancestor.'

There was a moment of complete silence before the man removed his mask. When he had done so, his face wore an expression of what might have been taken for friendly concern. 'I'm truly sorry, Doctor,' he said in his normal tones. 'We have troubled your rest. I can't think how I came to forget that your room was beneath this one.'

'Thank Heaven you did forget,' said I. 'What is to be done with you, you vile creature? I am utterly staggered.'

At this Lady Fairfax broke into sudden laughter. 'That is altogether understandable,' said she. 'My dear Dr Watson, you have been scandalously put upon. How am I to explain? Perhaps I may show you this.'

She handed me a tattered volume on whose cover I made out the legend, 'Plays of Terror and the Macabre'. I turned over its pages with a dawning comprehension which became complete when I reached, set out in cold print, the very words I had just heard Sir Harry pronounce. 'You are acting', was the best I could find to say.

'Correct, my dear fellow,' smiled the dreadful inquisitor of a minute before, cracking his whip against a battered escritoire – I saw now that the room was half full of such items of discarded furniture. 'I think I told you how my poor wife misses the theatre, and this sort of tomfoolery was the best we could devise by way of a substitute.'

'Last night,' I said feebly – 'last night I heard Lady Fairfax protesting in a strain I could have sworn held nothing simulated.'

'Quite true,' said the lady pleasantly; 'last night I was tired after my travels, too tired for this sport.'

'I will interrupt you no longer,' I declared, and brushing aside the apologies of both, took myself out of that room as fast as I could. Doubtless I had made a fool of myself, but I was saved from the self-regarding shame that that thought usually brings by commiseration towards Lady Fairfax. Nobody could have failed to see that her object that night had been, not entertainment, but distraction from thought of what the next day might hold in store.

It was a day that began auspiciously enough, with a blue sky faintly veiled in mist, so often the prelude to a blazing noon. By eleven o'clock the shooting-party was on its way towards the wood. Besides myself, it included the Fairfax brothers and half a dozen neighbours, but not Captain Bradshaw, whom I had just heard explaining to a bewhiskered farmer that the recurrence of a bowel complaint, the effect of a germ picked up in India, forbade him to attend. Happening to catch my eye as he said this, he had hastily looked away, and with reason; I have never met a worse liar. The only servant present was a ruddy-cheeked youth carrying a rattle to put up the birds.

The sun was hot and high as we moved into the shadows of the wood, where there were many small noises. Almost at once Miles Fairfax stumbled at some irregularity of the ground, and but for my out-thrust arm might have fallen.

'Are you all right?' I asked.

He hobbled a pace or two. 'My damned ankle. I seem to have twisted it.'

'Best let me have a look.'

This natural suggestion seemed to fill him with wrath. 'I haven't broken my leg, curse it!' he cried. 'I don't need surgery! I'll be all right directly and will catch you up. Go on, all of you. Go on!'

It seemed we had no choice but to do as we were told. Presently the rattle sounded, flocks of pigeons took to the air and the guns blazed merrily away. I held my fire, maintaining a keen look-out and staying as close to Sir Harry as I could without forming one target with him. The party trod steadily on, deeper into the wood. I caught various movements among foliage, but none were of human agency. I had begun to fear, not what might happen, but that nothing would, when we reached a clearing some seventy yards across. At once there came the smart crack of a rifle-shot and Sir Harry cried out and fell. I was thunderstruck, but after a glance at the baronet's prostrate form I shouted to the party that they should lie flat and keep their heads down. They obeyed with alacrity. Another shot sounded, but the bullet went wild. I faced in the direction from which it had come and walked slowly forward.

'Aim here,' I called, indicating my chest. 'Here.'

A third report followed; I heard the round buzzing through the air ten feet above my head. The fourth and fifth attempts were no better. When I had gone some twenty yards there was a receding flurry in the bushes. I followed at a run, but still had seen nothing when two shots rang out almost together and a howl of pain followed. Within a minute I had found what I sought – Bradshaw and Carlos each covering with a rifle the prostrate form of Black Ralph.

'Well done, lads,' said I, grasping each by the arm, then turned my attention to the would-be assassin. My first good look at the scoundrel showed him to be of simous and ape-like appearance, and there was something animal in the way he whimpered over his injury. This was nothing much; a bullet had creased his

knee-cap, temporarily incapacitating him but not, which would
have been the case had it struck nearer, crippling him for life. All
in all he was infernally lucky.

'Whose shot was it?' I asked.

'I'm not certain,' said Bradshaw.

'I am certain,' said the Spaniard with a gallant bow. 'It was
yours, Captain. Most brilliant, with a moving target at that range.
And now you may leave it to me to deliver to the authorities this
piece of filth.'

Sir Harry's wound was lighter – a gash in the upper arm which
had not bled excessively. When I reached him, he was being
tenderly comforted by his brother Miles, whose whole nature
seemed transformed, and who gave me such a look, compounded
of remorse for past conduct and a firm resolve for the future, as
I shall never forget. On our return to Darkwater Hall, the wife's
joy at her husband's safe homecoming affected us all, notably
Bradshaw. I received so much praise for my supposed courage
in exposing myself to Black Ralph's fire that I was forced at last
to explain that it was undeserved.

'The rifle is the key,' said I, the recovered weapon in my hand.
'Like all its fellows, it's inaccurate. So when it was stolen I knew
the culprit was someone ignorant of firearms. Then, when your
tea-cup flew to pieces yesterday, Lady Fairfax, I knew more. To
get a bullet out of this thingumbob between you and me at
something like eighty yards the firer must be either a brilliant
shot with many hours of practice behind him – impossible – or
a very bad shot with the luck of the devil, one who had the luck
of the devil again an hour ago; that staggered me, I must say. So
you see, while Black Ralph was aiming at my chest I was safe. If
he had just let fly at random he might conceivably have hit me.'

Bradshaw seemed dissatisfied. 'But even the most inaccurate
weapon in the world is dangerous at short range,' he observed.

'Indeed it is. That was why I kept my distance till there were
no more shots in the locker. But of course I knew who was the
villain of the piece within minutes of arriving in the house, despite
all the questions I asked.'

'By deduction?' asked Miles Fairfax with a friendly smile.

'Certainly not. I knew Black Ralph was a criminal, one glimpse of him was enough to show me he was a dangerous one, and everybody else I saw was simply incapable of such a monstrous deed as the one he tried to perpetrate today. It was obvious. And I thank God for that fact. In a case of the least difficulty I should have been the sorriest of substitutes for Sherlock Holmes.'

Accompanied by Bradshaw, who told me he felt he had vegetated too long, I caught the evening train for London, where we supped pleasantly at the Savoy.

If I were recording here one of Holmes's adventures I should lay down my pen at this point, but since I mean to ensure that nobody shall see this account until fifty years after my death, I will take leave to say a little more.

I have been less than frank with the reader. By this I do not merely mean to confess that, in this narrative as in others, I have done what Holmes himself once accused me of doing and concealed 'links in the chain' – the scheme I devised with Bradshaw and Carlos for apprehending Black Ralph is the most glaring example – in order to make a better story, though I hope the finale thus produced is not 'meretricious'. Nor do I mean to discuss the view, put forward by a Viennese colleague to whom I recently recounted the outline of this story, that Sir Harry Fairfax's amateur theatricals might have been something other than what I had taken them to be, and in some abstruse way – which I could not wholly follow – connected with his failure to produce an heir. But it is all too certain that he was still childless when, some ten years after the Black Ralph affair, he met his death in a riding accident, leaving his brother to inherit with sorrow the baronetcy and estates he had once so ardently coveted.

Enough of that. What I have to reveal is of another order altogether. The interview with Dolores, as set out above, is a lie. She did indeed impute to Carlos a groundless jealousy of Sir Harry. But the manner of this, and its circumstances, were wholly different from what I have implied. The two of us were in my bed. Even in these easy-going days of the third decade of the twentieth century I would not care to publish such a confession. I dare hope that the reader of the 1970s will find it unexceptionable; a vigorous bachelor of three-and-thirty, such as I then was, a beautiful and passionate girl, and an opportunity – is there anything there to outrage delicacy?

Dolores, what was it in you, or in me, or in both of us that brought it about that in your arms I experienced a joy more intense and more exquisite than any before or since? Was it that we were so different from each other or that we shared a strange communion of spirit? Was it the season? Was it – contrary to appearance – the place? To me, that is the real Darkwater Hall mystery, as impenetrable and as wonderful now as it was then, forty years ago.

John H. Watson, MD
Bournemouth
April 1925

The House on the Headland

I had done myself pretty well that evening in the coffee-room at the Irving. After a couple of ounces of caviare, I had enjoyed a superb grouse and wound up with a hot-house nectarine, sharing a bottle of the '26 Aloxe with my neighbour. Others at the common table, I had noticed, were in the same mood. In those fateful August days, there were those of us who were not at all sure where we should be a month later, nor even that the Irving would still be in existence. For the moment, however, as the conversation buzzed under that magnificent ceiling, all seemed cheerful and reassuring.

As we sat over a glass of vintage port in the members' lounge, I mentioned this air of ease to my table-companion. In truth he was much more than that; he was and is one of my closest friends. Although he plays only a brief part in this story, I must say something of him. His name is Roger Harvey, his age the same as mine – forty – and his employment somewhere in the Overseas Office, somewhere very remote from my own corner of that institution, somewhere he has never spoken of, even to such as myself. My obvious deductions were shortly to be confirmed.

He nodded agreement with my remark. 'Most of them still can't really believe it's coming, or can't take it in.'

'But it is?'

'Oh yes,' he said, with a look I knew well. It meant that he was certain, but was not to be asked the grounds of his certainty.

'Shall you be staying in Whitehall?'

'For another week or so. Then I disappear. And you?'

'I've heard nothing precise. I imagine there will be plenty of work for my section.'

'Indeed there will,' said Harvey in a grim tone. 'Not at first, perhaps, but later – no doubt of it. I must leave you shortly; I have a lot of clearing-up to do at the office. But if it reveals anything one-twentieth as remarkable as what I came across yesterday, I shall be very much surprised.'

'You sound mysterious.'

'I mean to. Excuse me a moment.'

My friend went to the hall, where his dispatch case was, and presently returned carrying a folder criss-crossed with pink tape.

'I found this where it should not have been,' said Harvey. 'Not so much misfiled, I venture to think, as hidden.'

'Hidden some time ago,' I suggested, looking at the condition of what he had brought.

'It's as old as we are – nothing in it that could be of the slightest interest to Master Hitler, otherwise of course it wouldn't have left the office.'

'What does this red disc signify?'

'Out of use now, but it used to mean "Destroy when acted upon".'

'Presumably not acted upon, then.'

'Oh, it must have been acted upon, my dear fellow. When you read it, you'll agree that whatever else might or might not have happened, what's in here' – he tapped the folder – 'would have been acted upon all right, though I missed any record of how. No, kept for what I'll call its curiosity value.'

I was gazing at Harvey. 'I'm to read it? Why?'

'Why not, if you've nothing better to do? It'll take your mind off our impending troubles. And you're pretty close to being its ideal reader: you're fascinated with the bizarre if anyone ever was, the business took place in your part of the world and you have a vivid imagination combined with strong nerves. I'll be interested to hear what you make of it. Forgive me now – I'll telephone and arrange a drink before I vanish. Give my love to Celia.'

'Thank you, I will.'

'I shall be sorry to miss your wedding. Good night.'

When Harvey had gone I found a bridge four in process of gathering, joined it and played on in the card-room till past eleven. The next evening I took my fiancée to dinner and the theatre, and so it was almost forty-eight hours before I set about slipping the tapes off Harvey's folder, with no great sense of expectation, for previous attempts of his to feed my taste for the 'bizarre' testified more to the goodness of his heart than his understanding of what might appeal to that taste. Only the previous month he had drawn my attention to a most commonplace tale of the supernatural in the *Cornhill*. But any distraction was welcome just then, with German troops reported on the move towards the borders of Poland and Celia visiting her widowed mother.

Before I open the folder, so to speak, you may care to learn a little about the person who has taken it upon himself to describe to you its contents. I will begin by explaining what Harvey had meant, in the lounge at the Irving, by my part of the world: the general area of the eastern Mediterranean. It is mine in a double sense. I was brought up in the family of a British diplomat in one of the coastal cities there. Although my name – Robert Chalmers – could hardly be more British, and I have never held anything but a British passport, my parentage is unknown. Picture me as fair-haired and blue-eyed, with something about the eyelids of those blue eyes that earned me the nickname of 'Chinkie' at school, but, when I grew up, contributed not a little (so at least I have often been assured) to what I can without vanity call my considerable success with women. It is this that has kept me single, but recently, as you already know, I have been taking steps to end that state.

Perhaps it is vanity after all that has led me to wander from my theme. Harvey had had in mind, of course, the second and, in the context, more significant sense in which the Levant is my place. My knowledge of Greek and Turkish, virtually that of a native in both cases, and the influence of my foster-father soon

secured me a place in the appropriate section of the Overseas
Office. I was thus already in possession of information necessary
to the understanding of at least part of the contents of the folder.
I knew, for instance, that after literally centuries of struggle and
in response to pressure from the Allied Powers (Great Britain,
France and Russia), Turkey withdrew the last of her troops from
the island of Crete in November 1898. One of the documents in
the folder proved to bear the name of a Cretan village and a date
in January 1899.

These documents varied in category and provenance. Some
were straightforward signals or decodes; others were reports of
assorted lengths, many of them copies of notes the British agents
in the field had delivered to what would in these days be termed
their control – the location of which I will not even now divulge.
What I had before me was an account of an operation assembled
from the control's dispatches to London and additional matter
supplied here which I will refer to as I go along. A more or less
connected story emerged. I have amused myself, having as I do
something of a literary turn of mind, by dramatizing that story
wherever possible. I assure you that I have neither added nor
altered anything of substance.

Let me begin with information from the official dossiers of the
two agents involved. The younger, Michael Courtenay, had been
born in 1870, educated at Rugby and Brasenose and recruited
by the Department (nowhere referred to by any fuller title) in
1895; he was expert in opening locked doors, safes and the like;
his interests, perhaps rather quaintly, embraced cricket and
the then new-fangled science of psychology. A photograph in
poor condition nevertheless showed him to have been a broad-
shouldered, heavy-featured young man with a determined look.
His superior officer was eight years his senior, Guy Barnes by
name, of similar education and a distinguished record of service
in the Department. With his unruly hair and wide eyes he resembled, I thought, a poet or musician rather than the severely
practical creature required by his trade.

Far above the head of either man it had been concluded that, however warmly to be welcomed on other considerations, the Turkish departure raised certain hazards for the Allies. It rendered the island more vulnerable to the intervention of third parties, of which the most likely was Italy, lately in aggressive mood, her disastrous Abyssinian adventure concluded only two years before – not that she showed at the moment any sign of an interest in Crete. The departure itself might be a feint, a prelude to return in greater strength – not that this was foreshadowed by any known development in Constantinople. What was quite certain was that the newly appointed High Commissioner for the island, Prince George of Greece, had arrived to take up his office on 21 December 1898, and hardly less so that he had enemies there and near by. All in all an unobtrusive intensification of vigilance seemed desirable. Together with his colleagues in the area, Courtenay received orders to keep an eye on comings and goings, to watch for and report anything which his two and a half years' local experience told him was unusual. He passed the message on to his village informants and settled down to wait in the little shipping office that disguised his true function.

He had only a short time to wait. Early in that January there came to see him a middle-aged fisherman whom I will call Vassos and who had shown himself to be reliable and observant. Courtenay asked for coffee to be brought. (He does not say so, but since in the Greek-speaking world nothing of importance is ever discussed except over coffee I have thought the inference a safe one, like others I have drawn here and there.)

'You have news for me, Vassos?'

'Yes, *kyrie*. I don't know what it means, but it is news.'

'We will try to understand it together. Speak.'

The visitor was silent for a short space. Courtenay thought he seemed agitated about something. (This he does say.) Finally he began: 'Last night I take out my boat to go to my lobster pots, near the side of the bay where there is the headland with the big house on it.'

'I know the place. Go on, man.'

'I beg pardon, *kyrie*. I have reached the pots but not brought out my lantern when a light flashes from the house. That surprises me because I think the house is empty, as it has been for over a year, but then I remember the chandler has told me three men have come to it a week ago. While I watch, the light flashes again, and it flashes on and off, on and off, twice, like that, and then all the house is dark. Then I look out to sea and there another light flashes, and again all else is dark, and this is much more strange, because now I hear an engine, a big one, and what must I think of a ship with a big engine all dark except for the flashes in these waters where there are so many small craft? So I wait, and soon the ship comes, and she is big, bigger than my cousin's *kayik*. She's just passing me when some more lights come on, at the landing-stage under the house, but they are dim, as if someone has smoked the glass of the lanterns, just enough to see by, except . . . The anchorage is too small for the ship to tie up alongside, so she turns and comes in stern first, beam on to me. When they're ready, some people disembark; they have the dim lanterns too.'

'How many?' asked Courtenay.

This harmless question evidently troubled Vassos. He swallowed and said, 'Either sixteen or seventeen, *kyrie*.'

'That's near enough. All men?'

'Ten at least, *kyrie*. With some I couldn't be sure.'

'Did you get a good look at any of them?'

Vassos said in a changed tone, 'Once there was a bright light for some seconds, perhaps a match, and I saw . . . I saw . . . no, I could not have seen.'

'What could you not have seen? What ails you?'

'No, *kyrie*, forgive me, I can't say. On the head of St Peter I swear it was nothing you asked me to look for.'

'Oh, very well. Did anyone see you?'

'Certainly not. I waited till they were all gone and then I paddled away; I didn't even row at first.'

'Excellent. Can you take me out there? We will be two fishermen who happen to be passing.'

'When, *kyrie*?'

'Now, if possible.'

After some thought, Vassos said, 'Better tomorrow morning, *kyrie*, I will speak to my cousin. Can you be at the harbour by six o'clock?'

'Yes. You've done well, Vassos. Here.'

'*Evkharisto, kyrie.*'

'*Parakalo. Kal' iméra sas.*'

A couple of hours after Vassos had left the office, a large, well-built young man with baggy trousers and a dirty face was riding an elderly donkey along the path that led from the base of the headland to the house at its tip. When still some fifty yards from his objective he found his way barred by a freshly painted iron railing with what proved to be a locked gate in it. There was a bell attached to this gate, but instead of ringing it, the obvious course, the new arrival tied up his mount to the railing and wandered in apparent perplexity along it first to his left, finding that it ended at a precipice, or rather projected a yard into thin air, then in the other direction far enough to see that it ran down a broken slope to the water's edge. Where it crossed naked rock each upright was rooted in a heavy cross-bar. Those three earlier residents had not wasted their week. The railing would not have kept out a determined and properly equipped intruder, but it was quite enough to see to it that idle curiosity remained unsatisfied. The intervention of some olive-trees and a dip in the ground gave a poor view of the house itself from the landward side of the railing, except that it appeared to be shaped like an L or perhaps a T and had one or more outbuildings close to it.

While the person with the donkey, who carried a pannier of fresh figs, was looking vaguely in that direction, a man came out of the little olive-grove. He wore servants' clothing and as he approached he called out in a Peloponnesian accent, 'What do you want, you there?'

The other swept off his straw hat and bowed. 'Greetings to your honour.' His accent was Cretan and rustic. 'Would your lordship care for some of my fine fruit? Two piastres for the whole.'

'We need none. We have our own supply.'

'One and a half piastres.'

'I tell you we need none,' said the servant, halting while still some yards short of the gate. If he had a key, it was not to be seen. 'Be off with you, fellow.'

'One piastre. My figs are the most delicious in all Crete. His highness the Count would much enjoy them.'

'Count? What Count?'

'Count Axel, your master, distinguished sir.'

'Count Axel is not here. Now go.'

The Peloponnesian turned his back and retreated the way he had come. After making a blasphemous gesture and muttering a number of imprecations, the unsuccessful vendor of figs resumed his donkey and went off down the path. Not a hint of menace, said Courtenay to himself, just total discouragement, designed to set the word going about that there was no profit to be had at the house on the headland. What meaning was to be attached to the implied denial of Count Axel's existence, followed by the explicit denial of his presence? – his existence, and his status as the recent purchaser of the house, having been easily enough established by earlier inquiry in the port. Perhaps no more than a simple desire to be obstructive. Axel – presumably a Scandinavian name. Could Sweden or Denmark have any designs in Crete?

Early the next morning an observer at the house could have noticed (and doubtless one or more did) the antics of a large fishing *kayik* in the waters close to it. The wind was steady enough, the sea calm, but some inexperience or ineptitude at sail or tiller saw to it that the boat, borne only by the current, drifted past the tip of the headland at a speed low enough to keep it within a couple of hundred yards of that spot for several minutes. Shouts and curses filled the air; men ran to and fro on the deck. Courtenay, crouched below the gunwale with his binoculars, saw no more than one thing of the least significance, but it was enough to make him send for Barnes.

'Bricked up?' queried Barnes on the evening of the next day. 'Are you sure? How recently?'

'I'm sure,' said Courtenay. 'Not being a bricklayer I couldn't tell how recently, but I'd wager it was brand-new work, certainly less than a year old. I'm still trying to find the man who did it. Of course, it might have been one of them.'

'There being no point in blocking a single window . . .'

'And no window-tax or anything of that sort . . .'

'We'll start looking in the morning.'

They looked for the best part of two days – through the stout naval telescope Barnes had brought on Courtenay's advice, their vantage-point a secluded spot on the far side of the bay from the house. It was established at once that the outbuilding noted by Courtenay had had at least two of its windows bricked up, and gradually that, to go by Vassos's figures, there were either five or six persons in the party who never ventured into the air. At morning, noon and evening someone emerged from the main house carrying a large tray covered with a cloth and disappeared round the corner of the outbuilding, to where the door must be, later retrieving it piled with empty dishes. Another visitor, on both afternoons, was a tall man with white hair and a complexion proclaiming an origin far to the north of where he now was.

'Count Axel,' said Barnes.

'Yes, but who's he going to visit?' asked Courtenay. 'Who can he be keeping in there? And why on earth?'

Neither had any idea.

They also looked through their telescope, taking alternate watches, for the best part of a night. The moon, approaching the full, gave them an excellent view. The man they had identified as Count Axel visited the outbuilding from 9.27 to 9.53. By eleven the house was in darkness and the grounds, as far as could be seen, deserted.

On the second afternoon, a messenger from Courtenay's office ran them down and said that a jobbing builder had called there, saying he was the man he had heard the English *kyrios* wished to see. Courtenay went and was back within the hour, looking well satisfied.

'There are three windows and the fellow bricked them all up,' he told Barnes. 'But he was very helpful about the type of lock he installed in the door.'

'It should present no difficulty?'

'None whatever to me. You it might take some minutes. My informant also told me what I needed to know about the way the inside is laid out, and supplemented our observations of the buildings as a whole. I'll pass it on to you later. Tonight?'

'Midnight. I believe you about that gate, but even if you could open it in one second you'd be certain to be spotted – there must be a twenty-four-hour watch on it. So it's a boat to the tip of the headland where you go ashore and I wait for you. We'll be in shadow till the very last minute. Will your inquisitive fisherman convey us?'

'Jump at it; he loves a bit of excitement.'

However, when the proposition was put to Vassos, so far from jumping at it he refused outright, and only a solemn undertaking that in no circumstances would he be required to leave his boat, together with a substantial increase in his fee, changed his mind for him. He would muffle his oars and be out of sight near the base of the headland at 11.45.

'There's one characteristic of the door I neglected to mention earlier,' said Courtenay as they approached the rendezvous. 'It has a hinged flap a hand's-breadth deep or more at the bottom.'

'Deep enough to allow a loaded tray to pass when the flap is raised.'

'That was how I saw it.'

'What do you expect to find, Courtenay?'

'Weapons. Ammunition. Perhaps explosives. Enough to cause the authorities to institute a raid.'

'Behind blocked windows?'

'I've been thinking again about that. Vassos had a very poor view of those people when they were landing. Half a dozen of them might well have been masked or hooded. They can't be expected to remain in that state for days on end, so they live where only one man can see them, their leader. Because if a servant saw them he might recognize them, or be able to describe them later, when the job, whatever it may be, is done.'

'Let's hear your views on the job,' said Barnes.

'Well, they have a strong enough force to seize a strategic point on the coast and hold it while their friends arrive in battalions. They certainly have enough to do for Prince George. I feel we'll learn the whole story in the next couple of hours.'

Vassos was waiting for them. When they reached his boat he said gravely, '*Kyrie* Cartnee, *kyrie* Barans, I entreat you not to do as you intend.'

'We have to do it, Vassos,' said Courtenay. 'It is duty.'

'I know nothing of that. Then you will go?'

'Of course. Do you expect us to turn back at this stage?'

'No, *kyrie*, but remember that I entreated you to.'

'Very well. Now let us move.'

By midnight they had reached the spot carefully chosen through the telescope. The two Englishmen disembarked; Vassos took his boat a few yards off into deep shadow. The climb ahead of Courtenay looked a good deal more formidable than they had had reason to expect, but he indicated that he could manage it and was soon out of sight. Barnes himself was in shadow and settled down to wait, till half an hour before dawn if need be. If Courtenay had not rejoined him before then, it was to be assumed, as agreed, that he had been forcibly prevented from doing so. In that eventuality, Barnes was to return whence he had come and inform the British authorities in the island. Meanwhile he was to be on hand to cover the withdrawal.

In fifty-five minutes he heard Courtenay returning. This surprised and dismayed Barnes: the junior officer was famous in the Department for his ability, unexpected perhaps in so big a man, to move over the most difficult ground in silence. Was he who approached indeed Courtenay? Barnes shifted position and drew his revolver.

Courtenay came into view, but it was not the Courtenay who had set off to climb the face of the headland. The dimly seen

figure lurched and tottered from side to side, as if almost over-
come by intolerable lassitude.

'Courtenay,' called Barnes, softly but urgently. 'Over here.'

With obvious, toilsome effort, the other changed direction and
took half a dozen weary steps towards the voice. Then he fell
forward and did not move. Barnes, revolver in pocket, ran to
him and turned him over on to his back. Blood was spreading
from a wound in his chest. The eyes were open. After a moment
they recognized Barnes; another moment later the whole face
took on a look of enormous loathing.

'Don't go up there,' said Courtenay.

'What did you find?' Barnes became aware that Vassos, disinclination to set foot on the headland forgotten, was at his side.

Courtenay made another great effort, this time to speak again.
'Terror,' he seemed to say, 'to fill . . .' After a single indistinct
further sound he fainted.

'He has seen,' said Vassos.

'Let's get him into the boat,' said Barnes.

When Courtenay was lying unconscious in the bows, Vassos
lifted his hand to help Barnes aboard. It was refused.

'Take him back and fetch a doctor,' said Barnes. 'You have
never seen this man before; you found him on the beach. Then
return here and wait for me. If I don't come by first light, everything is changed. Go to the English bey in the town and tell him
what you know.'

Vassos signified consent and rowed away into the darkness.

Since Courtenay had not been pursued and no observable
alarm had been raised, it seemed probable that he had killed or
otherwise silenced his assailant. At any moment this might
become known; Barnes must hurry. Here was his only chance,
for once Count Axel's men were alerted no outsider would ever
afterwards be able to reach the objective unseen.

Barnes, taxed though he was by the ascent, managed to do so.
He stood in shadow at the corner of the main house and listened
for five minutes; nothing and nobody stirred. When, after another
five minutes, he rounded the further corner and came in view of

the outbuilding with the bricked-up windows, he at once caught sight of a human body lying near the door in full moonlight. With the utmost speed he went to it and dragged it into the comparative darkness under a carob tree. It was that of a strongly built man in his thirties with Courtenay's knife still deep in his side. Barnes turned the corpse face down and made for the door of the outbuilding. Its lock had not yet responded to his attentions when, behind him, he heard another door open. In no time he was hidden and watching.

A lamp approached from the house. Soon Barnes was able to recognize Count Axel in a white dressing-gown and Turkish slippers. His look of pleased expectation changed to one of mild puzzlement when, it could be assumed, he noted the absence of the man now lying under the carob. He glanced about for a moment while Barnes crouched very still and hoped very much that the small patch of blood where the man had first lain was small enough not to be noticed; then, evidently deciding that the matter could be left, the Count took a key from his dressing-gown pocket, opened the outbuilding door, entered, shut it behind him, and relocked it.

At once Barnes hurried over and went on with his work. The lock was confoundedly stubborn and the need for complete silence a severe constriction. Some seven or eight minutes went by before the lock allowed itself to be turned. In that interval it occurred to Barnes that Courtenay must have been attacked while re-locking the door, then that that was precisely when he could not have been attacked, or not effectively, because his wound was in front. So he had allowed himself to be disabled by an antagonist who had met him face to face. But his reflexes were known to be outstandingly quick. What had deprived him of the initiative?

Slowly Barnes pushed the door open an inch, two inches. Inside it was almost dark. He pushed further. A little light came through gaps in the curtain that covered a portal at the far end of a short passage straight in front of him; beyond it, he had learned, lay the main room of the building. On each side of the passage were smaller rooms, just then seemingly deserted. Barnes crossed the threshold and shut the door. Soon he was standing at the portal in an excellent position to see what was on the other side of the curtain without being seen. Some rhythmical movement and the sound of heavy breathing could be heard, but no speech. He put his eyes to the most promising gap.

A lamp, the Count's or another, gave illumination that, while not bright, was clear enough. The room held five day-beds or couches, each with an occupant. All of these were naked. All were female. On the couch nearest Barnes there lay a girl of about twenty-five with pretty brown hair and three legs, two normally placed, the third, somewhat withered, growing out above the left hip. Opposite: was it two negro women or one? – at the shoulders certainly two, at the hindquarters as certainly one; it was easy to see why Vassos had been undecided about how many people had landed that night. Next to the two or the one, another double entity was disposed, a slim girl of about the same age as the first, evidently an Asiatic half-caste with exquisite features and the look of being some months gone in pregnancy; emerging under her left arm was something like the top half of a five-year-old child, which now stirred in its sleep. It was impossible to tell anything as to the age of the fourth occupant, because it – she – had no face, none, that is, in the human sense, only as we speak by analogy of the face of a dog or a horse or, more applicable, a tapir.

This being was actually the last to come to Barnes's attention. The first rocked and strained in Count Axel's arms, and Barnes had thought her normal, her face, a true face unlike that other poor creature's, half-turned in his direction, but now, when he gazed at her again, that face turned away, and as it did so another began to come into view, another face on the same head, a Janus-head, another true face that gaped its mouth and half-closed its eyes in pleasure.

Somehow Barnes took himself out of that building without being heard, somehow he climbed and ran and stumbled down the headland without serious injury; he was bruised and bleeding in twenty places when he came to the boat and Vassos. He had waited till he was out of hearing of the house before letting himself start to sob and whimper and managed to keep almost completely quiet after they landed, though he let Vassos give him raw brandy and bread and hot goat's milk and put him to bed and sit up with him for the rest of the night. He gives these details himself in his report, a painful chronicle with its abrupt swings from the style of a conscientious, highly trained officer to that of a sensitive man still in a state of shock and semi-hysteria. But, as he says, he could not afford to wait till such time as he might feel better: he must have orders, and a replacement.

For Courtenay was dead, had died in a monastery hospital within an hour of arriving there. It was on hearing this news that Barnes, again by his own account, wished most fervently that he had killed Count Axel when he had had the chance. But if he had, what would have happened to those occupants of the outbuilding? At that time in that place, they would almost certainly have been quietly slaughtered, and it would have taken a bold man to pronounce them better off dead. I am not as confident as Roger Harvey that Barnes's report was acted upon, though to be sure orders to do nothing constitute action.

In any event, no answer to his request appears in the folder. The final document is a signal from the Stockholm police; Count Axel had large estates near Karlskrona; he had not resided in Sweden for thirty years; late in 1898 he had fled inexplicably from a house he owned in Portugal, leaving it full of possessions. Even in those days it could hardly have been easy for him to kidnap or buy his company and then keep it hidden; now, with governments and police quick to trace any missing person, none of it would be possible.

One small item that puzzled Barnes I can clear up. Courtenay's last words to him had nothing to do with terror; he was trying to say a single word that I, with my Ancient as well as Modern Greek, can identify, though I have never encountered it: teratophilia, erotic attraction to monsters. No doubt Courtenay had run across it in his psychological dabblings. It stands for an inclination bound to arouse abhorrence in those fortunate enough not to share it. Nevertheless I have pondered on it and other matters a good deal these last days, since reading the contents of that folder. I have felt I have had to. Consider: I was born in June or July 1899, in the Levant; nobody living knows exactly when or where. My colouring is Nordic. I have what might be an Asiatic eye-characteristic. Also consider something nobody living knows in detail but I: near my right hip I have an old scar, very old, the relic of surgery carried out so early in my infancy that my foster-parents, who started to care for me when I was six weeks old, did not know, or said they did not know, the nature of the operation. I have read that the tendency to bear twins is strongly inherited. Finally consider what has occurred to me as I write these lines: whence do I derive what Harvey called my fascination with the bizarre?

That has decided me; I will write to Celia to break off our engagement. I have no idea whether the tendency to bear twins, or near-twins, is inheritable through the male line, nor do I propose to find out. But I must do more. I feel that an office job is unsuitable for a healthy man, even one of forty, in wartime. When I meet Harvey for our farewell drink tomorrow, I will ask him for an introduction.

Note: Acting-Sergeant Chalmers, R. F., of the Royal Rifle Regiment was killed in France in May, 1940 when, showing complete disregard for his own safety, he attacked an enemy tank with hand-grenades. He was awarded a posthumous DCM.

To See the Sun

I – *Stephen Hillier to Constance Hillier, Wheatley, England*

Albergu snt. Ioanni,
Nuvakastra,
Dacia
31 August 1925

Darling Connie,

Well, I was always pretty sure I had the wisest of wives, but never has the truth of that proposition become as clear to me as this afternoon on the journey from Arelanópli. I had known in advance that there were no railways in this part of the world, and precious few motor-cars; I was quite unprepared for the roads. In many places, and almost everywhere in the foothills and higher, they simply don't exist, except round the larger towns, which are few and far enough between. The equipage that brought me here was of a piece with them: a veritable box on wheels, iron-tyred wheels at that, a couple of scraggy horses straight out of Browning, 'every bone a-stare', and at the reins an unshaven fellow in a sheepskin jacket that looked as if he had made it with his own far from fair hands – and not taken it off since its first day on his back.

Our ride took us through some of the wildest and most beautiful scenery in Europe – distant peaks wreathed in cloud, great pine-forests that shut out the sun, mountain streams in white traceries down almost sheer cliffs, and sudden vistas of the green plain far below. But it was hard (or so I found it) to appreciate these delights at their true worth, or even to take them in at all, while being perpetually flung from side to side and bounced into the air only to be dropped an instant later on to an unpadded bench that grew harder with each descent. My attempts to contrive a cushion out of my travelling-rug were an utter fiasco, and when, after what seemed like many hours, I reached my destination, I had a violent headache and a sick feeling in my stomach, a dull pain racked every muscle and I could have sworn I was bruised from head to foot. Last but not least, my eyes, full of dust and pollen, stung and itched intolerably. How *very* wise of you to have stayed at home!

Now all my ills are a thing of the past. A bath, which incidentally revealed my almost complete bruiselessness, a change of clothes, and food and drink, have between them set me up again, and my eyes, though still a little bloodshot, have responded well to careful bathing with boracic solution. (Bless you for remembering to pop the tin into my luggage!) Although this place is nothing more than a village inn, it's excellent of its kind – spotlessly clean, bone dry and providing quantities of plain wholesome food and the sturdy red wine of the region. Far from uncomfortable, too; I write this at a table by the window of a pleasant, light room of fair size, furnished with a handsome and ample bed, its mattress a little hard (that one expects) but commendably free from lumps. The landlord is a sterling chap with a swarthy skin and the unexpected blue eyes I've come across before in remote parts of the northern Balkans. He and his smiling, apple-cheeked wife have made a great fuss of me, bringing me plates of patties and bowls of fresh fruit quite unasked and providing enough hot water to bath a horse.

The first shades of dusk are here and I must pause to light my candle. With the passing of the day, what I see from this window has changed a little and goes on changing as I write. Beyond the dark-red roofs of the peasant cottages, sharply sloped against the heavy winter snows, there's a level grassy stretch something like a mile across (though it's hard to be precise) and bounded by an irregular line of low hills that give place to higher hills, these being in turn topped by summits of what must be pretty considerable elevation, seeing that Nuva-kastra itself can't be much less than two thousand feet up. Until a few minutes back, the expanse of the plateau, broken here and there by a farmhouse with its outbuildings, a mill, a church, at one point a tiny village of tiny houses, had a warm and invit-ing look, and the distant mountains, though indeed wild, seemed to offer a noble mystery, a kind of primeval innocence. But now, how remote, how lonely everything seems! Imagine what it must feel like to be a wayfarer on that exposed plain with night closing in, even more to be lost among those desolate ravines and crags, beset by strange sounds and half-fancied movements in the dark! What makes us think that hidden forces are likely to be benevolent?

Some people would say I'm overdoing it rather. Somebody called Constance or some such name would go further and accuse me of childish romancing, that old bad habit of mine. Well, it's possible. I'll see how I feel when I come back from this evening's expedition. Nothing elaborate, hardly more than a stroll before dinner. I have a good hour to kill, it's a clear evening and anyway I must get out and about. I'm so rested that I'm restless. (Can those two words really be connected?) Or perhaps I'm simply impatient to start my investigation. You must bear with me about this business, darling Connie. You must do more than that; I know (how well I know!) that you consider the whole thing to be the most perfect piffle imagina-ble, and you're probably right, but do, like the sweetest as well as the wisest of wives, wish me luck in my search for the vampire.

This won't go off till the morning (if then!) so I'll leave it open and add any new information of interest before I finally post it. Meanwhile, I give you my love, I give you my thoughts, and my heart is joined with yours even though you are so far away.

II – *Countess Valvazor's Journal*

31 August 1925 – The undirected uneasiness, the small vague fears I have been subjected to over these last weeks, sharpened tonight into foreboding: I sense the approach of danger. What kind or degree of danger still eludes me, but I hardly care if it should prove to be mortal. I take a long look at this statement now that I have committed it to paper and ask myself in all honesty whether it is true. Yes, I say, I believe it is. I am weary beyond all expression, and I have nothing to look forward to in my life. If only I could appeal to God to help me to endure! But everything is over between Him and my wretched self, and I am alone in perpetuity.

Again I reread what I have just written, and am struck equally by the self-pity in it and its quality of – what shall I call it? – determined hopelessness, refusal to consider any prospect of alleviation. In the impossible event that a stranger ever comes across these lines, he could think no differently. But, stranger, I would cry to him, these repulsive characteristics are part of my condition. They poison everything, they come between me and everything I once enjoyed: food and drink, literature, art. Here I am surrounded by beautiful objects, or so at least I regarded them at one time. Now, an abominable mist hangs over them, coarsening the outlines, tainting and muddying the colours. Poems I loved in the past are no longer intelligible; they are full of words that have lost their meaning for me, references to feelings I cannot remember. Come, whatever you are, whoever you are, do what you will with me, so long as you sweep the mist aside, make me see the way I used to see, help me to escape from myself.

My call has been heeded – no, impossible, for the unknown has been moving towards me since the middle of the month at latest. But all the same, now, without question, something, somebody, one or the other, is at hand. And this is no fancy – as I write these words there are sounds of movement under my window. What visitor is here?

Is it Death?

III – *Stephen Hillier to Constance Hillier*

Castle Valvazor,
Nuvakastra,
Dacia
Later, 31 August

Darling Connie,

A new address calls for a new salutation. Well, your brainy husband has brought off the most stunning *coup*, as you can see. Here's how it came about.

Fifteen minutes' walk from the inn brought me to the front door of the castle, which I must explain isn't a castle as we at home think of it but a large and splendid house, in this case in a sort of Byzantine style, all domes and pillars. (Early seventeenth century, I heard later.) I'd been intending just to have a look round and sample the atmosphere, and certainly the place looked sinister enough in all conscience, with the moon not yet risen and an owl hooting in a fashion that sounded more than just dismal. There was a lighted window on an upper floor that somehow caught my attention, and though I'd had no intention of paying a call until the next day I suddenly found myself at the great front door operating an enormous wrought-iron knocker. Two minutes later I was talking to Countess Valvazor – in Dacian!

To have got inside without an appointment was a sufficient surprise; these old families aren't usually so accessible. Then the countess herself – all I'd been able to gather from the embassy in London was that the castle was occupied by someone of that style and name, someone older, I'd rather thought, than the youngish, expensively dressed woman in front of me. Quite striking, I suppose, if you like that aquiline type. But the real shock came when she led me out of the hall, which was about the size of a church and full of tapestries and suits of armour and goodness knows what, and into a (comparatively) small parlour opening off it. There are old pictures and old chairs and so on in here too, but also a cigarette-box, a typewriter, a gramophone and records (including some of Paul Whiteman, it turned out) and among other magazines (you won't believe this) a copy of the *Tatler*! I'd just about taken all this in when the countess spoke to me again. She said she agreed it made a slightly bizarre sight, but she said it *in English*! Perfect English, too, or rather perfect American. It shouldn't have been as surprising as all that, after the *Tatler*, but it was, just the same.

Well, she went on to explain that she'd been educated in America, and she was very nice about my Dacian, and she said I'd said I was a scholar, and I said the Dacian word *skolari* was the nearest I knew, but really I was just an amateur, a dabbler in popular mythology, and I told her a bit about the book, and in no time . . . Look, my old Constance, I may as well do things in style and set this out like a proper story, so far as I can. It'll save time in the end, because I want to keep a detailed record and this way I won't have to make a separate set of notes. And I think even *you* will find parts of it mildly interesting, or at least odd. Here goes.

The countess asked, in effect, 'What brings you to Castle Valvazor?' I sort of jumped in with both feet and mentioned vampires, and she said, 'Oh, so you know about us! I suppose we must be quite famous, even in England!'

What a relief – I should have told you that she spoke in a completely friendly, natural way. I said, 'Only among the well informed.'

She said, 'For the moment, perhaps. Of course I'll be glad to tell you everything I know, and let you see the family documents.'

I thanked her, and offered my cigarette-case, and she took one, saying she adored State Express. Then she asked me where my luggage was. (Actually she called it 'baggage' in the American style.)

I said it was in the – sorry. I said, 'In my room at the Albergu Santu Ioanni.'

Without a second's thought she rang a hand-bell and said, 'We always keep a guest-room ready.'

Can you imagine how I felt! I tried to protest; I said, 'You mustn't let me impose myself on you.'

'I'm doing the imposing,' she said. 'We get so few visitors here, and most of them are boring relatives. I'm being practical, too; it'll take you at least a whole day to get through the archives.'

I murmured my thanks (I was really quite overwhelmed), and then the maidservant or housekeeper who had answered the front door came into the room. Name of Magda, it seems; about fifty; typical Dacian peasant stock; obviously devoted to the countess. Arrangements to fetch my things were quickly made. I gave special instructions about the letter to you I had left in my room (I have it in front of me now), and handed over a ten-florin note to compensate the landlord of the *albergu* for his trouble. (I had already paid for a full day's board.) And that was that. So here I am, installed as a guest in the house of the most celebrated family of vampires in the whole of Dacia!

When Magda had gone, I said to the countess something like, 'I have to admit I know virtually nothing about you, just that you're the only child of the late Count and that you're the mistress of this castle and its estates. Do you live here alone?'

'Not quite,' she said. 'But I am the last of the Valvazors, this branch anyhow. I don't imagine I'll be around here very much longer.'

I asked her why not.

She said, 'The kind of life my family used to live in this house is becoming a thing of the past. The Great War has changed everything. Very soon I shan't be able to survive. In fact I spend most of my time putting the place in order so I can sell up and get out.'

'I'm sorry to hear it.'

'Don't be,' she said. 'There was a lot wrong with our old ways.' I didn't know quite how to take that, but she went on straight away to ask, 'How are you on the family history?'

'Well,' I said, 'I begin of course with Benedek Valvazor, who terrorized the whole province two hundred years ago.'

'Of course nothing,' drawled the countess with a smile. '*We*

begin with Tristan the Wolf in the late seventeenth century.' Seeing
my look of surprise, she went on, 'Surely you must know of him?'

'Oh yes, but only as a warrior against the Turks.'

'He was that too, but he was, or should I say his corpse, was
beheaded and burnt and the ashes thrown into the air over
running water in 1696.'

'But he died in 1673,' I protested, sure of my facts.

'Right. The story never really leaked out because the king was
hard on superstition, and a thing like that would have made him
really mad.'

I nodded thoughtfully. Gregory IV had been on the throne at
the material time, and his opposition to all forms of pagan belief
and practice (and of course anything even remotely to do with
vampirism comes under that heading) is a byword among hist-
orians of eastern Europe.

The countess said, 'There's a whole raft of stuff about Tristan
in the files.'

'Excellent,' I said, still thinking.

'Benedek too. But the star of the show is Red Mathias.'

'Ah. The only vampire known to have been dispatched by a
bishop.'

'We have an eye-witness account by the bishop's chaplain.'
She was obviously quoting from memory when she went on, 'So
dreadful was the cry when the stake reached the heart that my
lord sank to his knees and begged me to pray for his soul forthwith and in that place.'

The utterly matter-of-fact tone in which she said this only
made it the more convincing; I wish you could have heard her,
Connie. Anyway, that wasn't the end of our conversation by a
long chalk, but it's as far as I can take you just now. I'm to present
myself for dinner in five minutes, and somehow I know that the
Countess Valvazor wouldn't take kindly to being kept waiting.
So I'll stop for now, but as always I have time to say that my
loving thoughts go out to you and a little piece of you is here in
my heart.

IV – *Countess Valvazor's Journal*

Later – It was not Death that came; I am tempted to call it Life. The change was complete and immediate, as soon as I set eyes on him. When – with what reluctance – I sent him away to make ready for the evening, I went instantly to the bookcase and took down the volume of Cantacuzinu I used to treasure so, and the pages fell open at 'Mary in Spring', and the tears sprang to my eyes just as they did in the past. Not content with that I hurried upstairs to the gallery and – I had almost forgotten where it was, but the moment I caught sight of the big Puvis de Chavannes, 'St Martin of Vertou in his Hermitage', I knew the veil had lifted; the work, by common consent our best picture, was restored in my eyes to all its old power and beauty. If I had needed proof, here it was.

My first impressions of him. Around forty, maybe a year or two older, rather tall, very dark – but I know that, anyone can see that. What else, what more? Honourable, brave, chivalrous, sentimental, a little shy at the best of times, a little cautious, a little fussy, enormously English. I find I forgot to say that, while far from being the best-looking man I ever saw, he is beyond question the loveliest one – no, the only lovely one. Every time he looks me in the eye, and he has a very straight look, I am afraid I will swoon.

A little shy at the best of times – and very shy at the worst of times, like on first meeting the love of his life; he knows that and the rest of it as well as I do. Shy, cautious, even conventional. I must make it easy for him. Certainly easier than I have made it so far, jolted with such violence by my feelings that I behaved as awkwardly as he, cannot remember anything I said for the first few minutes. I must have inquired his business, overridden any protests he might have made against the notion of becoming my guest – I do remember the feebleness of his attempt to seem anything but delighted – and no doubt discussed some of the Valvazor history. During our conversation I discovered something more about him: he is an interesting man. This quality is not necessary in somebody one loves – from what depth of experience do I write that? – but it is very agreeable. I was naturally full of curiosity about his remarks on vampires and what led him to study the subject. By this time I reckon I had ceased to blush and stammer and fall over my own feet like an infatuated schoolgirl.

'The whole thing fascinates me,' he said. 'The idea of a creature once human, now no longer so, and yet in theory and on a low plane immortal, somehow protected from the destructive effects of time, existing at all only at night, its only desire to feed on human blood, driven by nothing else but fear, fear of the sun, fear of the crucifix and of the stake through the heart – it isn't believable in these modern times and it isn't in the least beautiful, but I feel its power, a sort of sullen, outlandish, desolate poetry. If I didn't, I should never have travelled thousands of miles in pursuit of it.'

'I understand,' I replied. 'It's so much part of the local tradition, or rather it was, that I can't think of it in any kind of elevated way without an effort. It's just there. Now, may I offer you a drink, Mr Hillier?'

'You may and welcome, countess,' he said with a smile and, when I handed him a martini cocktail of my own making, sipped it attentively and pronounced it excellent.

'You were saying a moment ago,' I observed after making sure he was right about my mixing, 'that your version of the vampire legend wasn't believable today. It's certainly hard to believe, but what's your alternative explanation? Take the story of Red Mathias, for instance. What really happened in that vault? I mean, these weren't superstitious peasants too terrified to see straight, nor mountebanks telling tall stories in the hope of picking up a few centimes – they were highly educated, responsible men. Are you going to tell me they were lying? What would be the point?'

He shook his head decisively. 'They weren't lying.'

'Then,' I pursued, 'Red Mathias was a vampire and the bishop destroyed him.'

'Not that either,' he said to my bewilderment, but went on, 'I can give you the answer in one word. Ergot.'

'Ergot,' I repeated. 'A fungus that grows on . . .'

'Rye. Yes. And the contaminated rye gets made into bread, and people eat the bread, and they go mad, for a time, until all the bad bread has been eaten. While they're mad they see things, they suffer vivid and detailed hallucinations. They have convulsions and die a good deal too. There was a famous case in Prussia in the time of Frederick the Great, when a whole village fancied its dead had risen from their graves.'

'I heard of something like that in one of the mountain villages.'

This surprised him. 'Not recently?'

'No, it was before I was born.'

'Now these hallucinations are very easily communicated,' he told me in the most charming professorial way imaginable. 'If one man says he sees something, his friends will say they see it too. So if the original hallucination is of a creature returning to its coffin just before daybreak . . .'

'Yes, but why should it be that rather than anything else?' I objected.

'An old folk-belief based on some long-forgotten incident such as the robbing or desecration of a grave. If this were Scandinavia people would "see" trolls and ogres.'

'It's possible.'

'As time went by more care was taken to prevent ergot from getting into the bread. The vampire has died out in the last thirty or forty years because of improved baking methods.' The smile he sent me then made me catch my breath. 'I see you're not convinced.'

'There must be something more,' I managed to say; 'something strange and unearthly. You're too reasonable, Mr Hillier.'

'I can assure you, countess,' he said, laughing, 'I'm not too reasonable to find the mystery still absorbing when I think I know the explanation. But I've digressed. The family history. What about Baron Aleku Valvazor?'

'My great-uncle. We have something.'

'I hope it's good. The accepted story is a sad let-down. All those promising tales about the young girls who died with the name of Aleku on their lips, and then he goes and dies himself, of typhus, and that's that.'

'I don't think he'll disappoint you altogether.'

'We shall see. That's a fine portrait of him in the hall.'

'I noticed you were examining it. You'll see more of him. I mean of course there are other pictures of him in the castle.'

He seemed to find this less than obvious, but remarked mildly, 'On the evidence so far, a remarkable-looking man.'

And there I have to stop. In a moment my beloved and I are to meet again, and I must strive with all my might to prevent myself from perpetrating some idiocy. But I want to say one more thing. Thank you. It's all I can say.

V – *Stephen Hillier to A. C. Winterbourne, St Matthew's Hall, Oxford, England*

Castle Valvazor,
Nuvakastra,
Dacia
1 September 1925

. . . This brings me almost to dinner-time yesterday. You'll have to forgive me, Charles, for telling my story in the strictest, most unadorned chronological order, without forward references to what I later did or discovered; I feel it's only in that way that I stand the remotest chance of making sense of it.

After a couple of wrong turnings (the place really is huge) I found my way to the parlour pretty exactly at the appointed hour. A short, wiry man of about sixty, who I saw at once wasn't a Dacian, rose politely to greet me. His name is Robert Macneil and he acts as a kind of steward, supervising the affairs of the castle and its estates and also acting as librarian – it was to fill this post that he had come to Valvazor in the first place. So much I had been told already; what I saw or thought I saw for myself was that, under a veneer of reserved amiability and a kind of donnishness more suggestive of the stage than any seat of learning I know, here was a very tough, determined fellow indeed.

Naturally I didn't reach this conclusion all at once; other things had a claim on my attention. Or rather . . . Old boy, I despair of conveying to you the brilliance of her eyes, the profusion of her glorious hair, the voluptuousness of her figure, anything about her in a way that will do it justice. I had fallen for her like a ton of bricks literally the moment I set eyes on her. At that stage I didn't dare to wonder about her feelings for me. No use telling myself I shouldn't be in my present state; it seems to me that, again literally, I had no choice. By the way, we've known each other long enough for me to be able to admit to you that I've made the lady sound less than sensational when writing to Connie. *Verb. sap.* No, I'm sorry, I shouldn't try to be flippant about it. Casual adventures aren't my style.

Well, the three of us dined in a modestly sized room that is clearly not the one in use on grand occasions; hardly a pigsty all the same. The vaulting overhead reminded me a little of that at the western end of the chapel at Matt's, though any resemblance must surely be fortuitous. We went from a delicious potato soup to chicken *konstanta* (with plum sauce) and thence to fingers of cheese dipped in a harsh local mustard. Two wines were offered, the red vigorous enough, the white a little thin, I thought, but the countess evidently preferred it. The Scotchman did most of the talking, and most of what he said was on the subject of vampirism. I'll just summarize those parts of his discourse which were wholly or partly new to me.

'Many details of the vampire legend turn out to have no basis in fact – I mean of course no basis in recorded statements, the testimony of alleged witnesses and so forth. For instance it's widely believed, even in parts of this country, that the creature casts no shadow, and no reflection in water or looking-glass. How could that be so? As is clear from its other attributes and activities, a vampire is flesh and blood, in however modified a form. Then the alleged protection given by a crucifix – nothing more than a sign of the Church's attempt to Christianize the essentially pagan rituals used to ward off or destroy the vampire. Which brings up another question – why should the being have to be in its coffin for destruction to be effective? Benedek Valvazor himself was decapitated and annihilated on the roof of this very castle. A spike or nail hammered into the skull is also held to be effective. There are other methods which strike one as bizarre in the extreme; the Cretan islanders, for example, boil the vampire's head in vinegar. It seems the only means generally found serviceable is exposure to direct sunlight. Causing total disintegration. Into dust.'

At this point in his remarks Macneil saw what I had that moment seen, that Countess Valvazor was looking distinctly uncomfortable, even unwell.

I said, 'What's the matter?' I think I may have shouted a little in my anxiety.

'It's nothing,' she said, and took a deep breath. 'I guess I am a tiny bit squeamish after all.' She managed a smile then. 'And those were my ancestors you were talking about, darn it.'

'Indeed,' said Macneil. 'How could I forget that? Countess, you haven't touched your food.' Here he too smiled, but in a very different, not altogether pleasant way. 'Eat it up, now.'

She shrugged her shoulders and did as she was told. At the end of the meal, the servant Magda brought in Turkish coffee, devilish sweet and strong. An *eau-de-vie* of the country, made it seemed from greengages, was also produced, but all three of us declined, Macneil because, according to him, he was off to bed shortly, having had a long day and being faced with an early start in the morning. He added that he would be in the castle library and at my disposal from eight o'clock onwards. Before finally departing he cautioned me against staying up too late, on the grounds that, even at these comparatively modest altitudes, a visitor found he needed his sleep. His actual leave-taking was civil enough, but the impression he'd made on me was by no means unequivocally favourable. I tried to convey this tactfully to the countess, who took my point at once.

'He has a great deal of authority around here,' she said. 'And as you saw we dine together. It must be hard for him to remember he's only an employee.'

'How did he acquire his authority?' I asked her.

She hesitated. 'He – how shall I put it? – he made himself useful to Baron Aleku.'

'Baron Aleku?' I said in surprise. 'But he's been dead for . . .' Half-bemused by amorousness as I was, I couldn't work it out.

'Robert has been here since 1890; thirty-five years ago. He's a clever man, a good organizer. But for him my life here would be impossible.'

'I think I understand.'

'Can't we forget him?' she asked softly.

In an instant I had no breath. All I could do was nod my head.

'Would you like to see some of the rooms?'

'Very much.'

The room we saw (though I saw little enough of it, at any rate at first) was the countess's sitting-room. I gazed at the pretty curtains and covers and cushions and agreed in lethargic tones that they were beyond doubt pretty. For whatever reason, my companion seemed equally distracted. She listlessly indicated another portrait of her great-uncle, less striking than the one I had noticed in the hall, then a larger picture which did catch my attention. This was an outdoor scene showing what I identified as a funeral procession moving across a stretch of parkland towards a one-storey building of somewhat grotesque design, no doubt a place of entombment. The light might have been that of a rainy day at the end of winter. I learned from the plate that the funeral was that of Baron Aleku Valvazor in the year 1891. For a few moments, without any clear reason, I experienced a feeling of the most profound depression. I spoke before I thought.

'Where did this happen?'

'Here,' said the countess with an inquiring look. 'In the grounds just outside this window.'

'And what I see there is some kind of . . . sepulchre.'

'There are Valvazors in it that go back to the sixteenth century.'

I made a non-committal noise. My interest had subsided again.

'The ceiling in this room is supposed to be very unusual.'

And then . . . My dear Charles, we should both of us have to be altogether different from what we are if I could tell you, even in outline, what happened then; you must use your own experience and your imagination. But this I will say, even to the loyal friend of Connie's that I know you to be: it wasn't so much that what happened then was better than any comparable experience of mine, it was more that there simply was no comparison. Afterwards, we agreed that in the very first instant of our meeting – but now, like an oaf, I'm once more on the point of embarrassing you. So, in the most strictly practical fashion, I'll do no more than state flatly that Countess Valvazor is called Lukretia (the Dacian aristocracy, like the Rumanian, are fond of stressing their links with Ancient Rome), that she's twenty-nine years old and, as you must know to appreciate what followed, that the setting was her bedchamber, a rather sombre room which she had done her best to cheer up with her gay cushions and rugs and so on.

It was late when I fell asleep. At once, or so it appeared, I entered on a series of vivid yet incomprehensible dreams. There were animals quite unlike any real or even legendary beast, and manufactured objects, large and small, of unguessable purpose. And the people, so many of them, so active, so unremittingly interested in me – what were they all doing? What was happening? Where and what were these places? Was I dying? At last a horrified voice that called in a strange tongue banished this troubling phantasmagoria: 'Aleku, you devil, you hound of hell!' – yes, Charles, 'tu kani d'infernu', those very words; I was wide awake in a split second.

Lukretia took some calming down. She said she had very little idea of what had caused her to shriek out like that, it had been too dark in her dream, but she knew it was something awful, something loathsome. I said it was over whatever it was, and she said it wasn't, and then – I must get this part down as near as possible *verbatim*, because although I don't understand it I know it's important.

She said, 'Will you do something for me?'

I said, 'Anything I can.'

'Will you pray to God and tell Him I thank Him for sending you to me? Because I've no doubt that He did. I thought He had abandoned me for ever, but now I see He hadn't after all. Tell Him that, too. You will, won't you?'

'Of course I will,' I said, 'but wouldn't it be better if you told Him yourself?'

'Oh yes,' she said, 'but in my state prayer is ineffective.'

'In your state? What state?'

'Of absolute sin.'

'Can't you confess it?' I asked, I hope as gently as I intended.

'The father won't hear me. We . . . there was a quarrel.'

'Then go to another father.'

She shook her head; she had a funny look I couldn't make out. 'Please do as I ask.'

'Gladly.'

'Promise me, Stephen.'

'I promise.'

'I'm going to hold you to it.'

When I slept again I didn't dream at all. For the experience I did have I can find no word; perhaps you know one. I was awoken by the sound of an enormous bell from somewhere overhead, somewhere quite near, still dying away as I listened. Lukretia hadn't stirred, I could readily see. But how could I see it so readily? Because the room had grown lighter. How? With light from outside, through the chinks between the heavy curtains, bright light. But that wasn't possible. We all carry a reasonably efficient clock in our head, and mine told me that it should still be dark out there. With my thoughts wandering slowly from festive illuminations to forest fires I put on a thick wrap of blanket-cloth (which I was soon to be mightily glad of) and hurried to the window. As I reached it the bell tolled again with an abruptness that made me blink. I pulled a corner of curtain aside and looked out.

What I saw (and I saw it, I wasn't drunk, I wasn't mad, and I certainly wasn't dreaming, I knew that as a normal waking man always knows it) – what I saw was the funeral procession of Baron Aleku Valvazor in 1891. No one who had seen the picture in the room next door could have been in the slightest doubt. Everything and everybody was there, the old priest, the young priest, the coffin on an odd-looking waggon drawn by six men pulling ornamental ropes, the family and friends, the more prosperous farmers and yeomen in their characteristic brimless hats, the peasants, all on a rather blustery, chilly February or March afternoon nearly thirty-four years ago. I could also see several figures that I was nearly sure weren't in the painting, like the one who must have been the artist himself furiously at work, an assistant at his side. And like Lukretia, clad in black, standing with bowed head near the entrance to the tomb and then suddenly glancing up and, as I recognized her, looking me straight in the eye.

I say I recognized her; she must have been nearly a hundred yards away, or quite that, but the light though not perfect was good enough and I had caught not so much any lineament as, more distinctively, a tilt of the neck that, after those few hours, I now knew well. But of course I thought of none of this at the time. Instinct made me turn away towards where I had left Lukretia and there was nothing, not only was she not there but the bed, the dressing-table, the pier-glass, the pictures, the sculptures, the brasses were all not there, nothing was there but stone walls and floor, the floor whose chill now struck through to my bare feet. I turned back to the window and there was nothing there either, just uncurtained panes and starlight and approaching dawn. Would you have lingered? Shivering and gasping with more than cold I was out of that grim spot pretty smartly, I can tell you, but finding my way back to the countess's room or to my own was a different kind of task. I wandered up and down the great staircases and along the twisting corridors for anything up to half an hour. By then I was very cold indeed. In the end I rounded a corner and almost walked into Macneil, who was dressed for the outdoors, indeed for the saddle. He gave me a look of surprise and suspicion.

'Where have you been, Mr Hillier?' he asked. His tone was almost accusing.

'I don't know,' I said.

After another look at me his manner softened a trifle and he said, 'Have you been sleepwalking?'

'I don't know that either. I found myself in a room I've no memory of entering. Perhaps I did sleepwalk.'

'What sort of room?' he asked gently.

'It was empty.'

'Completely empty?'

'Yes.'

'Oh,' he said. 'Now I mustn't keep you standing here on this chilly floor. The countess sends you her apologies.'

'Apologies?' I said. 'What for?' I dare say I sounded rather stupid; it was how I felt.

'She received a message to say that her old nurse was dying and was asking to see her, and so she hurried off. As she would. It's a fair drive, nearly to the border of the province. I'd expect her back some time in the afternoon. And now I must speed you on your way before you catch your death of cold. Down to the end there, Mr Hillier, turn left, and your room's in front of you. I hope to see you later if you feel well enough.' And he turned his back and went.

After a couple of hours in a warm bed, a comfortable bath and a large breakfast of scrambled eggs with strips of smoked mutton, hot rolls with quince jam and scalding coffee, I felt – well, still puzzled and wary, but I had got over the painful bewilderment that had gripped me earlier. I had another look at that picture of the funeral, and was more than ever sure I had *seen* what it portrayed, had not in any sense been dreaming. Next, a visit to the library, high-ceilinged and of ecclesiastical atmosphere, Macneil the complete professional in leather cap and taped-on cuffs, and informative. Much of interest, a few surprises, selective list enclosed. He (Macneil) was very proud, and with reason, of their Codex Palatine, which it seems no less a person than Dietrich Dittersdorf came all the way from Budapest some months ago to consult. I should have loved to hear more of all this, but you'll understand I had a more pressing concern. When I had duly admired the Codex, I broached the matter.

'Tell me, Mr Macneil,' I said, 'it was in 1891, was it not, that Baron Aleku was buried?'

'Indeed,' he replied; '25th February 1891, Ash Wednesday.'

'It seems to have stuck in your mind.'

'Odd how these things do.' He was smiling that smile of his. 'I was there, of course.'

I won't pretend I showed I was ready for that. I must have gaped. 'Were you, by George!' I said before I knew it. 'I hadn't quite realized you'd been in these parts for so long' – though you remember I had heard about it from Lukretia. 'Perhaps you can tell me which members of the family were also present. Out of interest.'

He was grinning now. 'You've been looking at that painting in the countess's sitting-room, haven't you, Mr Hillier?'

'Yes, a fascinating piece.'

'Oh, do you think so? I've always found it rather ordinary. However. Yes, there was the countess dowager and her sister, Count Zoltan and Countess Elizabeth, their three sons, of whom the eldest was to be the present countess's father, Baron . . . Baron Horvath on the dowager's side and Baroness . . . it's gone, and the Rumanian cousins, those were the . . .'

'Yes. Thank you.' I realized I had had a fat chance from the beginning. 'I must have been mistaken. I mean you're right, it isn't a very good painting.'

'If you want to know more about Aleku, I could show you the mausoleum after luncheon – you know, where he's buried or is at rest.'

I thanked him and accepted, though I hardly expected there would be much to see, and he picked up a shallow pile of grey folders that evidently held what he considered most likely to be of interest to me. I thanked him again for his trouble; he said that as a result of years of diligent subject-indexing it had been no trouble at all. (Librarians are much the same everywhere, eh, old boy?) Then, opening one of the folders, he muttered a question about the state of my Hungarian, and I saw fit to call it rusty, which I hope you'll take as a pardonable exaggeration, or rather as whatever the opposite of that is. (Understatement. I must pull my brains together.) Accordingly, Macneil had the kindness to run over the main points of what had been an address given before the inner college of St Ladislas' at Peks by a certain Dr Bela Hadik in 1913.

The speaker's main theme is apparently that the powers of the vampire and also its weaknesses, its limitations, can be rationally explained. On this view, the vampire is not in any sense dead, rather it has entered upon another kind of life, its activity confined to the hours of darkness but itself made potentially immortal and ageless. We are to remember that the victim of a vampire's attack loses very little blood, and yet soon afterwards, perhaps after a second attack, perhaps not, is dead. Of what malady? Later he rises from the dead and functions once more – walks, talks, thinks, is capable of great physical exertion. In his turn the victim becomes the predator and himself imbibes blood, not much, and not often. For what purpose? Hardly for nutriment; no corporeal frame of that size could possibly subsist on such a meagre diet. Day-to-day sustenance must be provided by more conventional food.

The postulate is that somehow, perhaps through the vampire's saliva, a peculiar element reaches the victim's bloodstream and multiplies within it. During the period of supposed death, actually suspended animation, a number of changes take place which curtail freedom of movement but confer enhanced strength and capability of self-repair and, it has been said, certain abnormal powers of the mind, such as the ability to detect malign forces at a distance.

At this point, just to contribute something of my own, however obvious, I put in, 'At any rate, the physical changes permit the creature to survive injuries that would kill an ordinary mortal and therefore, if he is to be destroyed, he must be damaged in ways no living being could withstand – impalement, decapitation, burning.'

'Indeed,' said Macneil, 'and just as the vampire transforms normal blood, so he needs something from it. Whatever that something is, it tends to overheat the body, so that during the warmer, daylight hours there must be not only rest but refrigeration.'

'For which purpose,' I said, 'a stone coffin packed with earth and laid in an underground vault would be as good as anything science could come up with till just the other day.'

He smiled at me again, but more pleasantly this time, like a schoolmaster at a pupil who has got it right for once. 'Exactly, Mr Hillier. Well, I think you have the heart of it there.'

I said with a show of detachment, 'Do you really believe any of this vampire stuff yourself?'

'Yes,' he said straight away.

'Have you seen any of it?'

Now he hesitated before saying firmly, 'No.'

'Do you believe any of *this*?' I tapped the folder.

'Maybe.'

'Oh, it's rather rot, don't you think? I mean it leaves out so much. You said last night that exposure to the light of the sun was the most effective means of destroying a vampire – widely believed to be so, that is. Is that accounted for here?'

'Not specifically.' He spoke as if he perhaps wanted to have done with the conversation. 'Further overheating of the body would no doubt result.'

I couldn't resist saying, 'To the tune of thousands of degrees Fahrenheit? If you'll forgive me, Mr Macneil, your belief seems to be founded on a wish to believe.'

'No doubt it does, Mr Hillier, but I'd like you to cast an eye on what I have here before you finally make up your mind on that point.'

'What is it?'

'Part of the only known statement on vampirism committed

to paper by a self-confessed vampire,' he said impressively, hand-
ing over a single yellowed sheet covered with brownish writing,
and added, 'The most secret document in this library. Even the
countess doesn't know it's here.'

No doubt I should have inquired into the last part of that, but
I was too eager to examine what I now had before me and
allowed Macneil to withdraw, muttering as he went something
about binding up a batch of pamphlets.

As I read, I began to wish more fervently than ever before
that the advance of science had reached the point at which books
and other printed or written material could be copied at the
pressing of a switch, for instance by some development of the
photographic process. This is 1925, though, not 1975, and I
have had to do what I could with pen and ink. As you see, I
started to transcribe the original, which is jolly simple Dacian,
but not simple enough, I suspect, for those whose knowledge of
the tongue is worse than rusty. Being simple it has lost little by
being translated, though I should add here that the writer was
obviously an educated man and that one or two words and
expressions, together with some slight formalities of construction, suggest a date in the last century, most likely its second
half.

Enclosure

Duminu wobisku. Preko wos ni par mizerikordi ni par pieti.
The Lord be with you. I ask you not for pity nor for mercy, but
for your prayers. You who are not accursed, pray to Almighty
God for my wicked soul. You who go out in the day, petition all-
loving God for His justice towards a child of His who lives in
loneliness and misery, who stays always in the same place and
who never sees the sun. Plead with Him that I have no choice in
the end but to take my loathsome refection, and to lie and dissem-
ble, which I loathe almost as bitterly, and suborn others to do evil
on my behalf, for if I do not I shall surely die at last, and there is
no life so miserable that it is not to be preferred to death. Say all

this to Him, for His will is that I cannot say it myself; why should one of my vile condition obtain such relief? Say to Him also that I trust in His goodness and expect His deliverance. On that day there shall come one who will.

Main letter

One who will do what? is no doubt the question you're asking yourself. I certainly asked it, and must have done so aloud, for Macneil, at my side again to write in an addition to the vast catalogue, expressed his ignorance and added that (as I had surmised) the following sheet or sheets were lost. He went on to say that he considered it to be about fifty years old, or a little less, and that it had been in the library when he first came, but with no press-mark or entry and no information as to its origin, merely a half-indecipherable note about a hearing before a quaestor or investigatory magistrate. Finally he asked me what I thought of the document. I told him I didn't know, which was and is no more than the truth. It might be a fake, it might be the ravings of a madman, but I can't believe it's either, but as to why, that again I don't know. Something about the handwriting bothers me; I've made a tracing of the first few words which you'll forgive me for not sending on.

Luncheon, consisting mainly of toothsome and expertly cooked river trout, was pleasant enough, enlivened moreover by much interesting talk from Macneil on the subject of local history; he has his own style of being agreeable. After the meal, as arranged, he took me over to the family tomb in the grounds. This, especially the interior, proved sadly unspectacular. It was strange none the less to see a plate in the wall with the legend *'Segnu Aleku Valvazor*, 1841–1891' and a Latin text mentioning eternal rest. Macneil told me that when – but this is another piece of talk which I feel instinctively calls for *ipsissima verba*.

'Not more than a couple of weeks after the burial,' he said, 'a party from the village came up and broke open the coffin and found . . . a corpse. A corpse showing unmistakable signs of decay, not Aleku in his habit as he lived. There were no more rumours after that.'

I was startled, and exclaimed, 'It took a damned lot of nerve to lead that coffin-breaking expedition.'

'Yes, nobody seemed to know who did. Not a local man, it was said.'

'When was this place built?' I asked him.

'In its present form it was completed in 1891. You're quite right, Mr Hillier, the year of the baron's death, by a melancholy coincidence much remarked on. No sooner had the Count prepared for a return to traditional practice by entombing the family dead outside the castle proper than his younger brother . . .' He spread his hands.

'Then there's a burial chamber *in*side the castle proper.'

'Oh indeed, an extensive one. I'd be happy to show it to you in the morning. I must be getting back to the library now; we take a large number of journals and I do so hate getting behind with them.'

We were strolling quite companionably towards the castle when he asked me something that filled me with suspicion on the instant.

'Are your whereabouts known to your people in England, Mr Hillier?'

I replied carefully and truthfully, 'No, at this moment not a soul has more than the vaguest idea of where I am.'

'Dear dear,' he said, 'a most unwise omission in a country like this. If I may, I'll send a man to the telegraph station. Tomorrow.'

Whether he does or he doesn't, my vaguely based conviction that nobody here should know of this letter, much less be given it to post, has become intensified. I'll be sure to get it off to you myself in the morning, along with one to Connie. Not that the story's over yet by a long chalk, I bet.

I write this in the parlour I described to you earlier. Outside, the colours of the lawns and shrubs are beginning to fade as evening approaches; Magda has just brought me a lamp. Still Lukretia has not returned. With Macneil's permission I brought

here the library copy of *De Mortuis Viventibus* by Lartius Cala-
sanctius, all of whose works I thought I knew; this one I'd never
even heard of, but I'm too strung up to do as much as open it.
Shameful of me. Perhaps I'll be more capable tomorrow.

I'll write again as soon as I have more news. Good luck with
the James Barnes Hitchens prize.

Yours aye,
Stephen

VI – *Countess Valvazor's Journal*

1 September 1925 – . . . The last was no dream, but a memory
of that fatal night, all except the moment when Stephen was there
in my place, helpless as I was, and I woke cursing Aleku for a
devil and a hound of hell. Now I have fed my hatred enough,
and can come to the events of this very evening.

After making my arrangements with Magda, I found Stephen
in the parlour with one of Robert's ancient tomes on his knee.
He sprang up and we kissed with every show of passion, but
I immediately sensed a constraint in him. And yet it was he
who, breaking the embrace, gave a look of misgiving and
mistrust.

'What's wrong?' he asked gravely. 'Is it your nurse?'

'I stayed with her till she died,' I told him, 'that's why I'm so
late. It was quite peaceful. A good death. I had to go, Stephen.'

'Of course.' His voice was so gentle that I wanted to kiss his
feet.

'I'm sorry I rushed off without seeing you, but I just didn't
know . . .'

'I understand.'

I tried to brace myself. 'If I were to ask you to go now, this
evening, not as far as Arelanópli but farther than Nuvakastra,
and wait there for me to join you, and if I said it was very important to both of us for you to do that, would you go?'

'After being told nothing more? Not even just how important "very important" is?'

'Meaning we . . . might never see each other again.'

'"Might"?' he said, still gently. 'How likely is "might"? Nine chances in ten? One in a hundred?'

'Oh, darling . . .' I felt great tenderness for him, and great exasperation. 'You'd have to have it all spelled out, wouldn't you?'

'Yes. Otherwise I might feel I was being got out of the way for some sinister purpose.'

'Sinister? I don't understand, Stephen.'

Now his look was stern. 'Neither do I. Last night I saw the funeral of Baron Aleku Valvazor in the year 1891.'

'You were remembering the picture in my sitting-room. That sort of thing often happens in dreams.'

'This was no dream. I saw it.'

'That's impossible,' I insisted.

'It happened. I watched it from your bedroom window. At least that's where I started.'

'How could you see anything?' I asked in bewilderment. 'It was dark.'

'Outside it was light. When the . . . performance was over I found I was standing in a strange, completely bare room in some other part of the castle. I had the devil's own job finding my way back, in fact—'

I interrupted him. 'All right, what if it did happen? How could it have anything to do with me and my sinister purposes?'

'It has something to do with you all right. You were there. I recognized you.'

'I was where?'

'At the funeral. In 1891.'

'Nonsense,' I said coolly. 'I was in somebody's dream in 1925. Somebody I had just made a certain impression on, if I'm not flattering myself. But I'm going to humour you. Let's suppose you're right: you weren't dreaming, you *saw* Aleku's funeral, though I'm far from sure what that means. You couldn't have seen me at it, because I wasn't born then. But you might quite well have seen this person.' And I opened my locket and showed him mummy's picture. 'My mother. She was there.'

'It was you,' he said, but he said it with lessened conviction.

'You took it to be me. Of course you did. You would take it to be me rather than a person you'd never so much as thought about. Aren't we always doing that? Taking someone for a person we know, even when the person doesn't look anything like the someone? Haven't you often done that? In your dreams?'

The truth of that observation obviously struck him with some force, and turned him almost sullen for the moment. 'Well, how did I get to that strange room?'

'Darling, you walked there in your sleep. How else could you have got there? I couldn't have carried you.'

'No', and a rueful grin.

'That's better,' I said, trying to sound as much like an English governess as I could. 'Now let's have no more childish talk of sinister purposes.' With that I kissed him in a very ungovernessy fashion.

A little later he said, 'All right – devilish odd, though,' but I knew already that I had disarmed his suspicions. With his cheek against mine he went on softly, 'But what was your real purpose? In trying to get rid of me?'

'That was rather silly. I wasn't trying to get rid of you. Did I sound like it?'

'Not much, no.'

'What I was doing was giving you the chance of ducking out if you wanted to. Making it easy for you.'

'But why should I have wanted to duck out, as you call it?' he went on as before.

'I don't know. Well, you might have. I had plenty of time for thinking on my trip, maybe too much, and in the cold light of day I found I just couldn't believe in last night. For myself I could, but I couldn't quite for you. I don't know why, you gave me no cause.'

'I say, Lukretia, really,' he rebuked me.

'Yes, I said it was silly.'

'Was that what was wrong when you first came in tonight? My God, what an absurd question.'

'I wasn't thinking.'

'You were not.' He drew away a little and looked me in the eyes, smiling. When he smiles his mouth stays firm; it would not be quite so lovely otherwise. He has a little scar shaped like a V on the left side of his chin. Perhaps he got it playing some game in school, in that 'quite decent' school in Sussex county. I looked back at him and he said, 'Would you like me to show you just how silly you were being?'

'Oh yes,' I said, 'I would. I'd like that very much.'

What followed was joy, unlike anything he or I have ever had in our lives before or have ever thought about, but still very simple joy. Afterwards there was peace, for me the first I can remember; I cannot speak for him. But it had to end. I got out of bed, put on a robe, went behind the screen and opened the champagne.

I could hear him laughing. 'Why all the concealment?' he asked.

'I was afraid if I didn't arrange it this way you might be distracted.' Back in bed I raised my glass to him and said in my native language, 'I wish you happiness your life long.'

'May your good fortune never fail,' he responded at once, raising his own glass. His Dacian is very correct, but his consonants are heavy in the English way. A delightful way.

There was one more thing to be done. I fetched the small scissors from my dresser and snipped away a lock of hair. 'Now your turn,' I said. 'No, let me do it for you.' When I had taken a lock of his, thick and strong, I held on to it and handed him mine. 'We're official lovers now and can only cease to be by exchanging these again. Is that English? By giving them back.'

'I follow you.' There was a sadness in his eyes which at another time might have troubled me. 'I'm glad we've done that. Is it a peasant custom?'

'Well, a custom anyhow, though it's dying out, as what isn't? But I'm fond of it. I've never done it before. You needn't go on holding that; the ceremony is concluded.'

I went back to the dresser and left the two locks and the scissors. Stephen was comfortably settled against the pillows with his eyes shut.

'Well, what do we do tomorrow?' he asked drowsily.

'Tomorrow we prepare for England,' I replied. 'And the day following we leave for England. And after however many days it is we arrive in England. And we go to London and see the churches and the palaces and the people, and we walk in the park and sail on the river. And in the country we go riding and we sit in the garden early and late.'

I cried then, but there was no one to hear me; Magda's potion certainly acted fast. Soon I made myself stop crying, for I had work to do, and tough work at that. I put on a gown of blazing scarlet and bedecked myself with my finest jewels. On my way out I bent and kissed Stephen's forehead. As I did so it occurred to me that there was really no hurry; those with whom I had business would stay till I came. I settled myself at Stephen's side and kissed his cheek, once, twice. By slow degrees a delicious languor stole over me; as I lay there I could no longer feel the pressure of the bed against my body; my vision clouded, so that I saw only vague coloured shapes without any meaning, and in my ears there was the sweetest melody I ever heard, in some sense under my control and yet at every turn delightful in its unexpectedness, always about to come to rest in a cadence of supreme poignancy before miraculously passing into fresh unbounded rapture. There was no name for the instruments that played it, nor for the bewitching odours that drifted to my nostrils. An inviolable warmth enfolded me. My well-being and happiness were both of them exquisite, and to be made perfect needed only a single small action on my part. And for its performance no volition would be necessary, nothing more than surrender to the onward flow of ravishment. Oh paradise, oh abode of the blessed . . .

Suddenly I was back in my dream, that cruel dream in which Aleku chained me to the dungeon wall in perpetual captivity, but now there was another beside me, gagged and blindfolded like myself, and I knew it was Stephen. I screamed and came to myself in an instant. After a second's inexpressible agony of mind I ascertained that, though my teeth had indeed been at his throat, they had not penetrated the skin and, as I watched with equally intense relief, the marks I had left began to fade. I got off the bed and knelt down and tried to say a prayer of thanksgiving, for I had no doubt about where that warning had come from, but not a word could I utter, as always. So I offered thanks in my heart; even He cannot prevent that. They were double thanks; I knew now for a certainty what I had been pretending was not certain, that I could not for ever, nor even for long, suppress the abominable craving that defines my state, and that Stephen would be in deadly danger as long as I could get at him. This knowledge has hardened my resolution to do what must be done. It must all of it be done; the danger to Stephen comes not only from me.

Writing this last entry has brought me pain, not least in detailing the lies I had to tell my beloved. But it has helped me relive some of the most wonderful, the only wonderful moments of my life, and after forty years I find it hard to break the habit of confiding to these pages what nobody else must know and what, thanks to Magda, nobody else will ever know. So now, goodbye. To whom, to what do I say those words? No matter.

VII – *Confidential Transcript of the Privy Inquest Under His Rectitude Quaestor Miron Filipescu, Nuvakastra, 3 September 1925, Extracts*

QUAESTOR: Fetch Prefect Sturdza.
REGISTRAR: Prefect Sturdza, in the name of Omnipotent God I charge you to tell the truth in all matters—
QUAESTOR: Hold your peace, registrar, and let the hearing

proceed. This is not a court of law; it is not even an official council. I pray God our business today never comes before any such body. Speak, prefect.

PREFECT: Thank you, your rectitude. I have here the paper brought to me at the police office by the witness Magda Marghiloman. I have satisfied myself that the handwriting is that of Lukretia Iulia Klodia Valvazor i Vukcic, Countess Valvazor of the same.

QUAESTOR: Good, good, Read it, man.

PREFECT: Yes, sir. 'In the year 1886, being then twenty-nine years old, I was forcibly reduced to the abject and abominable state of vampire by my father's brother, Baron Aleku Valvazor, who also debauched me. For four years thereafter we continued our hideous practices to the horror and shame of my parents and at growing risk to ourselves. The danger was not from the subsequent activities of our unfortunate victims, who were made away with when they had served their turn, but from the number of unexplained disappearances in the surrounding country. The village people would have come for us one fine day.

'At the end of that period, early in 1890, the Englishman Robert Macneil arrived at Valvazor, ostensibly to serve as librarian and nothing more, but though my father would never admit it I have always been certain that, through some intermediary unknown to me, he had obtained Macneil for another purpose, namely to protect his brother and daughter from the otherwise inevitable consequences of their vile acts. At any rate, Macneil soon set about an elaborate deception. He procured a middle-aged man – a Bessarabian corn-factor, I was told – who resembled Aleku closely, or closely enough, and somehow lured him here. Having caused it to be given out that the baron was gravely ill with typhus fever, he administered to the unhappy stranger a fatal dose of one of those poisons that leave no exterior sign. A pair of local women, chosen for their ready tongues, were brought in to prepare the deceased for burial. A funeral was then elaborately staged and the stranger laid to rest in the mausoleum that my father had refurbished for the purpose. The behaviour of the peasantry on this occasion was gratifyingly credulous, but Macneil would leave nothing to chance. With every appearance of spontaneity, though in fact at his instigation, a band of villagers broke open the tomb after a sufficient interval and found, not the untouched, immaculate form they had been half-expecting, but what could only have been a dead body. To all appearance, Baron Aleku was no more. No such stratagem was thought necessary in my case; I was then quite undistinguished in horror.

'Thereafter the ingenious and industrious and unspeakable Macneil saw to it that those whose blood we drank were brought from far enough away for Castle Valvazor not to be an object of suspicion. So matters continued for decades; I grew inured to my uncle's embraces, even – forgive me if you can – developed a taste for them. To my status as a creature altogether depraved, beyond the reach of divine mercy, I was perfectly indifferent. Then, one night, the night of 31 August, all was changed. God or His messenger spoke to me in a dream, commanding me to make an end to the evil and holding out hope, if I heeded the commandment, of my soul's salvation. At once I was resolved; I made preparations and, as soon as opportunity presented itself, I struck.

'Late the following evening, 1 September, I came upon my uncle and Macneil in the small parlour. Having contrived Macneil's brief but sufficient absence from the room, I took a hammer and drove a large iron nail into the back of my uncle's head, not remitting my blows until the point had emerged through the right eye. I had been less than certain whether this would prove enough to secure the demise of such a one, but very soon such extreme and dreadful changes had taken place in him that I could no longer be in doubt. So perished a creature of the utmost infamy, and so who knows how many innocent men and women were spared a terrible fate.

'When Macneil returned to the room he expressed violent loathing at what he saw. He went on to utter various taunts and threats, which changed to entreaties and attempts to strike bargains when he saw what I intended. To no avail; my duty was clear and my determination absolute.

'In all save immaterial particulars this account is true and complete, and that is the sufficient and necessary reason for offering it to you as guardian of good order. You must take it or leave it as it stands. I shall not be available for questioning.

'Under my hand and seal, Lukretia Valvazor.'

QUAESTOR: Thank you, prefect. Well, that is at any rate clear. We will defer other considerations till we have more evidence before us. Fetch Dr Eótvos, if he is composed enough to address the inquest.

DOCTOR: Yes, sir, I think so, your rectitude. I must emphasize that the need for haste and secrecy has meant that my findings are necessarily tentative and rather general.

QUAESTOR: That is understood. Please go on.

DOCTOR: One body appears to be that of a man of extreme old age, perhaps as much as ninety years old. This I surmised from the state of the hair, the teeth and one or two other parts that had to some extent escaped the process of decomposition undergone by the remainder, which was so advanced that the corpse could not be moved as a whole and had to be examined on the spot. And yet among the remains of the alimentary canal there were fragments of partially digested food that could not have been swallowed more than an hour before, perhaps two at the most. Human physiology, human . . . what happens when a man dies . . . will not allow of such a thing.

QUAESTOR: Do you wish to rest, doctor? Very well. Are you saying that this was not the body of a human being?

DOCTOR: No, sir; well, not quite. There had been forces at work on it that I cannot guess at, producing effects I would have thought flesh and blood incapable of and have most assuredly never seen or heard the like of. Is that satisfactory? Thank you, sir – the other body was human in every respect. I identified it as that of Mr Robert Macneil, well known to most of us here. The . . . unusual factor in this case was the manner of death. The head was almost separated from the trunk, but not as the result of any blow from a weapon. The two had been *pulled* apart.

QUAESTOR: In your opinion, could a human being have done that?

DOCTOR: No, sir; well, again, it might be possible for a professional strong-man, but certainly not for a normally developed female, which I take to be where your question tends. I should add that the right humerus, the bone of the right upper arm, was at one point not merely broken but shattered into thirty or forty pieces, some of them barely visible to the naked eye. No weapon, nothing inorganic here either; the bruising showed it to be the work of a human hand, or something shaped like a human hand, in a squeezing motion. As before, impossible for a normal person, man or woman.

QUAESTOR: Could we amend that and say, impossible for a normal person in any state known to medical science?

DOCTOR: That would do very well, your rectitude.

QUAESTOR: Excellent. Thank you, doctor; you may retire. Fetch the witness Magda Marghiloman.

REGISTRAR: She will tell you nothing useful.

QUAESTOR: How do you know? And what do you suppose I might find useful? Now, Magda, if you are sensible this will take no more than a minute. You heard the prefect read the document your mistress gave you. Tell us where you were when she gave it you.

WITNESS: In her ladyship's sitting-room, your rectitude.

QUAESTOR: What happened after that?

WITNESS: She kissed me, and she gave me the locket with her lady mother's picture, and she said goodbye . . .

QUAESTOR: All right, Magda, we can pause here and no harm. Go on when you can.

WITNESS: . . . and I went out and left her there.

QUAESTOR: What time was this?

WITNESS: About midnight.

QUAESTOR: And that was the last you saw of her. Where is she now, Magda? Where is your mistress now?

WITNESS: She has gone away.

QUAESTOR: Magda, we all know she has gone away. What we desire to be told is where she is. At least, that is the question we are asking.

WITNESS: I do not know the answer, your rectitude.

QUAESTOR: Quite so. And in your opinion, Magda, just your opinion, is there anyone who does know?

WITNESS: No, sir.

QUAESTOR: Very well. Now, you heard the prefect mention a certain Mr Stephen Hillier, an Englishman, who was reported to be in Nuvakastra four days ago. We have been absolutely unable to discover where he went after that. Have you heard or seen anything of this man?

WITNESS: No, sir.

QUAESTOR: In fact, you have no news or other information about him whatever.

WITNESS: Nothing whatever, sir.

QUAESTOR: And, again in your opinion, Magda, everybody would say the same, everybody at Castle Valvazor, that is.

WITNESS: Everybody, your rectitude.

QUAESTOR: Thank you, Magda, that will be all. Registrar, clear the chamber. None to remain except Prefect Sturdza, Dr Eótvos and yourself.

Now, gentlemen, we are all Dacians, indeed we are all from round about, and my feeling is that we can settle this in no time. The only matter of the smallest complication touches Mr Hillier. We have to admit the possibility that he was somehow involved in the events at Valvazor. If so, we are bound to think it more than possible that he is dead. Should that be the case, we could expect to be told nothing to that effect by any of the castle people. The first we should hear would be an inquiry from his family in England – if he has one, if they know he came to Nuvakastra. Unless that happens, which God forfend, I say we do nothing. As things are, what reason would you give, my dear prefect, for detaining Mr Hillier, searching for him, mentioning him?

However, these are all remote contingencies, of the sort we jurists love to pursue, but of little practical import. I will wager our man is well out of it, and we are no less well rid of him. If, by a chance more distant than any we have considered, he has departed from this place having learned of these recent oddities, we need feel no concern. Left to himself he will keep his mouth shut, you may be sure.

As for our corpses, or rather our corpse, for Baron Aleku has been dead for thirty-four years, has he not? – as for Mr Macneil, he met with an accident from which he died. He fell down the stairs, drowned in his bath, what you will. Would you consent to certify that, doctor?

DOCTOR: Gladly, your rectitude.

QUESTOR: As for Countess Valvazor, she has disappeared. And that at least is a fact. We shall see no more of her in this life.

REGISTRAR: Or the next.

QUAESTOR: Amen; I wish I were so sanguine. I suggest to you, prefect, that a couple of trustworthy fellows saw the countess making for Arelanópli yesterday morning, would you agree? There will be the question of the inheritance to be settled. I look forward to that, not least to the arrival of some innocent cousin from Philadelphia, as it might be, to take possession of his property, like a young man in a ghostly tale.

Well, unless I have missed something, our business is concluded. Prefect, you will see to it that all documents are burnt. *All* documents.

DOCTOR: May I ask a question, your rectitude? Do you believe the countess's story?

QUAESTOR: Must I believe anything? If I must believe something, then what else is there? And now, gentlemen, I invite you to take wine with me. There is that in what I have heard this evening that drives me almost irresistibly to a fortifying glass.

VIII – *Stephen Hillier to A. C. Winterbourne*

Hotel Astoria,
Budapest,
Hungary
6 September 1925

My dear Charles,

It's no good, I shall have to tell someone, no, not someone, you, before I go mad, or die of I don't know what, grief, or horror, or something like bewilderment, which I never thought could become an emotion as intense and as painful as the others. Sorry, I'm probably not making much sense. Let me concentrate on matters about which there can be no dispute.

On the 3rd, Friday morning, I left that castle and made the rotten journey to Arelanópli, where I took the first available train out of Dacia. It was a stopping train and I had made no arrangements to visit Hungary and it cost me a fiver to be let in, but I would cheerfully have paid ten times as much just to get out of that beastly country. I must say the Astoria is a very decent place and the servants are most considerate, appearing not to notice what I'm afraid must have been my obvious distress of mind, meeting without question my desire to take all meals in my room (not that I've wanted very much to eat) and leaving me alone as far as possible. As a result I'm better, well, better than I was, though not exactly chirpy at this stage. I reckon I shall be able to face a long journey in a couple of days and then will probably make for Paris, anyhow somewhere as unlike where I've been as possible. I can't face Connie yet awhile; it's not that I don't – no, I won't go into it now, I think you'll understand when you've read what I have to say.

I remember at the end of my last (God knows how I managed to get it posted) I told you I was in the parlour trying to read and waiting for Lukretia. Charles, I want to skip over what happened that evening (there was nothing that can't wait till I see you) and come to the next morning, I suppose about seven o'clock. That night I hadn't dreamed at all, so that waking suddenly, as I did, was like being in a single instant thrust from a dark dungeon into the sunlight; the whole of that charming bedroom was ablaze with the sun. It made me blink. I felt at the same time sluggish and on edge, strung up, for a moment unable to remember where I was. It took me longer than that to piece together what had happened or must have happened before I fell asleep and later. I decided at last – Lukretia had given me champagne; there had been some drug in the champagne; I had succumbed to it; she had left the room; she had not returned. Possessed by a sudden urgency I jumped out of bed and dressed as quickly as I've ever done in my life. On the dressing-table there was an envelope with my name on it, also the lock of my hair had gone (explanation later). I put the envelope in my pocket and hurried out.

Downstairs, I found the parlour door shut, locked fast. I called repeatedly, but no one came, nor was there at first the least sound; I had the sense that I was alone in the castle. Then, faint but insistent, there came to my ears an irregular banging or slamming sound, as of an unfastened shutter caught by the wind, indescribably desolate. I found the cause soon enough, in fact a long glass door giving on to a small terrace at the side of the building. In the grip of the acutest dread, yet not knowing what it was that so afflicted me, I advanced through the doorway. The air was already warm; I could hear insect noises and the song of birds. A statue of a naked nymph or girl holding a lamb in her arms, no doubt a copy of a Hellenistic original, stood off to one side. I moved out of the shadow cast by the house and into the full light of the sun; it was very strong. A fitful breeze was stirring the dust on the flagstones. My eye fell on what might have been a thin wisp of dark hair, no more than four or five strands, but it had disintegrated before I could reach it. A thought too terrible to think was beating at the inside of my head. I remembered the envelope I had picked up and tore it open; there was a single sheet of writing inside. This is what it said.

My only dear love,

'I have to go away and you will never see me again in this life. Anything that could drive me from you must be very powerful, very strong, and it is, so strong that I must not tell you what it is. But I am allowed to tell you what it is not. It is not your fault, neither in yourself nor in any deed or word of yours. It is no shortcoming in the love we feel for each other. That love has been the only true thing in my life and the means of deliverance from all my sorrows. It, and you, have made me happy in such a way that what other happiness I have known seems to me trivial and dull. And that means that the shortness of our time together matters much less to me; I hope, I know, that this will be a consolation to you.

Now I must go. Don't try to find me; I cannot be found. Don't try to learn more about me; think of me as you knew me. We may meet after all in a million years from now; I think perhaps God intends that. Goodbye, heart of my heart.

Your Lukretia

Remember your promise. *Duminu wobisku*.

And with the last two words the unbearable thought declared itself. I reached into my pocket again and brought out the tracing I had made of the first phrases of the document Macneil had shown me in the library. There was no question about it; the hands were the same. I knew now what had troubled me at the time: my unwitting perception that the writing was feminine had been up against my conscious assumption that what was in front of me was the work of a man. And I knew much more besides.

I won't try to describe my feelings. I went back indoors and knelt down and prayed for Lukretia's soul, as I have done on retiring and rising ever since and will continue to do for the rest of my life. Then I found Magda, or she me. She asked me my pleasure. I told her I wanted to be packed up and out of the place in the shortest possible time, and she set about it as if she was no less interested in my early departure than I was. How much had she seen and heard over the years? In the last thirty-six hours? I didn't want to find out. After our first question and answer neither of us had anything to say till we were standing outside the great front door and a grim-faced fellow in an overall was loading my bags into a sort of wagonette. Even then Magda and I exchanged only a word of thanks as I tipped her and a word of farewell, but right at the last she gave me a look saying as plainly as words that we were united by our loss, and I hope I returned it adequately. Before the driver had whipped up his horses the door of the castle shut with a crash. Macneil didn't appear, which suited my book all right.

I'm sorry to bother you with all this, old boy, but perhaps you see now why I had to tell you, or felt I had to tell you, and why I don't feel like coming home just yet. I'll probably see you about the 18th or the 20th. Thanks for listening!

> Yours,
> Stephen

PS: I wonder if I could ask you to keep this and my last under lock and key. Matt's is a jolly decent place, I know, but one can't be too careful.

IX – *Stephen Hillier to Constance Hillier*

> Hotel Astoria,
> Budapest,
> Hungary
> 7 September 1925

Dearest Connie,

It must be a week since I wrote. As you can see, I've been on the move. I didn't stay long at that Castle Valvazor place, which I soon found was a thorough wash-out. In my last letter I wasted your time (and a lot more of mine) with all those stories about

Tristan the Wolf and Red Mathias and eye-witness accounts. Then when I went through the archives the next morning there was nothing there at all, just the dullest and most conventional family documents you can imagine. I complained about it at luncheon, or rather said I thought I must have been looking in the wrong place, and the countess said no, I'd seen all there was, and more or less admitted she'd spun me a yarn to induce me to stay on for a bit and cheer up the company. Well, I saw her point about the company, but I ask you! I hung on another night out of politeness and invented an engagement in Budapest. I want you to promise never to mention Countess Valvazor. Seriously. If you do I won't reply. I mean it was such a sell and such a bore.

In a way, though, my visit wasn't wasted. It set me thinking about this whole vampire business, made me take a second look at it, if you know what I mean. And, well, I've come to the very reluctant conclusion that you were right about it and I was wrong. It's nothing but a string of peasant superstitions that don't hang together and haven't even got the merit of being charming. What on earth possessed me to imagine there was a book, a serious book, to be written on the subject? I'm afraid it'll annoy old Charles Winterbourne, but I'm going to wind up my research. Something on, say, early Hungarian literature would be far more the sort of thing. I've been looking round the museums here and already have something to go on.

This is a fascinating city. I expect you knew it was originally two cities, Buda and Pest. The royal palace at Buda is very fine, with over eight hundred rooms (not that I've been in them all!). Near by stands the church of

I'm sorry, dear, I'll have to break this off if I want to catch the post. I'll be off again in a day or two. Will drop you a line as soon as I can.

> In haste, with love,
> Stephen

Affairs of Death

To trade and traffic with Macbeth
In riddles and affairs of death . . .
    – *Macbeth*, IV v

Leo IX, a native of Alsace, succeeded to the Papacy in AD 1049.
Four years later he gathered an army of Italians and German
volunteers and led it in person against the Norman invaders
who had occupied Sicily and southern Italy. The papal forces
were defeated and the Pope captured and imprisoned for some
months.

My gaolers released me without notice on the morning of 26th
October. They acted without explanation also, merely indicating
in their vile French that I was free to go. Their continued and
studied lack of respect for my person, however, suggested unwilling compliance with outside pressure, which could have been
nothing but the intervention of the Emperor. The prospect of this
had been all that sustained me through the tedium and discomfort of my captivity. Henry had held his hand on purpose, of
course, partly to emphasize his disapproval of my recent actions,
partly without doubt as a reminder that in some sense I owed
my enthronement to his good offices.

My delight at returning to Rome was tempered by apprehension about what might have been in store for me there. But I
found the City perfectly quiet and Hildebrand the Benedictine
had kept everything safe. I had sent ahead and he was waiting
up for me in the yellow saloon, where a cold supper had been
laid. He greeted me with a precise blend of reverence and warmth.
He was a little thinner since June, I thought, perhaps a little
harder too. He had seen much of the world for one who was still

barely thirty years old, enough at least to understand Germany, and that was much.

I had not asked for a doctor, but he had caused one to be present, a Greek by the look of him, with a white beard to signify great knowledge. He prodded me, took my pulse, looked at my tongue. When he made to bleed me I threw him out.

'Let me bring him back tomorrow, Lord,' said Hildebrand. 'You are not well. Those Norman pigs have starved you. Was your highness at least dry?'

'Most of the time. I need rest and good food, fresh food.'

'Assuredly. Eat now, Lord. You enjoy these little birds.'

'No, I am too tired. Pour me wine.'

As he handed me the cup, he said quietly, 'I thought to have no ceremony. It seemed not to be called for.'

'No indeed. Even these few are too many. Have the goodness to remove them.'

One inclination of his head and it was done.

'Hildebrand, who would have thought that an uncouth rabble like that could put those brave fellows of mine to rout? The Supreme Pontiff a common prisoner. Arrest them all, my boy, all who are in Rome; hunt down the others and fetch them here. All – Gerard, Frederic, Valerian, Florentinus, Otho, the Spaniard and the one with the stutter. All my captains, all those who robbed me of victory. Confine them here. All of them.'

'There, be calm, Lord. They shall be fetched, all of them.'

'See they are.' I coughed a trifle and took some water, then more wine, with a sparrow's wing to nibble at. 'Well, what waits tomorrow?'

'Many things, great and small. None pressing. Few pleasing. Some plaguing, as Peter Damian rebuking you for usurping the Emperor's function by your activities as a soldier.'

'Never mind him.'

'Perhaps we need not, but your highness had better mind an accusation of heresy from Michael Cerularius.'

'There must be something in the air of Constantinople that rots the brain. Does Michael, a mere bishop, really know no better than to offer a direct challenge to my authority? I shall have to cut him off altogether.'

'He will have earned it, Lord. Now one pleasant matter. There is a king in Rome, most eager for an audience with your highness. I think I never saw one more truly eager, high or low.'

'What king?'

'Of Scots or Scotland, Macbeth by name. Having quite given you up, as regrettably some few had, he had petitioned the Cardinal Vicar-General for an audience and professed himself overwhelmed to learn he might after all be privileged to be received by your highness. He was most particular that you must consult your own health and comfort in the matter. A touching rogue. It might amuse you, Lord.'

'Amusing or not, I will see him. Of course I will. I must make any friends I can. If he cares to call on me I will receive the king of Vinland. How is he attended, this Macbeth?'

'Most suitably, by someone I took for a kind of freebooter. He was here, King Macbeth was in Rome, three years ago on purpose to see your highness, but you were abroad then, peregrinating beyond the Alps.'

'Yes, yes. Such persistence merits reward. Arrange it.'

'It is done, Lord. Provisionally. Noon, not tomorrow but the day following. Now your highness must retire,' said Hildebrand, calling servants. 'And sleep late.'

When, not much refreshed even by twelve hours in a good bed, I rose the next afternoon, Hildebrand was soon in attendance again with, among much else, information about Scotland. The country, or the territory inhabited by Scots, was confined to that part of the mainland of Britain which lies north of the Firth of Forth. Here and over neighbouring regions from the furthest shores of the Irish Sea to those of the North Sea, there ranged at different times bands of Irish, Picts, Scots, Britons, Angles, Cumbrians, English, Danes, Norwegians contending in prolonged and obscure struggles. That part of northern Europe had been a turbulent place for centuries and seemingly still was.

At first sight Scotland was no concern of mine. The Church

was well enough established there, and Macbeth had shown himself well disposed to her in the dozen years of his rule. I had no means of controlling events. There was only one bishop of the Scots, at the unwalled city of St Andrews, and his influence was purely local. What monks there were had no power. Clearly, the key to control of the Scottish Church lay in the sovereign. If I could win some personal regard from Macbeth, I might be laying the foundations of something that might, again, prove useful in any future trouble with England. And that there would be trouble with England sooner or later, perhaps in my time, perhaps after many years, I had not the slightest doubt.

I hardly know what I had expected to encounter the noon following, certainly not the tall, fair-haired, blue-eyed figure in his late forties who was presented; I thought he might well have had a Norse ancestor as well as Norse neighbours. His companion, introduced by my usher as Captain Seaton, short, broad, heavily bearded, with a look of stupid ferocity, was much more my idea of a Scotchman. As the two knelt before me I bestowed on each a salutation appropriate to his rank.

So as not to overawe my visitors excessively I had received them in a small throne-room built two centuries before by my predecessor Agapetus II and not two storeys high, none the less worthy of its function with sumptuous new frescoes, sculptures in the round and jewelled appointments. The soldier, if that was what he was, kept his eyes straight in front as though fearful of taking in his surroundings; his master glanced here and there without disrespect, without astonishment either, his attention soon caught by the most unusual piece on view, a grotesque carved-oak Calvary the bishop of Rennes took out of some church there and sent me for my forty-seventh birthday, my first after being consecrated.

The king's dress gave further mild surprise; not deer-skins and foot-rags but a rich gold-edged surcoat that would not have disgraced the Emperor Henry himself, an inner garment of dark-red silk, high Spanish shoes, a short, stout cross-hilted sword, plain but with some elegance in the workmanship, and below the throat a curiously shaped crucifix, evidently silver but of a pretty bluish tinge, which I promised myself I would have off him before he took his leave. What manner of tribal chieftain was it who wore these things?

As was my custom when receiving royalty, I had had my seneschal install near the dais and at right angles to it a heavy chair with a high and elaborately carved back representing scenes of martyrdom. Mounted on a shallow platform, it was in no sense a throne but it did elevate the monarch in occupation a sufficient distance above the commonalty. Here King Macbeth sat, well enough at his ease with his blue eyes reverentially lowered. Without much confidence in being understood I asked in simple Latin a question about his earlier visit to the City.

Unexpectedly once more, he replied in fluent and correct French, the language of my childhood, 'I was desperately disappointed to be unable to pay my respects to your highness. I had to be content with distributing money to the poor of Rome.' His accent was no worse than that of my late captors, indeed much resembled theirs.

'Your majesty's skill in the tongue is remarkable.' No more so than his having discovered my own familiarity with it.

'Thank you, Holy Father. I have been fortunately placed. It so happens that over the past two years or so I have sheltered at my court a number of French-speaking fugitives from England, and I sent myself to school with them. After all, this conversation, however memorable to me, would have been much restricted otherwise. My Latin is rudimentary, and I doubt if your highness' Gaelic is much better.'

I laughed, partly in unconcealed appreciation of this speech. Those fugitives had of course come in the first place from Normandy, but after my recent experiences it would have been less than tactful to mention even the existence of that place. As for having learned French, he had not done so in order to be able to converse with me, whom he had been prepared to face three years before in ignorance of it and whom he had not expected to see at all this time. No, his conversational target had in the first place been Duke William, universally understood to have been promised the English throne by King Edward as soon as it fell vacant, and therefore a most interesting personage to any king of Scotland. But would William desire such a meeting?

'Doubtless you made other visits on your journey here, your majesty?'

He was on the defensive at once. 'Yes, Holy Father, one such, but it was of no importance, not even comparatively so.'

'Nevertheless I trust enjoyable.'

'I must ask your highness to pardon me,' he said, blinking fiercely.

This time I suppressed a smile. It was as clear to me as from a full description that what he had visited or attempted to visit was indeed William's court, and no less so that he had been rebuffed – unseen, I judged, for it took no more than a glance to show that here was someone to be reckoned with, not the refined soul he took himself for, a barbarian still, but a remarkable barbarian. I said smoothly, 'We hear pleasing reports of the state of Scotland under your majesty's stewardship.'

'Your highness is too gracious. And you bring me to the object of this interview, or the secondary object, the first plainly being to be granted your blessing, Holy Father. For reasons that will appear, I had felt driven most urgently to come to Rome even when I took your highness to be absent. To find you present after all, to reach you, I see as a distinct mark of divine favour.'

An ardent blue-eyed stare went with this. I began to cough for a moment and shifted position on my throne. Talk of such matters has always unsettled me. It might have been a little sharply that I said, 'Please go on, sir.'

But he hesitated for a moment before continuing, 'I hope to be forgiven for making what must be an unusual request. It is that a clerk should be sent for to record the substance of what, if permitted, I shall say.'

I gave the necessary directions and waited.

'I suppose you know little of Scotland, Holy Father. It is a remote and obscure place, its people wild, ignorant, credulous, superstitious, not brutal but childish. They have no notions of probability, of consistency, of what is real and what is fancied. My reign has not been untroubled and some of the events in it, and even more those attending its inception, were violent, confused and ambiguous. Not long after I am dead the generally accepted account of it, of my reign, is likely to deviate absurdly and irrecoverably from historical fact. A like process has already distorted the years of my predecessor's rule. With your leave, with your help, Holy Father, I intend to set on record the truth of these matters and to have that record lodged in the bosom of the see of St Peter, where it will be safe for ever. This it was that brought me here. What I have to say may also attract your highness' passing attention, for all Scotland's distance from the centre of the world.'

That last stroke, accompanied by a different kind of glance, caused me to reflect that such men as this were not very common anywhere, not even in Rome. Just then a clerk appeared, a Benedictine, and on my nod settled himself at Macbeth's left side. I spread a hand in invitation.

'Some things are seen, some things are put out of sight. It is seen that old Malcolm II, King of Scots, fortunate, victorious, praised of bards, had no son to follow him, but that he ruled so long that by the time he died his grandsons were grown up. For the succession, it is seen that he favoured the eldest, Duncan. This, when he might have chosen the third in age, myself, or even the fourth and youngest, Thorfinn Sigurdson, son of the Norwegian earl of Orkney. By the ancient custom of our royal house the eldest prince has no firm right to succeed, and I had a better claim, a double claim, a claim not only through my own lineage but also through that of my wife Gruoch, granddaughter of King Kenneth III, whom old Malcolm had deposed and killed. Such a claim as hers is also admitted by our custom.

'All this is seen. It is further seen, though ill remembered, that old Malcolm made over to Thorfinn, with the title of earl, two fiefs on the mainland, this as a means of restraining him, of placating any ambition he might nourish. The old man had not reckoned that, once on the throne, the foolhardy Duncan would try to recover those places by force of arms. Scotland ran with blood, much of it that of my own people, some of it my own blood; I carried a sword for my king as a commander of his armies. There seemed no end to be hoped for.

'Then one morning thirteen years ago Thorfinn's Norwegians burst upon the Scots from the rising sun at Burghead in Moray and cut them to pieces on the beach in ten minutes. Duncan fled and I and a party of my followers fled with him. Moray was my fief; by secret paths I led him to an abandoned fort at a place called Bothnagowan. There, on an August night, we seized our chance, a dozen of us, and surprised him as he lay asleep out on the rampart, and stabbed him to death with our daggers. With no delay I had myself proclaimed king and was crowned at Scone, made peace with my cousin Thorfinn, made him my friend. Indeed, he had been my friend before, he who always does what he has said he will do. And the Scots hung up their arms.

'This too is seen by some. What is not seen, what is already forgotten, what is put out of sight is Duncan as he was. Comely I grant him, with a bright eye and a curved lip, very like my father-in-law, as my wife often noted; both men were descended from Malcolm I, dead these hundred years. However, in all else Duncan was a wretch, mean of spirit, vengeful, I think a little mad. No one was safe from his sudden rages. Wasteful and indolent. Unclean in his person – he stank under our knives, not only from fear. Not kingly. It is put out of sight that his nickname of the Gracious was a jest, a taunt.

'Now Scotland is safe and at peace. This has not been customary. So fierce and prolonged have been her inner conflicts that, of her last nine kings, only old Malcolm my grandfather died in his bed. The future holds some hope. Having no issue I have taken as my son the fruit of my wife's first marriage, young Lulach, a strong, honest boy of twenty-one. I mean him to succeed me. Duncan's sons, Malcolm and Donald Bane, whom I generously spared, shelter in the household of Siward, the English earl of Northumberland, a cousin of their mother's. They show no signs of moving to unseat me, nor can they ever contrive it while my friend and ally Thorfinn lives. Let them try and welcome. I will defend my country to my last breath.

'That all this is true I, Macbeth, King of Scots, swear on my honour.'

Indicating to the scribe that his formal statement was finished, he went on in a different tone, 'There remains the heavy matter of the killing of Duncan. It was done *more Scottico*, not in malice, it was done for Scotland, not for my advancement, it was done as an execution, not as a wanton slaying, but it was murder. If I am to bear the blame . . .'

In an oddly irritating gesture he fumbled with the crucifix at his breast. I told him briskly.

'Of that you and I will speak in private, your majesty, at a later hour.'

Macbeth gave a slow nod, his thoughts on old wrongs and enduring hazards. It was more than half to himself that he said, 'Already they are telling one another that my gentle Gruoch had a hand in Duncan's death, when in truth she was in my castle at Dunkeld, over sixty miles away. If it were not for this record, who could guess what might be believed of me in centuries to come? That I took innocent lives, that I murdered my friend, murdered children, that I consorted with witches and saw visions, that I – how to put it? – supped full with horrors.'

Here he turned briefly to his man Seaton and in a strange language spoke what I took to be some words of courteous apology for subjecting him to so much incomprehensible talk. The fellow gave a grunt of oafish surprise and faltered out a few harsh, graceless syllables, staring vacantly as he did so. Poor, poor King Macbeth; if that was his chosen associate, what must his daily company at home have been like? I would forgive him his murder; indeed, to have confined oneself to a single such lapse in a country like Scotland, assuming the impression I had formed of it to be even moderately fair, indicated commendable restraint.

There were, of course, other considerations, other than the obvious diplomatic ones. A man likes to show mercy whenever possible. Then, at our private audience early that evening Macbeth relieved me of what might have been an awkwardness by tactfully producing unasked a quantity of gold and suggesting that I should devote it to pious purposes of my own choosing. And, when all is said, one soldier is bound to feel a certain kinship with another. It was with a full heart that I pronounced him absolved and wished him a safe return, and I allowed him without reluctance to keep the dainty crucifix he seemed so attached to.

The next morning Hildebrand came to me with Macbeth's story written out fair. 'Evidently, Lord, a considerable person.'

'More so than his position calls for. I hope for his sake he sits as securely as he appears to believe.'

'Time will show.'

'Time will show many things of greater moment than the devices of a Scottish desperado, however engaging.'

'Is your highness instructing me that this is not to be put into the permanent archive?'

'We agreed to keep it as sparse as possible. Extract whatever is needed.'

'As your highness pleases. I hope you feel your time was not wasted.'

'It was most diverting, and we have the man's goodwill.'

'True, Lord. And now some news of your captains. Five are confined. Valerian died by his own hand before he could be secured. Frederic is believed to be at large in the Emperor's domain. I have somebody competent at work.'

'Let the matter be settled and over. It seems well it should be done quickly.'

HISTORICAL NOTE

Macbeth ('fair, yellow, tall') first visited Rome in the year 1050. This visit, unlike his second three years later, is vouched for by documents. In 1054 his armies were defeated near Scone by those of Earl Siward, but he continued on the Scottish throne another three years. Then his ally Thorfinn died, and shortly afterwards Malcolm Broadhead murdered him. Macbeth's stepson Lulach became king, but after a few months Malcolm murdered him too and took the crown, ruling as Malcolm III. Macbeth and Lulach were buried in the island of Iona, the ancient resting-place of the Scottish kings.

The health of Pope Leo IX had been shattered by his captivity and he died the following year, 1054, though not before he had proceeded with the excommunication of the Patriarch of Constantinople, thus making final and permanent the split between the Western and Eastern Churches. He was canonized as St Leo in 1087.

Hildebrand became Pope Gregory VII in 1073 and also achieved sainthood.

Mason's Life

'May I join you?'

The medium-sized man with the undistinguished clothes and the blank, anonymous face looked up at Pettigrew, who, glass of beer in hand, stood facing him across the small corner table. Pettigrew, tall, handsome and of fully moulded features, had about him an intent, almost excited air that, in different circumstances, might have brought an unfavourable response, but the other said amiably,

'By all means. Do sit down.'

'Can I get you something?'

'No, I'm fine, thank you,' said the medium-sized man, gesturing at the almost full glass in front of him. In the background was the ordinary ambience of bar, barman, drinkers in ones and twos, nothing to catch the eye.

'We've never met, have we?'

'Not as far as I recall.'

'Good, good. My name's Pettigrew, Daniel R. Pettigrew. What's yours?'

'Mason. George Herbert Mason, if you want it in full.'

'Well, I think that's best, don't you? George . . . Herbert . . . Mason.' Pettigrew spoke as if committing the three short words to memory. 'Now let's have your telephone number.'

Again Mason might have reacted against Pettigrew's demanding manner, but he said no more than, 'You can find me in the book easily enough.'

'No, there might be several . . . We mustn't waste time. Please.'

'Oh, very well; it's public information, after all. Two-three-two, five—'

'Hold on, you're going too fast for me. Two . . . three . . . two . . .'

'Five-four-five-four.'

'What a stroke of luck. I ought to be able to remember that.'

'Why don't you write it down if it's so important to you?'

At this, Pettigrew gave a knowing grin that faded into a look of disappointment. 'Don't you know that's no use? Anyway: two-three-two, five-four-five-four. I might as well give you my number too. Seven—'

'I don't want your number, Mr Pettigrew,' said Mason, sounding a little impatient, 'and I must say I rather regret giving you mine.'

'But you must take my number.'

'Nonsense; you can't make me.'

'A phrase, then – let's agree on a phrase to exchange in the morning.'

'Would you mind telling me what all this is about?'

'Please, our time's running out.'

'You keep saying that. This is getting—'

'Any moment everything might change and I might find myself somewhere completely different, and so might you, I suppose, though I can't help feeling it's doubtful whether—'

'Mr Pettigrew, either you explain yourself at once or I have you removed.'

'All right,' said Pettigrew, whose disappointed look had deepened, 'but I'm afraid it won't do any good. You see, when we started talking I thought you must be a real person, because of the way you—'

'Spare me your infantile catch-phrases, for heaven's sake. So I'm not a real person,' cooed Mason offensively.

'I don't mean it like that, I mean it in the most literal way possible.'

'Oh, God. Are you mad or drunk or what?'

'Nothing like that. I'm asleep.'

'Asleep?' Mason's nondescript face showed total incredulity.

'Yes. As I was saying, at first I took you for another real person in the same situation as myself: sound asleep, dreaming, aware of the fact, and anxious to exchange names and telephone numbers and so forth with the object of getting in touch the next day and confirming the shared experience. That would prove something remarkable about the mind, wouldn't it? – people communicating via their dreams. It's a pity one so seldom realizes one's dreaming: I've only been able to try the experiment four or five times in the last twenty years, and I've never had any success. Either I forget the details or I find there's no such person, as in this case. But I'll go on—'

'You're sick.'

'Oh no. Of course it's conceivable there is such a person as you. Unlikely, though, or you'd have recognized the true situation at once, I feel, instead of arguing against it like this. As I say, I may be wrong.'

'It's hopeful that you say that.' Mason had calmed down, and lit a cigarette with deliberation. 'I don't know much about these things, but you can't be too far gone if you admit you could be in error. Now let me just assure you that I didn't come into existence five minutes ago inside your head. My name, as I told you, is George Herbert Mason. I'm forty-six years old, married, three children, job in the furniture business . . . Oh hell, giving you no more than an outline of my life so far would take all night, as it would in the case of anybody with an average memory. Let's finish our drinks and go along to my house, and then we can—'

'You're just a man in my dream saying that,' said Pettigrew loudly. 'Two-three-two, five-four-five-four. I'll call the number if it exists, but it won't be you at the other end. Two-three-two—'

'Why are you so agitated, Mr Pettigrew?'

'Because of what's going to happen to you at any moment.'

'What . . . Is this a threat?'

Pettigrew was breathing fast. His finely drawn face began to coarsen, the pattern of his tweed jacket to become blurred. 'The telephone!' he shouted. 'It must be later than I thought!'

'Telephone?' repeated Mason, blinking and screwing up his eyes as Pettigrew's form continued to change.

'The one at my bedside! I'm waking up!'

Mason grabbed the other by the arm, but that arm had lost the greater part of its outline, had become a vague patch of light already fading, and when Mason looked at the hand that had done the grabbing, his own hand, he saw with difficulty that it likewise no longer had fingers, or front or back, or skin, or anything at all.

Mr Barrett's Secret

I

It must have been in the January or February of the year 1845 that I first became aware of the connection of Elizabeth, my first child and eldest daughter, with the man Robert Browning. Had I had the least intimation of what was to follow, I should have forbidden its continuance in any form, and have prosecuted my interdiction with unswerving tenacity. Nevertheless, full knowledge of the future that awaited Elizabeth and myself would surely have led me to bless that divine provision whereby it is not given to us to see as far as the next tick of the clock.

A letter, addressed to Elizabeth in a strange hand, arrived by the early morning delivery at my house at 50 Wimpole Street, a circumstance in itself very far from unusual. More especially since the publication by Moxon of her *Poems* in two volumes the preceding August, my dearest Ba (to use her family pet-name) had grown used to receiving correspondence from persons unacquainted with her. Many came from America and other distant parts of the world; the letter in question had been posted in London.

In characterizing just now the style of the writing on the envelope, I used the word 'strange' advisedly. It was not only unfamiliar to me; it was peculiar, extraordinary, odd. And yet in its very singularity there was a principle I seemed to recognize from some distant part of my life, from long ago. Possibly, too, I was aware of an indefinable threat or menace lurking in it, remote but real; more likely, however, I am allowing later events to sophisticate those first memories.

Whatever I might have thought, then or afterwards, there was no doubt that Elizabeth was delighted with her letter. I had scarcely finished breakfast before I was urgently summoned to her room on the third floor of the house.

'Dearest papa!' she cried, rising from her sofa-bed to embrace me in lively fashion. 'You will never guess what a marvellous gift I have had in the post this morning!'

'You are bidden to take tea with our young Queen,' I suggested, smiling.

'It's a trifle soon for such a thing, though doubtless that and much else will come in time. No, I am the recipient of a poem by Mr Robert Browning, a most beautiful and wondrous poem in which he exalts me to the status of a queen, but a queen of poetry and of the making of poetry. Oh, it's such a poem, darling papa, so full of the loveliest affirmations of devotion, so eloquent, so rich in the spontaneous vitality you know I prize above everything.'

'And this comes unprompted? As a spontaneous tribute?' I asked.

'Not quite, it's true. You may remember that in my poem "Lady Geraldine's Courtship" I referred to Mr Browning along with Mr Wordsworth and Mr Tennyson as a man whose writings place him next to the Gods.'

'So you did. And now he sends you a whole poem by way of return.'

'Well, there of course,' said Ba merrily, 'uncultured fathers and others of a sad literal disposition of mind will insist that the thing's only a letter, you know, nothing but a rather long and flowery letter, dash it all, the work of some modish popinjay with a fancy for extravagant compliment', and the dear girl's voice and demeanour became for the moment a fanciful but truly comical travesty of my own. 'But this is a letter with the beauty and tenderness of a poem, a true poem. Enough! – you shall see and judge for yourself', and she made to hand me the closely written pages, but snatched them quickly back and read from them in a high thrilling voice, '"I love your verses with all my heart, dear Miss Barrett", oh, and, "Into me it has gone, and part of me it has become, this great living poetry of yours", and a little farther on . . .'

'I shall never see to judge for myself,' I laughingly protested, 'if you persevere in your recitation', but I believe she was too much engrossed in those pages to hear me.

'Yes, he speaks here of, h'm, h'm, "the fresh strange music, the affluent language, the exquisite pathos and true new brave thought', and again, "I do, as I say, love these books with all my heart – and I . . .", but there I think he goes too far.'

A blush mantled her pale cheek. What had Browning written that she had not cared to let me hear? I know not, for I never saw that letter at last. But some of the phrases in it that I had been permitted to hear, the references to fresh strange music and to affluent language (affluent! a curious epithet, many would say, in this connection), remain lodged in my mind to this day. So did the general kind of expression employed therein. Once again, I felt I had received a warning or a premonition; once again, however, I may in saying so be looking ahead to what then lay in the future.

Certainly, at the time my strongest feelings were pleasure in my dear Ba's pleasure, heightened by satisfaction that her gifts of versing had been recognized by one I knew to be a poet of sorts, and by a reasonable hope that there might lie distraction from the melancholy and low spirits that had afflicted her increasingly as she grew past her first youth – at this time she was approaching her thirty-ninth birthday. My main concern, however, was as always for her health. This had never been truly sound since, at the age of fifteen, she had fallen victim to a mysterious incapacitating ailment that also afflicted her two younger sisters. As it proved, they were able soon to cast it off, but Elizabeth perhaps never wholly recovered, and within three months she had developed measles. Thereafter she spent much time confined to her room, even her bed, and I have always thought that the resulting seclusion and immobility were what first led her to the writing of verses – a healthier remedy than the opium which she came to consume, sometimes, I fear, in distressingly large doses.

Elizabeth's first letter to Browning further cheered me. I had been concerned lest, with all the refreshment of pleasure and interest in life the man's words might have brought her, she had perhaps become over-excited thereby, brought to an unhealthy access of sentiment. The dry terms of her answer, composed without any assistance but confided to me, were greatly reassuring. She spoke of her high respect for Browning's own ventures into poetic composition, saluted him as a fellow-craftsmen, told him that he would remain in her everlasting debt if he would draw her attention to faults in her manner of composition – nothing of the dreamy palpitating stuff in which he had evidently indulged himself. The correspondence continued. I had pressing concerns of my own at that time, in the City, relative to my affairs in the West Indies, and to be candid I was not sorry that my dearest Ba seemed to have found someone who might unwittingly share the burden of emotional obligation to her that I had inescapably (if gladly) acquired.

So matters stood for a couple of months and I was more than content. Elizabeth had acquired a companion who might prove more durable than her poor much-loved brother, known to her as Bro, lost sailing off the Devon coast at the age of thirty-three, and one who was nearer at hand than the excellent Hugh Stuart Boyd and John Kenyon, the latter known to me since our days at Cambridge and Elizabeth's benefactor and distant kinsman. Her letters to and from Browning, of which I was told nothing of substance, grew more frequent, but I saw no harm in that.

Then, in May of the same year, 1845, the two were to meet; he was to visit her at two o'clock in the afternoon of the 20th. I raised no objection; at that time I had none to raise; at two o'clock that day I was engaged in the City of London. I had left my Ba in her room as usual reclining on her sofa, surrounded by her simple furniture, most notably her beloved books on shelves built by her brothers, and with her spaniel, the well-behaved Flush, close beside her. As her father I could say to myself that, for all her large brown eyes and splendid thick dark hair, she was not what the world would have called beautiful. The black silk she wore at this season accentuated the pallor of her ivory complexion. She looked small and defenceless (she stood only an inch over five foot), eagerly desiring and yet deeply dreading the advent of the scoundrel* who had so artfully insinuated himself into the very springs of her being.

Before I departed, I counselled Elizabeth to remember that this young man, six years her junior, must be as apprehensive as she of the coming encounter, and that, whatever might betide, he ardently desired her welfare, and doubtless more. What else could I have said or done?

'I see that Mr Browning's visit was a success,' I remarked some hours later as I took tea with Elizabeth in her room.

'Oh yes, it was most pleasant and valuable,' she replied from her seat on the sofa. (I occupied the armchair by prescriptive right.)

'How did he impress you?'

'He was most affable, and from the beginning there were no constraints. We had lively talk for something above an hour.'

'Upon what topics?' I asked.

'Oh, a great many, from poetry to politics.'

'Very likely. I was hoping you might particularize a little.'

'Oh . . . ah . . . he renewed his affirmations of regard for some of the things I've written, especially . . . especially "A Dream of Exile" and "The Rime of the Duchess May" and others. Truly, he was most . . . I could not have wished for a more . . .'

'No lady,' said I with a smile, my hands on my knees, 'is on oath when her father questions her on her conversations with an eligible young gentleman; indeed, she need say nothing at all. But, my dearest Ba, you and I have always been closely attached; pray do a little to indulge the curiosity of an old man and a loving parent. No doubt Mr Browning did converse with you of this and that; but what did you make of him, in what frame of mind

---

*Note: I am now satisfied that the abusive term *scoundrel* is unjust, together with the following clause, and that they represent nothing more than a transient, though once deeply felt, emotion of mine. – E. B. M-B.

do you look forward to his next visit, if there is to be one, did you like him?' And Flush, at her side as always, raised his dark liquid eyes to hers as if to say that he, too, would have welcomed some information upon this head.

She looked at me for a few moments in silence, and it was not hard to imagine something of the battle of emotions that raged within her. Then she rose to her feet and held out her arms to me, and we embraced; I remember thinking how thin her small frame was, like a sheaf of ropes. Urging Flush to make room, she drew me down to sit close to her on the sofa and took my hand in hers.

'Dearest papa,' she burst out in her high voice, almost as thin in its way as her figure, 'Mr Browning is such an impressive, inspiring man, he has quite bowled me over with his ardour and strength. I swear that within a minute of his arrival I was in continuous suspense to see what he should say next – I learnt what it meant to be hanging on someone's lips. He carried within him so passionate a flame that I felt almost scorched by it,' etc., etc.

'I gather from this that you do wish to see him again,' I interjected when I thought it timely.

'I am quite set on it', and she went on without pausing for breath, 'and this, all this, from a great poet, many say the greatest of our age!'

Soon I had seen and heard enough for the time being. In a light tone I counselled the dear creature not to allow her thoughts to proceed too fast, to beware of placing an extravagant hope upon the sequel to a single brief meeting, and to consider that Mr Browning must have many other concerns in his life than an occasional visit to a fellow-rhymer, however highly regarded. When she seemed calmer I left her. I had some thinking of my own to do, and a hope hardly less extravagant than any of hers to consider.

For despite the very great depth and strength of my fatherly love, and the warm affection in which I had always held her, there was no gainsaying but that Ba's feelings for me, however welcome and however takingly expressed, were inappropriate in their degree. To put the matter in less abstract terms, she was nearly forty; while delicate of constitution she had the inner power of endurance shown by many other members of her sex;[*] as just demonstrated she was by no means indifferent to male charm; the isolation in which she lived was fully explicable but unnatural. To put it coarsely and more shortly still, she needed a man.

Perhaps Robert Browning was destined to be that man. For the time being I tried to look no further into the future. Mr Browning's letters continued to arrive at 50 Wimpole Street at an accelerating rate, and so did he in person for strictly delimited weekly visits. Dear Ba looked forward to each with what I may perhaps term a steady crescendo of expectation. She seemed happy. Her health was visibly better than it had been for years. All the same, I knew that there was more than a salubrious concern in her expressed desire, expressed indeed in previous years but never so pressingly as now, to winter out of England, in Malta, Pisa, Madeira. I would listen to any suggestion. Not having it in my nature to be either inquisitive or effusive, I was content meanwhile to allow matters to take their course. Nevertheless I knew my daughter was aware that, at least in principle, I was not unfavourably disposed to her association with the man who admired her so extravagantly, though I did wonder a little at not being invited to meet him.

II

That September, I was dining at the Reform Club, to which I had been elected a few years previously, when I was delighted to recognize my old friend John Kenyon at a nearby table. We arranged to take a glass of claret afterwards in the gallery on the

---

[*]Not by any means all of them, alas. My dearest Mary, Elizabeth's mother, had died seventeen years before this at the age of forty-seven. – E. B. M-B.

first floor. His large, stout figure was soon seated opposite me. A half-bottle decanter of the wine arrived and we filled and raised our glasses.

After we had exchanged one or two trifles of family news, he asked after Elizabeth, with whom as I have said he was remotely connected, his great-grandmother having been the sister of Elizabeth's great-grandfather. Kenyon had been most kind and helpful to her in the past, encouraging her in her poetical work, visiting her frequently and introducing her to Wordsworth, an old man then though not yet Poet Laureate, and to Miss Mary Russell Mitford, authoress of that famous book, *Our Village*.

'Elizabeth is well,' I told Kenyon in answer to his inquiry. 'Her cough is always diminished in the warmer weather, indeed this summer it appears to have vanished completely.'

'Let us hope its absence continues,' he said.

'Indeed we must.'

'To make that happy sequel more likely, it's much to be desired that she goes somewhere more clement than England for the winter.'

'Yes, Malta seems for the moment to be the favourite, at your suggestion, I'm informed. As I said to the dear girl's aunt the other day, if she does go I'll consider very seriously a visit to Jamaica.'

'Your and my ancestral home.'

'Just so. And the seat of substantial business interests of mine, at which a closer look might be valuable.'

I was about to elaborate this point when it was borne in upon me that Kenyon was hardly listening. His attention seemed to have settled on something or someone at the far end of the gallery where we sat. What it was I could not see. Turning back to me he said, his kindly florid face showing animation,

'Elizabeth still receives letters from the poet Browning and exchanges letters with him.'

'So she does,' said I, somewhat amused at the confidence with which he made this statement.

'But when you and I last talked, you and he had yet to meet.'

'That is still a pleasure deferred.'

'It need be deferred no longer, I think, or perhaps only for a few more minutes. Robert Browning has this moment joined a small company up there. He's not the chap to stand on ceremony, and I've no doubt he would welcome the chance of making your acquaintance.'

'My dear Kenyon, I hardly feel—'

'Surely a golden opportunity, here on neutral ground.'

'I must ask you to excuse me. But I will, if I may, satisfy my curiosity about how the fellow looks. The cut of his jib, as I believe it's called. Which is he?'

'He's not in our view, but he took the chair nearest to the corner, facing this way. A small man, dark, impeccably dressed.'

Kenyon looked at me in some wonderment as I rose to my feet and strolled away along the gallery. I had very little idea of what had sent me on this slightly whimsical errand, until for a matter of a few seconds, and for the first and last time, I had sight of Robert Browning. His glance at me was brief, without hostility and without interest. Before I was past him his face grew lively at some remark from one of his party and he laughed and quickly answered. I moved on at the same pace and had soon completed the circuit back to my seat.

'You saw him, then?' asked Kenyon, alert for my answer.

'Yes. As clearly as I see you.'

'And you're satisfied he has no horns sprouting from his forehead.'

'Completely.'

'I'm glad to hear it. But he has a very dark complexion, didn't you think?'

'I suppose it might be called that.' Perhaps I spoke somewhat mechanically.

'So much so that I've heard it said he has Creole or coloured blood.'

'What an absurd suggestion.'

'Is it not, of one of the most cultivated men one is likely to meet? If required I could testify that, on the best authority, there's

no truth in the tale. But, by an odd coincidence, it is true that
Browning's family, like ours, has connections with the West
Indies. More particularly, his paternal grandmother came from
a family with extensive plantations and many slaves in St Kitts
in the Leeward Islands, on the far side of the Caribbean. You
must know that Browning senior, Robert's father, became a clerk
at the Bank of England and is far from wealthy, though he seems
content to support his son's poetry. The son and his sister grew
up in New Cross, south of the . . . But whatever is the matter,
my dear fellow? Are you unwell?'

'I beg your pardon,' I said as best I could. 'You're aware of my
asthmatic tendency – I fear I'm suffering a mild attack, nothing
for serious concern . . . perhaps the ventilation in this part of the
building . . .'

'Of course we must get you home at once. I'll summon the
porter and get him to go out and secure a cab to convey us.'

Over the next few days, giving out that I was indisposed, I kept
to my room when at 50 Wimpole Street, leaving the house from
time to time to make certain inquiries. At the end of this period,
about the middle of the month, I went to Elizabeth's room about
midday, having first made certain we should not be interrupted.

She greeted me amiably enough, though with something less
than the warmth I had long grown to expect. 'Dearest papa! Are
you quite recovered from your disorder?'

I thanked her for her solicitude, assured her I was myself again,
and thereafter came straight to the point. 'I regret I must inform
you, Elizabeth, that it will not after all be possible for you to
spend the coming winter abroad.'

From her reception of that announcement, I could see easily
enough that its drift came as no great surprise to her, though her
disappointment was as evident. 'May I know your reason for
this decree?'

'I am not bound to furnish a reason, but I will do so. My advice
is that the discomfort and strain of the double journey would
probably more than undo any beneficial effect of a few weeks in
a warmer climate, not to speak of the various dangers attendant

upon any foreign travel and sojourn.'

'I am willing to take that risk.'

'I am unwilling that a daughter of mine should do so.'

'I am of age, papa.'

'While you reside here and remain unmarried you will continue to be bound by your father's wishes.'

'Those conditions may not obtain for ever,' she said with a show of resolution.

'Indeed they may not. Is this a warning that they're about to end?'

She hesitated, then shook her head firmly but with despondency. 'No.'

'In that case I'll repeat that I sincerely wish things could have been otherwise touching your visit abroad, and I bid you good day.'

'Oh, papa.' With one of her nimble movements, Elizabeth barred my path to the door. 'Please, dear papa, will you not be open with me and tell me the whole truth?'

Now I hesitated. 'I very well remember,' I said, 'discussing with Mr Kenyon, your friend Mrs Jameson and yourself the possibility of your wintering on the Continent, this on more than one occasion, and your taking my side against the proposal, declaring you were just as well off in your own warm room, and the upheaval would not be worth while. Suddenly, the upheaval has become worth while. Why?'

She made no answer, but her cheeks flushed.

'When you're ready to answer that question,' I said as gently as I could, 'I will answer yours, and speak plain. I can only hope that day soon comes.'

I should never have given that promise. To keep it would have been to divulge my secret, and that I could never have done, not to Ba. Sometimes now I wish devoutly I could have brought myself to *speak plain*; more often I thank my stars I had the sense to keep my own counsel. But I must not indulge in idle fancies.

To my surprise, far from being dashed by my steadfast performance of my duty in at least forbidding her Continental visit,

Elizabeth seemed cheerful and philosophical, content as always with being at home, surrounded by her family. That at any rate was what I told myself; I told myself many falsely comforting things. I find it almost impossible to believe that over all those months nothing of significance took place; nothing, that is, of which I was directly aware, except the abduction of Flush by ruffians and his eventual expensive recovery. The threatened loss of a dog! To be sure, I should have been greatly dashed if the attempt had succeeded, but there was a disparity between this and what I eventually did suffer so great as to be almost comical.

III

Early in the following August, everything changed, or rather, much was brought to light. I had found Robert Browning's continued regular visits to my daughter tolerable while they remained of specified duration. That day he overstayed his time and overstepped the mark. In a flash he shattered the protective shell in which I had encased myself. As soon as he had gone I hurried to Elizabeth's room in a towering rage, but the rage was directed inwards. No truer word was ever spoken than that there is none so blind as he who will not see.

Without preliminary I exclaimed, 'It appears, Ba, that *that man* has spent the whole day with you.'

'But papa, there was a storm, as surely you noticed. Mr Browning stayed only until the rain had stopped.'

'Confound the rain. To the devil with the rain. This reckless behaviour is insupportable. I will not have it. It must cease. Do you understand me?'

'I'm not sure,' said my daughter. 'Is it your meaning that Mr Browning is never to visit me here again?'

With renewed warmth, and no hesitation, I retorted, 'It is, it is. He is not to cross this threshold while I live, not for a hundred storms. He must never . . .'

'Dearest papa, you are overwrought. Come, let me sit you down here and make you see you're with one that loves you and will take care of you. Now what are these imaginings? For you seem to think Mr Browning is a sort of demon. Yet it's not so long since you seemed to tolerate his visits quite willingly and even, I thought, to welcome his addresses to me. Something has happened to change your mind. I beg you, tell your Ba what it is.'

'I cannot. Nothing has happened. But you are never to see that reprobate Browning again.'

'Mr Browning is an honourable English gentleman with none but the highest notions of what is right and proper. Or have you heard some lying tale to the contrary?'

'Nothing of that sort,' I had to answer. 'He is . . . he's simply not fit.'

'You refer presumably to his lack of a personal fortune.'

'You know there's very little that could be of less moment to me than any such consideration. In itself, that is. But the consequence of his lack of means must be that he lacks the sensibility required of him in his dealings with a personage such as yourself.'

'I can assure you that Mr Browning yields to no one where sensibility is concerned.'

'He attended no university.'

'His wealth of knowledge would challenge any who have. And since when was attendance of a university a guarantee of sensibility?'

'He is six years your junior.'

'Oh, stuff. Mama was four years older than you. Tell me the truth, father; why have you taken so strongly and so suddenly against poor Mr Browning? I remember so well how happy you were on my account when he first appeared.'

'That was before . . . I will no longer permit his visits. Oh, Ba,' I burst out, 'pay heed to what I say as never before. I beg of you, be guided by me. I don't know what you and he are to each other, and I swear to you I don't wish to know, but let there be no more of it.' I stared at her and spoke with all the earnestness of which I am capable, 'In the name of God, my daughter, banish the man Robert Browning from your life.'

Truth is so terrible, even in fetters, that for a moment I thought I had won. Then Elizabeth turned away from me and said in level tones, 'I will not. Robert and I love each other. If God is to be brought into the matter, let Him part Robert and me, for nothing human will. If you try to prevent his entry into this house, I will leave it forthwith and trust to Mr Kenyon or Mr Boyd to help me. Now please go.'

So ended my last conversation with Elizabeth on this subject, in fact our last conversation worthy of the name in this world. On Saturday, 19th September, 1846, she left my house for ever, having a week earlier been married without my knowledge to Robert Browning at St Marylebone Parish Church. Soon the couple, taking Flush with them, were in Paris. Three weeks later they had reached Italy.

I suppose I had all along regarded it as inevitable, but to have such a thing happen, however clearly foreseen, is utterly different. But what else could I have done, knowing what I knew?

Let me set in order what I knew and if need be whence I knew and know it.

1. Robert Browning is of very dark complexion. (Kenyon's phrase; my own observation.)
2. It has been said in London that he is of Creole or coloured blood. (Kenyon.)
3. His ancestry includes a West Indian grandmother. (Kenyon.)
4. The style in which he expresses himself, while correct grammatically, is fundamentally different from that of a true-born Englishman, not merely in his choice of words, but in his way of putting them together and their movement in his verses. (My own reading of the last-named and memory of what I heard of his first letter to Ba, also my glimpse of its cover.)
5. Mine is a slave-owning family domiciled in Jamaica for many years, indeed Elizabeth was the first for some generations to have been born in England.
6. I am myself of dark colouring.
7. Elizabeth is indeed of pale complexion, but there are distinct

olive or sallow tints in that pallor. (Witness my personal pet-name for her.)

8. No West Indian person can be certain of his or her pedigree.

9. By a phenomenon known, I believe, as atavism, plants and animals have a tendency to reproduce earlier types. (My own observations in Jamaica.)

10. The laws of heredity are at present not well understood, but a child will often resemble its grandfather or grandmother rather than either of its immediate parents. (Common knowledge.)

It surely stands to reason and to common experience, requiring no further argument, that the presence of Creole blood on *both* sides of a union *must redouble to an incalculable degree the chances of Creole blood in the issue.*

No doubt in days to come the question of the colour of a human being's skin will seem no more and no less interesting than the colour of eyes or hair. Here in England in the reign of Queen Victoria, those days must appear impossibly far off. By the very same consideration, how could I tell my daughter that the combined heredities of herself and Browning might – very likely would not, but still *might* – produce black offspring? How could I go so far as to say I had a reason for trying to forbid their further association? The result must have been not only to destroy Ba's love for me, as the bearer of the worst of bad tidings, but also to place at risk her prospects of happiness. The latter I could not face. Better for all three concerned that I should continue to appear to my dearest Ba, and perhaps in time to the world, the very epitome of a selfish, obstinate, unreasoning tyrant. That is the part I must continue to play until my death. I resolve to do so and to keep my secret.

I pray that the Italians may be a more tolerant people in this regard than the English. They are after all a darker-skinned race than we.

Wimpole Street,
October, 1846

IV

Until now I have resisted all temptations to add to the foregoing. I subjoined not a word even on that blackest day in November, 1850 when Elizabeth's *Poems* in two volumes appeared in a new edition that contained a section entitled *Sonnets from the Portuguese*, evidently addressed to the man now her husband. I could bring myself to do no more than hastily glance through these poems; they seemed to me of a most improper, indeed disgusting intimacy, but it was not that which wounded my feelings. The title is intended to puzzle or misdirect the reader, but if it had been specifically meant to cause me pain it could not have been more artfully devised. For 'little Portuguese' was my own personal pet-name for her, kept a secret between the two of us, an affectionately teasing allusion to her pale honey-coloured skin. The thought of her violation of this precious confidence, of my name for her being, so to speak, filched away and handed to a man who, whatever else may be said of him, had known her for only five of her forty-four years – there are no fitting words. The first shock brought a return of the asthma from which I had suffered earlier in the year, and even now the hurt remains keen.

But for the moment, in the face of a second, graver blow, I am incapable of such Stoical forbearance. Yesterday I was in my dining room at 50 Wimpole Street when I heard from the hall the unmistakable sound of a child's laughter and screams of delight. These were noises quite foreign to my house. I at once connected them with the known presence in London, not merely of my estranged daughter and her husband on their third visit, but of their six-year-old son, the child whose very existence I had tried to efface from my mind. Knowing what I must do, I inhaled several deep breaths; then, willing my head not to renew its trembling, I opened the dining-room door and strode into the hall.

There, on all fours in imitation of a lion or some such beast, was my son George Moulton-Barrett, and, retreating from him in feigned alarm, there was my grandson, Robert Wiedemann Browning. We stared at each other for what seemed an eternity, but was probably no more than two minutes. I could think of nothing to say and doubt whether, in any case, I could have spoken a word. The little lad facing me, whose looks reminded me strongly of my dead son Edward's, could have served as artist's model for a picture of a typical English boy, with the unambiguous fair colouring that that implies.

At last I turned and went back into the dining room, having mastered my strong desire to pick the youngster up and hug him to my breast. When I was breathing more or less normally I summoned George there. He stood before me, serious, dependable, the one of my sons I most respected.

'Whose child is that, George?' I asked, still not finding speech easy.

'Ba's child, father,' he answered.

'And what is he doing here, pray?'

'He is waiting, sir, waiting until it's time to return to his mother. I mean to take him on the short journey in a few moments. Would you come with us?'

'I fear not, George. Truly I cannot.'

'Papa, I beg of you. It would make Ba so happy.'

'No, my boy. Leave me. And kindly remove the child forthwith.'

When I heard the front door shut after the two, I lowered my head into my hands and may possibly have shed a tear. So it had all been for nothing, I said to myself. What I had taken for facts had not all been facts, that or my conclusions from them had been erroneous. But if I truly thought I had been wrong, why had I refused to go to Ba with George and her son?

After a troubled night, I awoke this morning with the answer rising to my lips. My daughter is now forty-nine years old and some months. In the nature of things, it must be unlikely that she could bear another child, so unlikely that I can rule it out, feel untroubled by any possibility. But I find I still cannot bring myself to come face to face with her, and with *him*. I could bear her silent reproaches, his silent triumph, but not their pity. *Her* pity.

Wimpole Street,
August, 1855

V

The above is of course fiction, but it contains much fact, the prime example being Mr Barrett's ten points.

With the exception of (4), all are matters of record. (9) and (10) certainly hold for the mid-nineteenth century, and I was told of (8) by a Jamaican friend in the 1970s. As regards (4), Mr Barrett had undoubtedly seen something in Browning's work which many would agree was there without thinking it the result of being an untrue-born Englishman. Further, it might be instructive to produce suitably recondite but representative extracts from Browning and, say, Wordsworth, Leigh Hunt, Byron, Keats, Hood, Beddoes, Tennyson, Clough and Arnold, and present them blind to a good class with the instruction to pick out which one was the work of a West Indian. The Browning sample might be the following excerpt from 'Nationality in Drinks', which Mr Barrett could easily have read, since it was first collected in *Dramatic Romances and Lyrics* in 1845:

> Up jumped Tokay on our table,
> Like a pygmy castle-warder,
> Dwarfish to see, but stout and able,
> Arms and accoutrements all in order;
> And fierce he looked North, then, wheeling South,
> Blew with his bugle a challenge to Drouth,
> Cocked his flap-hat with the tosspot-feather,
> Twisted his thumb in his red moustache,
> Jingled his huge brass spurs together,
> Tightened his waist with its Buda sash,

> And then, with an impudence nought could abash,
> Shrugged his hump-shoulder, to tell the beholder,
> For twenty such knaves he should laugh but the bolder;
> And so, with his sword-hilt gallantly jutting,
> And dexter-hand on his haunch abutting,
> Went the little man, Sir Ausbruch, strutting!

Other facts in my story include Browning's first letter to Elizabeth and the extracts from it; the paraphrase of her reply; Mr Barrett's membership of the Reform Club; his asthmatic weakness, including the severe attack of 1850; Browning's visit in August, 1846 and the reason offered for its prolongation; and Mr Barrett's meeting with his grandson. 'The Portuguese' was certainly Browning's pet-name for Elizabeth; there is no evidence it was ever her father's.

With one exception, I mean the thoughts and feelings I attribute to Mr Barrett to be sincere on his part, truthful. The exception is his final paragraph, where his explanation for not wanting to face Elizabeth and Browning strikes me as distinctly thin. His 'real' motive is more likely to have been fear of betraying his jealousy at seeing the two unequivocally together, with their offspring. (Not a sexual jealousy: I have never believed that he harboured a guilty passion for his daughter.) And perhaps he was still obsessed by his theory. Anyhow, he died in 1857 at the age of seventy-two; Elizabeth survived him by only four years.

I myself think it most unlikely that Browning, any more than Elizabeth, had some 'Creole' blood, though, if he had had, Victorian literature and the world in general would be that much more interesting. He would have been the English member of a great trio of European coloured writers of the nineteenth century, the others being Alexander Dumas père (black grandmother) and Alexander Pushkin (black great-grandfather), both of whom can be taken as sharing something of his spirit.

A few additional facts may be of interest. In 1972 I gave a talk on Tennyson to a literary society in Barnet. I was glad that what

I had to say was entirely favourable to the poet, because my audience included his highly articulate ninety-three-year-old grandson, Sir Charles Tennyson (1879–1977), though that is by the way. In the closing stages of the meeting, the secretary of the society took me aside.

'Now I know Tennyson wasn't the same person as Browning, but we have a Mrs [I forget] in the audience, a descendant of Browning's brother. Would you like a word with her?'

'Very much,' I said.

The word I had with the lady was not memorable, but I was most interested to find she was black, especially when I checked afterwards and found that Browning had no brother. None known to history, that is.

Boris and the Colonel

I

Edward Saxton was the Fellow and Director of Studies in English at a small Cambridge college, and concurrently a lecturer in that subject at that university. His special interest, on which he had given a course for over fifteen years, was the work of Thomas Gray, William Collins, Oliver Goldsmith and lesser poets of the eighteenth century who were then collectively regarded as precursors of the Romantic movement. The events recounted here took place in 1962, when Edward was forty-five years old; a thin, rather tall figure with a perceptible stoop.

He still lived where he had done when his wife had died suddenly two years earlier, in what called itself an old mill house in a village some miles east of Cambridge. He had a green shooting-brake and used it to drive himself to and fro most days during term. One such day in late spring found him in the college room he used for teaching, a few minutes before his first pupil was due.

This pupil was unlike his others in more than one way. To begin with it was a girl he expected, an undergraduate at one of the women's colleges. Also unusually, she was so interested in her subject that, over and above a weekly tutorial hour with her own Director of Studies, she had come to an arrangement whereby she showed her work to Edward four times a term. This was due partly to his personal qualities and partly to her third point of singularity, a family connection with him.

Lucy Masterman was a niece of Louise, Edward's dead wife, child of her elder brother, now in her second year at the university and nearly twenty years old. She was sturdy, dark-haired, rosy-cheeked, with large watchful brown eyes, a feature she had shared with Louise. She still retained the artless manner she had shown as a little girl, though Edward had sometimes thought she found it came in handy when dealing with grey-haired scholars like himself.

That manner was in place when, punctual as ever, she arrived. Indeed, that morning it was slightly more marked than usual, if anything, but when he looked back afterwards it seemed no time at all before Lucy was reading him her essay, and scarcely longer till she was illustrating her set theme, 'Gray's use of the rhymed quatrain in his *Elegy*'.

> Far from the madding crowd's ignoble strife (she read)
> Their sober wishes never learned to stray;
> Along the cool sequestered vale of life
> They kept the noiseless tenor of their way.

Lucy's comment was that the simple inhabitants of Gray's village might have been surprised to receive such a weighty tribute, with its heavy, regular rhythms and its tendency to epigram. A stanza such as the following, she went on, might have sounded more comfortable and comprehensible:

> But if one should return whose errant mind (she read)
> From rustic toil once took him far abroad,
> All then would labour merely to be kind,
> And crave his presence at their humble board.

The excitement that filled Edward on hearing these last four lines was quite unfamiliar to him, and it was not paralleled by anything that happened later. It had reached its full strength almost at once, and he could not remember afterwards how he had restrained himself from giving way to his feelings. For a moment he was young again, when anything had seemed possible. As Lucy paused, he asked her to stop for a minute in tones suited to a real command, and in an uncharacteristic movement got up and paced the floor.

'Did you know, Lucy,' he said in his diffident tenor, when nearly half that minute had passed and he was himself again, 'that that stanza appears nowhere in any received text of the *Elegy*?'

She blushed easily, as he had noticed. She did so now. 'I thought it might be a cancelled stanza from one of the extant manuscripts.'

'The so-called Eton manuscript has seven such stanzas, none of which even approximately resembles in any way the four lines you have just read me.'

Her blush deepened but she said nothing.

'In any case Gray would never have written those lines,' he pursued.

'You seem very sure.'

'So would you be, my dear, if you were once to hear in them what I heard. Read them aloud again.' As soon as she had finished, Edward said, 'There. Does that sound all right to you?'

'Well . . .'

'What about the rhymes?'

She looked at her page again and this time noticed something. 'Oh.'

'Precisely. *Mind* and *kind* are perfectly acceptable, if a little trite. *Abroad* and *board*, despite the words' similarity to the eye, are not acceptable, as any speaker from the west of England or Ireland or America outside the South would spot immediately.' If Edward's habitual manner had anything vague or preoccupied in it, there was nothing of either to be seen in him by this time.

Lucy perhaps saw this. She said tentatively, '*Abroad* rhymes with *Claude* and *Maud*, and . . .'

'And *fraud*. And *board* with *abhorred* and *harpsichord* and what you will. No poet of the eighteenth century, certainly not one as fastidious and well educated as Gray, could even have contemplated such a false equivalence.'

'So my sententious quatrain is a fake.'

'I'm afraid so. The work of a contemporary speaker of standard English, at a guess, possessing a good but not intimate knowledge of English poetry of the period, and more certainly a defective ear. Now. To begin with, not your work, Lucy?'

'No. I found it in a cupboard in one of the guest bedrooms at home among some sheets of typing paper, which was what I'd really been after, the typing paper. I'd come across it there ages before and I'd just left it and forgotten about it until I needed some, some typing paper. You know how you do. And it was just there in with the other sheets, the sheet with that stanza typed on it.'

'But who'd typed it, who'd written it, have you any idea?'

'Not really. Some guest, I suppose. I'm often not there, you know, at home. Most of the time, in fact.'

'Can I see it, the paper you found?'

Lucy hesitated. 'I chucked it away. Probably somebody going in for one of those weekend competitions in the *New Statesman* or somewhere. You know – write some lines in the manner of this or that well-known poem.'

'Very likely.' This explanation, like the rest of Lucy's last couple of remarks, did not satisfy Edward, but the light fog of boredom in which he habitually lived had begun to seep back in, and for the moment he could not understand or quite believe in the animation of his first response to what now seemed four rather ordinary lines. 'But . . . what made you put it into your essay like that, in a way that suggested as strongly as possible that it was a bona fide part of Gray's poem?'

'Oh, that was just rather silly.' Lucy showed some discomfort at being asked such a question. 'I was wondering if you'd spot it, but I knew you would and of course you did as soon as I finished reading it, didn't you?'

'Almost. But I still don't quite see what you hoped to gain from your little deception.'

'Nothing at all. It was just a joke.'

Edward's response to this information suggested he was no stranger to jokes, but had got out of the habit of responding to them. Perhaps he had come to find it an effort to laugh. 'I thought as much,' he said, laughing now. 'But it seems to have recoiled on your own head, Lucy dear.'

'What? Oh, I see. Yes, I suppose it has a bit. In a way.'

'Well, I think we might get on with things, don't you?'

And in no time she was citing the carrying-over of the sense between the sixteenth and seventeenth stanzas as the only case in the entire poem, and pronouncing on the significance of that. It was a well-written essay, one that showed some real feeling for literature, as Lucy's always were and always did. When she had finished reading it and discussing it and its subject with Edward, they agreed that for next time she should consider the justice of Johnson's remark, 'In all Gray's odes there is a kind of cumbrous splendour which we wish away.'

She was rising to go when Edward said to her, 'Have you really no notion at all who it was that put together that piece of pseudo-*Elegy* you found?'

'None whatever, I'm afraid. As I said, I'm not usually there.'

'It might have been interesting to know.'

The matter was left at that for the time being.

Some weeks later, Edward was sitting in the common room of his college drinking a glass of sherry before dinner. He regularly did so whenever he dined in college, and he did that most nights, not because he particularly enjoyed either the fare or the company but because he preferred them to the alternative, a solitary meal prepared by himself in his kitchen at the old mill house. He was on visiting terms with several married couples both in Cambridge itself and in the country outside, but he was not the kind of man to attract or to welcome any kind of regular arrangement for getting himself fed by friends. Now and then he dined out in another college, and once or twice a term he spent the weekend at the house of his brother-in-law, but the evening in question was what his evenings generally were.

The presence in the armchair next to his of Roger Ashby, the Fellow in Modern European History, had over some years become an expected part of those evenings. Edward had no objection, except when Ashby commented on what he saw as the similarity of their situations, having divorced his wife four years previously and not remarried. This proved not to be one of those occasions. Instead, so to speak, he asked in a meaning tone if Edward had seen the newspaper that day.

'Not yet,' said Edward. He had explained more than once to Ashby that he held off doing so until the time of his final snack and his nightcap at home.

'Thing in it that's bound to interest you. A fellow claims to have discovered some previously unknown lines from Gray's *Elegy*. Which if I mistake not is a poem that lies within your field, my dear fellow-toiler?'

'Very much so. Does the paper quote the passage in question?'

'Yes, but I fear . . . Ah. Excuse me.'

While Ashby crossed the room and returned to his seat, Edward felt in himself an onset of that same excitement that had visited him when Lucy started to recite her spurious stanza. Now as then, he found it hard to sit still.

'Yes,' said Ashby, turning to the middle pages of the captured newspaper and clearly preparing to read the relevant part aloud.

Edward forestalled that by saying, 'Let me see if I already know how those lines run.'

'I thought you said you hadn't yet—'

'Nevertheless, I have a feeling I may know them. You can hear me if you would.'

Ashby gave in with a fairly good grace, and said nothing while Edward recited verbatim what he had heard from Lucy at that tutorial. This feat of memory drew no appreciation from Ashby, who kept his eyes on what was before them and moved his head tentatively in small lateral jerks. 'Is that all?' he asked finally.

'Yes. Am I right?'

After a headshake of greater amplitude than before, Ashby said, 'Well, it might be best if I simply read you what's here.'

'I'd sooner see it with my own eyes,' said Edward. He had a well-founded distrust of the other man's willingness or ability to read anything aloud without oral annotations of his own. The words on the page proved to be set out in a way that obscured their function as part of a stanzaic scheme, but he soon rectified that in his mind and read:

> Should one retrace his steps whose foolish dream
> From righteous labours lured him far astray,
> None but would hail him as he drove his team,
> And court his company at close of day.
>
> Secure all night within his peasant cot,
> Each morn he treads the land that gave him birth,
> And contemplates some not unhonoured spot
> To house his weary bones in native earth.

Edward had fully taken in these lines before it occurred to him to do as much as glance at the surrounding matter. This informed him that the two stanzas quoted had come to light among a packet of manuscript papers in the library of a London house whose name meant nothing to him. The authenticity of the documents was uncertain, but was being checked by experts in eighteenth-century literature and in the history of writing materials. The finder of the papers wished to remain anonymous while verification was still proceeding, but was himself a well-known authority on the poetry of the period.

Some minutes had gone by since Edward had begun to read, a longer interval than Ashby normally let pass in silence. He turned out to be on his way back from the buttery hatch carrying two glasses of sherry, and soon overrode Edward's protest that a single drink before Hall was as much as he allowed himself.

'Have you formed any opinion on the authenticity of those verses?' asked Ashby.

'My first tentative impression,' said Edward carefully, 'is that their author is unlikely to have been Thomas Gray.' His mind was still perturbed at this unlooked-for sequel to the Lucy stanza, as he called it to himself, and what it might mean.

'You are clearly not one of the experts consulted by the anonymous finder. Which is a little surprising, isn't it? Given your well-known eminence.'

'Thank you, Roger, but there are quite a few others of at least equal eminence.'

'Really. Perhaps less ready than you to detect a forgery.'

'That's possible too, of course.'

'Whereas a successful forgery would be worth a great deal of money.'

'These days a reasonably careful and physically prepossessing forgery of such a famous poem, even if openly acknowledged to be a forgery, would be worth a substantial sum, especially in America. It would be interesting to have a look at that manuscript. I wonder whether—'

What Edward wondered competed unsuccessfully with the buzzing of the internal telephone. Answering this was something Ashby seemed to like doing. He threaded his way across the room between couples of old dons and young dons and a parson or two and spoke into the instrument. When he hung up his eyes were on Edward.

'Call from Suffolk for you in the lodge,' said Ashby. 'A Miss Masterman.'

Edward was picking up the receiver in the porter's lodge in much less time than he had taken over the newspaper. He was breathing quite fast as he gave his name.

'This is your favourite pupil and relative,' said the familiar youthful voice. 'How are you?'

'Fine, but why aren't you in Cambridge?'

'Revising for exams, of course. You could give me a tip or two there, especially over the Metaphysicals. It's been simply ages since we saw you down this way. I was just thinking, if you happen to be free, why don't you turn up at your usual time on Friday?'

'My dear Lucy, I can't think of anything I'd rather do.'

The warmth of Edward's response was clearly a little surprising to Lucy. 'Oh,' she said. 'Well, that is good news, I must say. I'm afraid it'll be deadly dull, just me and the aged parents.'

'Couldn't be better.'

'Couldn't it? I was going to offer an inducement, but it seems you don't need one.'

'What sort of inducement?'

'Just, there's a bit more to tell you about, you remember, that Gray's *Elegy* thing. You know, that cod verse I stuck in my essay.'

He very nearly screeched at her to tell him instantly, but thought he had better refrain in the circumstances. Instead, he asked her, 'You've seen the paper today, have you?'

'Well yes, but what about it?'

'Look again. Page 7.'

'A second and more successful attempt, or at least a subsequent one.'

Lucy had settled herself on the floor of her parents' drawing room in one of those squatting attitudes impossible for any normal male west of Suez. 'Are we sure about that? If it matters, that is.'

'That sort of thing always matters,' said Edward from the sofa. 'No, we're not sure, how could we ever be, but there's a strong suggestion in the fact that this time he avoids the cockney rhyme we noticed in your text. Presumably he noticed it too. Could I have another look at what you've shown me?'

'My text, golly!' said Lucy, passing him the typewritten sheet.

'M'm. Yes, this is a workpaper all right, leading to fair copy, probably with one or two precursors. Earlier efforts to you.'

'Thank you, Uncle.'

'How certain are you that there are no other bits hanging about somewhere?'

'As certain as I can be without taking the bloody place apart brick by brick.'

'All right, Lucy. Well, there it is. I'd give a lot to know who it was that cooked up this stuff.'

'Would you? What would you do if you did know? What good would it do you?'

'Put it down to interest. Or instinct. I just want to know.'

'Would it help to know who typed what you've got there?'

'What are you talking about, of course it would. A hundred, a thousand to one they're the same person. Why? Surely you're not going to tell me you know who it was? I don't think I could stand another shock.'

Lucy jumped up from the rug and seated herself next to Edward, turning her top half round towards him in her best unselfconscious style. 'I'm afraid I have been rather saving this up to tell you face to face.'

'Like the typescript. All right, but please keep it as short as you can.'

'Of course, what do you take me for? The first thing was me tracing the typewriter. That was easy.'

She brought out a sheet that, while a little crumpled, resembled in its general appearance the one he already held. Edward compared them.

'The typings are certainly very similar,' he said after a minute or two.

'More than just very similar. Look at the "d" in *mind* and *abroad* and so on. The bulgy part has got a little break in it near the bottom. You see? And the "s" all over the place, too far over to the right. And the "h". Almost like an "n".'

After a shorter interval, Edward said, 'Yes, I do see. But what . . .'

'It belongs to my dad. As soon as I saw it, the original one, I thought I knew it. Somebody staying here for the weekend borrowed it off him one afternoon. Would you like to know who it was?'

'Oh, I suppose I might as well, now we've come this far.'

'Good. He's called Colonel Orion Procope.' She spelt the surname. 'Three syllables, stress on first,' she explained. 'Strikes a chord?'

'There's a restaurant in Paris called something analogous, but I'm afraid I've never heard of any such person.'

'I've an idea there's a Sir in front of most of that or perhaps a Lord hanging about somewhere, and I'm pretty sure there's an MC after it. Evidently he did something jolly gallant in the desert. Any better?'

'Sorry.'

'Well, I had a shot, at least. Mind you, the colonel, which is how he likes to be addressed – Colonel Orion Procope has rather got the look of, you know, someone who changes his name about a bit. Anyway, you'll have the chance of judging such things for yourself in a little while.'

'What!'

'My turn to be sorry,' said Lucy, neither sounding nor looking particularly sorry. 'Yes, he's coming to dinner. I promise that's the last of my surprises.'

'For this weekend at least. Well, that's a comfort.'

Before they went off to change, Lucy released some further crumbs of information about the gallant colonel. He lived no great distance away, across Suffolk, near the coast; having never married, he lived there on his own, 'apart no doubt from the occasional fisherman', according to Lucy; he got invited over for the weekend a couple of times a year, for dinner or Sunday lunch two or three times as often; he might never have been invited at all but for his apparently lonely situation, 'and he most likely wouldn't have been even so, if Mum weren't such an old softie'; he had first met Lucy's father in the course of some 'strangulatingly boring' piece of business in the City of London; he had never been known to say much about his history.

Edward had his usual room at the eastern end of the house, usual at least since Louise's death. For some months after that death, he had thought he would never have been able to come down here again, but when once he decided to try, it had not proved so difficult. These days, in fact, the place was only fitfully one where he had known some happy moments with her; he valued it more for itself, for its spaciousness, though it was not very grand or very old, and its silence. He liked this part of East Anglia too, never sunny for long, but at some time every day full of light from its enormous sky, which Constable had never forgotten.

Of course this was Lucy's place too. Now that she was momentarily out of his sight, he found it easier to think of her as an entire person, easier too to consider with some objectivity her resemblances to her aunt, seen in her colouring and the look of her face with its round eyes and arched brows, and felt rather than seen in the way she held herself, upright but with head a little bowed. He now doubted the truth of his earlier impression that the glance of those brown eyes had grown more direct recently. But was he accurate in supposing that he saw her first of all as a version of Louise?

He was tying his tie at the dressing table when out of the tail of his eye he caught a distant movement through the east window. He soon saw a car descending a low hill in the nearer distance. For a few seconds it vanished before reappearing and entering the short driveway, an expensive-looking car sprayed a very dark blue picked out with crimson. After it drew up, just beyond rather than below where Edward was standing, nothing happened for a short time. Then a youngish man in a dark suit and a chauffeur's cap got out of the driving seat and another about Edward's age out of the passenger's seat. What could be seen of the latter showed him to be an average sort of man in a dinner jacket, not tall, not short, with a mop of brown hair that seemed to have kept most of its colour, but there was something about the presumable Colonel Procope that made Edward draw cautiously back from his window.

There was no trace of that something to be seen when in due course the two men met. Indeed, the colonel made a favourable impression with his generally straightforward manner and the restrained warmth with which he greeted the three Mastermans. When he came to Edward, he managed to convey satisfaction at meeting one he had heard good reports of. He was quite unmilitary in his appearance, which by including a remnant of stubble by one ear and a loosely tied tie rather suggested some colleague of Edward's, or the popular idea of one. It might perhaps have been said that he talked a little too quietly for perfect manners.

The first patch of conversation that Edward remembered afterwards came during dinner, and was preceded by a brief warning look, or glare, at him from Lucy.

'Oh, colonel,' she said, 'I am right in thinking, am I not, that you got a medal for something brave you did in the war?'

Before answering, Procope moved his eyes to her and only then turned his head, a slightly disconcerting trick Edward had noticed in him before. 'A medal?' he echoed with humorous pomposity. 'Come, every Tom, Dick and Harry gets a medal. What they gave me was a decoration, what? The old MC, you know. In fact, Lucy girl, you know perfectly well.'

'I wanted to be sure because one of my college mates I happened to be telling about you said she was pretty sure she remembered her father saying he'd known somebody with your name or something like it in the war in North Africa somewhere.'

'When you've got your breath back, tell me what unit he was in.' The colonel made a vaguely conspiratorial face at Lucy's mother, Kate Masterman, who beamed back at him. The two were certainly on good terms, Edward thought, but in no more than a companionable way, without any trace on Kate's side of the old softie of her daughter's description.

Lucy seemed to search her memory. 'Could he have been a Desert Rat?'

'Certainly he could. I had very little to do with them. They were strictly the Seventh Armoured; I was with the Tenth. Most of the time.'

'Of course, Edward was in the desert too, weren't you, uncle?'

'Only for a couple of weeks,' said Edward discouragingly. He had seen his share of action, but had got no nearer 'the desert' than Anzio in Italy.

If Lucy had hoped to drive Procope into some sort of corner, to force him into undue reticence or talkativeness, she was disappointed. In five minutes or so he had shown that he had either experienced fighting in North Africa at first hand or been thoroughly briefed by somebody who had. Whichever it was, Edward could see nothing at all in him of any kind of man that might have tried to fake a couple of Gray's *Elegy* quatrains. On the other hand, it had to be conceded that he did look a bit like one given to changing his name about, as Lucy had put it. Edward felt this strongly enough to see something false in the chummy au revoir the fellow sent Kate when the two women left the table.

So, what with one thing and another, Edward was more than adequately surprised to hear Procope say, almost as soon as the door was shut, 'I gather you're a great authority on Thomas Gray, Dr Saxton. The chap who wrote the *Elegy*.'

'I suppose one might put it like that. Nice of you to anyhow, colonel.'

Procope made one of his faces. 'Well, it's true. Now you obviously think Gray's pretty good as a poet, otherwise you wouldn't have bothered to turn yourself into an authority on him.'

'Yes, at least pretty good.'

'Sorry. Of course, I know I'm a complete what-you-may-call-it, a layman, an amateur, but I've always been fond of the old hoary-headed swain and the rest of it. Time was when I could have repeated whole chunks that I'd got by heart. Don't you worry, Toby, I'm not about to start polluting your dining room with a poetry recital.'

Toby Masterman made some inoffensive remark. To Edward's eyes he looked indisputably more like a military man than his guest, but like nothing positive that could be thought of, stout, almost florid, unlike his dead sister with a completeness once mildly comic to Edward and now the cause of mild thankfulness. The only surprising thing about him was that he had produced Lucy.

After a laudatory word or two about the port now in circulation, Procope said with renewed vivacity, 'Things being as they are, I consider myself lucky to have run across an expert like you, Dr Saxton, just when there's been this thing in the paper about some extra verses of the poem seeming to have turned up from somewhere. You must have seen that, naturally. Tell me, off the record, so to speak, what did you think of them, those verses? I quite see you may prefer not to commit yourself until you know more about the thing.'

Edward tried to remember that the question had come from the apparent author of the verses in question. 'Well,' he said cautiously, 'as regards poetical merit, what I saw struck me as distinctly below par, below the general standard of the *Elegy*, but then what Gray wrote is so familiar that one can't be sure. What I'm trying to say is, it's hard to compare the known with the unknown.'

'I'm pretty hopeless myself when it comes to anything like that. But I value your opinion, welcome it too, because it throws some light on a question I have to admit interests me more, the authenticity of those eight lines. Taking into account your first reaction to them as poetry, do you think they're Gray's work or not? As far as you can tell.'

This seemed to Edward one to fend off. 'That's more difficult,' he said. 'Not really one for me at all. I don't know enough about Gray's lesser contemporaries to be sure.'

'You're too modest, Dr Saxton. You must have some feeling one way or the other.'

'I wouldn't like to commit myself to any such feeling without looking at the stuff again.'

'That's easily arranged.' Procope brought out a wallet from which he carefully took a neat newspaper cutting. 'It just so happens, as they say.'

Edward tried to feign a pleased interest as he looked again at what Roger Ashby had shown him earlier that week. He felt himself blushing to a degree that might have rivalled Lucy, and did his best to put on a fit of coughing. It was extraordinarily hard to read the printed words as opposed to looking in their general direction.

'I'm sorry, Toby,' said Procope, 'we'll be finished in a minute.'

'Take your time, I'm quite comfortable as I am.'

'You saw the piece, did you? What do you think?'

'I think the port is with you,' said Toby.

Possibly because he was seeing the stanzas in changed circumstances, Edward all at once found in them something he had not noticed before, something that brought on in him a more intense agony of dissimulation. He decided he had to speak and might as well speak the truth.

'In my opinion these lines are not the work of Thomas Gray,' he said.

'Ah! Thank you! Thank you, Dr Saxton, for delivering the kind of verdict that I slightly hoped you would see your way to.'

Instead of frankly goggling at the colonel, Edward tried to look no more than politely interested and expectant.

'As I told you just now, I'm a total amateur in literary matters, interested as I may be in one or two of them, but even so, or perhaps for that very reason, I find it pleasant when a professional confirms my subjective judgement.'

This time Edward managed to say, 'Yes, I see.'

'I take it you've been approached by whoever's concerned and asked for your expert opinion? No? Well, they'll come to you, never fear. When they do, I hope you'll denounce this impudent fabrication. As before, that's only a, what did I say, a slight hope of mine, a modest one. Because, although the matter has aroused my curiosity, it matters to me personally not at all whether those lines are genuine or spurious. Not one scrap. I haven't even taken a bet. What do you say to that, Toby?'

'I say we should consider joining the ladies.'

When the colonel had departed and Lucy slipped away to bed, Edward forgathered with Toby and Kate for a nightcap in a corner of the drawing room. Outside the house the stillness seemed absolute.

'Interesting sort of chap, Colonel Procope,' said Edward experimentally.

The experiment was not a success. Kate said she thought the colonel was rather pathetic, Toby said more apologetically that neighbours had become thin on the ground, and the topic lapsed before Edward could get out his prepared quip about the fellow reminding him of some dishonest smallholder. A moment later Kate asked Edward how he thought Lucy was looking, at which point Toby shifted in his chair in a way suggesting that there had been enough recent discussion of his daughter to last him for a bit.

This time Edward spoke guardedly. 'She looks fine to me,' he said, and was not surprised to hear from Kate that mere outward looks were a trifle compared with inner wellbeing or the lack of it, and that it was here that Lucy gave grounds for concern, having just broken suddenly with an altogether suitable near-fiancé.

'About nothing at all,' said Kate. 'All of a sudden he became a frightful bore.'

'For my money he'd been that all along,' said Toby. 'Full of, well, full of what there was of himself. Damn it, the girl must be allowed to make a mistake and change her mind now and then. She's not twenty yet.'

'It's much more than that, as you know. She's thoroughly discontented with her whole generation of young men and always has been. You'd have thought Cambridge would have opened her eyes, but from that point of view it's been a total washout.'

'Oh, Katie, give the poor little thing a chance. She needs time.'

'If there's anything I can do,' said Edward.

'It's sweet of you, dear Edward, but I get the impression that where that girl's concerned you're impossibly distant and grown-up. Oh, she's very fond of you, of course, so she ought to be, but as a remote sort of uncle-figure, which after all is what you are. You do enough for her by encouraging her interest in literature.'

And that ought to be enough for any uncle-figure, thought Edward a little later as he undressed in his single bedroom. He switched off his light and looked out over the soundless landscape. In a corner of his mind were an excitement and something to be looked forward to with a tiny thrill. The excitement was from Gray and Procope, the something was the prospect of conferring again with Lucy. But a thrill of any size that arose from that prospect could be no more than a function of habit and memory.

'And I'm quite sure he meant it,' Edward told Lucy the next morning, by way of winding up his account of the conversation with Colonel Procope.

'But he can't have,' she said.

'On one assumption, it would indeed be all one to the colonel whether those stanzas are genuine or not. It would not concern him either which they are shown or taken to be. Let's see if you can find grounds for . . .'

He stopped speaking because she seemed to have stopped listening. They had reached the gate of the small paddock, which they now entered. Lucy clinked the handle of the pail she was carrying, not loudly but it appeared loudly enough to attract the attention of a large horse standing by the far hedge. This animal at once came trotting over to them with what to Edward was excessive eagerness. Seen close to, it looked about the size of a full-grown elk, reddish-brown in general colour but with black mane and tail and large off-white teeth. These it showed prominently while it breathed noisily at them, butted Edward in the chest and without ceremony set about bolting the contents of the pail.

'You remember Boris,' said Lucy and, when Edward looked uncomprehending, added a trifle impatiently. 'You know, after Boris Godunov.'

'I thought it was Virginia, after Virginia Woolf.'

'That was the little mare I had ages ago. She's gone. It's Boris now.'

Indeed it was Boris now, in the extra sense that Lucy's attention was all directed that way, with none to spare for Edward. Presently she threw a rope round the horse's neck and in a flash was on its back. For a moment she sat there very still and straight and seeming taller than before; Edward almost caught his breath at her look of dignity and power. Then she was off, away, just a girl trotting and cantering her horse round her father's paddock. He, Toby, had prophesied that the horse would be disposed of about the time she found herself a man.

As soon as he profitably could, the man she was with at the moment said, 'Now, Lucy, I want you to do a little experiment for me.' While she shut the gate behind them he took out his copy of the stanzas, but did not at once hand it over. 'Try to forget that this might or might not be part of Gray's *Elegy*. See if you can manage to forget the fact that it's in verse, which shouldn't be all that exacting considering the lubberly way the paper has set it out. Now. You've no idea what this might be, you've just this moment come across it written on a pad. Right, here it is.'

Lucy halted on the gravel drive to read. He thought it marvellous that she found no evident difficulty in doing so without artificial aid and in what was not much better than average daylight, living as he did in a world where everybody wore glasses, most of them all the time, like himself. In his eagerness he tried to prompt her by suggesting she should attend only to the meaning of what was in front of her, but she spoke at the same time, and with a shake of the head at his own ineptitude he told her to go on.

'What it *says* . . . if somebody who went wrong or went to the wrong place should retrace his steps, come back to his starting-point, he'd be perfectly . . .'

'Secure. The best word out of however many dozen it is. Though not at all Gray's kind of thing, a sort of pun, Latin *securus*, *se* plus *cura*, free from care, also modern *secure*, in a state of security, not at risk from hostile undercover moves or surveillance.'

'In fact the message of the whole thing seems to be . . .'

Edward was too excited to notice that he had again interrupted. 'The message. That's what it is. A message. Well done. It suddenly hit me last night. What is the characteristic of that newspaper and no other, almost no other anywhere? All right, there are several, but the one that interests us is that it goes all over the world.'

'*Far* astray.'

'If you wanted to send a message to somebody you couldn't locate, perhaps you couldn't even say with any certainty what country he was in, what better means could you think of? Almost, what other means at all? Exposed as a forgery or not, you really could afford to be indifferent. You might even leave drafts of it lying about.'

'Provided your man saw it.'

'Admittedly you'd have to take your chance on that, but you might be able to bet he'd see that paper every day. Of course he'd have to have some sort of interest in literature thrown in, but with a thing like the *Elegy* it wouldn't have to be a specialized one. And if there's silence at the other end you just have to think of something else. You're no worse off.'

They had reached the road before Lucy said, 'All right, let's have the rest of it, whatever it is.'

'How do you know there's more to come?'

'By not being blind or deaf. Come on, Uncle – shoot.'

'Very well, here goes. One. Colonel Orion Procope, MC. When I told you I'd never heard of anybody called that, I was speaking the truth. But I'd only to catch sight of him to be pretty certain I'd seen him before, and in some kind of sinister context. Nothing more specific than that till this morning when I woke up remembering who he was and where I'd seen him. I still couldn't remember his original name, and I knew it wasn't him in the flesh I'd seen, just a few photographs, which did nevertheless belong to a sinister context.

'Two. Guy Burgess and Donald Maclean. Do they mean anything to you, Lucy?'

'Not much. Weren't they Communist spies, years ago?'

'Eleven years ago to be precise, in 1951. At any rate, that was when they were exposed and fled to Russia, where they still are.'

'Oh yes, our security coppers made a frightful boob.'

'Not really. It was the weekend and they couldn't get hold of anyone to sign the warrants for the arrests. Respect for the law.'

'Something pretty boobish about that.'

'I agree it could never have happened in Russia.'

'M'm. I accept the rebuke,' said Lucy. 'But how did you know about the warrants?'

'It's not a secret. But the answer to your question takes us to Three. Edward Saxton, D.Litt. Where's this pub I've heard so much about?'

'You can see it from here.'

'So I can. Before we get there, let me just say that about that time I did a bit of work for MI5, to be known henceforth between you and me simply as the company, if you follow me. I'm not in your league as an unfolder of mysteries, but I won't tell you the rest till I've a glass of beer in my hand.'

It was cool, dark and quiet in the saloon bar. Edward and Lucy took their drinks over to a window that gave a view of an unfrequented stretch of road and a green hedgerow with woodland beyond it, all with their colours sharpened by the mild sun. No petrol fumes lingered, only country scents. Edward sipped beer appreciatively.

'One can get tired of drinking wine day in and day out,' he said. 'Though not very soon, I suppose. Now, let me go on briefly. Years ago I helped the company a bit over the matter of defective patriotism among former Cambridge men – you may remember that both Burgess and Maclean had been undergraduates at that university. There were others never or not yet brought to book, half a dozen of them, among whom was the man now known as Colonel Procope, who escaped prosecution for lack of evidence. Nothing could have been proved either against his close friend, perhaps more than close friend, whom I knew as Green, but evidently Green was up to something our side didn't know about, because he cleared off to Russia too, just three weeks after good old Guy and Donald. Green read English at Cambridge, which isn't exactly incompatible with an interest in literature, though I agree—'

'I take it Green is still in Russia. But if he gets the colonel's message he'll soon be on his way back.'

Edward frowned and looked worried. 'I wish we could do better, but I don't think we can at the moment.'

'So what's our next step?'

'I don't honestly see we've got one. What we have is surmise, and nobody seems to be even contemplating anything illegal, I'm sorry to say. It would be interesting to have a tap put on Procope's telephone, but also out of the question. All we can do is keep our eye on the paper.'

'Would it help if we knew how he got them to print that stuff?'

'I'll have a word with the company. About that and other matters.'

Lucy looked at Edward, who held her gaze. She said, 'I'd never have taken you for a . . .'

'Careful.'

'. . . tradesman as well as an expert on Gray.'

'Tradesmen come in all sizes and shapes. What time is lunch?'

As they were on their way out, the landlord nodded politely to Edward and said to Lucy, 'How's my old friend Boris?'

'Oh, he's fine, thank you, Mr Littlejohn.'

'Have you taken him on a proper excursion yet?'

'I thought next week, perhaps.'

'He'd enjoy it,' said the landlord, who with his neat suit and generally scrubbed appearance looked like the citified person he was not. Laying a polished horseshoe on the counter, he said, 'Anyway, here's a present for him.'

'Oh, he'll absolutely love that. I'll nail it on his stable door.'

II

Revision, especially of the Metaphysicals, and bad weather combined to put off the day on which Lucy ceremonially nailed the horseshoe to Boris's stable door. But when that day came it was so clear and bright and the forecast so promising that she planned a proper excursion for him and her on the morrow.

She was up at six and, with her old tweed coat over her nightdress, fetched the horse to his stable facing the kitchen and put chaff and corn in the manger for him. A heavy dew sparkled on the grass, the sky was a slightly veiled but cloudless blue, and there was the kind of hush everywhere that she had noticed before at the start of a fine hot day. She got more or less ready before cooking herself a substantial breakfast of fried egg, bacon and tomatoes, no more than sensible before a day's riding. By this time the paper had arrived and she glanced at it as she ate.

Her eye was caught by a short item saying that the supposed additional stanzas of Gray's *Elegy*, the discovery of which was recently reported, had been shown to be a modern forgery. The finder's request for continued anonymity was being respected. This information revived Lucy's almost-lapsed interest in the matter, and even brought her a mental picture of Colonel Orion Procope being completely indifferent to the news, but she dismissed it and him from her mind in the course of making sandwiches with fresh Cheddar, chopped onion and plenty of sweet pickle. This done, she prepared a thermos of tea, leaving enough tea over to take up to her parents' bedroom with some arrowroot biscuits she privately considered dead boring.

The grandfather clock in the hall struck eight; time for grooming and saddling up. Lucy's saddle, a birthday gift, was of army pattern, which meant among other things that it had plenty of hooks on which to hang a haversack with her provisions, a nosebag with Boris's stuff, her black fisherman's sweater and a blanket of his. She was ready, and of course he knew it at once and made for the outdoors. A minute later she was walking him down towards the road, quite a striking figure in her twill jodhpurs and man's shirt, hair drawn back under a dark-green scarf, with the upright posture Edward had noticed.

As the sunshine grew stronger, the two of them were making good time, mostly over grassland or greenwood floor, so good that Lucy began to think she would fulfil her hope of reaching the coast before turnabout time and showing Boris the sea, perhaps taking him for a gallop along the sands if the tide was right, for a paddle if not. She had been talking on and off to him since they started, and when she mentioned these possibilities he turned his ears back to listen, but on being asked how he felt about them he simply took no further interest.

From earlier outings with Virginia, Lucy was confident that somewhere along their line of march she would find a good place for a rest, and sure enough not long after one o'clock they came to a shady spot with a patch of turf next to the road and a culvert over a stream, only a little one but enough to water Boris and wash the dust off his feet. Then, having loosened his girth, she put on his nosebag and he munched contentedly, swishing his tail against flies. She ate sandwiches, drank half her tea and read a chapter of her paperback copy of *Dr Zhivago*. Before they moved on she got into the saddle and let him crop grass for a few minutes.

Lucy was expecting to come in sight of the sea quite soon when she realized she was heading more or less directly for the village near which Colonel Procope lived. A glance at the map she carried in her haversack showed her that by the shortest route she was about two hours' easy riding-time from it. That route, however, involved a longish stretch of road and, although Boris never complained, she knew he preferred to avoid road travel where possible, so a few minutes later she turned aside on a more roundabout approach. Only then did it occur to her to wonder how long it was since it had first entered her head to seek out the colonel and what she hoped to achieve by doing so. She found no answer to either question, and soon put them aside in favour of taking in the look of sunlit greenery and wild flowers and the lulling pleasure of having a healthy, strong, good-natured horse under her. But she still moved along a curving path that led to Procope's village.

When at length she reached it she found little to see: a few smartened-up cottages, some boring modern houses, a church decorated in the usual flint, but also a post office, and that was obviously her first port of call. With the sound of rock music in her ears, she tied Boris to a convenient rail and went inside among picture postcards and toffee bars as well as stamps and telegram forms.

Instead of a fat old woman with glasses and a pencil stuck in her hair, Lucy found a fresh-faced one little older than herself, in dark slacks and a tee-shirt bearing the name and device of a brand of American cigarette. No less unexpectedly, this person reduced the music to almost nothing without being asked, and smiled a welcome.

'Colonel Procope?' she said at once when the name was mentioned. 'Straight down the hill over there, lane at the bottom on the left, a bit under a mile along on the left. Say twenty minutes' walk. I suppose it'd be quicker on horseback. That is your horse out there, is it?'

'Thank you. Yes.'

'Work at a riding stable, do you?'

'No. No, he's my very own horse. I keep him at home and look after him there myself.'

'That's nice,' said the young woman vaguely. She looked out of the window and then over her shoulder before glancing at Lucy and away again. 'You, er, excuse me asking, but would you be a great friend of his worship the colonel?'

'Certainly not. My parents see him occasionally but only as a neighbour.'

Lucy thought this description sounded pretty hollow, but it evidently reassured the other girl, who said with another smile, 'I thought you weren't, well, his type, kind of thing. Er, he's not exactly popular round here at the moment.'

'What's he been up to?'

'Not that he's ever been very highly thought of in these parts, but just the other day, see, he went too far. One of the village lads, young Tommy, well, he's only a boy, really, not too bright if you know what I mean, anyway, Tommy was playing round the colonel's place, just like a kid, you know, he wouldn't be doing any harm, and his nibs flies into a tremendous rage, shouts at him, says he'll give him a thrashing if he doesn't make himself scarce that minute. Then laughed and said he was only joking.'

Lucy thought for a minute. 'Did Tommy tell you all this?'

'His mother had to like drag it out of him.'

'Rough luck on poor little Tommy. Did he say anything else?'

'No. Oh, there was one bit, he said there was something funny about the shed in the colonel's garden.'

'M'm. What sort of something funny? I suppose he didn't say.'

'Not really. Something about a hole. His mother said he sounded frightened.'

The girl behind the counter herself spoke with sudden reluctance, as if she repented a little of having been so informative. Lucy took her cue, bought a couple of chocolate biscuits and departed.

Twenty minutes later the biscuits were inside Boris and he was standing in the shade and out of view while Lucy, also out of view, sat looking down on Colonel Procope's domain. This consisted of a small stone-dressed cottage of no particular consequence, a couple of wooden outbuildings and a fragment of land with a spinney at one end and an open gateway on to the road or lane. This was a rough-and-ready affair that on one hand became no more than a track and on the other led to a bridge across a considerable stream. On the far side of the little valley, a more serious road led westward towards Ipswich, Cambridge and other important places.

Nobody was to be seen moving around or near the cottage, not even through the modest but serviceable pair of field glasses that Lucy habitually carried in her haversack and had hitherto shown her nothing more dramatic than the odd pair of nesting waterfowl. It was more than likely that there was nobody in the cottage either. The sense of adventure that had uplifted her since she had reached the village began to subside, leaving her with a half-memory of more childish would-be exploits, adventures of the mind founded on reading and day-dreaming. She was on the point of calling off her fruitless vigil, remounting Boris and making for home – it was too late now for any trip to the coast – when a large dark-blue car she had glimpsed across the valley came into her view again making for the cottage. In due time it slowed up, drove through the gateway, stopped, and set down a figure she recognized without her field glasses as the eccentric colonel. Lucy had calculated that one or other of the outbuildings must be a garage, but if so Procope made no immediate use of it; instead, he went and unlocked the door of a small shed. Seen through her glasses now, he looked carefully about him before going inside. Though Lucy had no fear of being seen as long as she kept still, she found this intensive survey disturbing in some way. It took a full half-minute to complete, at the end of which time he did enter the shed and no doubt locked the door after him. There was no sign of the younger man who had acted as chauffeur in the past, nor of anybody else.

Lucy waited without result. She was again about to leave when she saw the door of the shed open and Procope emerge. After locking up once more, he gave a somewhat abbreviated repeat of his all-round scrutiny, then moved to the front of his cottage, which was out of her view, and presumably went in at the front door. When another ten minutes had passed without incident, she left her observation post, went to reassure Boris, who stood placidly tethered to a handy tree, and walked down the grassy slope towards Procope's abode, expecting any moment a challenging shout at best. None came. Still nothing happened when she reached the shed and peered in through a small window.

The interior was dark, and her own reflection kept hampering her attempts to see inside, but quite soon she found a vantage point that gave her a limited view. It was not so limited that she failed to make out part of a shallow trench dug in the earth floor of the shed at one end. So that was the hole young Tommy had seen: a trench. But what was a trench doing in a shed? Was it a trench?

Lucy's heart had begun to beat fast. Trying not to think, only to act, she hurried back to Boris and rode in a sort of semicircle along the slope, down and back till she was approaching along the lane from the village. At Procope's gate she dismounted, having done just enough thinking to run up an elementary story about finding herself in the district with time to spare and paying a call on the off chance that he would be at home.

The front door of the cottage had an old-fashioned bell pull that set up a tuneless jangling somewhere inside. Nothing happened for so long that Lucy had almost made to ring again when the door was flung open to reveal Colonel Procope.

The declining sun clearly illuminated a look of eager welcome on his face which very soon gave place to puzzlement, consternation, anger if not more. 'What do you want?' he demanded. 'What are you doing here?'

She had her back to the light; she was far from his mind; her hair was hidden; he had never done more than glance at her. These points occurred to her later; for the moment she was aware only that he had not recognized her. It seemed to her suddenly important to remain unrecognized. 'I'm sorry, sir,' she said, trying to look as well as sound rustic and gawky, 'but I wondered if my horse could have a drink of water.'

'Certainly not! Get out!' He was shouting and glaring, his fierce eyes doubly strange under the brown thatch of hair. 'If you don't, if you're not gone by the time I finish talking' – his voice rose to something like a scream and a fleck of saliva hit her cheek – 'I promise you I'll set my dogs on you *and I won't be calling them off!*'

There was no need on Lucy's part for any mimicry of someone badly disconcerted and frightened. She was back in the saddle, and had cantered a hundred yards towards the village, before she had time to reflect that any available dogs of the sort implied would assuredly have made a tremendous noise at the first sound of an unexpected visitor. Later still it occurred to her that no horse needed to be taken in search of water with a whole river a bare hundred yards away, but that was not going to matter now.

She arrived back at the post office in time to get some change and was soon on the telephone to Edward's college, to the porter there who advised her to ring the old mill house, then to Edward himself who listened to her account of events without asking any questions, except where he would find her on his arrival in something under the hour. Lucy went to the saloon bar of the designated pub on the far side of the village green, which was nice enough but not as nice as Mr Littlejohn's, and very slowly drank a half-pint of shandy (heavy on the lemonade).

Bit by bit her excitement ebbed away and with it all pretence of certainty, all her former sense of having happened to catch Colonel Procope on the point of committing some fearful atrocity. He had responded with surely disproportionate anger to a stranger's innocent intrusion, for such it had been to his knowledge, and had perhaps shown something of the same earlier to young Tommy. There were a dozen possible explanations for that. He was secretive about his shed, inside which he had dug a trench, and that trench might to a fevered fancy like her own – she admitted it now to herself – have been a grave. And it might have been an unknown number of other things besides. He, the colonel, had fabricated eight lines in the general style of a two-hundred-year-old poem to send a message to a friend who quite likely had been a spy. What had Edward called the basis for that notion? Surmise, perhaps leaving a ruder word unspoken. What he would call her more recent notions Lucy dreaded to think.

Her heart sank further when at last he arrived. She knew immediately from the way he looked round the bar, spotted her, came over, greeted her with a touch of solicitude, that he had not taken her tale seriously. He had turned up for merely avuncular reasons, to give her moral support and to calm her down. His manner was studiedly non-committal when she acted on his request to go over things again.

'So according to you,' said Edward after listening to her, 'you surprised the colonel just as his friend Green, having received and acted on his message, was about to walk in, be killed and be buried in the garden shed. Well now, why would the colonel want to kill his old mate after so elaborately persuading him to come all this way?'

'I don't know,' said Lucy, adding stoutly, 'but that doesn't mean there couldn't be a reason.'

'True, as far as it goes. How, do you think, would the colonel have known so exactly when Green was due after his long and difficult journey? And how might he have induced Green to call on him?'

'He's on the telephone.'

'True again. If Green was indeed going to appear, he might do so at almost any hour of any day out of, let's say a hundred.'

'Yes.'

'But you happened to come along and poke your nose in at the precise time he was expected.'

Lucy said forcefully, 'That's right, perhaps I did, and it's no argument against the manifestation of an unlikely coincidence to notice that such a manifestation, though perfectly possible, is unlikely.'

'True a third time. I think. Now I'm going to have a large glass of whisky. What about you? Would you like something of the sort yourself?'

'No, thank you.' She was slightly astonished. 'What, what for?'

'To strengthen you against a coming ordeal, or what may very well turn out to be one. We're off back to the colonel's place to see what we can catch him at.'

'Oh, are we? Wouldn't it make more sense to wait till dark?'

'He'll be on his guard then, and I want to see the ground in the light. The sooner we're there the better.'

When Edward had returned from the counter with his whisky, she said, 'Have you told, you know, your friends in the company about any of this?'

He hesitated briefly. 'No.'

'Because you don't want to look ridiculous. As ridiculous as you think my story is.'

Dropping all lightness from his manner, and focusing his attention on her in a way he had never done before, he took her hands in a loose but strong grip. 'I think it only just conceivable that your story has any substance in it at all. And that's how you feel yourself, isn't it? But I'd be a fool if I didn't follow it up. And I'd be worse than a fool if I didn't do something to repay the trust you showed in me when you asked me to help you.'

She was not sure she understood all the meaning behind his words, but she caught his tone immediately and responded to it. 'I'm ready whenever you say.'

He gave a wide grin with his eyes fixed on hers, another new expression, and squeezed her hands for a moment. 'Good. Now where's that horse of yours?'

'I suppose you mean Boris. He's on the green outside here, or he was when I last looked.'

'Yes, I thought I saw him,' he said without much conviction, half got up, remembered his whisky and drained it. 'Right. Order of march. You lead on Boris. I follow in my trusty shooting-brake, which I should like to pull up and put somewhere out of the way a couple of hundred yards short of the objective. Is that possible?'

'We'll pass a bridge over the river on our right. After that I'll dismount at a point where you should be able to drive off the road.'

He nodded and they left without further ado. Outside they parted in silence, Edward to his car, Lucy to Boris, who showed no resentment at having had to put up with a pretty dull hour, though he was obviously dying to be off somewhere. Before she put her foot in the stirrup she said to him,

'Now this is probably going to be nothing at all, but on the other hand you may find yourself having to do something pretty serious and grown-up, and I'll be relying on you. Are you ready for that?'

He tossed his head in a twisty, sporty way that showed he was ready for anything.

'Okay. Walk march.'

Behind her, she heard Edward start his engine but did not look back. Down the slight hill they went, left into the lane, up to the bridge. The light was still strong, but anyone would have known that evening was not far off. Colonel Procope's cottage came into sight. Soon afterwards, Lucy dismounted as arranged and led Boris to a point in somebody's field where he would not be disturbed and could not be seen from the road. Here she tied him to a fencing post by a rope long enough to let him graze wthout getting tangled, gave him some bread she had been saving and stroked his forehead and down to his nose. She told him to stay quiet and not to worry, because she would be back for him. Her heart was beating fast again, this time from fear, not of the colonel or whatever he might do but of his doing nothing, nothing out of the ordinary, of his turning out to be up to nothing worth all this fuss.

Edward's demeanour, when she joined him in the lane, quite failed to reassure her. His air of serious concentration, his vigilant peering ahead and around, showed her again that he was doing no more than humouring her and was perhaps already rehearsing his indulgent rebuke of her overheated imagination, fondness for sensational fiction and more. So what actually happened when they got to the cottage came as a surprise as well as a shock to them both.

Before Lucy had had time to do more than wonder what Edward had in mind, someone indoors gave a loud scream. It was a different sort of sound from anything she had heard as part of any film or imagined from reading any book; it might have come from a man or a woman or even an animal, and it set up a violent tingling at the back of Lucy's neck, hot or cold, she could not tell which. There were other noises too that might have been bodies striking against furniture. Somewhere at the back a door opened. Edward caught her arm and led her a few yards in that direction before dropping into a crouch behind an evergreen bush and pulling her down beside him. They heard a shout or two, not nearly as loud as the scream, and then a man unknown to them came out through the doorway in an irregular walk, very much like somebody trying to make his way along the deck of a ship in rough weather. He had not gone far when he collapsed on the ground near a water butt, though his arms and legs still moved.

So far, things had seemed to happen slowly, but now they greatly speeded up. Another man, one with blood on his forehead, one recognizable as Colonel Procope, came running out of the cottage and flung himself on top of the man on the ground. It was hard to follow details, but soon a voice said or called something and the first man no longer moved. The colonel got to his feet and stood for a moment, swaying slightly and panting and looking down at the other, who was dead; Lucy had never seen death before, but she found she knew it when she saw it. Then the colonel took the corpse's wrists in a businesslike way and started to drag it face upwards towards the shed.

'That's Green,' Edward muttered to Lucy and at once sprang up and ran towards the two figures. She followed. Procope turned and saw Edward and gave him a blow that sent him down into an all-fours position. Lucy went for the colonel, who hit her on the side of the jaw with his fist. She too went down, afraid she might be sick, able to see but not very well, as if through a flyscreen. By the time she was fully herself again, Colonel Procope had shut the door of his expensive car and was driving off, scattering gravel from under his tyres as he turned into the lane. Edward followed, but some distance behind, and when Lucy reached him he had already given up the chase.

'Damn,' he said. 'He can't get far, but he might—'

'You never know. Come on,' she said, running past him.

He came up with her. 'I'll never catch him in my car.'

'I've got another idea' – one she thought was hopeless but was going to try.

'It's no good.'

'Just run.'

Lucy soon forged ahead. She had won both the 100 yards and the 220 in her last year at school, but she had run no faster then than now, despite her riding clothes. Her speed may even have increased when she saw ahead of her that, in his haste, Colonel Procope had overshot the bridge and was now backing and trying to turn his car. At one point he must have stalled, for she heard the high rattle of the starter. Then she had run far enough, and at her best speed hurried to Boris, unhitched him and got him back to the lane in time to meet a flushed and gasping Edward.

'Get up behind me,' she said from the saddle. She could see the colonel's car crossing the bridge.

'What are you—'

'Do as I say.'

He managed it somehow. Apparently unaffected by the double load, Boris made good time down to the river and stoutly set about carrying them across the ten-yard stream. The water, so cold it burned, reached her knees. That was the end of her remaining sandwiches. Edward's arms were fast round her middle. She heard the approaching sound of the car. Then they were across and Edward swung himself clear and scrambled up the short slope to the edge of the road, putting his hand inside his jacket as he moved. He turned and faced the oncoming car and what happened next seemed to happen all at once. Lucy heard a loud noise between a pop and a sort of sharp crash and again, although she had never heard a revolver fired before, she recognized it. The car swerved away from her, then towards her, narrowly missing her before it ran on to the verge on the river side and stopped there as suddenly as if it had run into a brick wall.

Boris, who had endured the events of the last minute with the calm of a police horse, blew down his nostrils. Edward turned to Lucy and took her hands more tightly than before. His look just then reminded her of the Edward of years before, when he had been a noted cricketer with, she remembered hearing, an aggressive batting style. For no reason she was aware of, tears sprang to her eyes.

'I'm not thinking of him,' she said, not knowing whether she meant Green or Colonel Procope or the two together.

'Neither am I,' said Edward.

Near them, Boris contentedly stamped and snorted.

III

'One bit of news,' said Edward. 'The bullet missed not only him but his car. Some shooting, what? I never could learn even how to hold one of those things.'

'Just as well. But what happened?'

'Well, let's say he spun the wheel round with some idea of spoiling my aim, saw he'd swung too far, went the other way, also too far, and drove straight into a hunk of stone he probably never even saw, fast enough to cause him to bash his head in on the inside of his car. Not a man to react coolly to sudden difficulty or danger, the late colonel. As earlier actions of his had suggested.'

Lucy looked out of the pub window towards the green hedgerow, more brightly sunlit now than when she had last seen it. 'I suppose we'll never know what Green had on him that made him worth the colonel's while to dispose of.'

'In the colonel's own far from infallible estimation. What a silly fellow, as well as a thundering nasty one. Our friends in the, er, our competitors were well advised not to trust him with anything of great importance. No, I think you and I probably wouldn't say thank you for being told the secret of Colonel Procope. What a damn silly name. Can I tempt you to another of those?'

'Thank you, Edward, in a moment.' She went on in bit-by-bit style, 'You know . . . when I telephoned you that evening, and got you to come out and meet me, I realize now it was all fantasy, really. I just wanted to have a lovely storybook adventure, with you in it. Schoolgirl stuff.'

Edward said quickly, before he could think better of doing so, 'I wondered whether it might be something like that, but it didn't bother me at all. I wanted to see you. That was enough.'

'Oh. But you brought your pistol with you.'

'So I did.' He laughed. 'Just company training. Motto, better safe than sorry. Well, your adventure duly turned up, didn't it?'

'It certainly did. That was just as well too.'

'You wouldn't have managed any of it but for Boris. How is the old boy?'

'Oh, he's fine, thank you.' She spoke hurriedly and without warmth.

'What's wrong? Come on, Lucy, is there something the matter with him?'

'No, he's as fit as a fiddle. It's just, I've decided to put him up for sale next week.'

'What?' Edward was genuinely amazed. 'What on earth for?'

'I think I'm getting a bit old to go on having a horse in that adolescent way.'

He nodded slowly. Something her father had said on that point narrowly failed to reach his consciousness. 'Well, I suppose you know best. Are you ready for that drink now?'

'Did anything more ever come out about that forgery?' asked Roger Ashby.

Edward looked up from his armchair and glass of sherry. 'Forgery?'

'Those verses from Gray's *Elegy*, wasn't it? Which you seemed convinced were the work of some forger.'

'Ah. My conviction proved to be well founded. At least it was confirmed by an announcement to that effect in the paper.'

'Really. I must have missed that. Who was the forger, were we told?'

'No. Probably someone quite obscure or even unknown. A mere amateur.' After some hesitation, Edward went on, 'Oddly enough, just the other day I happened to run across the fellow who brought the verses to light. Bumped into him at a social gathering. He struck me as rather uncommunicative. My impression was he realized he'd been taken for a ride.'

Ashby did not ask for a clarification of the last phrase. 'I'd give something to know how he got a load of tosh into the paper. Friends in high places?'

'Perhaps a kindred spirit. A colleague of mine is looking into it. Now I must leave you for a while. I have to see a man about a horse.'

'A *horse*? That doesn't sound like your kind of thing at all, Edward.'

'Oh, not to lay a bet, I assure you. I'm buying the animal. With a view to giving it back to the vendor as a sort of present.'

'Somebody's birthday?'

'I suppose you could call it an engagement present.'

A Twitch on the Thread

'It must be wonderful, never to need help. I simply can't imagine what it's like.'

'I have quite a job myself.' Daniel Davidson tried to match his wife's bantering tone. 'You of all people surely realize I need help constantly, every other waking moment. Every other sleeping moment as well, I expect I'd find if I could be around to check.'

'Oh, come on, you know what I mean – outside help.'

'My kind of help comes from outside too, but yes, darling, of course I know what you mean. How are you feeling this morning?'

This was a regular breakfast-table question that usually got a short non-committal answer. Today it drew another question. 'How do you think I'm looking?'

Daniel surveyed his wife. He saw a pretty, fresh-complexioned woman in her early thirties with thick brown hair, quick eyes and a mouth that had an upward turn. At the moment she seemed to be forcing it to droop at the corners, but without much over-all effect. 'You look fine to me,' he said, 'but then . . .'

'But then I always do. My jolly little face, as you once lyrically called it. All bubbling over with the joy of spring. Have you never thought, Daniel, even for a moment, that I might be putting it on, really honestly never? It doesn't matter if you have.'

'Only to start with. Very soon not at all.' He had no need to ask what it was that she might or might not have been putting on. 'But you still haven't told me how you're feeling.'

'Oh, absolutely terrible, thanks,' said Ruth Davidson comfortably. 'As you've no doubt noticed, I've given up trying to get the voice right. No point in sounding a perfect misery as well as being one. But it's more I wasn't cut out for being one. As if it was happening to the wrong person. I'm sorry, my love.'

'New stuff no good, then?'

'It's a bit early to tell, of course. But I'll stick my neck out and say, well, the clouds might be lifting just a bit. You know there's nothing I'd rather tell you than something more definitely cheerful, but we've been through that and come back again too often.' Ruth took their used tea-mugs across the little basement kitchen to the sink and poured water over them. With her back turned, she said to Daniel, 'The same as there's nothing I'd rather be than just an ordinary woman with a husband she likes a lot and also fancies. I hope you don't need any convincing of that.'

'None whatever, darling,' said Daniel carefully. The care was needed to prevent the least hint of acknowledgement that he had heard very nearly all of this before, and not just in its general drift but down to its finer detail. 'When are you seeing Eric?' He had asked his wife that before, too, with a succession of other names at the end of it.

'We thought today would be about right. It is two weeks since he started me on these new things, but of course I can always hang on till perhaps I know more definitely how I feel.' Ruth checked herself before she could betray how small a hope she had of any profit in hanging on.

'You've made an appointment, have you?'

'Two o'clock. I don't mind cancelling it if you reckon I should.'

Daniel stated firmly that he was sure it would be the right thing to keep the appointment, partly to help Ruth out of taking a sort of decision, but partly because he had taken to Dr Eric Margolis on sight and was starting to believe he might actually do something for her, so presumably the more she saw of him the better. Eric had shown himself to be different from his various predecessors by a businesslike approach that offered no parade of that quality. He claimed merely to have had a good deal of experience and some successes in the treatment of depressive illnesses like the one Ruth appeared to be suffering from. That had sounded good or possibly good to Daniel and still did.

Although it had been nearly six years before, he still remembered often enough and clearly enough the afternoon his wife had come to him in his workroom and, with profuse apologies for interrupting, had confessed that she felt wretched most of the time and often tense and nervous, all without any reason she was aware of. In his experience she seldom wept, but she had wept a good deal while she told him she had hoped never to have to burden him with this and he tried not to give any sign that he had known something like it all along. For once, for a few minutes, he had seen and heard her without – what? Without the face and voice she showed to the world, or rather with a different face and voice, not the real Ruth but another Ruth he dreaded to encounter but had never seen again. Perhaps Eric Margolis had found out how to do so and how to lay to rest that pitiful, driven creature. Meanwhile, he, Daniel, would go on as before, acting as closely and continuously as he could on his wife's appeal not to raise the matter himself in any form.

Reflections of this sort filled the part of his morning that was not taken up with rounding off and revising his article on the ethics of punishment. At noon he gathered his papers and went to take his leave of Ruth. He knew she would tell him if she wanted his company for the Margolis trip and as usual she had evidently decided to manage on her own, so he said only that he would take his piece in to the office and very likely go round to the Sussex for a sandwich with one or two of the lads.

Wearing a red tie to go with his red-and-white check shirt, Daniel smoothed back his long fair hair and left the house, a large healthy-looking man with bright blue eyes that sometimes had a distracted look, hardly believable as the comprehensive-school science-studies teacher he had been before his marriage. The house he left was part of a mid-Victorian terrace that ran dead straight for two hundred yards before reaching the larger street with its coffee shops, little Italian and Greek restaurants, newsagents and video libraries. On the corner opposite the dignified pub stood the hardly less imposing tile-fronted Underground station he was making for.

He had nearly reached it when he caught sight of a middle-aged man standing outside it studying a piece of paper that perhaps bore directions. This and the style of his belted raincoat suggested a foreign visitor of some sort, and Daniel knew he had never seen him before, so it came as a considerable surprise when the man glanced up at his approach and evidently recognized him.

'Hello there, Leo,' said the stranger in an American accent. His expression combined pleasure, astonishment and some less agreeable feeling. 'You're a long way from home, aren't you?'

'What? My name is Daniel Davidson. I'm sorry, you must have mistaken me for somebody else.'

'You're telling me you're not Leo Marzoni? But . . . Talk some more. Please.'

'I don't know what you want me to say. I'm afraid I don't know you.'

'But it's Leo's voice except for the British accent.' By now the man in the raincoat was plainly agitated. 'If you're . . . Mr Davidson, you must have a double. Maybe a twin brother?'

'I have no brother. And no double that I know of. I'm sorry, I can't help you.'

'Sir, would you be good enough to tell me your profession? Your job?'

'Certainly. I'm a clergyman.'

'A clergyman? You mean a priest?'

'A priest of the Church of England, yes.'

'Oh my God,' said the American very quickly. 'Pardon me,' and he hurried away round the corner of the station and was seen no more.

This response to notice of his calling disconcerted Daniel for longer than having been mistaken for Leo something. There were doubtless a number of humdrum possible explanations for that mistake, or apparent mistake, such as researching the British character or winning a bet. Nothing of the sort would account for the unfeigned alarm the man had shown at the end. But Daniel soon forgot the question in the course of travelling from western parts of the capital to somewhere nearer the middle. His reasons for going in by tube included a clear financial one and a confused but strong one to do with what he felt his life should be or include, but on this trip his powerlessness to help his wife was enough to think about.

What with one thing and another, he was more than usually conscious today of being a bloody parson, as in unregenerate or inattentive moments he was still apt to think of himself. At the newspaper building, the features editor greeted him with his usual staunch cordiality, demonstrating to whom it might concern that he, Greg Macdonald, was not the sort to think any the less of a chap merely because he had seen fit to become a rev. Or so Daniel sometimes fancied. The other, smaller man in Macdonald's office had been about to depart, but changed his mind after grasping who and what Daniel must be. While Macdonald read through the article on punishment, this smaller man kept glancing at Daniel in a manner he perhaps believed to be unnoticed. His general air suggested someone thrown by chance into the proximity of an astronaut or serial killer. Daniel had grown used to that kind of reaction, though it seldom took such visible form.

Macdonald finished his reading and nodded weightily for a time. Then he said, still weightily, 'Very good, Dan. Well up to your usual high standard. Thank you.' He went on more buoyantly, 'Just a couple of small points. Mosaic law. They'll think that's something to do with mosaics. Can we call it the law propounded or whatever by Moses?'

'Will they know who Moses was?'

'They'd better. Enough of them will. This is a serious newspaper. Right, if you've no objection. Oh yes. Penology.'

'They'll think that's something to do with pricks,' said the small man, laughing aloud and looking Daniel in the eye.

'Oh Christ, you're still here, are you?' Macdonald twisted round elaborately in his chair. 'Didn't you hear me say the *Sun* ran it one day last week? Well, I did and it did. And there is the telephone if you think of anything more.'

'Nice talking to you,' said Daniel as the small man finally went.

'Number three on the showbiz desk,' said Macdonald. 'Sorry about that. I hate that clever baiting stuff.'

'It's a form of respect really.'

'I suppose you get a lot of it.'

'Not as much as I'd like, or ought to like.'

'You mean it's better than indifference.'

'I suppose that's what I mean,' said Daniel. 'But there are grades of indifference too, you know. I prefer it when it's founded on a fact or two. Now I'm pretty well indifferent to the Pope, let's say, but I'm clear about who he is.'

'I don't know a hell of a lot of fellows like you, Dan, but you're the only one I do know that doesn't mind talking about religion. And yet, it's funny, you look to me more like a cricketer or a racing-driver than . . .'

'Than a bloody parson. I know you mean that kindly. Will the study of methods of punishment do you instead of penology?'

When they got to the Sussex, they found already there the elderly urchin who was the assistant editor and the distinguished-looking scholarly type who was the astrologer, the latter said to be the chief agent of the paper's healthy and still rising sales. Their greeting to Daniel was heartier than Macdonald's had been but also more uneasy, as if he had just come off none too well after a charge of kerb-crawling. But they were tremendously unselfconscious about asking for whisky in his presence, and did not even glance at his ginger beer when it came, let alone at each other. Daniel sympathized with their embarrassment, which he saw as no reflection on them, and respected their efforts to hide it. Very soon it would all have worn off, and he had almost stopped noticing it in them at any stage, and about time too.

He and Macdonald carried their sandwiches over to a small

table by the wall. After a couple of minutes Macdonald said,

'You read the latest piece from that chap the Bishop of Kesteven, sounding off again?'

'Yes, thanks. Do you want me to write something about it or him? I wouldn't be the only one.'

'That doesn't matter to us. I thought it might come in nicely for your next. The importance of individual responsibility. Made to measure for you, Dan.'

'It might be fun to have a crack at it. And him.'

'What's he like? Do you know him?'

'A bit, yes. "Call me Barry" Kesteven is a pleasant, talkative fellow a few years older than me, say early forties. He'd make a useful video-shop proprietor, the sort that puts aside stuff he thinks you'll like. Not at all what you might expect from a servant of the Devil.'

Macdonald grinned a little fixedly. 'Do you mean all that seriously?'

'What, that the Devil exists, et cetera? You bet I do, mate, and I'd advise you to take the same line yourself if you know what's good for you. All right, I'll do Barry. You'd better send me a xerox, if you would, of what he actually said or wrote. Can I get you a drink?'

Daniel went and came back with another ginger beer for himself and another whisky for Macdonald, who asked, 'How long is it now?'

'Oh, it must be . . . Sorry, it's some time since I worked it out. Well, it'll be eight years this coming 10th August. No, actually that was the day I took my last drink, so it has to be the 11th I started on the ginger beer.'

'Was that before or after you met Ruth?'

'I'd just got through my second week off it when she turned up. That was the way round things were in those days.'

There was no trace of staunch cordiality in Macdonald's voice or manner when he asked, 'How is she these days?'

'Much as usual, but there are signs she's starting to get a little more cheerful.' Daniel always said something along those lines anyway when people asked something like that, merely to avoid spreading gloom.

'Good,' said Macdonald when nothing more seemed to be on offer. 'I hope I didn't . . .'

'Absolutely not. It's just that no news is no news.'

When Daniel got back home he thought several times of telephoning Eric Margolis to make quite sure that as regards Ruth's state of mind there was indeed no news, but each time he decided against it. The Davidsons' bottom two floors of the house were empty. They had lived there since a few weeks after their marriage, and for some time after that he had wondered occasionally how a baby might have been fitted in there, but he never wondered about that now. He made himself a pot of tea and waited for Ruth to come back. When sufficient time had passed, he decided she must have gone on to see someone, perhaps her sister in Westbourne Park. The couple who lived on the upper floors were both out at work, and the only sounds he could hear came from outside the building. When he had finished his tea, he went up to the ground floor and into his workroom above the kitchen. There, in a spot beside the desk from which he could see the trees at the end and along the side of the small garden, he knelt and prayed as he did a couple of times every day. After thanking God for his mercies, he petitioned as always for removal or alleviation of Ruth's sufferings by any fitting means, spiritual or physical or a blend of the two. Then, with a few reminders from his notebook, he appealed for the various forms of divine help needed by some of his parishioners. Finally he went through his list of late afternoon and evening visits, telephoning to check one or two doubtful cases.

Before he went out to start his round, Daniel rang Eric after all and was told Ruth had seemed to show no spectacular improvement if indeed any had been measurable. But, said Eric with ferociously guarded optimism, the possibility of some turn for the better some time in the future should certainly not be ruled out.

II

Over the next few weeks nothing changed much. Ruth's state continued to give grounds for modest hope that it might one day mend. Daniel's article on the utterances of the Bishop of Kesteven drew some correspondence in the newspaper and an approving reference in the *Spectator*. Daniel himself officiated at two weddings and several cremations, gave a communion service on the Thursday mornings, read the *Church Times* every Friday, attended the monthly meeting of the Parochial Church Council, prepared and delivered a weekly sermon.

One Saturday morning he was typing out such a sermon when Ruth came into his workroom and said, 'There's a man watching the house.'

He got to his feet. 'Sit down and tell me about it, darling.'

'I haven't started going mad,' she assured him cheerfully, 'if that's what you're thinking. There just *is* a man watching the house. Most interesting.'

'What sort of man?'

'The funny thing is, I haven't been able to see his face, he's got sunglasses on for one thing, but I've got the feeling I know him. You see what you think.' On the way to their bedroom, which was on the same floor at the front, she said, 'I suppose he might be waiting for somebody or have decided he could do with a bit of a read, but to me he looks like a man watching the house. I don't know, perhaps having mistaken it for another house. There, see?'

What Daniel saw without difficulty was a man of about his own size and shape, wearing sunglasses as noticed and holding a newspaper that hid another part of his face. After a short inspection it became hard to believe he was actually reading his newspaper and quite easy to agree with Ruth about what he was up to.

'How long ago did you spot him?' Daniel asked her.

'It must be getting on for ten minutes now. He hasn't moved since.'

'I don't think I know him.'

At that point, the man on the pavement tucked his paper under his arm and took off his glasses and wiped them. Daniel moved to get a better view, perhaps over-abruptly or unduly fast; anyway, just then the man looked up and at last showed his face, or enough of it to be recognizable by somebody with good eyesight at that sort of range. This Daniel had. He also had strong nerves, which helped him not to respond to what he had seen in a way many might have, with a cry of surprise or alarm. As it was he gave a violent start and drew in his breath sharply.

Ruth caught him by the arm. 'What's the matter?'

'Oh God, didn't you see? Surely . . .'

'Daniel, what is it?'

'You didn't see.' With great reluctance he looked again where he had been looking before, and saw no one. 'The . . . fellow seems to have gone now.'

'Who was he? Did you know him? Please tell me.'

'In a minute. Let's go back next door first.'

In his workroom once more, he made straight for his desk-chair and sat, thinking to himself that if there had been drink in the house he might very well have made straight for that instead. Ruth took the only other chair in the room. When he was breathing normally again, he said,

'I'm sorry, my love, I didn't mean to frighten you, but I had a bit of a scare myself. Just for a second I could have sworn that the chap outside was me, or the dead spit of me, or very nearly, to an uncanny degree. Quite a shock in a way. Of course I realize now he was just very like me. Nothing terribly odd about that. My face is the sort of face a lot of chaps have.'

'I don't think so,' said Ruth, 'but then I'm biased. Anyway, I've got it now, he wasn't just very like you, he was the absolute image of you, he was your double. You were right the first time: he was you.'

'I thought you didn't see his face.'

'I didn't have to. I could tell by the rest of him and the way he was standing. I almost got it the moment I saw him the second time because I'd seen you in between. You thought he was only, how did you put it, very nearly the image of you because all the millions of times you'd seen his face before it was the wrong way round. In your mirror.'

'Maybe,' said Daniel. 'Well, plenty of people have doubles. But . . .' He paused abruptly.

'But why should one of them come and spy on the other?'

Before Daniel could have spoken, the front-door bell rang.

'Don't answer it,' said Ruth.

'It's all right, darling, I promise you.'

Daniel went and opened the door. His double stood on the step, fair hair worn a little shorter than his own but still left long and parted in the same place, bright blue eyes, generally healthy looks, perhaps half an inch shorter, dressed differently but not so differently.

'You must be the Reverend Daniel Davidson.' The accent was American.

'I am he. And you must be Mr Leo Marzoni.'

'Correct. But I'm not only that, I'm your twin brother. Did you know I existed?'

'No.'

'Nevertheless I do, as you see, and that is what I am. But I have the advantage of you: I knew about you already. If you like to ask me in I can tell you more.'

'Please come in,' said Daniel mechanically. 'I'm sorry, I wasn't thinking.'

'Oh, you're forgiven,' said his visitor, with a sudden smile that communicated no warmth. 'The circumstances are out of the ordinary.'

Ever since he heard the bell ring, Daniel had been under the delusion that his words and actions were proceeding of themselves, without any need of his premeditation or will. He felt powerless to behave otherwise as he moved back to allow the man called Leo Marzoni to cross the theshold, and did no more than note his own instinct or whatever it was that told him that the other could not be what he said or seemed and that his coming here meant some incalculable harm. These feelings showed no signs of lessening while he took the stranger into his workroom and introduced a startled but not obviously frightened Ruth. Daniel found himself pronouncing words of reassurance to her and others meant to be explanatory about twins and doubles, and went on to tell her something of the American he had run into some weeks previously. Marzoni, on the other hand, appeared to find the situation little more than exceptional, striking, perhaps difficult. In a straightforward style he apologized for his various antics, for having had the absurd idea of waiting to catch Daniel as he came out of the house and especially for having panicked just now and taken off down the street before having the sense to turn back. He added that he would tell his story in full when they had all had a little time.

By the end of this recital, Daniel had begun to struggle free of his impression that events were taking place somewhere that, despite obvious resemblances, was not the world he knew. But he only really came to himself when the three of them were sitting in the kitchen over cups of coffee and the man he must learn to think of as his brother had duly begun the first instalment of his story. Several instalments were to follow; later, he was able to fit them together in his mind.

Leopold Marzoni was now thirty-eight years old. He had been brought up by a couple whom he treated in every way as his parents and whom he loved as a son, but he could not remember a time when he had not known that he was not biologically their son. He understood from them that he had been born in Brighton, England, and taken to America in infancy. His true mother had died soon after giving birth to him and to his twin brother. Leopold's foster parents had purposely avoided making the least move towards locating or even inquiring after this brother, whom they assumed to have also been adopted but no doubt reared in England. They had felt it their duty to tell Leopold this much, but had also impressed upon him that any attempt on his part to find his twin would be a dubious and almost certainly useless undertaking. Although he could remember, in his childhood, treating a British brother as an invisible companion in times of solitude, he had hardly given the real person a thought for thirty years.

So far, indeed, had that person been from Leopold's mind that he had said nothing of any twin brother when a neighbour, Irving Rothberg, had announced a forthcoming trip to England. But when Rothberg had come to see him on his first day back home and had spoken excitedly of having seen and talked briefly to an Englishman who was Leopold's replica, the latter had given his twin more than a thought. At once he had acted counter to parental advice and set about finding the Englishman in question.

'How did you manage to do that?' asked Daniel.

'It was easy, given Irving's memory. He remembered your name and the fact that you were an Anglican minister, so I got on to your General Synod and they delivered right away. It seems there's a Daniel Davies in Liverpool, but I ruled him out. Too old, for one thing. You must have had quite a shock, Daniel, when Irving sprang into your path and started calling you Leo.'

'I suppose it might have helped if I'd known I had a twin brother.'

'But your foster parents didn't tell you.'

'I didn't have foster parents in your sense, Leo. I was brought up in an orphanage, by an orphanage.' Without either of them being more than half aware of it, Daniel and Ruth joined hands as he said these words. 'They couldn't have been kinder or nicer to me or have done more for me than they did, but no, they didn't tell me I had a brother.'

'I see.' Leopold Marzoni looked almost grim, or at least as though he was coming to a less straightforward part of his tale. 'Not merely a brother, but a twin brother, as you said. And not merely a twin brother, but an identical twin brother, such that you and I look exactly alike. And I mean exactly alike, more alike even than most other identical twins. The nail on your left middle finger is smaller than usual, like mine. Your left eyebrow takes a little turn upward at the end and so does mine. And do you by any chance have a mole shaped like a horseshoe just below your navel? So do I.'

'And the pair of you don't merely look alike, you sound alike,' said Ruth. 'You have the same voice. One moment it talks with an American accent and the next it turns British, but it's the same voice, from the, I don't know, from the same part of the mouth, with the same little hesitations.'

'So Irving noticed,' said Leo, still rather sombrely. 'But you and I, Daniel, we don't merely look alike and sound alike. To understand the extent of our likeness, you need to know something about twins in general, okay? It's pretty solid stuff, so you'd better be sure you want it. No objections? Good, very good. For ease of digestion I'll give it to you in bits. Here comes Part I.'

Most cultures (said Leo) had greeted the occurrence of twins with hostility and even dread. Comparatively recently, attitudes had improved and serious study been possible. This had defined the difference between identical twins, who were always of the same sex, and the much commoner fraternal twins, who were often of unlike sex and no more similar than ordinary brothers and sisters. The difference was primordial and intrinsic.

Monozygotic or MZ twins, popularly known as identical twins, were the separate fruits of a single fertilized ovum that for some reason still under study had split into two. The name emphasized the fact that such twins have identical genes, are clones of each other. Fraternal twins were the product of two discrete fertilized ova and had only half their genes in common. Psychologists, biologists, geneticists and others interested in heredity had studied twins for many years. More lately, research had focused on MZ twins who had been separated soon after birth and reared apart. These individuals were rare, but there were probably a few thousand of them in the contemporary Western world, and recent investigations at Minnesota University had tracked down and studied more than a hundred of them.

Such was the gist of Part I. Daniel respected his twin's seriousness of purpose, while far from clear what that purpose was. At any rate, by the time Part II began he was seeing Leo as just a man and not as some kind of unearthly visitant.

When such twins were subjected to a full comparison (Leo continued), the close similarities between members of a pair in physical attributes, such as height, fingerprints and hair colour, might have been predicted. What was rather more surprising was the similarity of non-physical attributes such as tolerance, self-control and sociability. But most people would have been very much surprised by something more than similarity in the case of what might be called biographical detail. For instance, such correspondences between a pair of twins as recorded in 1979 included the following, selected from more than thirty such:

('I've been over this so many times I have it off by heart.')

Both men, aged thirty-nine when studied, had married a woman called Linda, divorced her and subsequently married one called Betty.

One twin had named his first son James Alan, and the other had named his James Allan.

Both had been employed by McDonalds and as a filling-station attendant.

Both had white benches built round the trunk of a tree in the garden.

'I'm particularly fond of that last one,' said Leo. 'I have fun imagining some guy who likes to think we're shaped by our environment rather than by our heredity explaining that either as a coincidence in itself or as the result of coincidental similarity in upbringing. Like the paddling in what comes next.'

From twenty-five resemblances in a study of a pair of female twins:

Both had fallen off a fence in childhood and bore scars in the same place.

One had a reasonless chronic pain in the right thigh, the other had a wasted muscle in the right hip but suffered no pain.

They folded their clothes in the same way, and when putting blouses and shirts in drawers, both did up every other button.

Both had developed the habit of walking backwards into the sea when going paddling.

'And just in the event that's not enough to convince you of something,' said Leo finally, 'and before we go any further, my wife, whom I married seven years ago, is called Ruth.'

'Does she look like me?' asked Ruth Davidson.

With only a brief hesitation, Leo said, 'My Ruth is roughly of the same physical type as yourself, fair-complexioned, vivacious in appearance if that's physical. But here, you can see for yourself', and he took a photograph out of his wallet and laid it on the table between them.

Ruth picked it up, studied it briefly and passed it to Daniel, who saw a pretty woman of about thirty looking rather like his wife, about as much like her as a sister of hers of similar age might have done, perhaps a fraternal twin. He got up and opened the French door into the garden. In fine weather like this the small kitchen could begin to get quite stuffy in the middle of the day. He filled a glass with tap water but set it down after only one sip.

'What sort of temperament would you say your wife has?' he asked Leo.

'As to temperament, well, what shall I say, not as vivacious as her appearance.'

'Depressive?'

'Well, Daniel, I think depressive just like that might be going a little far, you know? But in the right direction. Let's say anxious, nervous, ah, apprehensive? Inclined to fear the worst, is that enough?'

'Yes,' said Ruth, avoiding her husband's eye.

After a silence, Leo went on, 'But I didn't come all this way just to compare notes with you, Dan. It's been wonderful and extraordinary finding you like this, but there's more than that at stake. First, though, do you want us to go to Minnesota and have ourselves examined by scientists? I have to say they'd pay our expenses if we did.'

'No, let's keep this to ourselves.'

'My thoughts exactly. Now, you no doubt recall that when you told Irving Rothberg that by profession you were a minister of religion, he became agitated, because my—'

'You're a clergyman too.'

'Correct, Daniel, and not only that, but a minister of the Episcopal Church, which is the name for the Anglican communion in the States, which makes me as close a replica of you as I could possibly be in that rather important department.'

'Which must have struck your friend Rothberg as a coincidence so far-fetched as to be uncanny,' said Ruth, looking at Daniel now.

'So that was how you knew about the General Synod and the rest of it,' he said.

'Correct again. Now . . . brother . . . do you want to go on a little further, or do you want to stop? For now, that is. Maybe you'd like to stop.'

Looking into the bright blue eyes that were so like his own as seen for dozens of years in mirrors, even looking into them quite briefly, made Daniel feel almost dizzy, if not terrified, then in more serious danger than he had ever thought of in his life before. But as soon as he could he said, trying to sound like a man filling in a form, 'I'd like to go on a little further, such as, when were you ordained, Leo? Of course you know the exact date.'

'Of course. It was March 22nd, 1985.'

'I was 4th April in the same year.'

'Not the same day, at least,' said Leo. He put out his hand in an odd gesture, as if he wanted to give comfort or reassurance, hesitated and drew back.

'Close enough. Nine, thirteen days. And one more thing, if you will. Was your ordination the result of a sudden decision or did you approach it gradually, through stages of belief and conviction and . . .'

'It was sudden. Do you want me to tell you about it?'

'No. No, not now. We've come a long way in a short time. I'd like to have a chance to adjust.'

'I hoped you were going to say that. In fact it wouldn't be

overstating the case to say I knew you were going to say that.'

'Oh, I knew it too,' said Ruth. 'That or something to the same effect. Easy enough to see it in his face, sorry, darling, your face, just before you spoke. Anybody could have seen it who happened to be watching you attentively.'

'Which you were certainly doing,' said Leo with a smile.

'Yes, I've been watching you both attentively most of the time we've been down here. And comparing how you look. Now there was a pair of identical twins at my school, at least they said they were identical and they should have known, but they didn't *look* identical much. They were dressed the same sometimes, but nobody ever had any trouble telling them apart. Well, one of them even wore glasses most of the time and the other didn't seem to need them. And one was fatter than the other. Identical – no, what's needed is a word meaning rather more alike than similar. That's what you two are to look at, all you are. Dozens of differences, mostly small, shape of lower lip, left ear, really both ears, where the nose starts – dozens of them. You'd only look *very much* alike at a distance, which is how you first saw each other. There.'

'I never realized you were as observant as that,' said Daniel.

'But what's it all in aid of, you mean. Just, you don't want the two of you to be too much alike, do you?'

Leo nodded vigorously. 'Right, Ruth, right.'

'It's true,' said Daniel. 'I want to be told we're not.'

'Here's another way we're not,' said Leo. 'I'd be – let's say I wouldn't give a damn if we were utterly alike in every way there is.'

'That would make us completely unlike in the most important way of all.'

'Like you said, old buddy, we need to have time to adjust. How are the two of you fixed for later? Can I take you out to dinner?'

'Thank you, Leo, but speaking for myself I don't think I'd feel comfortable. Too much risk of you and me being stared at. You come here.'

Leo grinned. 'I see I mustn't forget that as well as being my twin brother you're an Englishman.'

'True enough. I was thinking we'd find it easier to talk with just the three of us.'

'Well, it's your town. Which I mean to go out and take a look at meanwhile. It's the first time I've ever been in it.'

They made their arrangements and Leo soon went off to the small hotel quite close by where he was staying, setting off on foot as a way of starting his look at London.

'He's got your walk,' said Ruth. 'Or you've got his.' She seemed charged up by recent events, her curiosity and alertness whetted.

'I suppose that's only to be expected.'

'Is that all you can say? Why don't you care for the idea of Leo and you being so alike? Does it give you a sort of weird feeling, doppelgänger stuff, anything on those lines?'

'Nothing like that at all. Plenty of things bother me, as you know, but I'm all right there.'

'I noticed you held back when he went to hug you just now.'

'Me being an Englishman again.'

Ruth frowned and moved her head to and fro at this. A minute later she said, 'Admittedly I haven't had much experience of husbands of mine meeting twin brothers they didn't know they had, but I'd have expected you to be full of questions and excitement and *wonder*, not the way you are now, as if you'd just had a packet of bad news.'

'I'm sorry, Ruth, I'd like to be like you about it, believe me, but bad news is exactly what I'm afraid I've had, or may be going to get.'

'You mean to do with JC?'

'Yes, that's what I – yes, yes.'

'But you can't tell me what or how.'

'I don't know myself, any more than I understand about him and me.' A tear started to run down Daniel's cheek and he wiped it away with his fingers. 'Sorry. If I did I'd tell you about it straight away, you know that.'

'Isn't there anything you can tell me?' she asked gravely.

'Probably nothing you haven't already seen for yourself, but anyway, one question I didn't ask Leo, in fact I expect you noticed me dashing in to stop him answering it before I had time to ask it . . .'

'. . . was if he was a godless drunk one minute and a very serious parson the next.'

Daniel hesitated. Then he said, 'All right, that'll do for the moment. At least if any of it wasn't or isn't true then I needn't worry about the rest. Now I suppose I'd better finish off my sermon for tomorrow. I'll be in for lunch but late. I've got to go and see Miss Rawlings first.'

'Is that the one with the killing eyes and the fantastic figure?'

'No, it's the one with the Edwardian false teeth and the face of a thousand wrinkles.'

He was on his way to the kitchen stairs when Ruth said, 'I wonder why he didn't bring his wife with him. Why he left the other Ruth at home.'

'Economy, I expect. If they're anything like us they have to watch the pennies the whole time.'

'Well, at any rate he's not unlike you. I wonder if they've got any kids.'

'We'll ask him.' Daniel retraced a couple of his steps. 'Doesn't it bother you, being like the other Ruth in temperament as well as looks and even having the same name?'

'Not a bit. You and he would almost certainly be drawn to the same kind of woman, and the name is nothing. Coincidence. Never make the mistake of underestimating the likelihood of coincidence.'

Daniel finished typing his sermon and went over the script pointing it like the text of a psalm and underlining words to be stressed. When he was satisfied, he put on his dicky and dog-collar, picked up his communion case and went out to his car, an A-registered Cavalier parked at the kerb. His parishioners had bought it for him and met some of its bills. Ten minutes later he was pulling up outside an unprepossessing but not actually awful block of flats. Since it was in quite a good area, not on any football supporters' track, for example, he left the car where it was, taking the communion case with him. Miss Rawlings had not so far asked for the service but he hoped she might one day, as some in her circumstances already had.

Miss Rawlings lived on the first floor, across a tidy, well-swept hall and up a stairway that Daniel had sometimes thought would have been the better for a couple of graffiti or some other defilement as a distraction from the overall style of the fittings. There was, however, enough of an unwanted smell coming from her room to offset this deficiency, strange and no more than disagreeable rather than straightforwardly revolting. As he made his way in, Daniel recited to himself supposed facts about the swift overloading of the olfactory sense in man.

Beside Miss Rawlings, sitting next to her on the couch of obsolete plastic, was a woman he knew quite well to be her widowed niece, but who looked at him with uncertainty and misgiving, in her fifties but at sea in the presence of a bloody parson.

'I'll be going then, Della,' she said reluctantly, her eyes on him. 'I thought I'd only just got here, but you seem to have company, don't you? Is there anything you want? I said is there anything you want?'

'Haven't you got that list I gave you?'

'What? Of course I have. I was just wondering if there was anything else. You know, anything else you wanted. You know.'

There was evidently nothing else, nothing on the tip of anyone's tongue at least. Looking successively at the other two as if of course it was no business of hers but she did hope they knew what they were doing, the niece left. Then, asked how she had been over the past week, Miss Rawlings began a narrative that worked up now and then to the level of mild complaint. Daniel had been ready for that. His unspoken agreement with the old lady was that she got a few things off her chest to start with and about the halfway mark it was his turn to talk about God, or at least to approach that subject. He listened now to what she was saying about the language of the girl at the paper-shop, superstitiously hoping that to do so might be repaid by her listening to him for as long.

Eventually Miss Rawlings said, 'My real trouble is I get these nasty times when I don't seem to see the point of somebody like me keeping going at all. I suppose you're going to say that's wrong, Mr Davidson.'

'A lot of people in your sort of situation do feel that from time to time.'

'That doesn't make it wrong or right, does it?'

'Let's just say it's unnecessary.'

'I don't remember ever thinking something because it was necessary. What was it – my sort of situation, you said? You don't know what it's like, how could you?'

Daniel saw that Miss Rawlings's eyes were bright over her fallen-in cheeks and the sharp nose that old age had made prominent. 'No, I don't,' he answered her, 'but now I come to think of it there are plenty of people not in your situation who can't see any reason for carrying on. I used to be one of them myself. Does that surprise you?'

'It's not the same thing at all, a young man like you.'

'Years don't matter, we can desperately need help at any time of our lives, and mercifully help is always available to those who ask for it.'

'I tell you, vicar, there's nobody who's going to help me. My niece and my grandnephew, and Ernie, oh he's marvellous, that Ernie, but what can he do, what can any of them do, they've got their own lives to lead. I need a person with me every minute of the day and night, and how could I expect anybody to put themselves in that position, if they had the time they wouldn't have the patience, how could they? No, I'm sorry, Mr Davidson, you're very good, but I just can't see any point in me going on.'

'You're forgetting God,' said Daniel. 'He'll be with you as long as you want him, he's got the time and the patience for everybody. You only have to ask him.'

'Oh, God,' said Miss Rawlings, by way of amused or weary reference, not invocation, 'don't talk to me about God. I tell you, he's never done nothing for me.'

'Have you asked him, have you prayed to him? It's the same thing, you know. And he always answers, did you know that? I was in such despair once I was going to kill myself, and at the last minute and as a last resort I prayed to God although I didn't believe in him then, but he answered just the same. I found I could . . .'

Daniel let his voice trail off. He had thought or hoped that the importance to everybody of what he was saying was so great and obvious that it was bound to reach someone who at any rate was used to hearing God mentioned. But it seemed that the bright eyes had sunk back into their sockets and the liveliness of manner gone again. A moment ago, the one room had looked neat and even cheerful, the single bed made and spread with a light green counterpane, the sink and draining board clear, with the clean crockery on its rack, a pair of flourishing potted plants on the sill. Now, he saw it as static and lifeless, like a model cell in an enlightened gaol. Poor Miss Rawlings. Even if he had had the required energy and insensitivity, he would still have not dared to tell her any more of the story of his first prayer, not just that it had been answered because he had truly wanted help, but what he had suspected more and more strongly ever since that moment, that God had planted in him the impulse to pray. Faith was offered before it could be accepted. He brought out his pocket diary and turned over some of its pages while he briefly made petition that Miss Rawlings should receive the gift of faith.

'Going, are you, doctor, I mean vicar?'

'Not just yet. There's still time for me to give you a hand with the forms for your new pension-book, that's if you'd like me to.'

'There's just a couple of places I'm not sure about. My niece looked it over, but you know, Mr Davidson, she's really a very ignorant woman, my niece. She's good about clearing the place up, I'll give her that . . .'

From the moment when Leo arrived at the Davidsons' that evening, Daniel felt certain that some disaster impended. Leo was perhaps conscious of a similar discomfort, not showing the buoyant disposition of that morning, when he had seemed to be at worst perfectly resigned to each successive shock of revelation. Daniel was at once drawn to him as one who must be uniquely sympathetic, and repelled by dread of one who constituted a threat to indispensable convictions. Was that normal, reasonable, to be expected in a man confronted with another who was limitlessly the same? Or was the whole concern no more than most singular and interesting? Nothing on paper or anywhere else gave guidance.

Not quite understanding why he did so, Daniel had spent the afternoon getting everything squared away in good time. After seeing to it that the church was ready for early service in the morning, he came back home and made a couple of telephone calls to fix the time of a cremation and brought his diary up to date. Then, as he did every fortnight or so, he wrote to his bishop, a prelate with outmoded ideas about his special responsibilities to those he had ordained. By a self-established tradition, Daniel devoted his final paragraph to a report on how God had seemed to him over the last weeks and how he thought he might have seemed to God. With feelings of guilt that no inner reasoning would dispel, he confined himself here to what he more or less certainly knew, omitting formless and very likely superstitious presentiments. When the letter had been made ready for the post, he straightened his parishioners file and tidied his workroom. He left as they were the photographs along his mantelpiece except for one showing the woman at the orphanage who, as he supposed, had been like a mother to him. She had been dead for nearly twenty years and the likeness was imperfect, but it was good enough to recall her to him when, as now, he picked it up and studied it. Lastly he knelt and prayed to be forgiven for having done so little to help Miss Rawlings and himself to be helped to face – what? Whatever might be in store.

While Leo and he were settling themselves in the kitchen as before, Daniel started to explain that Ruth would come down in a few minutes when she was ready, but Leo finished his sentence for him. Daniel shifted uneasily in his chair.

'Ah, come on, Daniel, there's nothing in that,' Leo went on. 'Only cause for worry if I couldn't see that coming. You and I could set up a great telepathy act, though. Do these identical twins have identical minds? Or maybe they have only one mind between them. We'd clean up. Too bad God wouldn't like it.'

'You don't believe in any of that paranormal stuff, do you?'

'Of course not, what do you think I am? That's one of the places God comes in very conveniently, isn't it? One word from him and there's no need to bother with that type of dreck for the rest of your life.'

Leo had spoken lightly, in keeping with his words and with his generously cut light-blue suit, darker-blue shirt and rather flashy sea-green tie. He looked altogether unlike Daniel's idea of a parson, even an American one. In fact he looked more like a successful insurance agent or travelling salesman than any member of the professional classes; Daniel recognized, or admitted to himself, that he must have something in his own general appearance that corresponded. Despite these things, however, Leo retained the air of uneasiness detectable as soon as he stepped in from the street. The smile accompanying his last remark seemed particularly forced. Before it had quite faded, he said,

'There was just one thing I wanted to tell you out of your Ruth's hearing, so here goes, why I didn't bring my Ruth to England with me, I thought perhaps you wondered about that.'

'Ruth did, my Ruth did.'

'Yes, she would, I see she would. Maybe I should have told you then, before, but the reason my Ruth isn't here is that she's with another guy. Been with him just two years now. You don't want to hear whose fault it was, even if I knew, it was like this other guy came along and sailed in and collected her. She liked me, but she liked him better. I didn't enjoy the next year at all, but I got through it without falling by the wayside and I'm over it now.'

Nevertheless Daniel said, 'I'm sorry, Leo.'

'Sure you are. I wouldn't have brought it up, but I felt you should know it. I didn't want you wondering, and when I thought about it, well, you needed to hear about something where we aren't the same, and right there is one sizeable thing. And don't forget the guy came along and he collected her, I'll swear she wasn't on the lookout for him or anybody, she wasn't driven out by her depression or anything else, so if you wanted to think my Ruth's departure says something about the likelihood of your Ruth departing you'd have to believe in Santa Claus. Or telepathy. Okay, the name's the same. Coincidence, my friend. Unless you have somebody called Janet in your life? No, I thought not. No more of this, then. I hope I didn't waste your time, Daniel.'

Now Daniel embraced his twin without hesitation and held on. He wondered that he had ever found it more than unfamiliar to be looking at and talking to a man so like himself in appearance. Leo had indeed followed or read his thoughts with remarkable accuracy, perhaps less remarkable in one so like himself on the inside as well. Of course. At this point Daniel pulled himself up as he remembered that Leo had just been talking of an irreparable loss. 'Would you like a drink?' he asked without further thought.

'Thank you, Daniel. If you mean a drink like coffee or lemonade, then not just now; if you mean like gin all the way through beer with any alcohol in it, then still no. But you have some of that kind of drink right here, do you?'

'No, there's nothing. I spoke without thinking. Neither Ruth nor I ever go near real drink.'

'Oh,' said Leo. He looked round the kitchen, seeming to notice the dresser with its rows of plates, the TV set and small low-built radio, the white-painted staircase leading up to the ground floor, the door to the dining-room, the open garden door past which came herbal scents and the distant cries of children. Louder and more sharply than before, he said, 'Did you never touch alcohol? I mean you yourself?'

'Oh, I touched it all right. Not to say bashed it. For years. Then I gave it up altogether.'

'Would you have called yourself a drunk in those days?'

'Yes. At least I agree that's what I was then. I should imagine plenty of people called me it at the time.'

Leo nodded his head, looked at Daniel for a moment and dropped his gaze. 'I don't quite know how to say this, but back then, did you believe in God?'

'No.'

'And . . . did your belief, was your coming to believe connected with your ceasing to be a drunk?'

'Yes,' said Daniel, looking back at Leo. 'It was all part of the same thing.'

'Daniel!' called Ruth's voice from the floor above. 'Darling, could you come up here a minute?'

Ruth was standing in the bedroom in an unfamiliar attitude, elbows crooked and right hand clasping left. She was smiling, with a look of settled anticipation, as if she had been watching him opening a parcel that contained a birthday present she knew he really wanted. She wore a freshly laundered white dress with a pattern of small blue flowers, one he had always liked her in but had not known her to wear for a long time.

'I was going to get you to guess,' she said, 'but then I thought that would be a bit silly, so I'll just tell you. You remember a couple of weeks ago I was boring you about some new stuff Eric had put me on, and I said it was early days yet but I thought there might be a slight improvement? – actually it was more than slight, but I was touching wood, and I've hung on all this time to try and be on the safe side, but anyway, still touching wood, I'm *much better*. Perhaps I'm still not quite what I was as a carefree schoolgirl, but I'm *much better*. I can see the point of things again. I thought I'd tell you before we—'

Daniel started kissing his wife. A few moments later she managed to say, 'Darling – Leo's downstairs. We can't—'

'So he's downstairs, as he'd probably say.'

'But . . . he's a parson.'

'So am I.'

'But an American parson . . .'

In the end it was not so many minutes before Ruth was again ready to receive their guest. Leo put on a wonderful imitation of a man who understood completely the British custom whereby married couples always held a thorough private discussion of the weather before starting the evening. Nearly all the rest of that evening passed quickly and not over-memorably in the kind

of semi-informative chatter to be expected of any new acquaintances with time to spare.

But not quite all of it. After Ruth had gone to bed, Leo gave
some details of his acceptance of the Christian faith and of how
this was connected with his renunciation of strong drink, and
Daniel responded with some details of his own.

III

'If you want to know what it's called, you can read it off the label
on the bottle,' said Eric Margolis. 'Remembering it afterwards,
of course. Why they give these things such jawbreaking names
beats me, unless for moral effect on the patient. If I put you on
something called B-23 you may not be gripped enough, but if I
say it's called chromopolyamineoxidase you're more likely to feel
you're being properly looked after. And why not? But to answer
your question: yes, this stuff is indeed reasonably new, in this
country at least. They've had good results with it in the States
and especially Australia, according to a man I know in Sydney
who actually understands these matters. It's a narrow-spectrum
deal; there are quite a few people it doesn't help at all, but those
it does help it helps a lot. Ruth sounds as though she's one of the
lucky ones.'

Eric's consulting room looked less like the traditional sort of
consulting room than the drawing room of a small but posh
hotel, with nothing overtly medical to be seen, not even a notepad. Eric himself, a lanky person whose small mostly bald head
was eked out with a dense beard, occupied an easy chair near a
low table on which lay two or three novels in their jackets.
Opposite him a similar chair held Daniel, sitting where he had
sat on a couple of previous visits and assorted lunatics and
neurotics on many times more. He said now, 'How long will she
have to go on taking this stuff?'

'Some time. It's no use putting even an approximate date on
it.'

'But there will be a date eventually, will there? Or will she be on it for the rest of her life?'

'That's most unlikely,' said Eric in his gentle voice, rubbing his fingertips together in the way he had, 'but at this stage I'm not ruling out anything.'

'But isn't there a danger she'll get addicted?'

'Addiction to a substance shows when somebody stops using that substance. Patients have come off this substance after a few weeks or a few years without serious trouble, as I told you. Some of them have felt funny or rotten for a while, which one can't discount, but nothing on the scale of a real drug hangover, like coming off, well, some popular tranquillizers and antidepressives, which some have said is worse than what put them on it in the first place. Ruth stays on till it's all right for her to come off.'

'I see. How do we know when we've reached that stage?'

'We get some idea when we try a controlled reduction of the dose.'

'M'm. If you don't mind my saying so, Eric, it all sounds rather hit-or-miss to me.'

'That's how it is. More miss than hit, too, though fortunately things are getting better every year. About point-one of one per cent a year. The gloomy view of the situation is that we're no nearer understanding how these materials work than we were twenty years ago, so we've no way of telling which one will help which patient, and the consequence of that is we chop and change and keep our eyes and ears open for anything new that might be good.'

'Thank you, doctor,' said Daniel. 'Would there be a cheerful view?'

'No. But there is a slightly less gloomy one this time round. Let's say we have scored a hit with Ruth. That means there's something like an even chance she can be kept as she now is while in the meantime she gets better. A mental illness, if a prolonged bout of depression can be called that at all, is only like a physical illness in a couple of ways, but one of them is that its victims sometimes make a full recovery. Thank God.'

'What sort of long-term chance do you give Ruth at this stage?'

'More than evens, Daniel. Substantially more. With her intelligence and good temperament she's beginning to shape up as one of my successes. The last, what, *area* to count your chickens in is the mind, but . . . I won't say any more. Just, there's a good deal of hope where before there was only average hope, average hope being better than no hope at all but not much. Well, unless you've got anything more . . .'

Eric stood up. Daniel did the same, but said, 'Actually there is one other item, but could we talk about it somewhere else? What about that pub down on the corner?'

'Not there if you don't mind. They know me there because I take the occasional arachnophobe or homicidal maniac there. We'll try another place.'

On their way to it, Daniel asked, 'Don't you ever take notes of what a patient says?'

'No, I take a secret tape which I turn on and off with a secret switch. Better all round.'

'Did you turn it on for me?'

'I should say not. Tape costs money, you know. Sorry.'

'That's all right, only my nose does feel a little bit out of joint.'

Eric's other place was another pub, an extensive pub where, at this early hour, there was room to sit apart. By way of a token of decorum, a concealed apparatus quietly played one of the more understandably neglected of Handel's operas. Daniel brought Eric the gin and tonic he had asked for.

'Aren't you having anything at all?'

'I'm not thirsty.'

Daniel spoke with enough emphasis to make Eric glance at him but not pursue the matter. Soon afterwards Eric said, 'What was this item you were going to raise?'

'Oh yes. Well, it's a bit difficult to put neatly. More a feeling.'

'Some quite important points are that.'

'Yeah. Well . . . I'm afraid it rather brings in philosophical things. Things to do with belief. You know, church doctrine.'

'To me, you can say anything you like about that. It's one of the great advantages of me from your point of view. But try not to go too fast.'

'Right.' Daniel paused again, then nodded to himself. 'Right. For all your professional pessimism, you'd agree that more and more drugs are being discovered every day and the field of their application is widening all the time.'

'Yes. Exponentially.'

'Is there any theoretical limit to their expansion?'

'I don't quite know what you mean by that, but if it's, will there come a time when there are no more drugs to discover, then I haven't thought about it but it's certainly a long way off. If it's, are there going to turn out to be parts of the mind and human behaviour that can never be reached by drugs, then I have thought about that but to little effect. Actually theory doesn't help much there, because the question takes us outside pharmacology and biology and any other ology and into, what you said, philosophy, where I'm near enough at sea. But you want something more than that.' Eric poked inconclusively at the slice of lemon in his glass. Then he said rather quickly, 'Nothing I've learnt in the sense of being able to write it down, write it out, none of it tells me there are any areas of consciousness beyond the reach of human modification, and if the resulting prospect displeases you, don't investigate recent findings on the results of physical interferences with the brain by surgery or accident or both at once. As for gene surgery, I've made a personal point of not investigating that.'

'But,' said Daniel. 'At least I hope there's a but.'

'Oh, there is, beyond argument and beyond fact. Something tells me, and I mean tells me, not just suggests to me – something tells me that that is not so, that there is a part of each one of us no man could ever touch. I am I and you are you and will remain so. Unalterably. That something is very old, many times older than pharmacology. In my case it goes back at least as far as Abraham. In yours, Daniel,' said Eric gently, 'you'll allow me to say it's a little more recent than Abraham. But your personal . . . something . . . is stronger than mine. God has blessed you, my friend. I needn't tell you to be grateful for that.'

After a silence, Daniel said, 'I remember you telling me once that mad or disturbed people whose troubles disappear under the right chemotherapy, that some of them get to feel so well or at least so all right that they reckon they can manage without, and are back to square one in no time. Could anything like that happen to Ruth?'

'Ah. Well, since she's not in hospital there's nothing to stop her cutting her dosage down or even out. But if she does she'll soon start feeling rotten enough to go back on it off her own bat. Whereas . . .'

'Whereas if she doesn't feel rotten we could be starting to win.'

'We've won the first battle already, but yes. My turn to buy a drink. Another zero for you, or something more substantial?'

'I . . . Could I have a glass of water?'

'Water coming up.'

When Eric was back in his seat, Daniel said to him, 'Just to sum up, or put it another way: those domains of thought and action traditionally annexed to free will are being more and more encroached upon by the development of drugs and other novelties, and at present no end to this progression is foreseen. Sorry to sound so cut-and-dried, but it's the way I'm beginning to think these days. Have I left anything out?'

'But,' said Eric.

'I hadn't forgotten about but,' said Daniel.

'It's just that my Church is more easy-going than yours,' said Leo.

Daniel shook his head. 'That can't be true as things are today. Years ago it probably was.'

'Even now I doubt very much if your boys and girls would have scraped a helpless, hopeless drunk off the street and not only brought him back all the way but encouraged him, and I mean encouraged, not just put no obstacle in his way but positively begged him to take holy orders.'

'Well, that's an excellent description of what our lot did for me only a short time ago.'

'Oh, great. So here we are with another piece of our lives that's been pretty much the same for us both.'

'Part of us that's the same.'

'Pretty much the same.'

'Exactly the same.'

'Because we're exactly the same.'

'Exactly the same.'

Daniel felt comforted by the complete identity of himself with his twin and their complete accord in the matter. As before they sat in the kitchen, at the table. He turned his head away and looked out of the open garden door. Outside it was very bright and very still, with nearer objects in deep shade, paving stones and a stone tablet, evergreen plants and small shrubs in stone urns and earthenware pots, coils of dark-green hosepipe that had left dark puddles and patches of damp. The sight seemed to Daniel to reflect the tranquillity of his life. At the same time it occurred to him that he had not noticed the stone tablet before. He fancied it bore an inscription, but it was too far off for him to be certain of that, let alone to read whatever might have been there. He was about to get up and go and look when he heard a small sound from the far side of the table and turned back towards it.

A replica of himself was facing him. Ears, eyebrows, hair and its length and arrangement, shape of face, ears, everything was as Daniel was used to seeing it in the mirror, although he strongly suspected that that summary could not be true in fact.

'Who are you?' he asked curiously.

'It's hard to find a single word for who I am,' replied what he recognized as his own voice. 'Or what I am. Nevertheless, if you and Leo are twins, you and he and I could be triplets. Quite conceivable, if you'll pardon the impropriety, vicar. As our brother recently explained to you, monozygotic twins come from a single fertilized ovum that has split into two. When one of those moieties splits again, we're presented with identical triplets and, as you may have read in various newspapers, there's no theoretical limit to the number of times that can happen, or be induced to happen. Are you with me so far, Daniel?'

'Yes.' Daniel might have added that what was being said to him was also to be heard, with total synchronicity, inside his head, but thought it advisable to keep quiet about that.

'Whatever their number,' resumed the being across the table, 'all the resulting persons or animals or vegetal entities are identical. The artificial process, known as cloning, has long been a botanical commonplace and one day, perhaps quite soon, may be practically as well as theoretically applicable to human beings. Compared with non-uniform organisms, clones offer an untold, unexplored range of advantages and possibilities. Some of these are of course social, even political, indicating a community as simple as an anthill or a beehive. But you and I, brother, aren't interested in that, in what may or may not actually happen in the future; our concern is philosophical and so timeless. When the uniqueness of the individual is found to be limited and finite, instead of universal and infinite, it ceases to be a usable concept. It follows that any ideas of free choice that may be nourished by a human unit, formerly known as an individual, are illusory and false. Your path to God, Daniel, was already there waiting for you. You had no alternative.'

The last few sentences had been audible only inside Daniel's head, and when he looked up he was alone in the kitchen. Aware of nothing more than his need to do so, he got up and at his natural brisk pace walked out of the house by the garden door. He made for where he had seen the stone tablet, but could not find it. At the moment when he saw it was not there to be found, darkness closed about him. He stood still for a short time, then, for greater safety as he thought, dropped into a crouching position. What was under his hands and feet now was not stone but bare earth. The darkness that surrounded him was intense but not absolute; there was enough light from somewhere to show him that he was encircled by a flat, featureless plain that reached to the horizon in every direction. He felt that his spirit was leaving him.

Still in darkness, he became aware that he was breathing unusually: slowly in, sharply out, pause, then again. At the same time he found he was lying on something smoother and softer than earth.

'Are you awake?' said Ruth's voice quietly.

'Yes. Yes, I'm awake now.' In the time it took Daniel to utter these words his mind had altered what he had actually and inexpressibly dreamt into the dialogue or dialogues at his kitchen table and what had seemed to follow, and then in turn he had forgotten all that and was left with nothing but a strong, heavy feeling of loss and sorrow. 'I must have been dreaming,' he said. 'Did I wake you?'

'I was awake. Are you all right?'

'Oh yes. Oh yes, I'm all right now.'

But he must have said it wrong, because she at once switched on her bedside light, came over and knelt down by him and took his hands. 'Was it a very horrible dream?'

'It was rather.'

'But it's all over now, darling. Let's go down to the kitchen and have a cup of tea.'

'Not there, not for me,' said Daniel in a rush.

Ruth glanced at him for a moment. 'All right, you stay here and relax. Don't you dare go to sleep again.'

'I won't, I promise I won't.'

'I'll be very quick,' she said after another pause.

Alone in his workroom a minute later, Daniel knelt down by his desk and started to pray. He thanked God for preserving him from whatever had seemed to threaten him as he slept and for taking from him all memory of it. Then he stopped, stopped the silent recital of words which was his habitual form of prayer in private. Always before, God had been listening to his prayers, or he, Daniel, had believed unquestioningly that that was so, which no doubt came to the same thing. Now, he found he could not believe that his words were going anywhere. But he went on silently forming them in his mind, this time ones that asked for help.

None had arrived by the time he heard Ruth approaching with the tea-tray. He went and sat on his desk-chair, then got up again and helped her set out the tea-things on the corner of the desk he kept clear for such arrangements. She pulled up her chair and sent him a look of great friendliness.

'You haven't been yourself since that night you and Leo sat up talking, have you?'

'No, I haven't,' he agreed.

'And this dream you had is more of the same.'

'It feels like that. In effect, yes.'

After a moment, she said, 'You'll have to tell me sooner or later, you know. And no, you're not keeping me up.'

'It's painful,' said Daniel.

'Yes. But I'm here.'

'Can I have some more tea?' When this was done, he went on, 'That night, Leo and I went over our lives in detail, starting as far back as we could remember, childhood friends, childhood ailments, schooldays, school friends, girls, university, first job, all that. Until we were in our middle twenties or so it was, well, let's call it reassuringly boring. Quite a number of resemblances, such as both of us having a close friend at college called Paul, both of us liking *The Tempest* best of Shakespeare's plays and thinking Horatio had more in him than Hamlet, but nothing on the scale of those twin brothers he told us about who had both independently had a seat built round a tree in their garden, nothing where anybody who heard of it wouldn't think it was a bit of a coincidence and that was about that, nothing *spooky*. In fact, as we went on I started to feel I was going to get away with it, I started to feel safe. Meaning, as you saw from the very beginning, I was afraid of Leo, not as a person but because of what he was, what he is. And I was dead right to be afraid of him, or at least to wish more than anything that he had never existed.

'I dare say I felt a twinge or two of a rather different sort when we got on to you, that's to say when I got on to you and he got on to his Ruth. But the first part of it was all right, in fact it was, well, pleasant to go over our early times and sort of relaxing to find they were rather like theirs, which you'd have expected with two very similar men in pretty similar circumstances and countries. I thought there might be trouble of one sort or another when, I forget which one of us it was, but something was said that could have led to us letting on about, you know, personal

things, private things. I closed up straight away, which was probably me being English again, but then he did the same thing, so
perhaps Americans have their own scale of things to keep quiet
about that isn't so different from ours. Or perhaps that's just
how Leo is. After all, we are twins.'

So far Daniel had spoken in an equable, controlled way that
was still not natural to him and included pauses in odd places.
By now he was sitting hand in hand with Ruth, who had listened
without any sign of wanting to speak. Soon he went on as before.

'I'd better come to the crunch, my love. When you start talking about boozing, serious boozing, you find there isn't a lot to
say. For reasons you don't understand and can't be bothered
with, it suddenly dawns on you that you've got to be drunk and
you set about getting there by the nearest available means. You
don't enjoy getting there or anything else about it, that's not the
idea at all. So there you are, drunk, and that's that. The rest is a
matter of falling over, throwing up, stealing, fighting, waking up
on a train you don't remember thinking about catching, let alone
getting on to, being locked in a police cell and, if you're not so
lucky, an epileptic fit or two to see you back to square one. Plus
some other people's chatter about tension and insecurity and
feelings of inadequacy. All serious drunks are the same, except
over details that can be mildly interesting, such as brainy places
to hide a bottle.

'Some people seem to get out of it on their own. I'd never have
managed it like that. Then one morning I woke up lying on my
bed fully dressed, doing pretty well for that time of day, in fact.
But I had nothing to drink and no money, so I realized I was
going to have to go out and walk some distance to the off-licence
to pick up two four-packs of large cans of Aalborg Original Brew
and charge them to the brother of a mate of mine. Then I suddenly
thought to myself I didn't want to do anything like that ever
again, and if I could get some support or some sign from somewhere that there was the slightest chance that I wouldn't, then
I'd really try not to, and I couldn't understand it then and even
after all this time I still don't completely, but I managed to get

down on my knees and pray. I'm still not sure what made me. I've never told you or anyone else this before, and there's not a lot of it I could tell anyone, but after half an hour I knew I had a personal understanding with JC that said that as long as I went on really trying he'd see me right. And he did. I can't say much more than that, except perhaps, if I can get it across, it was a special, one-off agreement between him and me, run up for the occasion, absolutely not any kind of standard contract. I think that probably gets it as far as it goes.

'So you can imagine how I felt when Leo told me about the arrangement he'd had with JC and it was exactly the same as mine, so exactly the same that I could tell what he was going to say next and I could have said the ends of his sentences with him, word for word. So my special understanding hadn't been special after all, I'd just been hearing about another of the same and if there was one then why not half a dozen or a million others? A standard contract, you see, maybe different in inessentials but the same in essentials; anyone with the correct set of genes will do to accept it, so *I* wasn't special after all either. But I wanted to think I was special, not because I was Daniel Davidson but because I was me, I was unique, I was an individual. But I'd just found out I wasn't an – I've said it already. So what was I?

'But Leo was delighted. It was what he'd been hoping for from the beginning, what he'd meant when he said he hadn't come all this way just to compare notes with me. For Leo, it was a kind of final proof of God's greatness, that in the universe he made there could be two or more things that were unique and identical at the same time. But God as I see him could never be as great as that, because he's bound by the laws of reason.'

Daniel looked into Ruth's face and saw in it hope, trust and fear, and lowered his gaze. He went on at the same even pace.

'There was an old Church saying that God would never let a Christian soul escape from him. It might wander to the ends of creation, but he would bring it back to him with a mere twitch on the thread. Whoever came up with that was probably thinking of something like a fishing-line, but to me God's thread has turned out to be the sort that controls the movements of a puppet. But whatever happens I'll always be grateful to him, because he sent me you.'

Ruth was crying. 'I wish I could believe,' she said.

'So do I, my love. Now what do you say to both of us going down to the kitchen and making some fresh tea?'

'I say yes.'

'Thank you for not saying anything while I was maundering on.'

'Daniel, you and I know it wasn't maundering.'

'Sorry.'

'At any rate, now I know why Leo went off in such a rush.'

'He had a lot to get back for. And his trip had served its purpose.'

Some weeks later, Daniel was saying to Greg Macdonald, 'You mean you do want another piece from me, is that what you're saying?'

'Well, yes, of course, I'd like to see anything you write, Daniel.'

'Ah, but excuse me, excuse me, but that's not quite the same thing, is it? You might *like to see* something I'd written, perhaps you would, and then again perhaps you wouldn't, but I was talking about me writing something for the *paper*. How about that, eh?'

'Okay, fine, fine with me, but what subject were you thinking of?'

'Listen, I'm a great believer in never doing a single stroke of work, however small, until either I've been paid for it or unless I've been promised payment, and thinking of a subject is work, right? As soon as you commission me, I'll make a start on thinking of a subject, as soon as you commission me.'

'All right then, Daniel. A piece of the usual length at the usual rates. Good.'

'What about an advance?'

After almost no hesitation Macdonald brought out his wallet, and after only a little more hesitation took from it a twenty-pound note. Daniel soon put down the glass he had been holding and had also been glancing at from time to time with great seriousness. This done, he set about ceremoniously stowing away his advance in his own wallet, but halfway through this operation the note slipped from his fingers and sideslipped to the floor. First holding up a hand to forestall any intervention from Macdonald, he retrieved the note successfully enough but not at all speedily. The performance drew laughter from near by, only a little but sufficient to cause Daniel to go and remonstrate with a group at the bar that included the urchin-like assistant editor and the stately astrologer. They were soon joined by the landlord of the Sussex, and then almost at once Daniel strolled back to where Macdonald stood, glancing condescendingly from side to side as he came.

'This place has gone down a lot,' he said.

Whatever hope Macdonald might have had of a word or two of thanks for somebody's generosity with money could clearly be abandoned. He said with a bright smile, 'Any first thoughts on a subject?'

Daniel, whose expression had grown abstracted in the past few seconds, frowned a little. 'M'm?' he asked with some impatience.

'You know, for your piece. Any ideas?'

'Oh for Christ's sake,' said Daniel, still with impatience rather than anger, 'what are you burbling about? All this . . . If you've got anything to say why don't you say it out in the open, for Christ's sake.'

'I was just wondering if there was anything special you felt like writing about for the paper.'

'Oh, that.' Now Daniel sounded contemptuous. Having said as much, he seemed at rather a loss, but soon rallied. 'If you're hoping for something about something like thoughts on stopping being a bloody parson, you're wrong.'

'I wasn't—'

'For one thing, you can't ever stop being a bloody parson once you are one. It's called being ordained. Ha! You're it for life, er,

old boy, and I'm not going to write about that. For one thing,'
he explained, 'it would be . . . bad form. I told the bishop so. Too
private, I told him. Now let's have the same again. My turn.'

Daniel gave a grunt of pleased surprise at finding he had a
twenty-pound note about him. His mood changed when the
barman turned out to be reluctant to serve him. The landlord
reappeared. Macdonald went out into the passage and activated
the telephone there.

'Ruth?' he said a moment later. 'It's Mac. Yeah, in the Sussex.
No, I didn't, he just came walking in here just a few minutes ago.
Yes, I'm afraid he is. Not so far, but I'd say any moment. Okay
now, I'll hang on till you get here. Ah, not at all.'

On his way back, Macdonald heard a confused shouting from
the bar.

Note: *Further information about identical or monozygotic twins
can be found in* Twins, *by Peter Watson (Hutchinson, 1981),
among other places. I have selected from Watson's account of
pairs of such twins who have been separated soon after birth and
brought up apart. Further details of the male twins Leo describes
(James Lewis and James Springer, born in Piqua, Ohio, USA in
1939) and of the female twins (Irene Reid and Jeanette Hamilton,
born in UK in 1944) are given on pp. 9–11 and pp. 49–52 of*
Twins.

*A research group to study the subject was set up under Profes-
sor Thomas Bouchard at the University of Minnesota in 1971.*

Toil and Trouble

I

Adrian Hollies was a literary agent, which is to say he was a director of a prosperous firm of such, Parkes & Richards Ltd of Princess Square, WC2. One afternoon in early May he was sitting in his office in their offices talking to a well-known senior client of the firm, the novelist Jack Brownlow. Or rather Brownlow, enjoying the advantage of his valued seniority, was mostly talking to Adrian. In fact at the moment he was asking him one of those questions that no successful literary agent really enjoys being asked.

'What's your honest opinion, Adrian? I mean, I take it you have read the whole thing.'

'Of course, Jack. Well, for what it's worth, I think it shows you at the top of your form. Er, that is the character of Tom and his extraordinary relationship with Sonia, not to speak of the affair with Amanda, especially the part where they all find themselves—'

'Because unless you feel quite wholehearted about it I think I ought to find someone who does to represent me. I'm not trying to hold a pistol to your head.'

Much, said Adrian to himself. Out loud he said, 'I haven't the slightest reservation. I've never been in any doubt about the quality of your work.' The second part of that was not quite true. At least twice in his nineteen years with Parkes & Richards it had crossed his mind, albeit without lingering there, that against appearances there might be something to be said for Jack's work.

After all, the first novel back in 1958 had been quite readable for a global best seller.

'One of the young fellows at Fortuitous Millennium,' said Brownlow now, 'was telling me they'd give me substantially better paperback terms there than what you managed to get me for my last one.'

'Was that Mark Skinner?'

Brownlow hesitated. 'Could have been, but I never really caught the name properly.'

'I think at your time of life, Jack, you'd do well to consider the advantages of sticking to the devil you know.'

The devil Brownlow knew, a small firm specializing chiefly in military history and reminiscences, had had the luck to publish that runaway success of 1958, and continued to publish him now he broke a little better or a little worse than even with his chronicles of elderly daydreams. To be sure, he was still something of a name, a quality that also helped to account for his continuance in the Parkes & Richards string. But both publisher and agent were also unwilling, out of compassion or cowardice, to bring him up against the fact that at the age of sixty-three he had ceased for ever to be the kind of literary property he had once been.

Brownlow had at any rate not cared for the last remark, had possibly sensed something of what lay behind it, but he had hardly begun the long process of asking for clarification when a nearby telephone purred. Adrian snatched it up with simulated annoyance.

'Yes. Yes, Tania. Oh, not again. How long ago? Well, I don't remember meeting him. Oh yes. All right.' In the next ten seconds Adrian got his face to run quickly through some of its less welcoming expressions. 'Mr Pennistone? No, that's all right. Well, if I said anything at all I meant it, including that. No, I remember it well. Your book is *unpublishable*, and when I say unpublishable I know what I'm . . . I'm sorry, but I happen to have *Jack Brownlow* with me at the moment, so perhaps you'll understand if I . . . Very well, if you say so. Of course.' Clunk.

However this performance might have affected the unlucky

Pennistone, it worked wonders for Brownlow, who did nothing more than extract from Adrian a promise to spend some thought and research on the possibility of a change of publisher, with special reference to an improved paperback deal. So all was as well as it could be.

'Can I see you put it in?' asked Brownlow finally.

This question surprised Adrian less than it might have done because he had heard it in these circumstances before. What was to be put in was the xeroxed typescript Brownlow had brought with him, and what this was to be put into was the firm's vaults for safekeeping.

'It's silly of me,' he said without encountering any opposition, 'but until that's done I can't help worrying that some joker might steal my only copy. Now there's one in here too I don't care if my house burns down. Most authors have their funny little ways and I suppose that's mine.'

After Brownlow had gone, Adrian thought for a time about him and his funny little way. It could be taken as showing a relentless determination to stay in touch with the reading public, a group seldom far from his thoughts, or just to continue to be counted as a writer. That was understandable enough in some-body with his history, but even total non-starters like Pennistone had their version of it. What was it about the almost always frustrating career of authorship that made them pursue it so obstinately, in the face of every disappointment and discourage-ment? By rights Brownlow would have packed it in a couple of books ago, decided to live on his fat, taken to drink, fallen down dead, even found something else to occupy him, but no, he was hellbent on going on writing his very own sort of terrible novel *and getting it published*.

At this point in his reflections, Adrian almost literally bumped into Derek Richards coming out of his office. Derek was the son of the co-founder of the firm and was widely said to owe his position in it to little but his paternity. Perhaps in compen-sation, he affected a wild-eyed, bardic manner that suggested a mind usually bent on higher things than representing writers.

Nevertheless there was a kind of distant friendliness about him.

'You managed to get rid of that old fart Brownlow, then,' he said.

'Unfortunately he left the typescript of a new novel with us.'

'Why can't he go back to his roots in where is it and stay there?'

'Bristol. I suppose he wants to feel he's still a writer.'

'You mean there was a time when he was one?'

'Enough people would say so and there must be some who'd say he still is.'

They crossed the entrance hall of the building. Derek said with an air of indifference, 'Yes, I've noticed that you literary agent fellows tend to, what's the word, *identify* with your clients. Now and then to a rather touching degree.'

'Maybe. You should hear what we think about the likes of Brownlow in our innermost thoughts.'

'But I trust you're not going to tell me.'

'Haven't you ever wished you were a writer, Derek?'

'Never, thank God. You have, I know. Be very careful that nothing happens to you, or you may find yourself writing it up.'

'Don't worry, nothing's going to happen to me.'

But evidently Derek was tired of the subject of writers and writing. 'So Keith Gordon has eluded both the arm of the law and the assassin's bullet,' he said.

'What? What are you talking about?'

'I got it on the News. A chunk of masonry squashed the conniving villain as he was about to enter his offices in the City. Apparently an accident.'

'Surely not. There must be hundreds of poor swindled sods dying to knock off an arch-shit like Thief Gordon. What were the circumstances?'

'You obviously wouldn't expect me to know all of them, but evidently there were plenty. So far they hadn't managed to find any suspicious ones. What seems to have happened . . .'

And for the rest of their short walk to the pub that was their undeclared destination, Adrian discussed with Derek the fate of the famously shady financier, and the very existence of Jack Brownlow altogether faded from his mind.

II

A couple of mornings later, Adrian was preparing to leave his comfortable Tufnell Park flat and go to work when the telephone rang. The girl he lived with, a picture researcher called Julie something, answered it.

'It's for you,' she told Adrian, chewing a croissant.

'Mr Hollies? Oh, it's Sergeant Chatterton here, sir, Metropolitan Police, Kilburn Division,' said a reliable youngish voice, which went on to elicit his agreement that he was the owner of a specified car. This part took place against a considerable distant accompaniment of ringing telephones, buzzing buzzers and general intramural clamour. The voice continued, 'We picked up the vehicle in question early this morning, sir. It had been malparked near—'

'I had no idea, I didn't even know it had gone,' said Adrian in a state of some consternation.

'No doubt you didn't, sir. We have good reason to believe it had been used in an attempted break-in at some premises in Maida Vale last night. I wonder, sir, if we were to send one of our cars to pick you up, if you'd be good enough to come and collect it, bringing with you the relevant documents just to formally establish ownership. We'll get a car up to you right away.'

Not more than twenty minutes later a white car with an orange stripe round it, labelled Police, duly pulled up outside the flat. Adrian picked up the required pieces of paper and looked about for Julie to kiss her goodbye for the day, but she had already left. Outside on the pavement he was greeted by a red-faced, solid-looking man in his middle thirties and a pale, taller, younger one. Both wore smart police uniform with peaked caps.

'Mr Hollies?' said the older policeman. 'Good of you to be

with us so promptly, sir. I'm PC Beaumont-Snaith and this is PC Llewelyn. This business must have come as something of a shock to you, sir, but don't you worry, it'll all be settled very shortly.'

With some vague idea of verification, Adrian said, 'I was rather expecting somebody called Sergeant Chatterton.'

'Ah, he'll be down at the station waiting for you, sir. I'm afraid poor old Chatty is a bit on the desk-bound side these days, eh, Taff?'

'Oh, indeed,' said Llewelyn with a chuckle.

'If you wouldn't mind getting in the back, Mr Hollies? Rather a squash, I'm afraid, but this week we're having to take one of our trainees with us everywhere we go. Chris, this is Mr Hollies. DC Fotheringay.'

'You're a detective, then,' said Adrian alertly to the large man in plain clothes as he settled himself next to him in the back of the car. He heard Llewelyn say something into a hand-microphone about returning to base.

'I'll tell you all about that, sir,' said the large man in a deep voice, 'if you wouldn't mind just picking up that file for me down there on the floor. It's a bit further than I like to bend, I'm afraid.'

'Of course.'

Adrian's fingers had not quite touched the grey cardboard oblong on the floor in front of him when a strong hand fastened on the back of his neck and propelled him bodily downwards. A sharp point penetrated the skin of his upper arm through jacket and shirtsleeve and, before fear could reach him, he felt himself floating into a region where there were no policemen and no car nor anything else in particular.

After a lapse of time impossible to measure, Adrian became aware that he was lying on rather than in a bed that was strange to him. By degrees he found that this bed stood in an equally unfamiliar, small, clean but barely furnished room. The light was dim but definite enough for him to be sure it came from some artificial source and not from the two windows, which were heavily curtained and, as he was to find later, blacked out with thick paint. At any rate, he had no difficulty in reading the few words typed on a sheet of paper he found on the bedside table beside an electric bell-push with wires affixed. The message ran, 'Don't try to get out. You won't make it.'

Adrian found that he was still dressed as he had been, apart from his shoes, tie and jacket, which proved to be ready to hand. There were two doors out of the room, the main one strongly and invisibly fastened, the other open and leading to a proportionately small bathroom with w.c., handbasin, shower, comb, soap and towels, all in good order. No razor, in fact nothing more. Adrian peed, washed his hands and face and combed his hair. On returning to the bedroom, he investigated a previously unregarded table near the main window. Under a white cloth it bore a plate of cheese sandwiches and a flask of whisky. Without premeditation he disposed of both and found them excellent. Then he put on shoes, tie and jacket again, pressed the bell-push and sat down on a padded chair facing the main door. Within a minute it opened and in came the two men Adrian knew as Beaumont-Snaith and Fotheringay. Both had changed out of their former clothes into cotton sweaters and denims. Their manner had ceased to be respectful without becoming hostile in any way.

'How are you feeling, Hollies?' asked Fotheringay in his bass voice. He perched quite companionably on the end of the bed while Beaumont-Snaith leant against the wall by the door.

'A bit heavy,' said Adrian. 'Sort of limp. I think perhaps I'm still dozy from that stuff you pumped into me. What was it?'

Fotheringay looked at Beaumont-Snaith, who told him not to do that and added, 'I just took what was given me and passed it on to you as ordered.'

After nodding resignedly, Fotheringay said to Adrian, 'Well, the next bit of orders is we take you along to talk to, er, the next one up from us, if you reckon you're ready for it. There's no great rush.'

'Oh good. But I'm ready for it.'

'Oh, yeah.' The big man made no move. 'Aren't you afraid, Hollies?'

'Naturally I am, but ever since I woke up about twenty minutes ago I've had a lot to think about, for instance what this place is and what I'm supposed to be doing here. Or rather what the chap you've mistaken me for would have been doing here.'

'Oh, so you reckon you've been mistaken for somebody else.'

'I know I must have been.'

Over by the door, Beaumont-Snaith pushed himself upright. 'I think it's time we fetched you along to meet the next one up from us, don't you, er, Fotheringay?'

Their way took them along an L-shaped piece of carpeted corridor in which and from which there was nothing to be seen and, except for the burble of distant traffic, nothing to be heard. All the same, Adrian sensed he was on an upper floor of a considerable building that stood on its own. Beaumont-Snaith, in the lead, knocked at a closed door and entered, followed by the other two.

A well-groomed, well-dressed man of about forty, who had been sitting behind a large desk writing something, put down his pen and took off his spectacles with an exclamation of pleasure, rose to his feet and extended a hand. 'Good morning, Mr Hollies,' he said affably, in decisive tones that seemed to Adrian in some way familiar. 'Do take a seat. So glad you could come.'

Without volition, Adrian shook the proffered hand and almost as spontaneously took the seat, a comfortable chair near and at an angle to the desk. He hardly needed to glance at the heavy furniture, the rows of books and periodicals or the Italian prints on the walls to perceive the ambience aimed at as expensive-professional. Beaumont-Snaith and Fotheringay were no longer to be seen.

'At this stage of the proceedings,' said the man behind the desk, smiling, 'I should of course press a switch and tell somebody offstage that I don't want any calls or visitors till further notice, which is acknowledged by the appallingly distorted voice of the somebody, but that would be going a little too far. Still, there is a switch I can press to cause something amusing to happen.'

No switch sounded, but after a moment sounds of ringing telephones, buzzing buzzers and the like were to be heard from a concealed loudspeaker or speakers. With another smile, this time an eager, guileless, almost childish one that might have heralded the repetition of some established old favourite, the unknown recited carefully against this background, 'Mr Hollies? Oh, it's Sergeant Chatterton here, sir, Metropolitan Police, Kilburn Division. I wonder if you'd mind confirming that you're the owner of', and vehicular details followed. In the middle of them the loudspeakers faded. 'There, now. What do you think of that, eh?'

'I think that whatever it is you're trying to do here you're doing it to the wrong man.'

'Oh, the *wrong man*. I see. But I'm afraid that's quite impossible, Mr Hollies. Well, let's just check, shall we? Here we are – Adrian Hugo Hollies, born younger son of Frederick Irving Hollies deceased and Diana Victoria *née* Barton, educated Westminster School and Trinity College, Oxford, blah blah *blah*, at present director of Parkes & Richards, et cetera. Oh yes. Er, current live-in girlfriend Julie Scharwenka, employed by Central Magazines plc. That is your life, isn't it . . . Mr Hollies?'

'Yes, but I still say all this couldn't possibly have been meant for me and there's still been a mistake, it must just have happened at an earlier stage, for heaven's sake. Surely.'

'Oh dear, I'm sorry to say that's not the case either,' continued Chatterton's voice for a moment before an abrupt return to the earlier stockbroking inflection. 'You'll have to take my word for that, my dear fellow. I was present when this thing was set up and you, Adrian Hugo Hollies of Parkes & Richards, were at the centre of the picture right from the beginning.'

'Oh. What is this *thing* you mention?'

'You know some of the answer to that already. A mechanism for removing you from your daily life and imprisoning you for an indefinite period somewhere you'll never escape or be rescued from.'

This silenced Adrian, but only for a moment. 'Is that all?'

'It's what you might have inferred unassisted. Some of the rest is that your experience here is an end in itself. Nothing is required of you in the shape of information, your signature to a confession or any other action or reaction. Whatever happens you stay. Yes?'

'I was going to ask, though why I should hope to get anything helpful out of you I don't really know, I was going to ask if this is supposed to be a punishment for something I've done.'

The man Adrian was always to think of as Chatterton shook his head. It was a rather handsome head, in fact his whole being radiated something like distinction. 'No,' he said firmly. 'I'll tell you what is true, that indeed you have done something that displeased somebody, but to tell you what it is or was would be to immediately forfeit the anonymity that is of the essence of this enterprise, and . . . and after all, punishment suffered without knowledge of either the offence or the offended party can hardly be called punishment at all. So, let's call it revenge. Somebody intends to satisfy himself – or herself – by retaliating upon your person for some wrong you've inflicted upon him or her.' Chatterton appeared less than pleased with this formulation, but after a pause continued fluently enough, 'And that satisfaction and that wrong correspond to no legal definition, otherwise my principal would no doubt have looked for redress through the courts.' He finished strongly and with an air of triumph, smiling as he spoke and springily adjusting his position behind the desk.

'You mean any sensible person would think that whatever it is I'm meant to have done is ridiculously disproportionate to all this elaborate and obviously very expensive bloody *fuss*.'

Chatterton looked wary. 'I'm sorry, Mr Hollies, I'm not sure I follow you.'

'Really? Well, just consider. I'm a literary agent and as such I must have inflicted a great many wrongs on people, or what they might see as wrongs. And in my private life I've done quite a few things I'm ashamed of, like many of us. But nothing on this *scale*. Unless your principal is mad. Well, is he? Or is she?'

The question seemed to flummox Chatterton a little. 'I'm afraid I can't answer that. Or rather, I can assure you between ourselves that for practical purposes he or she is . . . is entirely sane.'

'Have I injured you?' asked Adrian quickly.

'Oh no, Mr Hollies, you've never done anything to me, anything at all. Why, you've never set eyes on me before, have you?' For a moment there, the shadowy presence of Sergeant Chatterton, and the absence of Chatterton QC or FRCS, was unmistakable. 'You and I have no quarrel.'

'So how much does this carry?'

But this time upmarket Chatterton was prepared. 'The organization will naturally see to it that I don't lose by this interruption of my more regular activities.'

'Such as resting, eh?' When this brought no reply but a huffy toss of the head, Adrian went on, 'How long do you expect this interruption to last?'

'That's easy,' said Chatterton with a less pleasant smile than before. 'As long as it takes.'

'As long as what takes? As long as it takes to what?'

'We have a modest programme arranged for you, Mr Hollies, but I'm afraid it would be premature at this stage to speculate on its likely duration. It'll last quite long enough to satisfy you, you'll find.' The last part was delivered in a tone that seemed to lack some of the required conviction.

'I see. I mean I see I'm not going to get anything out of you if you can help it. Why did you have me fetched along here, to this room?'

'If you really want to know, removing any unhelpful theories you might have formed about the reason for your presence here, impressing you with—'

'But leaving a big question mark over the disparity between size of punishment and crime.'

'From our point of view there's nothing unhelpful about question marks being left in your mind,' said Chatterton with some complacency. After a pause he added in a different tone, 'And I wanted to have a look at you.'

'I hope the sight's been worth the trouble.'

'Aren't you frightened, Mr Hollies?'

'One of your underlings asked me that. I told him of course I was, but I was trying not to let it interfere with my powers of observation and thought.'

'Admirable. If true.' Chatterton paused again before hurrying on, 'I've got news for you, Hollies. You won't be done any physical harm. Nothing actually painful's going to happen to you, nothing . . . *messy*, you understand?' Then, with yet another change of mood or idiom, he continued, 'But before this is over you're going to wish that all you had to put up with was something along those lines, something painful in that way, something that really . . . *hurts*. Right, I've said enough already. Ah, here we are.'

A door opened and the man earlier called PC Llewelyn, no doubt summoned a few moments before, came into the room. He entered in a lounging, rolling fashion before a kind of military yelp from Chatterton smartened him up in an instant. Coming to something like a posture of attention he said loudly, 'Yes, sir.'

'Wake up, Llewelyn.'

'I'm sorry, sir, truly I am.' This was said in a noticeable Welsh accent. The fellow had taken his jacket off but still wore his uniform trousers. Although there seemed to be no other definable change in his appearance, he looked uncommonly scruffy.

'Convey Mr Hollies back to his room and secure the door.'

'Right, sir.' Llewelyn at any rate spoke sharply.

Adrian looked from one to the other of the two as they went through their performance. His expression evidently offended Chatterton, who gave him a curt nod of dismissal and gestured impatiently to Llewelyn to remove him.

His return trip along the corridor was less smooth than the outward journey. Scruffy or not, Llewelyn was quite strong, and provided unnecessary encouragement to continue to move by means of a hand clamped on his upper arm. The door of the room he had woken up in was ajar and Llewelyn's hand propelled him across the threshold. Before the door could be shut Adrian said clearly,

'The devil damn thee black, thou cream-faced loon!'

Llewelyn stared back at him with a look of puzzlement,

surprise, dismay or of all three, but for a moment he neither spoke nor moved.

'Whom we invite to see us crowned at Scone.'

At this, Llewelyn scowled ferociously and gave Adrian a push in the chest forceful enough to send him staggering and almost falling. When he had recovered himself the door was shut and, he soon discovered, fastened. His instinct was for setting about getting it open again, but he had no way of doing so, certainly no quick or non-noisy way. No such decisive move would in any case make sense without knowledge of where he might find an exit from the house. And a means of using it. If any. It looked as if he might as well heed the advice he had received on waking, that he would not escape by his own efforts.

The scrap of paper bearing this message was no longer to be found. The remains of his snack had likewise been cleared away. The bed had been remade. A more thorough look than he had earlier ventured showed him pyjamas, fresh underclothes, shirts. Their mundane practicality seemed designed to dishearten him. With head bent he moved slowly round the room a couple of times, then halted and for some minutes stared at the wall in an unfocused manner. After that he sat down on the bed and paused a moment before dropping his head into his hands and rocking slowly to and fro. Anyone looking at him would have said that a thoroughly wretched man, if not a despairing one, was sitting there. Presently Adrian drew his legs up on to the bed and lay down on his side with his knees drawn up and his hands clasped. Unexpectedly, he slept.

There passed another immeasurable tract of time. At its end, at the sound of the door being unlocked, Adrian sprang up and stood beside the bed, smoothing his hair and straightening his tie. When all four of the men he had previously seen came into the room, they found him facing them in a posture of defiance.

After sending him a look of peculiar distaste, Chatterton moved over to one side, as if to underline his supervisory status. 'Come along, Hollies,' he said sharply.

Fotheringay and Llewelyn began to move forward, but Adrian

eluded their grasp. 'Let me come of my own accord, please. I'm quite capable of setting one foot in front of the other.'

'Oh, good show, sir,' said Fotheringay, 'but anybody can see you're terrified. Why not admit it?'

'What, terrified of you?'

Fotheringay's immediate response was to punch Adrian in the stomach. He collapsed on to the bed. 'That was quite unnecessary,' said someone: Chatterton.

'Just a tap, that's all. Look, he's getting up already.'

'Our orders are not to hurt him physically.'

'There won't be a mark on him, if that's what's bothering you.'

By now Adrian was facing them again, still panting and groaning, half doubled up, but back on his feet, and was allowed to make his own way out of the bedroom, round a couple of corners in the passage and into a room of about the same size but partly subdivided by a grey-painted screen on rollers. Two men were visible: after a first glance one of them went behind the screen and the other led an unresisting Adrian over to a corner where there stood a narrow backless couch of the sort to be met with in doctors' consulting rooms.

'Take off your jacket and shirt and then get up on here, please.'

Adrian followed instructions and successively had his blood pressure taken and allowed auscultation of his chest. Both exercises were rapid but thorough.

'Now sit up and take a series of deep breaths as I tell you, please.'

He felt the small cool circle of the stethoscope applied in turn to various parts of his back.

'Thank you. Please get dressed and sit on the chair.'

'Well?' asked another voice.

'His heart and circulation appear excellent. His blood pressure is above normal, but then he's obviously in a condition of extreme tension, if only as shown by his respiratory rate.'

'So there's no real risk?'

'In an undertaking of this kind there's *always* a risk, but if you mean am I prepared to take this risk then yes, I am.'

'Good. Let's get on with it, then.'

'Mr Hollies? Mr Hollies, I'm going to put you to sleep for a couple of minutes, nothing more than that. When you wake up you'll be in one piece and still here. Do you understand? Oh well, here goes.'

When Adrian came to himself after what he suspected to be only a short time, he was in some discomfort. He had been strapped into a chair in a way that prevented him from leaving it and also bound his wrists to its arms. More noticeably, his head was tightly clamped and what felt like pieces of sticky tape had been applied to his eyelids to prevent even their slight closure. A large screen of the TV type, at present blank, filled most of his vision. He must have made some movement because almost at once a voice spoke to him from behind his chair, the voice of the man who had seemed to be some sort of doctor.

'How are you feeling?'

'Restricted.'

'No nausea or trouble with breathing?'

'I've never felt better in my life.'

'Bravely spoken, Mr Hollies. Happy viewing.'

As he spoke, a thrumming click sounded, the screen in front of Adrian lit up and in a moment, with excellent definition and lifelike colour, images began to appear.

The first of these, that of an attractive young woman, Adrian found pleasant enough, and he had no objection when, smiling at the camera, she proceeded to undress, nor did he find what immediately followed any worse than embarrassing. When other persons joined her, however, he very quickly started showing signs of discomfort and not long after of distress. When a cry of pain sounded from the direction of the screen, he struggled to free himself and to turn his head away. Within a couple of minutes he was making anguished sounds and, as far as was possible to him, thrashing about. A female scream of terror and his own scream rose together, at which point the film froze and two or more men seized him and gagged him. But as soon as the coloured shapes were again in motion and appropriate sounds to be heard, he was able to show how much clamour could be created by a gagged man, especially in the forms of shrieks and inarticulate noises of protest and pain. In the end the man who had last spoken hurried forward and, with the screen now darkened, silence fell.

This time Adrian woke up lying on his bed. His eyelids were sore, his eyes ached and his lower lip was swollen and tender; he remembered biting it and feeling blood trickle down his chin. Despite these things he felt comfortable and languid, and guessed he was under some sedative or painkiller. He was alone. Presently, taking his time, he pushed himself upright and round until he was sitting on the edge of the bed. He had not long to wait.

The door clicked a couple of times and opened to admit the supposed doctor, who was now wearing a suit and tie. He looked closely at Adrian and said, 'You should be lying down.'

'I can get all the rest I want. I'm not going anywhere.'

The doctor was not listening. He brought from his jacket two small containers and handed them over. 'Take two of the round red ones to stop things hurting, not more than six in twenty-four hours. The white ones will calm you down and also help you to sleep. Dose of two, maximum six a day, got it?'

'Are you off somewhere?'

'I have things to see to.'

When the doctor had gone, Adrian went into the bathroom and came back holding a glass of water. Before he could have taken a pill there was the unexpected sound of a tap on the outside of his door.

'Come in,' he called. At the sight of Chatterton and Fotheringay he got up not very steadily, seized a chair by the back and ran at them with it, calling to them to keep their hands off him.

Fotheringay twisted the chair out of his grasp. 'Sit down, Mr Hollies,' he said easily.

As he sat on the bed again, Adrian said, 'Will you tell me something? Please?'

'Maybe.'

'Those, those things you made me see, they weren't real, were they?'

'Well . . .'

'When those men, when they forced the girl to do what she did, that wasn't really happening, was it? Please tell me.'

'We weren't on that side of it, Chatterton and me.'

'I mean, when they started . . . started . . . that poor girl,' said Adrian, and burst into tears, racking sobs he seemed at the same time to be trying to restrain. 'Sorry,' he gasped after some moments – 'sorry, I thought I could just ask you in the ordinary way, but when it came to it . . . I found I couldn't. Sorry.'

'Don't let it get you down, Adrian,' said Fotheringay. 'It was all trick photography, what you saw. Bloody amazing what they can do these days, you know. Must have cost somebody a fair packet, mind. But anyway, no call for you to fret like you're doing now.'

'No, but when he thought it was for real,' said Chatterton.

'Absolutely,' said Fotheringay. 'Oh no, I fully appreciate that.'

An awkward pause supervened, during which Adrian seemed to pull himself together and each of the remaining two waited for the other to proceed. In the end it was Fotheringay who nodded resignedly and spoke up.

'Er, Chatterton here and me, we got talking and we came to the conclusion we don't want to go on with this any longer. "This" being the kind of play-acting or pretend caper or make-believe we've been going in for up to now. Now we've got to know you a bit we reckon you've had a raw deal, and we're sorry, right? The thing was, we were both without a job, down on our luck, when this bloke comes along and throws cash around like he's got three arms and says there'll be more to come if we just look after somebody for a couple of days and go on according to this kind of script he's got for us, if you see what I mean. We say okay. But . . .'

Chatterton now broke in. Throughout what followed he stayed much closer to his police-sergeant persona than to the urbane self Adrian had first seen. 'The background is that Mr X had set everything up for a whole programme of unpleasant experiences aimed at punishing somebody he'd taken a real dislike to – lucky for you that you only got as far as the first of the series, there was a lot worse to follow. Then right at the last minute the job's off. The central character's suddenly not around any more.'

'Being as he's dead,' said Fotheringay.

'Anybody I know?' asked Adrian.

'Let's hope not, for your sake.'

'Keith Gordon,' said Chatterton. 'Also known as Big Thief. He had the misfortune to be under a couple of hundredweight of stonework when it fell off his office roof. Apparently it was a genuine accident.'

'I heard about it,' said Adrian.

'The word is he'd been warned it was unsafe but was too bloody mean to have it seen to,' said Fotheringay.

'Act of God,' said Chatterton contentedly. 'Who managed to get it right for once. Well now, Mr Hollies, imagine where that left our Mr X. He'd laid out oodles of funds and in the twinkling of an eye it was all going to be wasted. Or was it? In his shoes I know I'd have gritted my teeth and called it a day, but here was another one that didn't believe in money going down the drain. So how about a replacement for Big Thief? To cut what must have been a long story short, the best he managed to come up with was A. Hollies Esquire, a real swine who turned out to be a literary agent. Not that I'm trying to make you sound un-important, Mr Hollies.'

'No, of course not.'

'Right. Anyway, what had you done to him?'

'I've never done anything much to anyone. What did he say I'd done?'

'I didn't deal with him direct, but there was something about gross professional misconduct.'

'In my part of the trade it's not worth cheating anybody. I suppose I could have told him a book he'd written wasn't worth publishing.'

'Could be, very well,' said Fotheringay. 'Something that don't matter, like a book. You remember I thought this bloke was crazy right from the start.'

'You said yourself it was out of proportion, didn't you, Mr Hollies? And have you ever physically abused a girl, as I was told last night? Of course you haven't. Nobody could believe such a thing who saw you reacting to what you thought was the real thing. Oh dear.'

'There's not much time,' said Fotheringay. 'We've said we're sorry. We're going to wrap this up. But you understand, Adrian, we want to protect ourselves. We request – that's all we can do in the circumstances, request you to assist us. You're a clever sort of fellow and you know about things like stories and writing scripts and that. Now you just get down to it and write a story for, er, for Chatterton here and me to learn, right, showing how you got the better of us and got out of here. Clocked one of us on the head, kind of style, and made a fool of the other, get the idea? Best you can do in the next hour or two. We'll help you any way we can, I give you my solemn word.'

'What about Beaumont-Snaith and Llewelyn?'

'Yeah, well I reckon Llewelyn'll do what we tell him, don't you, Chatterton? As regards Beaumont-Snaith, he took a nasty bang on the head just now when we were discussing what to do, so could be he'll turn out to fit into the scheme quite smoothly. We'll just have to see how it goes, won't we?'

'Wouldn't it be simpler,' said Adrian, 'if we all just pretended to have gone through the whole programme?'

Fotheringay nodded slowly with eyebrows raised. 'Okay, but only if you fancy spending a couple of months pretending to be a nervous wreck after it, which is what you would have been. And us trusting you to do it, of course. No, I reckon we'd all be better off with Plan A.'

III

'And I presume Plan A went reasonably well,' said Derek Richards the following week.

'That's what I presume too,' said Adrian. 'We started off by cleverly buggering up the closed-circuit TV system, which natu-rally I'd assumed was there from the start. Then I luckily turned out to know a bit of karate, anyway enough of it to put paid to Beaumont-Snaith. Marvellous name, that. As for it going well, I've had no complaints, though I must say if I'd been one of them I wouldn't be feeling all that easy in my mind.'

'How about the doctor?'

'The ex-doctor was going to disappear somewhere abroad whatever happened, on account of a previous piece of his doctor-ing having gone seriously wrong, and duly did, in a flash. He was a real ex-doctor, by the way, quite a different figure from the others.'

'What tipped you off about them?'

'Well, the general way they spoke and carried themselves and the rest of it, as if they were on the green, in mummers' parlance. If you were brought up in a theatrical household as I was, it's unmistakable. You must have noticed, when you turn the TV on or switch channels at random, how quickly and certainly you can tell whether it's acted, however straightforwardly, or real life. I realized rather late on that those chaps talked like coppers in telly plays, not actual coppers, though that was right in a way, but I had plenty of time to take in that they were camped-up villains too. Then when Chatterton took two actorial phrases from me in quick succession without turning a hair I knew I was right, and confirmed it by firing a couple of lines from *Macbeth* at Llewelyn and getting a shock-horror reaction. He must have carried a spear some time in a rep production of the Scottish play as they call it because they think it's bad luck even to call it by its right name, let alone quote from it offstage. They're all grossly superstitious.

'What else did I know about actors as a tribe? That they were fluent but slow on the uptake, conformist, emotional and senti-mental, impressionable, above all impressed by acting, so wrapped up in the theatre that to see a part played with conviction, in other words hammed up a trifle, affected them more than the real thing ever could. So I set about acting my head off in the part of the decent, plucky little man who stands up to the big bullies even though he's scared to death and who can put up with his own sufferings but not somebody else's. And it went down a treat, didn't it?'

'Don't undersell yourself, dear boy. You showed some real pluck as well.'

'I found I could miss a lot of that film by rolling my eyes up. And it's easier when you're acting. I must go.'

'Where does Julie think you were?'

'With A. N. Other. She had a fling with S. O. Else so that's all right. We were having a difference at the time. I was only away for one night.'

Adrian left Derek Richards in his office and went upstairs to his own. He had not told Derek or anybody else about how, immediately on returning to his desk, he had telephoned that Pennistone whose pitiable book on the world of high finance he had so rightly dismissed out of hand, nor how he had given Pennistone notice of his return, just that and no more, nor how half a minute's complete silence at the other end of the line had been the only response.

Afterwards, Adrian had been as satisfied as he cared to be that he had identified the man Chatterton had stagily called Mr X and that there was nothing more to be expected from that quarter. He wished only, and that not very ardently, that he could have known the whereabouts of the house he had been taken to in a drugged state and brought back from with his head, however willingly, in a bag.

But there was one more thing. With the obstinate punctuality of the unwelcome, Jack Brownlow arrived no more than a couple of seconds after the agreed hour, full of fraudulent apologies for taking up the firm's valuable time. He settled himself down in a chair by the window with a self-importance suggesting his conviction that, in the years that lay ahead, visitors to this office would be told in hushed tones that that was the self-same chair *Jack Brownlow* used to sit in. No doubt for a similar reason he wore his usual archaic suit.

'Did you manage to glance at those rough xeroxes I dropped in the other day?' he asked when he was ready to.

'Yes I *did*.' Instead of going on to say that he had thought he recognized them as the opening pages of Brownlow's last novel, and had had to check to make sure they were not, or not quite, Adrian went on to say, 'I don't know how you do it.'

Luckily Brownlow made no offer to explain how. He said, 'That's a relief. I just thought it was time I made a clean break with the sort of thing the public expect from me.'

Adrian made some reply. This time what he did not say was that he had got an idea for a sort of thriller that began with a kidnapping, something he would gladly part with if Brownlow thought it was time he made a clean break with the sort of thing the public expected from him. Another lecture on how novelists should stick to their own experience might be too much to bear.

Captain Nolan's Chance

A PLAY FOR RADIO

Principal Characters (*denotes a fictitious person)

CAPTAIN LEWIS NOLAN	*In his late twenties. An upper-crust Irishman brought up in Milan.*
LORD ROBERT CECIL	*In his mid-twenties. [later Lord Salisbury]*
CAPTAIN IVOR MORRIS	*A few years older than Nolan. I see or hear him as a fairly posh Welshman. 'Ivor' is my invention. I cannot find Morris's true Christian name nor much about him, but a Capt. Morris certainly led the 17th Lancers at the charge, which he survived though grievously wounded, and was certainly a close friend of Nolan's and a fellow-enthusiast for cavalry.*
COUNT ROGACHEV*	*In his thirties or forties.*
LORD LUCAN	*Mid-fifties.*
LORD CARDIGAN	*Late fifties. A 'plunger', an aristocrat who spoke with a distinctive jargon or accent, pronouncing R as W and interlarding sentences with loud and meaningless exclamations of 'Haw haw'.*
JOSEPH*	*In his forties or fifties. Speaks with*

	an accent differentiating him from Russians, e.g. Polish or Ukrainian.
LORD GEORGE PAGET	*In his mid-thirties. A gallant soldier, later a general.*
SIDNEY HERBERT	*'Secretary at War' in the 1852 cabinet of Lord Aberdeen.*

Sequence 1 – London

We are in Pall Mall in the year 1854. A cab draws up.

CABBY: Here we are, gents. Retrenchment Club. Oh, thank you, captain. You two gentlemen going to be off to fight them Rooshans?

NOLAN: One day, maybe.

CABBY: Well, give 'em a bang on the boko from me. Good night, sir.

The cab moves off. During the exchange NOLAN *and his companion have alighted. They cross the pavement, mount some steps and enter the lobby of the club. A* PORTER *approaches.*

PORTER: Good evening, gentlemen.

NOLAN: We're here to see Lord Robert Cecil. We are Captain Lewis Nolan and Captain Ivor Morris. His lordship is expecting us.

PORTER: If you'll be good enough to wait a moment, sir, I'll inform his lordship that you gentlemen have arrived.

NOLAN: Thank you kindly. (*A moment.*) Ivor, for God's sake: this fellow is younger than you or me. Sure he comes from a grand family and they say he's a coming man, but there's no side about him at all. He's always been interested in the Eastern Question, that's Turkey and Russia and the rest of it. And the lad's fond of horses, do you understand.

PORTER: (*Approaching*) Would you come this way please, gentlemen.

They walk through part of the club.

PORTER: Captain Nolan and Captain Morris, your lordship.

CECIL: Thank you, Hawkins. Thank you for coming, Nolan. So this is the estimable Captain Morris. All I know about you, sir, is that you're a childhood friend of Lew Nolan here, and that you share some of this mad Irishman's delusions.

MORRIS: I'm afraid there are one or two subjects, my lord, on which neither Lew nor I is quite sane.

CECIL: That's a relief. I pass my days with sane people and believe me it's hell. Now sit down and let's have a drink. The sherry here can just about be swallowed if you grit your teeth, or you might prefer a little brandy.

Fade down and fade up in the main dining-room of the club.
CECIL, NOLAN *and* MORRIS *are at a table by themselves.*

CECIL: What's being said about the appointment of Lord Lucan to lead the cavalry?

NOLAN: Well, unlike the other generals he has seen active service.

CECIL: Oh, I didn't realize that.

NOLAN: Twenty-six years ago. He did well enough then.

MORRIS: And then, on April Fool's Day, if you please, it's announced that Lord Cardigan is gazetted Brigadier-General in command of the Light Brigade. Now Lucan's a difficult fellow, but the word is he's a good tough officer. But Cardigan, he's . . . may I speak plain, sir?

CECIL: Please do.

MORRIS: Lord Cardigan is a lunatic, that's the kindest thing you can say of him. Arrogant, reckless, obstinate, brooking no opposition, a damn fool, and unfortunately as brave as a lion. And in the 17th Lancers I'm to be under his command. The thought of that frightens me.

NOLAN: Which doesn't often happen to Ivor Morris. And my lord Cardigan wants me as his personal assistant, his A D C.

CECIL: Are you going to take the job?

NOLAN: I'll see the fellow in hell first. You know, my lord, when I think that the British cavalry list is full of brilliant and experienced officers in the prime of their careers, not one of whom has been given a command in this expedition, because their service has been in India – well, I want to weep.

CECIL: Before you collapse altogether, Nolan, you'd better have a glass of port.

We have moved to the port-drinking room of the club. NOLAN *is well away.*

NOLAN: It's my belief that, properly led, cavalry, especially light cavalry, can do anything.

CECIL: Is it your belief that cavalry could break an infantry square?

NOLAN: Yes, even that – sir. There's not just the one key to it, but two. The first is the man; well, the British army knows about him and how to train him. The second is the horse, and the British army needs a lesson or two about how to train a horse.

MORRIS: You mentioned leadership, Lew.

NOLAN: That comes later.

CECIL: When we talked before, Captain Nolan, you mentioned kindness as the basis of your system.

NOLAN: That's it, my lord. A horse should never be punished or startled, but shown he can trust the man on his back. I'll see if I can find you a copy of my book, *Nolan's System for Training Cavalry Horses*, it's all in there.

MORRIS: I'm afraid Nolan is something of a fanatic on the subject, my lord.

NOLAN: Ah, to hell, you're as bad yourself, Ivor.

MORRIS: All right, I may be pretty bad, but I have to admit in all honesty that my lads in the 17th are second to none as cavalry soldiers, and even some of the Hussars are pretty fair.

NOLAN: Oh, they're not all hopeless.

CECIL: You think they'll give a fair account of themselves against the Russians?

MORRIS: I think so, my lord, yes.

NOLAN: If they get the chance.

CECIL: M'm. I hope you're right.

We are in the same place but time has passed. All three men are slightly foxed.

CECIL: I think one more glass, don't you? Well, no doubt we could go on about horses all night, but I didn't invite the two of you along here just for that. Let me put it briefly. Now perhaps Lew Nolan has told you, Captain Morris, I concern myself greatly with the activities of Russia in the Near East. I scent a grave threat to our interests there and further afield. This affair now in the Black Sea, it may prove to be no more than a skirmish, a preparation for something larger. There's a devilish crafty fellow in St Petersburg called Count Rogachev whom I don't care for the sound of one little bit. Very powerful in an underhand way and a deadly enemy of England and jealous of our possessions overseas. I see in him a grave danger to our country.

MORRIS: Lew and I promise to throw this Count Rogachev into the Black Sea as soon as we set eyes on him, my lord, but what can we do meanwhile?

CECIL: I'm sorry, I think I was a little carried away. What the two of you can do for me meanwhile, my dear Morris, is to compile a report for my eyes only on the fighting qualities of our troops – morale, state of training, whatever may signify. They haven't fought a serious war for forty years – how would they resist a powerful and determined foe? You've told me something already; I need to know more. Will you do it?

NOLAN: We'll do all we can, sir.

CECIL: As it comes to you, nothing fancy. The telegraph would be quickest, but you'd have to resort to code.

NOLAN: We'll find a way, my lord, never fear.

Sequence 2 – St Petersburg

We are in a reception room in a palace. Men and women are chattering and laughing, eating snacks and drinking. JOSEPH, *a dignified butler, is supervising the serving of drinks.*

JOSEPH: A glass of champagne, my lady? Your excellency?

EXCELLENCY: Thank you, Joseph. Always on hand when you're wanted, eh?

JOSEPH: (*In undertone to* SERGEI, *waiter*) Two champagnes, Sergei, quick. And a napkin.

SERGEI: (*Nervous*) Yes, Mr Joseph.

EXCELLENCY: Splendid stuff. Yes, my dear, I always say it's a blessing the French can't fight half as well as they make champagne.

LADY: They fought well enough under Bonaparte.

EXCELLENCY: Until our Russian lads broke their spirit. Before you were born, Tania. I was just a young subaltern then. Yes, and Wellington finished Bonaparte off at Waterloo. I doubt if any British army could manage such a thing today.

LADY: Have you visited the Crimea yourself, uncle?

EXCELLENCY: Not as yet. I hope to go in a week or so . . .

COUNT 1: Well, as for our armies in the Crimea, they have only to wait for the British and the French to die of cold and fever and thorough incompetence, especially at the top. Their Lord Raglan and the others are drunk from morning to night.

COUNT 2: As I see it, Prince Menschikov need only hold firm and use his guns whenever he can. Our Russian artillery will settle things, as always.

COUNT 3: Allies? The flower of England, France, Turkey and Sardinia, if you please. A pitiful polyglot rabble, sir.

ROGACHEV: (*Calling imperiously*) Joseph, over here.

JOSEPH: (*Calling*) At once, my lord count. (*To* SERGEI) Come, Sergei – when Count Rogachev calls, you move fast.

ROGACHEV: Yes, colonel, I think this news makes the prospects for our little scheme look quite encouraging. (*To* JOSEPH) Some vodka for the colonel. No, just soda water for me.

JOSEPH: Here we are, sir. (*To* SERGEI) Some vodka for the colonel . . . Oh, bless my soul.

ROGACHEV: Joseph, if you've got a moment . . .

JOSEPH: (*Gamely*) Of course, your honour.

ROGACHEV: . . . just find my secretary, would you, and tell him to start assembling the select company straight away in the small parlour. And Joseph.

JOSEPH: Yes, my lord.

ROGACHEV: Of course we shall need refreshing there too, you know.

JOSEPH: Of course, your honour, I understand. (*To* SERGEI) Get those glasses changed at once, they're filthy.

SERGEI: Yes, Mr Joseph.

Fade down and up to small parlour. Half a dozen men are talking in low tones, ROGACHEV *comes in and all fall silent.*

ROGACHEV: Most honoured, your royal highness.

PRINCE: My dear Rogachev, I wouldn't have missed it for anything.

ROGACHEV: That's kind of you, sir. Well . . .

All sit.

ROGACHEV: Thank you all for leaving the party to come along here. I'll keep you away for as short a time as I possibly can. In fact I have only two points to bring before you for the moment. The first is that I'm now in possession of what I think is conclusive evidence of the low state of training and the very poor morale of the British forces fighting – if that is the word – in the Crimean peninsula. That's more important than—

GENERAL: Count Rogachev, may I put in a word here?

ROGACHEV: Please, let's hear your views, general.

GENERAL: Thank you. Well, fighting is certainly the word for what the English infantry were doing on the 20th of last month at the battle of the River Alma.

VOICES: Oh, that. Yes, we've heard a lot about that. Oh, the Alma.

GENERAL: Yes, the Alma. Those men showed not merely courage but blind courage in the way they went on advancing over the river and up those slopes in the face of withering fire from our guns, roundshot, grape and canister. They fell in masses but

they kept advancing. Does that indicate very poor morale?
Count Rogachev?

ROGACHEV: No more, general? Thank you. Accounts of that engagement seem to vary. Major?

MAJOR: My information is that the 'heroism' of the British has been somewhat exaggerated and misinterpreted. We should not forget—

ROGACHEV: The British so-called heroism is something of a myth called into being by way of excuse for the incompetence and timidity of our own commanders.

GENERAL: Nonsense, they're both fine soldiers. I've served with 'em.

ROGACHEV: It's touching, isn't it, the way the army always stands together, no matter what. If I may just finish this point, the state of an army's infantry is a far less telling indicator than that of its cavalry, who are likely to be a little less brutish by nature. Of course I speak myself as a cavalry soldier . . .

VOICES: Quite right. Of course. Hear hear. About time too.

ROGACHEV: Thank you. And – the British cavalry is in such a state, despite its fine uniforms, that their generals dare not use it, it seems. Major.

MAJOR: Yes, my lord. At the battle of the Alma, which has made such a profound impression on the general here, the famous British cavalry stood by and did nothing. The previous day at the valley of the Bulganek, their Lord Raglan ordered their cavalry to retire before they had even drawn their sabres. What humiliation!

A handbell rings.

ROGACHEV: I beg your pardon, major. Please continue.

MAJOR: The rest is detail, my lord. The theme that emerges is that their cavalry are frightened of our guns.

Voices express assent. Double doors open and JOSEPH *and* SERGEI *come in with drinks.*

ROGACHEV: Ah, Joseph, quick about it, now. Champagne for His Highness, vodka, and for me I think a small glass of still white wine. Well, gentlemen, this comes at a timely moment. Consider the victory our Cossacks will win over the British lancers and hussars and dragoons when they meet on the great plains below the Himalayas! A toast – your royal highness, my lords, gentlemen, I give you – the imperial conquest of India!

VOICES: India! We'll show 'em! To victory! Long live the Czar!

ROGACHEV: Joseph, my trusty friend, you shall join our toast! Pour yourself a glass of wine and raise it on high!

JOSEPH: Thank you, sir, but I beg your lordship to excuse me. My wretched stomach . . .

Pause.

ROGACHEV: Oh, very well. But you should see a doctor about those insides of yours, do you hear me?

JOSEPH: Oh yes, your honour.

ROGACHEV: See to it. (*Raises voice*) Is it your wish that I put our plan before the High Command at their next meeting?

VOICES: Yes! As soon as may be! Don't let's delay any longer!

GENERAL: Have you a date for this Indian escapade of yours?

ROGACHEV: I soon will, general.

We are in a smallish office with an open window overlooking the Neva. Hooter noises, etc.

PEMBERTON: (*Friendly*) But you didn't manage to get the date.

JOSEPH: Not yet, Mr Pemberton, I'm afraid. It's not easy.

PEMBERTON: I imagine not.

JOSEPH: Especially not since Count Rogachev became watchful. I was a fool to get out of drinking that toast. I just couldn't . . .

PEMBERTON: What does he suspect, Joseph?

JOSEPH: Not the truth, or I wouldn't be here now. No, he merely thinks I don't love him, which is true. I must be more careful to prevent him from seeing what I really feel about him.

PEMBERTON: How can you be sure nobody's watching you?

JOSEPH: Because I don't trip over a little man in a mask every time I turn a corner. It's strange how a people as deceitful as the Russians should be so bad at anything to do with spying. Don't worry, Mr Pemberton, I'll get you that date.

PEMBERTON: Well, it can't be for a few months yet, with winter coming on. In fact now I think of it . . .

He shuts the window.

PEMBERTON: That's better. What is it?

JOSEPH: I just hope you're right about those few months. I wouldn't trust Rogachev not to get troops over the Himalayas in dead of winter by balloon. Well, a little bit of judicious eavesdropping should settle the matter.

PEMBERTON *has opened and shut a drawer and now tosses a packet of banknotes on to the table between them.*

PEMBERTON: I'll look forward to it. You'd better count them.

JOSEPH: No need, Mr Pemberton.

PEMBERTON: Very well. You know, I think you'd do this work for nothing.

JOSEPH: Maybe. Maybe.

Sequence 3 – The Crimea

Near Balaclava, 17th October, 1854. In the distance a large force of Russian cavalry is manoeuvring back and forth. In the foreground a large force of British cavalry is advancing at a walk and trot. The troopers are chatting among themselves as they ride.

TROOPERS: Glory be, we're going to have a smack at 'em at last. We'll show those Russki swine who's master. About time too. Who do they think they are? Our turn now, eh?

SERGEANT: (*From near by*) No talking in the ranks. And watch your dressing there. Smartly now. Sit up straight and take a pride in it.

OFFICERS: (*From out in front*) Halt! Halt the 17th. Halt the Scots Greys. Halt the 11th.

The entire cavalry division halts.

SERGEANT: Right, settle yourselves, lads. Remember they're watching you. Prepare to charge. Now's the time to say your prayers. Listen to your orders, listen to the trumpeter, and do what you're told. Now, all quiet. Steady. And God bless us all.

Some moments pass in silence.

NOLAN: (*Muttering*) What the devil are you waiting for, Lord Lucan, you great ninny, you aristocratic booby, is it reinforcements from God's angels you're wanting? (*To colleague*) Will you just look at that ground now, boy, and tell me if you ever saw country better suited for a cavalry charge?

COLLEAGUE: You're right, Lew, it's ideal.

NOLAN: No narrow lanes, no woods, not as much as a damn hedge to jump, and as for the going, you couldn't wish for better at Newmarket. And we're all here. What's the matter with Lord Look-On? God, it's driving me mad.

COLLEAGUE: Keep your voice down.

More moments pass. Then the Russian cavalry in the distance start booing, jeering, laughing. Their trumpets can be heard.

NOLAN: The bastards are about to withdraw. I'll not stand it, so I won't.

He gallops off.

We are up with LORD LUCAN's *headquarters group, half a dozen officers with orderlies.*

STAFF CAPTAIN: They'll be forming column in a minute, sir. In order to retire.

COLONEL: Lord Lucan, I beg you, order the charge before it's too late.

LUCAN: I know your feelings, colonel, but you must know I cannot charge. I must follow what Lord Raglan has laid down. The Commander-in-Chief has stated most categorically that I must in no circumstances attack.

COLONEL: He's not here now, sir. It's a golden opportunity to deal a deadly blow.

LUCAN: Colonel, I have my orders.

NOLAN: (*Approaching*) Lord Lucan . . . Lord Lucan . . .

LUCAN: Who's this fellow? (*To* NOLAN) Who are you, sir?

NOLAN: Captain Nolan, at your service, my lord. Now if no one else will do so, I have to tell you to your face that by failing to attack the enemy when he's at our mercy you have neglected your duty, sir. Whatever your orders may have been, the responsibility of taking the war to the enemy is paramount and overriding.

LUCAN: How dare you, sir. Pray withdraw immediately.

NOLAN: You're supposed to be the general commanding the cavalry division, not a damn nursemaid. Back there are some of the finest soldiers in the world, and you're letting them just sit and chew their nails. You're a disgrace!

The last speech is broken into by protests, etc., from LUCAN, COLONEL *and* STAFF CAPTAIN. NOLAN's *last words are shouted as he is hustled away.*

LUCAN: I've a mind to have that insolent Irishman court-martialled.

COLONEL: I think it would do no good, my lord.

LUCAN: As I put it in my recent memorandum: It is not the duty of light cavalry needlessly, without authority, to engage the enemy.

COLONEL: Just so, my lord. Shall I have the Retire sounded?

LUCAN: Thank you, colonel, if you would.
COLONEL: (*To* TRUMPETER) Sound Retire.
TRUMPETER: Sir.

The trumpet-call rings out.
The waiting British cavalry hear the trumpet-call from the front.
The men are furious.

TROOPERS: The Retire! I can't believe it. Damn that cowardly
    swine Lucan to hell! Some general. Lord Look-On is right.
    We'd have cut 'em to pieces. Aren't we ever going to get a
    smack at 'em?
SERGEANT: (*Shouting*) Silence in the ranks! (*To* CAPTAIN) You
    can't blame 'em, sir.
CAPTAIN: (*Shouting*) Squadron will move to the right in column.
    Squadron will retire, 3 Troop leading. Walk march. Smartly
    there! (*To himself*) Oh God.

Fade out cavalry moving at walk.

Sequence 4 – London

Official building in Whitehall or somewhere. CECIL *is walking*
along a corridor on the way to his office. DANVERS *comes up.*

DANVERS: Good morning, my lord.
CECIL: Morning, Danvers. Has the mail from the Crimea arrived?

They walk along the corridor together.

DANVERS: On your desk, sir.
CECIL: The only thing in this whole mess and misery that seems
    to work is the mail service.
DANVERS: They say bad news travels fast, sir.

They enter CECIL's *office.*

CECIL: They're right there. (*Opens packet*) But for the electric telegraph we might still be living in a fool's paradise.

DANVERS: I hear, my lord, that in a few months we shall be able to get our news direct from Balaclava.

CECIL: If we still have anybody there to send it. (*Reading*) Oh dear.

DANVERS: I'll leave you, sir.

CECIL: Don't go far.

DANVERS *goes.*

CECIL: Oh, Lew, you are a positive wonder. More than just a clever fellow with a bribe. How do you do it? It's supernatural.

NOLAN: (*Voice fades up*) Greetings to my pious friend. Our bishop here is in very bad odour. Two days ago our loyal clergy were all keyed up to spread enlightenment among the heathen. It was a perfect opportunity. But alas, my lord bishop hummed and ha'd and did nothing. Our clergy were furiously disappointed. I myself remonstrated with my lord, who retorted with dignity that he had specific orders from my lord the archbishop to refrain from any attempt to spread the holy word without specific orders. What can a true believer hope to do?

Our clergy are in a very bad state, the kind of sullen discontent that precedes real trouble. Unless they get the chance soon to do something effectively evangelical their spirit will be lost. This is very urgent. Please advise me. Your reverend friend and brother. PS The bishop from Wales is as usual. He awaits the coming of his yacht from England with his French cook on board.

CECIL: The bishop from Wales? Oh – Cardigan, of course!

Knock at door.

CECIL: Come.

DANVERS *enters.*

DANVERS: From Lord Clarendon's office, my lord, by special messenger.

CECIL: Thank you, Danvers.

DANVERS *goes.*

CECIL: (*Opens envelope. Reads*) 'I thought you might like to see the enclosed. Please understand that it is a matter of the strictest confidence between us. G.V.' Thank you, George. Now—

PEMBERTON: (*Voice fades up*) Our man reports that Count Rogachev seems most interested and well informed as to the state of training and morale of our troops in the Crimea, with particular reference to our cavalry. This is no academic interest of his but an essential feature of his scheme to bring about a Russian invasion of India. A plan for this has been laid before the Imperial High Command, but our man is still unable to learn the proposed date of the move. What seems certain is that Rogachev sees as vital to his plan the supposed, or real, disinclination, or inability, of our troops to resist a determined and forceful adversary, especially . . .

CECIL: Especially where cavalry is concerned. Indeed. What else?

We are in a beau-monde London house during a party. Men and women are talking and moving about, e.g. up and down staircase.

HERBERT: Well, my dear Cecil, this is most pleasant, happening to run into you like this.

CECIL: It's good of you to say so, Herbert. For me, it's more than pleasant. You're the very man I was hoping to see.

HERBERT: You don't say. How delightful. Well, what can I do for you in the next couple of minutes?

CECIL: Very quickly – you remember this fellow Rogachev I was asking you about?

HERBERT: Rogachev? Oh yes, that Russian count fellow. What about him?

CECIL: That scheme of his for the invasion of you-know-where. What do the Cabinet make of it?

HERBERT: Make of it? They make nothing of it, Cecil. If they've heard of it at all, they've forgotten it.

CECIL: They think it of no account?

HERBERT: None whatever. Heaven knows what they do think of account. Keeping income tax down to sixpence in the pound, most likely. Well, must be off.

His voice is lost for a moment in the noise of the party. Then we hear it again.

HERBERT: (*Calling*) Oh Cecil!

CECIL: (*Approaching*) Yes, Herbert?

HERBERT: Just remembered – I was talking to a fellow in the Horse Guards the other day, and your friend Rogachev came up in conversation. Apparently he tried to get into our Light Dragoons some years ago, and they turned him down. No leg for a boot or some such jargon. That's all.

CECIL: My dear Herbert, that is most interesting.

HERBERT: (*Fading*) Just thought I'd mention it.

CECIL *is in his office with* DANVERS.

CECIL: (*Dictating*) The Muscovite priest we spoke of . . . was once refused entry to one of our seminaries. Full stop. Hence perhaps his contempt for our clergy. Stop. Your remarks on their low spirits are noted. Stop. Recommend you do your utmost to encourage some demonstration of their superiority to the ungodly, comma, whatever your bishop or archbishop may say. Full stop. No, comma: or not say. Full stop. Would you read the last phrase back, Danvers?

DANVERS: Whatever your bishop or archbishop may say, or not say.

CECIL: Or not say. Whatever Lord Lucan or Lord Raglan may order you to do, or fail to order you to do. That is a little strong perhaps.

DANVERS: Shall I strike it out, my lord?

Pause.

CECIL: No. No, keep it. Address to Captain Lewis Nolan – HQ
  HM Forces – Crimean Expeditionary Force. Priority. And that
  means priority with you too, Danvers, so down to the telegraph
  office you go like a bullet.
DANVERS: Immediately, my lord.

                                                    He leaves.

CECIL: No leg for a boot!

He collapses in laughter.

Sequence 5 – The Crimea

*The British forces outside Sebastopol. Before dawn on the 25th
October. A bitterly cold night, wind howling, sentries stamping
their feet, etc.* NOLAN's *tent.* MORRIS *approaches it.*

NOLAN: That you, Ivor?
MORRIS: It's me right enough.

He enters the tent.

MORRIS: What a night!
NOLAN: At least we're out of the wind in here.
MORRIS: Did you hear we lost an officer last night? Major Willet.
  Dead of cold or exposure or whatever you call it.
NOLAN: I can believe it. Do you know, I wish I was in Balaclava
  town this minute. They've got fires down there. Girls too for
  all I know. And liquor.
MORRIS: *I* wish I was in Sebastopol, in the bloody fortress with
  the Russkis. Snug as a bug in a rug I'd be. With the occasional
  trifling inconvenience of a British shell possibly disturbing my
  slumbers.
NOLAN: Without the faintest chance of a British soldier coming

to stir me out of 'em. When will they learn? It doesn't matter how long you bombard a place, you might as well be whistling at it unless you send a storming party in, horrible men with swords and bayonets and pop-guns to kill whoever's stirring. I wonder if the point ever strikes that perfumed idiot Lord Cardigan.

The British siege-guns are bombarding the Russian fortress of Sebastopol. LORD CARDIGAN *and a couple of* OFFICERS *ride up.*

CARDIGAN: Ah, I see. Those fellows down there are our men, and they are firing at the Russians. Is that correct?

OFFICER: That's correct, my lord.

CARDIGAN: Yes. Well, why don't we drive them away?

OFFICER: We seem not to have the forces sufficient to undertake such a difficult operation, my lord.

CARDIGAN: I have never in my life seen a siege conducted on such principles. Or lack of them. Without an assault this cannonade is useless. Huge sums of money have been blown away in ammunition; time, which is of the most vital importance, has been squandered, and nothing whatever has been gained. What is to be done next?

OFFICER: We await orders from Lord Raglan, sir.

CARDIGAN: No doubt you do, my boy. Well, it's back on board the *Dryad* for me. Some miles away, it's true, but I might as well be back in Whitehall for all the good I can do here. And at least on my yacht I can be dry and warm.

Back in NOLAN's *tent.*

NOLAN: (*Fade up*) . . . and not counting the Sebastopol garrison, there must be twenty thousand Russian troops out there, infantry and cavalry and heaven knows how many guns.

MORRIS: Under General Liprandi, who it seems is an aggressive sort of customer.

NOLAN: I rather fancy the sound of him. It's worth crossing

swords with a bastard like that, if we ever get within ten miles of him.

MORRIS: The Lord will provide.

NOLAN: He'd better. Otherwise we'll have to provide something ourselves.

MORRIS: You know, Lew, I've been thinking about your telegraph message from Robert Cecil. The last sentence, where he as good as told you to do anything you could to get our fellows a chance to hit the Russkis with everything they've got. Easy for him to talk like that in London, isn't it? I mean—

NOLAN: Oh, the lad's heart's in the right place, but he's never seen action.

MORRIS: Action, what action?

NOLAN: Sure, he's no notion what inaction's like either, British army-style, courtesy of Lord Look-On. Oh, it's hopeless, Ivor.

MORRIS: The only thing he can think of to do is get us all out of bed an hour before dawn to 'stand at our horses'. There's the aggressive spirit for you.

NOLAN: Right, let's go and stand at the poor nags. They must be as miserable as we are.

LUCAN *and his staff walk their horses through the gloom.*

STAFF OFFICER: All present and correct, my lord.

LUCAN: Thank you. Who's that?

PAGET: (*Calling as he approaches*) George Paget here, Lord Lucan.

LUCAN: Good morning, Lord George. Lord Cardigan not appeared yet?

PAGET: I expect he's still on his way from his yacht, sir. I'm deputizing for him. Getting quite used to it.

LUCAN: Let's move on to the artillery emplacement. They may have news there.

They ride on.

PAGET: (*Surprised*) Hullo!

LUCAN: What is it?

PAGET: There are two flags flying from the staff. What does that mean?

STAFF OFFICER: Why, that must be the signal that the enemy is approaching.

PAGET: Are you quite sure?

A great cannonade of British [light] guns starts up. We hear sounds of battle but no close engagement.

LUCAN: If the Russians storm the heights there's nothing between them and Balaclava but our cavalry.

PAGET: What are your orders for the Light Brigade, Lord Lucan?

LUCAN: Lord Raglan has done nothing, not even sent word. It must be our first duty to defend the approach to the town of Balaclava.

PAGET: Orders for the Light Brigade, sir!

LUCAN: Lord George, you will take the Light Brigade into reserve.

PAGET: My lord, please give us something to *do*, something active.

LUCAN: Kindly carry out my order at once. I will go forward with the Heavy Brigade and the Horse Artillery to make threatening demonstrations and using my guns as long as my ammunition lasts. Forward, the Heavy Brigade!

Bombardment. Two great explosions. Sounds of Turkish infantry in retreat.

STAFF OFFICER: Lord Lucan, most of our squadrons have come within musket range.

LUCAN: So I see. I must withdraw the whole cavalry division to the slopes of the Causeway over yonder. Proceed by alternate regiments. Send an order to Lord George Paget.

Cavalry on the move.

CARDIGAN: Morning, Lord George. Beautiful day.

PAGET: It is now, my lord.

CARDIGAN: H'm. How goes it?

PAGET: Not well, sir. In fact damn badly. The Russians are out in overwhelming strength, all our gun emplacements have fallen, the Turkish troops have run for it, we've lost command of the heights, and it looks as though we're going to lose Balaclava too. And the cavalry division has been moved out of the way.

CARDIGAN: That wretched Lucan again.

PAGET: Not this time, my lord, in fairness. Specific orders from Lord Raglan. We were in an excellent position before. Now there's only a few hundred Highland infantry under Sir Colin Campbell and a few dozen Turks to face the Russians.

CARDIGAN: I've no confidence in any of 'em.

Russian cavalry on the move.

LUCAN: On the order of Lord Raglan, eight squadrons of dragoons under General Scarlett are to be detached from the Heavy Brigade towards Balaclava to support the infantry.

CAMPBELL *addresses his troops.*

CAMPBELL: Men, remember there is no retreat from here. You must die where you stand. But for the moment you don't stand at all. Everybody down flat and don't get up till I give the word. And when you do get up, both ranks be ready to fire. We'll give those Russkis the shock of their lives. Make sure every shot tells.

Russian cavalry charging.

CAMPBELL: On your feet, men! Front rank, aim! Fire!

Volley of musketry. Confusion among Russian cavalry.

CAMPBELL: Rear rank, aim! Fire!

More of the same.

CAMPBELL: Get back in line, there! Damn all that eagerness! Let
'em come to you! Front rank, aim! Fire!

More of the same, followed by Scottish cheers.

CAMPBELL: Had enough, you Russian dogs? Ay, get yourselves
out of harm's way while you can! I don't blame you!

British cavalry on the move.

SCARLETT: Halt!

MAJOR: Looks as if we're not needed here after all, General
Scarlett.

SCARLETT: What do you mean, major? What about that lot up
there?

MAJOR: But that's the main body of the Russian cavalry, sir.
Thousands of 'em.

SCARLETT: Well then, they won't be expecting an attack from a
few hundred.

MAJOR: But they're uphill from us, and the ground between is
badly broken.

SCARLETT: Two more reasons why they won't be expecting us.
And look!

MAJOR: Surely they're not halting there.

SCARLETT: Preparing to outflank us. We won't give 'em time.
Now's our moment, while they're not moving. Come on! (*He
draws his sword.*) Trumpeter, sound the charge!

Trumpet sounds. SCARLETT's *force charge the Russians and a
great fight ensues.*
The Light Brigade are halted not far away.

PAGET: Smash into 'em, lads! Well done, old Scarlett!

CARDIGAN: These damned Heavies will have the laugh of us this day, Paget.

PAGET: Not if we move at once, my lord.

CARDIGAN: Lord Lucan's orders are that we are on no account to leave this position.

PAGET: Can't we attack without orders, sir?

CARDIGAN: Who are you to ask such a question?

From among the great fight comes the sound of English, Scottish and Irish cheers as the Russian force breaks and flees.

TROOPERS: They're running for their bloody lives! We can cut 'em to pieces as they are now. Surely they'll let us forward? What are we waiting for?

MORRIS: (*Rides up to* CARDIGAN.) My lord, are you not going to charge the flying enemy?

CARDIGAN: Certainly not, Captain Morris, we have clear orders to remain here.

MORRIS: But, my lord, it is our positive duty to follow up this advantage.

CARDIGAN: No, we must remain here.

MORRIS: I implore you, do, my lord, allow me to charge them with the 17th. See, my lord, they are in disorder!

CARDIGAN: No, no, sir, we must not stir from here.

MORRIS: (*Turning away*) Gentlemen, you are witnesses of my request.

PAGET: We're all with you, Morris. But it's no good.

MORRIS: My God, my God, what a chance we are losing!

LUCAN *and his staff.*

NOLAN: (*Riding up*) Lord Lucan, sir, message from the Commander-in-Chief, sir.

LUCAN: Kindly read it aloud so that all may hear.

NOLAN: Sir. (*Reads*) Lord Raglan wishes the cavalry to advance rapidly to the front. Follow the enemy and try to prevent the enemy carrying away the guns. Troop Horse Artillery may accompany. French cavalry is on your left. Immediate. Signed by the second-in-command.

LUCAN: I see. Or rather I fail to see. I can see nothing. From here, neither enemy nor guns are in sight. I know the enemy are in possession of guns of ours captured at the emplacements, and there are guns, Russian guns, at the end of the North Valley with the remnants of their cavalry. Which guns are meant? And is there to be no infantry support? Cavalry to charge artillery? Absurd.

NOLAN: Lord Raglan's last words to me were that the cavalry are to attack immediately.

LUCAN: Attack, sir? Attack what? What guns, sir?

NOLAN: There, my lord, is your enemy, there are your guns.

LUCAN: The Russian guns. At the end of the valley. Very well.

NOLAN: Will that be all, Lord Lucan?

LUCAN: Thank you, Nolan.

NOLAN *rides over to* MORRIS.

NOLAN: Good day, Captain Morris. Are you now in command of the 17th?

MORRIS: Good day, Captain Nolan. Yes, my superiors are all off sick.

NOLAN: We are to charge the Russian guns. Have I your permission to ride next to you?

MORRIS: By all means . . . Lew – you mean those Russian guns down the valley?

NOLAN: It's our chance come at last, Ivor, our chance to show the world.

MORRIS: Oh. Very well. We must do what we can.

LUCAN *rides up to* CARDIGAN.

LUCAN: Lord Cardigan, in pursuance of this order from the

Commander-in-Chief, you will advance down the North Valley with the Light Brigade. I will follow in support with the Heavy Brigade.

CARDIGAN: Certainly, sir; but allow me to point out to you that the Russians have a battery of guns in the valley on our front, and batteries and riflemen on both sides.

LUCAN: I know it, but Lord Raglan will have it. We have no choice but to obey.

CARDIGAN: I understand, sir.

LUCAN: Advance very steadily and keep your men well in hand.

CARDIGAN *rides over to his staff.*

SERGEANT: (*Calling to* TROOPERS) Right, pipes out there now. Don't disgrace your regiment by smoking in the presence of the enemy.

PAGET: I hope that doesn't apply to me, sergeant. I'll wager there isn't another cigar like this in all Balaclava.

SERGEANT: I think it's up to you, sir.

PAGET: I don't want to set a bad example.

CARDIGAN: (*Rides up*) Lord George, we are ordered to make an attack to the front. You will take command of the second line, and I expect your best support – mind, your best support.

PAGET: You shall have it, my lord.

CARDIGAN: In the first line, the 13th Light Dragoons, 11th Hussars, 17th Lancers. Second line, 4th Light Dragoons and the 8th Hussars.

STAFF OFFICER: Very good, my lord.

The regiments form up. CARDIGAN *draws his sword.*

CARDIGAN: (*Quietly*) The Light Brigade will advance. Walk march. Trot!

The troops set off, clearly audible owing to a sudden lull in firing.

*Then the distant guns crash out. As the first shots arrive, wounded
men and horses cry out.*

NOLAN: Oh, what have I done? Sweet heaven, forgive me!

He pulls ahead of MORRIS.

MORRIS: Get back in line, Lew! We've a long way to go and must
   be steady! (*Shouts*) Come back!

NOLAN *overhauls* CARDIGAN.

CARDIGAN: Here, captain, get back to your place in the line!
   Captain Nolan, get back, I say!
NOLAN: Now hear me, all you men!

*The rest of his words are drowned in explosions. A final one is
very near.* NOLAN *is hit. His horse wheels and begins to gallop
back through the oncoming Light Brigade.*

MORRIS: (*Horrified*) Oh Lew! Oh God, oh God!

From NOLAN
'*There burst a strange and appalling cry, a shriek so unearthly
as to freeze the blood of all who heard him. The terrified horse
carried the body, still shrieking, through the 4th Light Dragoons,
and then at last* NOLAN *fell from the saddle, dead.*' *The tumult
of the battle fades to nothing.*

CARDIGAN: That fellow Nolan behaved like a damned insubor-
   dinate dog, Scarlett. And a coward, too. Imagine the fellow
   screaming like a woman when he was hit.
SCARLETT: Say no more, my lord; you have just ridden over
   Captain Nolan's dead body.

Sequence 6 – London

A convalescent home. CECIL *is visiting* MORRIS.

CECIL: You look remarkably well, Morris.
MORRIS: Yes, my lord, I probably do, for a man who's had his head cut open here and there.

They laugh ruefully.

CECIL: How long will they keep you in this place?
MORRIS: I think they want to see me walk before they decide.
CECIL: (*Tentatively*) If it's not too soon to ask you – what do you think happened at Balaclava?
MORRIS: Well, my lord, Lew Nolan was never an easy fellow to understand. He was behaving very oddly even for him when he rode up beside me just before the charge. But I've no doubt in my mind that about as soon as he read Lord Raglan's order he decided to misdirect Lord Lucan. A great chance for Lew to test his theory about cavalry.
CECIL: But he underestimated the Russian artillery.
MORRIS: And his own feelings. Poor Lew hadn't seen as much of the business of war as I had, and I reckon the sight of what those first shells did to our fellows and their horses was too much for him. It was a horrible reminder that cavalry are flesh and blood, not just part of a theory. I think when he was hit he was in the middle of telling us to turn back.
CECIL: (*Slowly*) Do you think he was influenced by my notion of bringing about something that would show our friends in St Petersburg the quality of British cavalry, their high morale and their bravery?
MORRIS: I couldn't say for certain, my lord, but I know he was powerfully impressed by it. Especially by your last message. He'd set his heart on proving you were right.
CECIL: (*Heavily*) I see.

MORRIS: My lord, have you heard whether the news of the charge has had any effect . . . back there?

CECIL: Not as yet.

Sequence 7 – St Petersburg

ROGACHEV *and his faction in conclave.*

ROGACHEV: Surely this 'charge of the Light Brigade' shows little but the blind stupidity of the British cavalryman.

GENERAL: It may or may not show that, Count Rogachev. What it certainly shows is miraculous discipline and magnificent courage.

ROGACHEV: So you witnessed it, general?

GENERAL: Your honour must know that I had not the opportunity. Nor the privilege. But a soldier need not be a witness of such a thing. For a soldier, to be told is enough.

ROGACHEV: We must beware of attaching too much importance to a single event. What is it, major?

MAJOR: I did witness that event, my lord count, from behind the battery which the Light Brigade were attacking. With all respect to the general, you have to see such a thing. Such a thing! (*Begins to break down.*) It was without parallel, it was unique, it was indescribable. The French general who saw it said it was magnificent, but it was not war. It was indeed magnificent, and it was war besides. (*Weeping*) Those noble fellows! If only we had ten such men in all Russia . . .

ROGACHEV: There, there, my poor major, what you need is a drink. (*Rings handbell*) Again, we must pay attention to the larger picture.

GENERAL: The larger picture is that, far from the British soldier being in a bad way, it is the Russian. Every man in our army, high and low, is dismayed and daunted and in a state of fear at the thought of an enemy who can do such things. We shall lose the war in the Crimea, we shall never defeat Turkey while she has such an ally, and India is safe from us while the British remain.

The double doors open. JOSEPH *enters with* SERGEI.

ROGACHEV: Ah, Joseph. Drinks for everybody, please. Champagne for his royal highness . . .

JOSEPH: At once, my lord. (*To* SERGEI) Champagne here . . . vodka here . . .

MAJOR: (*To* GENERAL) If you call for a vote now, sir, you will assuredly carry the day.

GENERAL: Will you support me?

MAJOR: Of course, and not only I.

GENERAL: Very well. (*Raises his voice*) I move that we petition the High Command to proceed no further with any plan to move against India. I call for a show of hands.

ROGACHEV: Immediately, general?

GENERAL: If it please your honour.

ROGACHEV: So be it. All present, please signify. For the general's motion, that the Indian plan be called off forthwith.

Hands are raised in silence.

ROGACHEV: Against, that we are still resolved to move against India.

Another pause.

ROGACHEV: In the circumstances I will not call for a toast.

PRINCE: Better luck next time, Rogachev.

ROGACHEV: I thank your royal highness for an impeccably British sentiment. (*Irritably*) That will be all, Joseph.

JOSEPH: Thank you, my lord count.

Sequence 8 – London

The Retrenchment Club. We move over to where CECIL *and* MORRIS *are sitting.*

CECIL: Well, Morris, you look well enough to take a glass of port.

MORRIS: Thank you, my lord. I think I could manage just the one.

CECIL: I suppose one or other of us has to say a great deal has happened since we last sat here.

MORRIS: Yes.

CECIL: Do you mind talking about it?

MORRIS: No. No, not at all, my lord.

CECIL: Can you tell me how many were lost in the charge? The reports I've seen disagree.

MORRIS: I know for a fact that 673 officers and men began the charge. Afterwards, only 195 answered at the first muster. I was not one of them, and many unwounded men had lost their horses and only turned up later. Altogether 113 men were killed and 134 wounded. But for the French attack that followed, there would have been many more.

CECIL: A hundred and thirteen too many.

MORRIS: Oh, most certainly, my lord, but what would you? And if it's any comfort, Lew Nolan would very likely have done just as he did do if you had never met him. He was a mad fellow.

Closing notes of the Last Post.

CECIL: Theirs not to reason why, theirs but to do and die. But not in vain.

PS to Captain Nolan's Chance

Ever since I first heard of it as a boy, I have suspected that the charge of the Light Brigade at Balaclava was the result not of a blunder but of somebody's intention. My recent look at the matter in some detail has confirmed me in this view. For instance, Cecil Woodham-Smith's excellent, very full study, *The Reason Why* (1953), leaves one with at any rate a strong suspicion that Captain Lewis Nolan deliberately and vitally misled the commander of the Cavalry Division, Lord Lucan, about the objective of the charge.

Nolan had a unique chance to do so. He was the ADC of General Airey, Lord Raglan's second-in-command and the officer who wrote down and signed the fatal message that Nolan delivered. Up on the heights overlooking the battlefield, Raglan and Airey and their staff, who included Nolan, could see both (1) the captured British guns Raglan actually intended the Cavalry Division to recapture; and (2) the Russian artillery battery at the far end of the North Valley. From his lower position, Lucan could see neither (1), an easily attained objective, nor (2), to be attacked only at great risk. He was thus vulnerable to Nolan's deception (and had negligently failed to acquaint himself with the Russian groupings).

The reason why Nolan misled Lucan, if he did, would clearly have been something above and beyond his amply documented zeal for action. He was also a fanatical believer in the unrealized powers of cavalry, especially light cavalry. This too is well documented; after a dazzling early career as a cavalryman he wrote not one but two books on the subject, and much of what I put into his mouth in the first sequence of my play is a close paraphrase of some views he expressed. But for good measure, and to contribute something of my own, I invented a small conspiracy that included Nolan and plotted to convince a sinister Russian cabal of the formidable fighting qualities of the British soldier, especially the cavalry soldier.

Two points might be added here. I hope my conspiracy and its doings are fun, but in the end I incline to the view I attribute to Morris in his last speech, that Nolan as portrayed 'would very likely have done just as he did do' if there had been no conspiracy. And as for whether the historical Nolan really misled Lucan on purpose, we shall never know. Still, I rather think he did. True, he had a lot of luck with the incompetence that surrounded him, but it was the sort of luck that comes the way of murderous maniacs.

With exceptions like Nolan's discourse, most of my London and St Petersburg scenes (sequences 1, 2, 4, 6–8) are fiction. The Crimean sequences, 3 and 5, are largely factual, here and there closely so. For instance, Nolan's face-to-face diatribe against Lucan, Cardigan's remarks about siege warfare, Paget's questions about the significance of the two flags (and the cannonade that interrupts them), Campbell's words to his men, Morris's exchange with Cardigan, the text of the order to Lucan (verbatim), Nolan's placing himself beside Morris, Lucan's talk with Cardigan just before the charge, the incident of Paget's cigar and Cardigan's orders immediately following, the momentary lull in firing, the circumstances of Nolan's death and what Cardigan and Scarlett say about it afterwards are all matters of record. That record comes chiefly of course from what survivors of the battle wrote about it subsequently, and if one sometimes feels that they remembered with advantages, the capacity of human beings to say memorable or melodramatic things at great moments should not be forgotten.

Morris's version of the numbers killed and wounded in the charge is taken from p. 272 of *The Age of Reform* (1938) by E. L. Woodward.

1941/A

I – *The Pacific Operation*

. . . The Imperial Fleet that sailed from the Kuril Islands in the last days of November was the most powerful naval force ever assembled. It consisted in the first place of eleven battleships. The largest of them, *Yamato*, in which Admiral Isoruku Yamamoto flew his flag, was at 68,200 tons displacement one of the two largest battleships ever built, the other being her sister ship *Musashi*, then uncompleted. Each of their nine 18.1-inch guns (the biggest ever carried afloat) fired shells weighing 3,220 pounds. Top speed was a remarkable 27 knots to a range of 7,200 miles.

With the exception of the sister ships *Nagato* and *Mutu*, each bearing eight 16-inch guns, the other battleships in the Grand Fleet carried 14-inch primary armament, altogether providing a broadside of eighty pieces. Speeds of 22.5–28 knots could be attained. All the above ships could launch up to three aircraft via catapult.

The accompanying carrier component was likewise uniquely strong at the time, consisting as it did of no fewer than nine vessels, from the impressive sister ships *Soryu* and *Hiryu* with their capacity of seventy-one aircraft each and their top speed of 34.5 knots, to the smaller *Taigo* with her twenty-seven aircraft and 21 knots. In aggregate these ships carried the prodigious total of 380 aircraft.

Six heavy cruisers, fourteen light cruisers, sixty-six destroyers and nearly one hundred other craft, including a sufficiency of tankers for refuelling purposes, accompanied the capital ships.

Divided into four forces under vice-admirals, this unparalleled armada set its course due east. It passed hundreds of miles to the north of the main Pacific base of the US Navy at Pearl Harbor, the objective of an earlier strike plan now superseded. The change of plan had been largely the personal doing of Yamamoto, who had never wavered in his conviction that Japan could only hope to defeat America in a short war, the shorter the better.

Thanks to miracles of organization and the most rigid security, the Grand Fleet assembled intact and on schedule off the Californian coast, far enough off to be below its horizon. The four forces maintained for the voyage across the Pacific Ocean had become two, separated by some hundreds of miles, in fact the distance between San Francisco and Los Angeles.

At first light on 11th December, the Japanese fleet commenced bombardment of these two prosperous and populous cities with every gun that could be brought to bear, while every aeroplane capable of flight took off on bombing and strafing missions into their harbours and business and residential quarters. Complete surprise was attained. Of the initial salvoes, one heavy shell struck almost the precise centre of what was at that time the longest single-span suspension bridge in the world, opened only four years earlier, the Golden Gate Bridge at the entrance to San Francisco harbour. The bridge sustained great damage and there was some loss of life.

After a prearranged interval, the two forces ceased fire, turned into line abeam and steamed inshore, a change of location designed partly to permit greater accuracy and to conserve aircraft fuel, but also, at least as important, to leave the helpless citizens in no doubt of who and what it was that brought them destruction and death. The ships of the battle-fleet went to their new stations and recommenced bombardment, whether of the cities themselves or of shipping and harbour and other installations. The aerial attacks had continued without pause.

Shortly before 10.00 hours a tender or other small boat was observed approaching the waterborne forces bearing a rough-and-ready white flag. This impudent excursion, which could have claimed nothing conceivable in the way of legal standing or significance, was swiftly and properly dealt with. On orders of the Admiral himself, the destroyer *Shimakaze* closed with the intruder at top speed and rammed her amidships, cutting her clean in two. The remnants rapidly sank, those persons who had survived the impact being helped on their way by small-arms fire and grenades from *Shimakaze*'s deck.

By then or soon afterwards, large parts of both cities and their outskirts were ablaze. Visibility on this clear, sunny winter's morning had at first been excellent; now heavy clouds of smoke drifted across the target and ascended hundreds of feet into the air. Massive explosions occurred at intervals. One especially severe and prolonged disturbance in the San Francisco area has been taken to indicate a seismic shock induced by the bombardment in an area notoriously subject to earthquakes, but material evidence is lacking.

Despite increasing difficulties of ranging and targeting, the Japanese warships and warplanes prolonged their assault on the two coastal cities until breaking off the action shortly before noon. Already large parts of the afflicted areas had been destroyed, and hundreds of thousands of their people lay buried in the rubble or lay dead or dying in what had been their streets. Sentimentalists have suggested that the attack was needlessly prolonged and excessive damage and slaughter inflicted, perhaps forgetting the first objective of the Californian operation, viz. the delivery of the maximum possible shock, not only locally but throughout the United States. It could be asserted with some confidence, in the light of subsequent events, that those Americans who lost their lives in and around Los Angeles and San Francisco did so, albeit unknowingly, in the service of their country.

When the cease-fire came and all aircraft were safely returned, the fleet drew off. The whole of it with one exception began the long voyage home across the Pacific under the command of Vice-Admiral S. Toyoda. The exception, the giant battleship *Yamato*, whose ammunition had been conserved, started off on her way to a fresh target some 3,500 miles to the south-east, a target of such importance that Admiral Yamamoto had insisted on attending to it personally.

The naval forces assaulting the Californian cities had met with negligible resistance. A number of obsolete US warplanes made feeble, uncoordinated attempts to close with the vastly superior Japanese aerial armament, but in almost all cases these were shot out of the sky at ranges too great for them to return effective fire. Even considered solely by the standards of warlike profit and loss, the Pacific operation was the most successful in history.

II – *The Atlantic Operation*

Twenty-one hours in real time after the Japanese had launched their first attack, at first light on 12th December, the German battleship *Tirpitz*, having eluded the vigilance of the Royal Navy in slipping out of European cover and crossing the Atlantic, commenced bombardment of the city of New York.

At 41,700 tons and with eight 16-inch guns as primary armament, *Tirpitz* was clearly a ship on a rather smaller scale than the mighty *Yamato*, and hers was a solitary adventure; nevertheless the damage and loss of life she inflicted were considerable and bore closely upon events.

Tirpitz concentrated her fire on the island borough of Manhattan, though she caused some damage to the US Navy Yard on the farther side of the East River. Her shells destroyed or severely damaged several of the city's loftier buildings, including the 102-storey Empire State Building. Two considerable fires were started. At a later stage, making up in boldness for what she lacked in firepower, *Tirpitz* actually sailed some distance up the Hudson, bombarding the shore at point-blank range with every gun available. A salvo from her secondary armament of 5.9-inch guns reduced the famous Statue of Liberty to fragments.

Amid growing but still largely ineffectual signs of resistance, *Tirpitz* discontinued the action just before 09.00 hours and

retired. Out in the North Atlantic once again she turned south-
ward, her mission in that ocean not yet accomplished. While in
transit she successively launched from her catapult the four
aircraft she carried, each of them an Arado 196A-3 twin-float
seaplane carrying two 110-pound bombs. The two-man crews
had been carefully selected and intensively trained for what was
perhaps the most important part of the entire Western opera-
tional sector.

It had been decided with some reluctance that a regular naval
attack on Washington, DC, though infinitely tempting, must be
ruled out as too hazardous. Approach via the Potomac River or
the Chesapeake Bay was finally rejected as too difficult and
remote, with a risk that the encroaching force might be trapped
and destroyed before it could withdraw. Such an outcome was
unacceptable in view of the necessity that the enemy be denied
any countervailing success, however small in proportion, on this
day of his humiliation.

Accordingly, the four seaplanes delivered a short-range, low-
level and deadly accurate attack on the White House on the late
afternoon of a day that had filled it with Service and civilian
chiefs of every description. No one who witnessed it would ever
forget the unheralded approach at nearly one hundred yards per
second of a warplane flaunting the insignia of a distant but hostile
Power and firing a machine gun as it came. The story goes that
one such round, penetrating a conference room by its shattered
window, struck the wheelchair in which President Franklin D.
Roosevelt sat and, ricocheting, hit and killed an air-force general
standing behind him. Whether literally true or not, the supposed
incident has great metaphorical force.

After completing a number of strafing runs at their target, and
having dropped on it their collective bomb-load, amounting to
something not far short of half a ton of explosive, the seaplanes
rendezvoused with the *Tirpitz*. Two airmen were lost. Those killed
in and around the White House ran into scores, but the moral
effect of such a daring stroke was incalculable.

Now, by an assiduously reconnoitred route, *Tirpitz* continued her long journey to the south. Round the tip of Florida she steamed, through the Yucatan Channel between Cuba and Mexico, then down the Caribbean to her third and final objective.

III – *The Combined Operation*

During the night of 16th/17th December, *Yamato* and *Tirpitz* took up their stations off the two ends of the Panama Canal, each vessel out of range of the shore defences. At a previously agreed time close to first light, both commenced bombardment of the sections of canal nearest them. After two hours the *Tirpitz*, whose primary ammunition had started to run low, discontinued fire, and a little later *Yamato* followed suit.

There were altogether six double locks in the canal system, each of great mass and strength. All lock walls rested on rock foundations and were over 80 feet in height. In the case of the outermost locks, the walls contained over two million cubic yards of concrete. Nevertheless the concentrated broadsides of the two great battleships caused multiple breaches in both. What with severe consequential flooding and damage to permanent installations, it was estimated from reports reaching the Washington office of the canal that, even under normal conditions, repair and reopening could be expected in months rather than weeks.

Before the preliminary investigations were complete, *Yamato* and *Tirpitz* had reached home and safety, having accomplished their part in the shaping of history.

IV – *The Sequel*

The Empire of Japan had declared war on the United States of America in a proclamation date-timed 11.30 p.m. on 11th December, but unfortunately delayed for some hours before it reached the US Government. At two o'clock that afternoon Joachim von

Ribbentrop, as Foreign Minister, had read out to the American chargé d'affaires in Berlin the text of Germany's declaration of war.

The combatant Powers continued in a state of war seven full days. At 11.00 a.m. on 18th December, President Roosevelt delivered an address to both Houses of Congress and, by simultaneous radio broadcast, to the nation at large. The text ran, in part:

It is with a heavy heart, my fellow Americans, that I stand before you this day. You will all share my feelings of shock, sorrow and indignation at the appalling carnage that resulted from the Japanese surprise attack on the cities of Los Angeles and San Francisco. The German raids on the East Coast cities of New York and Washington, DC, though smaller in scale, were no less dreadful and demoralizing. In the nation's capital I myself came under enemy fire, for a single instant only, but long enough to kindle in me a special sympathy with those men, women and children who really suffered.

America was still reeling from these heavy blows when the news arrived of the virtual destruction of the Panama Canal. That canal . . . is in a very real sense America's lifeline. Denied it, my Service heads advise me that the possibility of one day defeating in war two such powerful and such implacable adversaries as Imperial Japan and the German Third Reich is not non-existent but is hopelessly small, far too small for the substantial risk of total defeat to be run. Therefore, as your Commander-in-Chief, I hereby order all American forces to lay down their arms totally, finally and forthwith, pending the signing of a peace treaty. My fellow Americans, the war is over!

Now, I call upon you all to join with me, at this late hour, in returning henceforth to our traditional path of neutrality amid foreign conflict. Let us forgo any thought of revenge and pursue the proud role of beacon of liberty and democracy, by whose light other nations may in the end return to the paths of peace and goodwill.

Necessary adjustments in the status of certain of our overseas territories, and in some of our domestic arrangements, are in the process of being settled and agreed. As soon as the details shall be finalized . . .

The adjustments referred to by the President turned out to comprise the cession to Japan of all America's Pacific territories, including the Hawaiian Group with the Pearl Harbor base, Guam and Wake Island, and to Germany of Puerto Rico, while the Panama Canal Zone passed under the tripartite authority of the United States, Japan and Germany. The domestic arrangements concerned were naval installations in the continental United States. The US Navy was to be progressively reduced to fishery-protection and coastguard vessels.

When these details were after some days released to the American public, some revulsion of feeling occurred, and there were riots and disturbances from ocean to ocean, though not as violent or prolonged as those that followed the original bombardments.

Besides, it was too late.

From *A History of the Second Great War, 1939/A–1943/A*
by Michael Bridgeman
Josef Goebbels Professor of Modern History
in the University of Oxford

Afterword

This piece by Kingsley Amis originally appeared as the Introduction to the 1987 edition of *Collected Short Stories*.

These are nearly all the short stories I have ever published; I omit 'The Sacred Rhino of Uganda' (1932) as uncharacteristic. I wish there were more of them, and not only because I should be that much richer if there were. For one to an extent committed to the novel of standard length (which I take to be in the region of 75,000 words) and to producing fairly regularly too, setting out on something of a different order of size, something that hardly need do more than get as far as a second page in order to have being, is a busman's holiday certainly, but still a holiday. From having to keep twenty Indian clubs in the air at once you suddenly find yourself given licence to get by with two. And if you drop one of those, what does it really matter? A couple of botched pages can be filed *sine die* or even scrapped; a couple of hundred – well, I hope it never happens to me.

If shorts are so angst-free, why not write more of them, perhaps switch to them? Partly because (for that very reason, I suspect) short-story ideas or starting-points come to me rarely, as can be seen. Novel ideas turn up with no greater frequency but, in their different case, quite fast enough (touch wood). Each sort of idea declares itself as such instantly, simultaneously with its dawning. For instance, the moment I thought of the word that Courtenay says to Barnes near the end of 'The House on the Headland' I knew I had a short story and also that it would be, or seem to be, a secret-service story. Whereas, when once in Tottenham Court Road a taxi hailed by an Asian ignored him and stopped for me instead, I knew I had a novel coming and also that it would be about a rich fellow of progressive views.

All the same, a glance will show that my kind of short story has a strong affinity with the novel; its scale is different but its internal proportions, the relative parts played by dialogue, narrative, description, are alike and make the two read alike. And the stories are telescoped novels in that it would be feasible, however savagely boring the result (and the process), to draw them out to near standard length. Potter's earlier life in the timber yard and something of his marriage could be stuck on to the front of 'Dear Illusion', but Sue Macnamara could not be brought into any of that and so the structure would be deformed. The one story here that has to begin and end where it does is 'Mason's Life' – almost true too of the four SF-drink pieces. Anyway, the things that only the short story can do, the impression, the untrimmed slice of life, the landscape with figures but without characters, make little appeal to me. This collection is really one of chips from a novelist's work-bench. I say so without complacency. A novel may, indeed in certain respects does, call for not only more sustained but also more intensive effort than a story; even so, a volume of Kipling's stories, say *Life's Handicap*, offers stiff competition on merit to *Portrait of a Lady, Tess of the D'Urbervilles, Almayer's Folly* or any other novel of the period. Well, few writers move with equal facility in both forms. Graham Greene seems to, though.

Mention of Kipling leads me to wonder whether, if he were today to produce 'Without Benefit of Clergy' or another masterpiece from the book referred to, he would find its magazine publication as easy as he actually did in 1890. Then and for long afterwards, weeklies and monthlies entirely or largely devoted to new fiction, for the most part short stories, flourished in both Great Britain and the United States. Now, notoriously, a tale of any length has to fight for a place alongside political articles, interviews with film directors, cookery columns and soft porn. Just as notoriously a hardback or paperback collection usually does worse commercially than a novel by the same author. This last fact was once explained to me by a publisher (not one of mine) as reflecting readers' dislike of having to acquaint themselves with a new set of characters a dozen times over in the course of the book, instead of getting shot of the trying task for good at the beginning. Can that be right? Have readers got worse? – after all, there are more of them. Or have short-story writers got worse?

– after all, writers of everything else have. But then novels go on getting read, or at least bought. But then again, not in hardback very much. Perhaps the vestigial puritanism that breeds reluctance to fork out £11.95 on a mere (book-length) story breeds outright refusal when the merchandise is a lot of little stories. Perhaps.

My other possible partial explanation takes account of another fact, that of course the short story of the 1980s is to be seen not only among tits and bums, etc., but also in those pale and sickly present-day equivalents of the Victorian fiction magazines, the periodicals subsidized by the Arts Council or one of its offspring. A writer, or any other kind of artist, who partly or largely need not depend on pleasing the public, who in effect has his fee guaranteed whatever the quality of his product, is tempted to self-indulgence and laziness. You may maunder on at your own sweet will in prose or verse (or something called verse) and get your money regardless. But when it comes to a book and the public, a larger public, is invited to pay the full price, even that of a paperback, it jibs. It turns to a novel, which as yet is unlikely to contain any material subsidized by the Arts Council.

The above has at any rate the merit of heeding a third fact: when people decline to buy something, they usually do so because they see insufficient merit in what is on offer. And word gets round; I should guess that the term 'short story' has become a fully fledged consumer-deterrent in its own right, like 'sensitive study' in a different context. Short-story writers need another Kipling to restore their image. But Rudyard resurrected would have a plenitude of more urgent business on his hands.

In reprinting these pieces I have followed the policy of altering nothing material, merely supplying omissions and rectifying stylistic and factual erros. In particular, 'Who or What Was It?' retains its original form of radio script. Let me say here that the broadcast had an interesting and mildly appalling sequel. My intention had been to fool listeners into thinking it was a factual account until three-quarters of the way through and then, with luck, induce them to suspend their altogether necessary disbelief for the last few minutes. The detail about the cross was put in partly to make incredulity inescapable and final. For some, it missed its mark most

grievously. An old friend, himself a novelist, the late Bruce Mont-
gomery ('Edmund Crispin') telephoned to ask if the story was true;
when I demanded to know how he could have thought that it could
conceivably be true, he disarmingly shifted his ground by saying he
wondered if I had had a go of DTs. A television producer telephoned
to suggest using it for one of a new series of programmes on the
supernatural. I asked how it was proposed to set about this. 'Well,'
came the reply, 'I thought we might start by taking the cameras
along to the pub.' I said, 'Pub! What pub?' and there was a great
silence.

The funniest and most frightening of these cases was a letter from
something calling itself the Religious Experience Research Unit at
Manchester College, Oxford, director Sir Alister Hardy, FRS. The
writer, who was not Sir Alister, said that he and his colleagues were
collecting examples of outlandish coincidences and the like, asked
for further details of my 'experience', and added that so far nobody
known to him had come across 'such a striking and remarkable
nexus of events as you describe'. I hope not. There was another
good bit about my having been (on one view of the matter) in two
places at once; that was comparatively straightforward, the man
said, an obvious case of 'bi-location'. You could not wish for a finer
example of the popular habit of thinking that giving something a
Latin name goes a fair part of the way towards explaining it.
'Mummy, there's a monk floating in the air – how does he do it?'
'It's called levitation, dear.' 'Oh, I see.'

I was tempted to string this fellow along, but compassion or
laziness intervened. Eventually, I believe, the Religious Experience
Research Unit or its scribes published a compendium of striking
and remarkable nexuses of events. If I have the right book in mind,
it received a great deal of respectful attention. In one way, this is
not at all surprising. All sorts of people are uncomfortable in a
universe where there seems to be nothing supernatural, nothing
beyond this life, no undiscovered forces, no God. I sympathize; I
find it none too cosy myself; but I do wish there were a little less
eager, cruising credulity about. I wish too, quite vainly, that such
people, other people too, would face a little more squarely what is
entailed by believing, or believing in, something.

Science-fiction fans among many will remember how, one night in 1938, Orson Welles put out an adaptation of his near-namesake's *War of the Worlds* over a New York radio station. It was cleverly done as a succession of supposed news broadcasts and, near the end, supposedly genuine commentators described the invaders from Mars horrifically battering their way into the city. According to the story, thousands of listeners panicked, fled along the streets, besieged bus terminals, drove off into the countryside. This showed credulity all right, stupidity too – 'news' of that sort would not be going out on just one channel, etc. But it also showed a certain consistency. If, for whatever inadequate reason, you really believe the Martians are coming, then you are behaving logically and appropriately by trying to run away, you are following out the consequences of your belief.

Nobody, as far as I know, panicked or drove to Cornwall as a result of my broadcast. But those who said they thought the story was true, or might be true, responded illogically and inappropriately. Consider: if you saw a man restoring to life another clinically certified as dead beyond the possibility of error (and that would be less extraordinary than what I described over the air), the appropriate response would surely *not* be, 'How very interesting. I might telephone that chap in a day or two and see if I can find out a bit more about it.' No; if you telephoned anyone it would be the Archbishop of Canterbury, you would fly to the Vatican, approach the worker of the miracle and say, 'Master, I will sell all that I have and follow you.' Those reactions to my broadcast constitute one more small piece of evidence that, when it comes to any debatable question of this sort, from the existence of ghosts to the value of palmistry, the line between belief and disbelief is becoming blurred. Is astrology true or false? Many would say that there was something in it, many more than take the slightest practical notice of its advice. Do you believe the flat-Earth theory? Yes and no. That way madness lies.

I have seen it said that the first three stories here are parts of an unfinished or discarded novel, and that 'Moral Fibre' comes from a draft of my novel *That Uncertain Feeling*. Neither is true.

Kingsley Amis